D1154073

RUSSIAN
CLASSICS

IVAN GONCHAROV

The Same Old Story

A Novel

Translated by *Ivy Litvinova*

RADUGA
PUBLISHERS
MOSCOW

Translation from the Russian
Illustrations by *Orest Vereisky*

First printing 1957
Second printing 1975
Third printing 1989

Printed in the Union of Soviet Socialist Republics

ISBN 5-05-002438-2

CONTENTS

FOREWORD

LIFE AND HOW TO LIVE IT*

An author explores life by two means—the intellectual, which begins with reflections on life's phenomena, and the artistic, the aim of which is to fathom the same phenomena and grasp them not with the mind (or, rather, not only with the mind) but with all one's being, intuitively as it is called.

The former, intellectual means requires the author to logically render the material he has studied, while the latter, artistic means allows him to express the essence of the same phenomena through a system of artistic images. A writer of fiction gives us a picture of life, not simply a copy of life but a picture transformed into a new artistic reality, and as a result the happenings that have attracted his interest are brought in sharp relief by the brilliant light of his genius or talent, and sometimes we can even see what lies behind them.

Presumably, a real writer shows life only in its artistic representation. But in actual fact these "pure" writers are not so very many, and it may even be that there are none at all. More often than not a writer is both an artist and a philosopher.

Ivan Alexandrovich Goncharov (1812-1891) has always been considered one of the most objective of Russian writers, a writer, that is, who does not let his own personal likes and dislikes influence his judgement of values. In his novels *The Same Old Story* (1847), *Oblomov* (1859) and *The Precipice* (1869), he portrays life objectively, indifferent as it were to both good and evil, leaving the reader to use his own judgement and pronounce the verdict.

This attitude of his is stated most clearly by one of the personages (an editor of a magazine) in the novel *The Same Old Story*. He says: "...a writer only writes something worthwhile when he is not

*English translation © Progress Publishers 1975.

carried away by self-absorption and prejudice. He must cast a calm, clear glance at life and humanity, otherwise he will express nothing but his own *ego*, which nobody cares a rap about." In his article "Better Late Than Never", Goncharov wrote: "As for myself, I have to say that I belong to the latter category, that is, I'm carried away by my 'ability to paint' (as Belinsky said about me)."

In his first novel, *The Same Old Story*, Goncharov painted a picture of Russian life on a small country estate and also in St. Petersburg in the 1840s. He could not, of course, give a complete picture of life both in the country and in the capital, which no writer could do anyway, because real life has many more aspects to it than any picture of it could present. Let us now see if the resultant picture is as objective as the author wished it to be, or have any secondary considerations made it a subjective one?

The dramatic content of the novel can be called a duel fought by the two main personages: Alexander Aduyev, a young man, and his uncle Pyotr Ivanovich Aduyev. It is a fascinating, dynamic duel, with now one side scoring a point and now the other. Each fights for the right to live his life according to his own ideals, which in the case of uncle and nephew are exact opposites.

Young Alexander Aduyev arrives in St. Petersburg straight from his mother's loving arms, clad from head to toe in an armour of lofty and noble impulses. He comes to the capital not prompted by idle curiosity but guided by his determination to give battle to all that is calculating, unfeeling, and vile. "I was drawn here by an irrepressible desire, by a thirst for noble activities," exclaims this fledgling, this naive idealist. And it is not just some one person that he challenges, but the whole world of wickedness. A poor little home-grown Don Quixote! And, mind you, a Don Quixote who has also read and listened to a lot of high-sounding rubbish.

The subtle irony with which Goncharov describes this young man whom he views with quite obvious mockery— his leaving home, the vows of everlasting love he makes to Sonechka and of his everlasting loyalty to his friend Pospelov, and his first timid steps in the capital—endears this young man to us, but the image already predetermines the outcome of the duel between the nephew and the uncle. Writers do not speak with irony about genuine heroes who are capable of performing great deeds.

And here is the opponent: Pyotr Ivanovich Aduyev, 39, a metropolitan, owner of a porcelain factory, a high-ranking official, a man with a sober mind and good practical sense. Goncharov endows him with a sense of humour and even sarcasm, but he himself does not treat this character with irony. And this makes us presume that he, the uncle, is the real hero of the novel, that he is the one the author invites us to model ourselves on.

These two characters who had attracted Goncharov's interest

were the day's most striking types. Even before the plot of the novel had quite taken shape in his mind, Goncharov wrote: "The encounter between the nephew, a dreamer with a mild character who has led an idle, sheltered life, and the uncle with his practical mind, gave me a hint of a motif that was only just beginning to develop in St. Petersburg. This motif was the faint glimmerings of an awareness that it was imperative to be a doer, engage not in routine work but in real, vigorous activity to fight the Russia-wide stagnation."

Goncharov very much wants to take this "doer" as a model for himself and, what is more, offer him as a model to the readers.

With what sparkle he wrote the dialogues of the uncle and nephew! How calmly, confidently and peremptorily does the uncle rout the nephew who is so impulsive but not armed with the terrible weapon of logic and experience! Every word of criticism spoken by the uncle is killing and irrefutable. It is irrefutable because what he says is true. The truth is grim, hurtful and pitiless sometimes, but it is the truth.

Take the episode where the uncle ridicules the "tangible signs of intangible relations"—the ring and the lock of hair which Sonechka gave her dear Alexander to take with him to St. Petersburg. "And is this what you carried with you over a thousand miles? You should have brought another sack of dried raspberries instead," says the uncle, and chucks these precious symbols of everlasting love out of the window. To young Alexander his uncle's cold words and action seem monstrous. Can he ever forget his dear Sonechka! Of course not. Never!

Alas, the uncle proves right. Very soon Alexander falls in love with Nadenka Lyubetskaya, he falls in love with all the ardour of youth, with all the passion which is part of his nature, recklessly and blindly. He has completely forgotten Sonechka. His love for Nadenka fills his whole life. His radiant happiness will last forever. And as for the business which his uncle is always talking about, what does he care for business when he spends all his waking hours at the Lyubetskys' country place? Oh, that uncle of his, he has nothing but business on his mind! He's so unfeeling. How can he have the heart to say that Nadenka, his Nadenka, this angel, this perfection, might jilt him! "Who, Nadenka?" Alexander cries, appalled. "That angel, that embodiment of sincerity..." And the uncle replies: "But for all that a woman—and she will most probably deceive you." Oh, these men with the sober, pitiless minds and worldly experience! The uncle proves right again: Nadenka does deceive him. She falls in love with a count, and gives Alexander his congé. The world is painted black for him at once. And there is his uncle with his: "I told you so."

Alexander fails with a crash in absolutely everything: in love, in friendship, in his attempts to write. Everything, absolutely everything that his teachers and books have taught him turn out to be so much rot, and with a faint crunch it is ground to dust by the iron tread of sober reason and practicalness. In the most dramatic scene where Pyotr Ivanovich and his wife come to see Alexander who, driven to despair, has taken to drink and gone to pieces, the uncle parries the nephew's self-defensive mumbling: "It was not I who invented all that I expect of you." And his wife asks: "Who then?"— "The age."

Here is the key to the behaviour of Pyotr Ivanovich Aduyev! The bidding of the age. The age demanded such behaviour. He says: "Look at the young men of today— what fine fellows they are! What mental activity, what energy, how deftly and easily they cope with all that nonsense which in your old-fashioned language is called *agitation, sufferings,* and God knows what else!"

This is the culmination of the novel. The opponent's decisive blow. Such is the age! "And is everybody bound to obey whatever this age of yours invents? Is all this so sacred, is it all so true?" Alexander makes a last feeble protest. "It is all sacred," his uncle replies brusquely.

The question of how a person must live—guided by his feelings or his reason—may well be called an eternal problem. There is one extremely significant passage in the novel.

Alexander says: "According to you emotions need controlling as if they were steam. Sometimes a little may be released, sometimes it must be shut off, the valve must be opened or closed..." To which his uncle replies: "Yes, not for nothing has Nature given man this valve—it is reason."

Through the whole novel the reader follows these two ways of living life. At moments it seems to us that Goncharov is advising us, in no uncertain terms, to live by reason and only by reason, or at least to use our reason to verify our feelings, as Salieri used algebra to verify his harmony. But that advice comes from a thinker, a man who reflects on life philosophically. Had Goncharov been only that he would certainly have proved to us that that is how we must live. But he was an artist before all else, and a realist artist at that. He portrays life as it is and not as he would like to see it. Being a true son of his age, Goncharov is wholly on the side of the older Aduyev, as he himself admitted when he said: "The duel of the uncle and the nephew also reflected the breaking up, which had just begun, of old notions and mores—sentimentality, ridiculously exaggerated feelings of friendship and love, poetised idleness, the family lie of affected, never really existing devotion... All this was outliving its day, and receding into the past: faint glimmerings of a new dawn appeared, of something sober, businesslike and sound."

Intuitively, Goncharov felt that the older Aduyev was a man of the new type. He was that indeed. And on him the writer pinned his hopes.

What sort of man was he, this Pyotr Ivanovich Aduyev, this model worthy of emulation, this sober-minded man of business? Historically, we've had him classified long ago: this was a new type, a capitalist, a man of business and sober calculation, who came to replace people who clung to their decrepit feudal ways.

In the novel, the older Aduyev always speaks of the need to be calculating in everything. In business. In friendship. In love. In marriage. And coming from him it never sounds discreditable. Even in art one must be calculating, and when his nephew tells him he is writing a book the uncle asks: "And are you sure you have talent? Without it you will merely be an unskilled labourer in the field of art, and what's the good of that? If you have talent—that's another matter. It would be worth while working. You can do a lot of good. That's capital—worth a great deal more than your hundred souls." Alexander gasps: "Do you measure that by money, too?"—"How else? The more people read what you write, the more money you will be paid."

This is calculation expressed in its most realistic form— money. Everything is measured with money.

"You seem unable to picture a moneyless tragedy!"

"Some tragedy, if it's not worth a farthing."

The measure of all values is money.

Goncharov the thinker and the sociologist wants to see the ideal in this new type of man, in Pyotr Ivanovich Aduyev. But Goncharov the artist will not let his vision become blurred. In fathoming the truth, the artist is, in a certain sense, more accurate than the thinker.

With a feeling of unquestionable superiority, from the heights of his experience, worldly wisdom and age, Pyotr Ivanovich Aduyev shatters his nephew's naive and pure faith in the "world of perfection", and shatters it very thoroughly. This is what now goes on in the soul of the once ebullient young Alexander:

"He inspected his life, questioned his heart, his head, and was appalled to discover that not a single dream, not a single rosy hope was left anywhere—all that was already behind him. The mist had dispersed, and he was confronted, as by a desert, by naked reality. Heavens, what boundless emptiness! What a dull, joyless prospect! The past had perished, the future was destroyed, there was no such thing as happiness. All was chaos—and yet one must go on living."

Alexander, reduced to a most pitiful state, tries and fails to commit suicide. Goncharov does not spare him, and strips him of all glamour. No doubt that's exactly what happens to people when they become so utterly disillusioned.

"At least teach me what to do now, Uncle!" Alexander cries in the extremes of helplessness.

"Do? Why ... go back to the country."

Cursing the city where he has buried his finest feelings and lost the strength to live, Alexander goes back to the country. He is defeated. It is his uncle who has won the duel. He has triumphed over Alexander completely.

It is a vain hope that in the country he will be resurrected. Resurrection is impossible, all he can have is a change of heart. And this is what does happen. Strange as it may seem, at home he begins to feel homesick for St. Petersburg, that same evil, sinister and soulless city which he cursed such a short while ago. New thoughts begin to stir in Alexander's changed mind: "In what way is my uncle better than I am? Am I incapable of finding a path for myself?.. I cannot stay here and perish... And my career, my fortune? I alone lag behind—and what for? Why?" And he rushes back to St. Petersburg to make his career and his fortune.

He writes to his aunt: "It is not a madman, a dreamer, a disillusioned person, or a provincial who is coming back to you, but simply a man such as Petersburg is full of, such a one as I ought to have become long ago."

I have long noticed this phenomenon: there are young men who are prone to idealise reality, who rant and rave against any sign of human weakness and demand ideal behaviour from others, but when they grow up and see their contemporaries who may not be so very ideal but who have advanced far ahead along their ordinary course of life, these young men suddenly clutch at their heads and start trying to catch up with them. They must catch up with them at all costs! And here these same sweet idealists turn into extremely practical men who will stop at nothing to attain their belated aims, and become far nastier characters than the people they have recently been accusing of all the mortal sins.

This is precisely what happened to Alexander. This naive, provincial idealist became a monster, pure and simple. Goncharov debunks his hero's claims to any charm completely. He seems to be telling us that such is the end of a man who enters life with spurious notions about it. First he bruises his ideal forehead against the realistic sharp corners of life, then this forehead hardens, a horny growth sprouts on it, and the man becomes a rhinoceros.

Let us see now, what were the fruits reaped by the winner, by Pyotr Ivanovich Aduyev, the author's favourite hero in whom he saw a man of business, capable of fighting the Russia-wide stagnation? Strangely and even alogically, the fruits of his victory are bitter indeed. This man with a realistic, sober world outlook has spiritually murdered his nephew to whom he was rather attached in his own way, and reduced the wife he loved to a shadow threatened with tuberculosis. At the end of the novel we find Pyotr Ivanovich planning to sell his factory, retiring and dreaming of one thing only—to go and live in Italy where he may be able to prolong the life of his wife.

The nephew has changed into the uncle, and with a vengeance too. The uncle has to a certain extent changed into the nephew. Quite involuntarily Goncharov, who tried to prove to us the advantages of sober reason and a calculating mind, now screams at the top of his voice that loving your fellow-creatures is more important than any calculations or business considerations in the world. Because he was a genuine artist, Goncharov saw no way out of this dramatic collision, no possibility of combining big business with the essentially human. The world of private enterprise is a cruel world indeed and it will take its toll of victims.

In the course of the whole novel a struggle was fought between Goncharov the thinker and Goncharov the artist. The artist won. And we have every right to place him with those outstanding 19th-century writers whose realism, to quote Friedrich Engels, "could manifest itself irrespective of views".

I would advise the people who ask themselves how to live to re-read Goncharov's *The Same Old Story*. To be sure, the novel does not give a straightforward answer to the question. But this old novel will greatly help the young to find the answers to some of the questions posed by our own 20th century.

Victor Rozov

The Same Old Story

Part One

I

One summer day the entire household of Anna Pavlovna Aduyeva, the owner of a modest estate in the village of Grachi, was up at dawn, from the mistress herself to Barbos the watchdog.

Anna Pavlovna's only son, however, the twenty-year-old Alexander Fyodorich, slept the sound sleep of youth. The house was full of fuss and flurry, but everybody went on tiptoe and spoke in whispers, so as not to wake the young master. If anyone made the slightest noise or spoke loudly, Anna Pavlovna was on the spot instantly like an infuriated lioness, roundly scolding, reviling, and sometimes, if very angry, even slapping the culprit as hard as her strength allowed.

In the kitchen frantic preparations were on foot, as if for a great company, although the Aduyev family consisted of only two persons—Anna Pavlovna and Alexander Fyodorich. In the coach-house the carriage was being polished and the wheels greased. All were busy, all worked in the sweat of their brow. Barbos was the only one who had nothing to do, but even he took part in the general stir in his own way. When a footman or the coachman passed him, or a maidservant scurried across the yard, he wagged his tail and sniffed energetically at the passer-by, while his eyes seemed to say: "I do wish somebody would tell me what all the fuss is about!"

Now, all this fuss was because Anna Pavlovna was seeing her son off to St. Petersburg, to work in a government office or, as she put it, to see the world, and let the world see him. A tragic day for her! And that was why she was so sad and irritable. Every now and then, in the midst of her cares, she opened her mouth to give some order, but stopped half-way through the sentence, her voice failing her, and turned aside to wipe away a tear, or if too late, to let it drop into the trunk in which she was packing her Sashenka's clothes. Tears had long been welling up in her heart, they lay like a weight on her breast, choaking her and threatening to gush up in torrents. But, as if saving them up for the last farewell, she shed them thriftily, a drop now and again.

She was not the only one mourning the coming separation—Sashenka's manservant, Yevsei, was also overcome with grief. He was going with his master to Petersburg, leaving the warmest nook in the house, behind the stove in the room of Agrafena, the prime minister of Anna Pavlovna's cabinet, and—what was still more important for Yevsei—her housekeeper.

There was only just room behind the stove for two chairs and a table, on which tea, coffee, and snacks were served. Yevsei had entrenched himself firmly both in one of the chairs and in the heart of Agrafena. The second chair was for herself alone.

The affair of Agrafena and Yevsei was an old story in the house. Like all such affairs it was discussed, with much slanderous gossip about the persons involved, and then, like all such affairs, dropped. The mistress herself was used to seeing them together, and they had enjoyed ten years of bliss. There are not many who can count ten happy years in their whole life. But now the hour of separation had struck! Farewell, warm nook, farewell, Agrafena Ivanovna, farewell, games of cards, coffee, vodka, cordials—farewell everything!

Yevsei sat in his accustomed place, sighing noisily. Agrafena, a scowl on her face, busied herself about the house. She expressed her grief in a way of her own. That day she poured out the tea fiercely, and instead of handing the first cup, very strong, to her mistress, as she usually did, she poured it away, as if to say "nobody shall have it", taking her mistress's scolding stoically. The coffee was boiled too long, the cream "caught", the cups slipped through her fingers. She did not place the tray on the table, she banged it down. She did not simply unlock cupboards and doors, she wrenched them open. But she shed no tears, she just vented her rage on everything and everybody. And this was quite in keeping with her character. She was never satisfied; nothing suited her; she was always scolding and complaining. But at this crucial moment of her life her character displayed itself in all its splendour. And it seemed as if no one annoyed her so much as Yevsei.

"Agrafena Ivanovna!" he wailed with a plaintive tenderness that did not quite suit his tall, closely-knit figure.

"Couldn't you sit somewhere else, you dolt?" she replied, as if he had never sat there before. "Let me pass, I want to get a towel."

"Ah, Agrafena Ivanovna!" he repeated languidly, sighing and getting up, only to sink back on to the seat as soon as she had taken the towel.

"He can do nothing but whimper! Sticking to me like a leech! A perfect pest, dear Lord!"

And she dropped a spoon noisily into the slop-basin.

"Agrafena!" came suddenly from the next room. "Have you gone mad? Don't you know Sashenka's still asleep? What are you doing—fighting with your beloved, by way of farewell?"

"You'd like me not to stir, sit there like the dead!" hissed Agrafena venomously, drying a cup with both her hands as if she would have liked to break it into pieces.

"Farewell! Farewell!" said Yevsei, heaving a mighty sigh. "The last day, Agrafena Ivanovna!"

"And thank God for that! Good riddance to bad rubbish! There'll be more room. Get out of the way, now, I can't move! Stretching out your long legs!"

He tried touching her on the shoulder—and didn't she give him what for! He heaved another sigh, but made no attempt to move. And he was quite right, that was not what Agrafena wanted at all. Yevsei knew this, and was not upset.

"Who will sit in my place?" he murmured, with another sigh.

"A wood goblin!" she snapped.

"God grant it! So long as it's not Proshka. And who will play cards with you?"

"Well, and supposing Proshka does, what of it?" she asked venomously.

Yevsei rose.

"Don't play with Proshka—anything but that!" he said in anxious, almost threatening tones.

"And who's to prevent me, pray? You?"

"Dear Agrafena Ivanovna!" he pleaded, putting his arm round what might have been called her waist, if there had been the slightest hint of a waist in her figure.

She responded to the embrace by sticking her elbow into his chest.

"Dear Agrafena Ivanovna!" he repeated. "Will Proshka love you as much as I do? You know what a rascal he is—he's after every woman he sees. And I—oh! Why, you're the apple of my eye! If it weren't the mistress's will ... oh!"

He groaned and made a gesture of despair. Agrafena could bear no more—at last even *her* grief showed itself in tears.

"Can't you leave me alone, you miserable wretch?" she said through her tears. "How you do go on! As if I would take up with Proshka! Can't you see nobody can get a word of sense out of him? All he thinks about is pawing wenches..."

"So he *has* been after you! The scoundrel! And you never told me a word! I'd..."

"Just let him try! As if I was the only female in the house! Me to take up with Proshka! What next, I wonder! It makes me sick even to sit next to him—the dirty pig. Free with his fists he is, and always trying to eat the mistress's victuals under one's very nose."

"Agrafena Ivanovna, if it comes to that—temptation is strong, you know,—better let Grishka take my place. He's a quiet, hard-working lad, he isn't one of your scoffers."

"There you go again!" shouted Agrafena. "Foisting me upon everyone, as if I was some... Get out! There's plenty of you men, and I'm not the kind of woman to throw myself at just anyone. You were the only one, you devil, I got mixed up with, as punishment for my sins, and I repent it ... and you keep on nagging at me!"

"God reward you for your goodness! It's a weight off my mind!" exclaimed Yevsei.

"Now he's pleased!" she shouted ferociously. "What's there to be pleased about, anyway!"

And her very lips turned pale with fury. Neither of them spoke for a few moments.

And then: "Agrafena Ivanovna," began Yevsei timidly. "Now what?"

"I was almost forgetting—I haven't had a drop since the morning."

"Is that all?"

"It's on account of my grief."

She reached for a glass of vodka and two huge hunks of bread and ham from behind a sugar-loaf on the bottom shelf of the cupboard. All this had long been made ready for him by her solicitous hands. She thrust the food and drink at him—you would hardly fling food to a dog so roughly. One hunk fell on the floor.

"Here you are—choke yourself! The devil take you! Quiet now, the whole house can hear you champing!"

She turned away from him with an expression of assumed disgust, and he began eating slowly, eyeing Agrafena from beneath his brows, and covering his mouth with his free hand.

In the meanwhile a *troika* drove up to the gate. The shaft-bow was fixed over the wheel-horse. The little bell, hanging from it, its clapper lolling from side to side, emitted hollow sounds, like the tongue of a drunken man, bound and flung into a cell. The coachman tethered the horses under a shed, took off his cap, and extracted from it a grubby towel, with which he proceeded to wipe the sweat from his face. Catching sight of him from the window, Anna Pavlovna turned pale. Her knees gave way, and her hands hung limp at her sides, although she had been on the look-out for the carriage. Mastering her emotion, she called Agrafena.

"Go on tiptoe, very, very quietly, and see if Sashenka's still asleep," she said. "His last day at home will go in sleep, the darling, and I shan't be able to look my fill at him. But no, you can't—you'd steal in about as quietly as a cow. I'd better go myself."

And off she went.

"Go yourself, since you're not a cow," muttered Agrafena, returning to her room. "So I'm a cow, am I? You haven't many cows like me, have you?"

Anna Pavlovna was met by Alexander himself, a flax-
en-haired young man in the pink of health and strength.
He greeted his mother cheerfully, but catching sight of the
trunks and bundles turned in silent embarrassment to the
window and began tracing designs on the pane with his
finger. A moment later he was talking to his mother again,
and even regarding the preparations for the journey with
carefree enjoyment.

"You shouldn't have slept so late, my love!" said Anna
Pavlovna. "Your face is all puffy. Let me rinse your eyes
and cheeks with rose-water."

"Please don't, Mamma."

"What would you like for breakfast—will you begin with
tea or coffee? I've ordered beef chops in sour cream. Will
you have some?"

"Anything you like, Mamma."

Anna Pavlovna went on with the packing for a while,
and then stopped, gazing wistfully at her son.

"Sasha," she said, after a short pause.

"What is it, Mamma?"

She hesitated, as if in vague terror.

"Where are you going, my love, why are you going?"
she brought out softly, at last.

"Where, Mamma? Why, to Petersburg, to ... to..."

"Listen, Sasha," she said, in agitated tones, placing a
hand on his shoulder, with the evident intention of making
one last attempt. "It's not too late to change your mind!
Don't go!"

"Not go? Impossible! Besides, the ... the clothes are
all packed," he said, at a loss for words.

"Your clothes! There, and there, and there ... look—
they're not packed."

She emptied the trunk in three armfuls.

"But, Mamma, what d'you mean? I'm all ready, and
now you want me to stay. What would people think?"

He looked unhappy.

"It's not for myself—it's for your sake. What are you
going for? To seek happiness? Aren't you happy here?
Doesn't your mother think all day long how to satisfy
your slightest whim? Of course you are of an age when
your mother's efforts to please you are not enough to make
you happy. And I don't expect them to. But, look around

you—everyone wants to please you. Marya Karpovna's daughter, Sonechka, too. Ah, you're blushing? How she loves you, God bless her, the darling! They say she hasn't slept for three nights!"

"Come now, Mamma! She only..."

"As if I couldn't see! Oh—I mustn't forget! She promised to hem some handkerchiefs for you. 'I'll do them all myself,' she said. 'I won't let anyone else do them, and I'll mark them, too.' What more could you wish? Don't go!"

He listened in silence, with bowed head, playing with the tassels of his dressing-gown.

"What will you find in Petersburg?" she continued. "Do you think you'll be as well looked after as you are here? Oh, my dear! God knows what you'll have to endure—cold and hunger and want—you'll have to bear it all. There are plenty of bad people everywhere, but you won't find good people so easily. And as for distinction—what's the difference whether it's town or country? When you know nothing of Petersburg life you think you are the first person in the world, living here. It's the same everywhere, dearie! You're well-educated and clever and handsome. The only joy left to an old woman like me is to look at you. You could marry, God would send you little ones, and I could dandle them—and you would have no sorrows or cares, you could live out your days in peace and quiet, envying no one. Perhaps things won't be so good there, perhaps you'll remember my words... Do stay, Sashenka!"

He cleared his throat and sighed, but uttered not a word.

"See!" she continued, opening the balcony door. "Can you bear to leave such a sweet nook?"

A cool fragrance came into the room through the open door. A garden planted with ancient lime-trees, dense thickets of wild rose, wild cherry trees and lilac bushes stretched from the house far into the distance. There were beds of gaily-coloured flowers among the trees, paths running in all directions; and beyond them lay the lake, softly splashing against its shores; one half of it, smooth as a mirror, reflected the gold of the morning sun, the surface of the other half was ruffled and of a deep blue, like the sky above it. Still further, the tossing, multicoloured cornfields rose in an amphitheatre towards the dark woods in the distance.

Anna Pavlovna, shading her eyes from the sun with one hand, pointed to all these objects in turn with her free hand.

"See," she said, "how beautifully God has adorned our fields! We shall take as much as twelve hundred poods of rye alone from these fields. And over there are wheat and buckwheat. The buckwheat is not as good as it was last year, probably the harvest will be poor. But look at the woods—see how they have grown! See how great is God's wisdom! We will get at the very least a thousand rubles for fire wood. And the game—the game! And it's all yours, dear son. I am only your stewardess. Just look at that lake—what splendour! It's truly divine! And the fish in it! The only fish we have to buy is sturgeon—the lake is teeming with ruff, perch and crucian—enough for ourselves and our servants. Look at your cows and horses grazing over there! You are the master of everything here, while there—who knows—everyone will lord it over you. And you want to run away from all this bliss—whither to, you don't rightly know yourself, perhaps—God forbid!—to your peril. Do stay!"

He said nothing.

"You're not listening," she said. "What's that you're staring at?"

He pointed in silent thoughtfulness to the distance. Anna Pavlovna followed his glance, and changed countenance. Between the fields the road wound like a snake, disappearing into the woods—the road to the Promised Land, to Petersburg. Anna Pavlovna was silent a few minutes, trying to master her emotions.

"So that's it," she brought out mournfully at last. "Well, never mind, my love! Go, since you long to leave this place, I will not keep you. You shall never say that your mother spoiled your youth and your prospects."

Poor mother! This is the reward for all your love! Is this what you expected? Ah, but mothers expect no reward. A mother loves without rhyme or reason. If you are great, famous, handsome, proud, if your name is on the lips of all men, if your deeds are renowned throughout the world—your old mother's head will shake with joy, she will weep, laugh, pray long and fervently. And the son seldom thinks of sharing his fame with the mother. If you are poor in spirit and intelligence, if Nature has set the brand of ugliness upon you, if you are sick, body or soul, if, finally, men repulse you and you find no place among them—there will be all the more place for you in your mother's heart. She will press her ill-favoured, misbegotten child still more warmly to her breast, she will pray still longer and more fervently for him.

Must Alexander be considered callous because he brought himself to part with his mother? He was twenty years of age. Life had smiled on him from the cradle.

His mother had petted and spoiled him, as mothers always do spoil an only child. His nurse had sung to him while he was still in his cradle that he would always be rich and never know sorrow. His professors had declared he would go far, and when he returned home from his studies, the neighbour's daughter had smiled at him. Even Vaska, the old tomcat, seemed to prefer him to everyone else in the house.

Of grief, tears and disasters he knew only by hearsay, as people know of some disease which has never come their way, and only lurks remotely among less fortunate folk. And so the future presented itself to him in radiant colours. Something seemed to beckon him from afar, though what it was he did not exactly know. Delightful visions flitted by before he could make out what they were. Blended sounds rang in his ears—the voice of glory, the voice of love. And all this kept him in a state of delicious agitation.

His home soon became too cramped for him. The beautiful countryside, the love of his mother, the adoration of his nurse and the whole household, his soft bed, the good food and the purring of Vaska—all these blessings which are so much appreciated on the downward slope of life, he cheerfully surrendered for an unknown full of irresistible, mysterious enchantment. Not even the love of Sonechka—first love, so tender and rosy—could hold him. What did he care for it? What he dreamed of was a great passion that knew no limits and inspired resounding feats. In the meantime he loved Sonechka with a moderate love while waiting for the great passion to come his way. He dreamed, too, of the services he would do for his country. He had studied diligently and extensively. His diploma testified to his knowledge of a dozen subjects, as well as half a dozen languages, ancient and modern. His fondest dream was to become a famous writer. His verses had astonished his friends. Innumerable paths lay before him, each more alluring than the other. He did not know which to set foot upon. Only the straight road was hidden from his eyes—if he had noticed it, perhaps he would not have gone away.

But how could he stay at home? His mother desired it, and that was only natural of course. Love for her son was the only feeling left in her heart, and it seized eagerly upon this last object. But for this, what would there have been left for her to do? She might as well have been dead. It has long ago been pointed out that the heart of a woman cannot exist without love.

Home life had spoilt Alexander, but it had not corrupted his heart. Nature had done so well by him, that the love of his mother and the adoration of those surrounding him had only affected the better side of his character, developing in him emotional susceptibility, and implanting in him an excessive trustfulness. Perhaps they were the cause of the first stirrings of vanity in him; but vanity itself is a mere mold, everything depends on the material we pour into it.

Much more unfortunate for him was his mother's inability, for all her tenderness, to instil in him a correct attitude to life, to prepare him for the struggle which lay ahead of him, as of everyone. But this would have required a skilled touch, a subtle mind and a great store of experience, not limited by the cramped horizons of rural life. For this she should have loved him less, not thought of him every moment of the day, not shielded him from every care and unpleasantness, not done his weeping and suffering for him when he was a child, she should have let him feel the approach of storms, she should have let him cope with them himself and think over his own destiny—in a word realize that he was a man. But how was Anna Pavlovna to understand all this—let alone to fulfil these requirements? The reader has seen what she was like. Would he like to take another look?

She had already forgotten her son's selfishness. Alexander found her repacking his clothes. Her cares and the

bustle of departure seemed to have made her quite unmind-
ful of her grief.

"Look, Sashenka, make a note where I am putting your
things," she said. "Right underneath, at the very bottom
of the trunk are the sheets—a dozen. See if the list is
right."

"Quite right, Mamma!"

"All marked with your initials—see! 'A.A.' And all
done by that sweet Sonechka. But for her our ninnies
would never have got them ready so soon. What next? Oh,
yes—pillowcases. One, two, three, four—a dozen altogether—that's right. Here are the shirts—three dozen. Just look
at that lawn! Pure linen—I went myself to Vasily Vasilyevich
in his factory. He chose the three very best lengths. Mind
you check the list, my love, when your laundry comes
from the wash—they're all new. You won't see shirts like
that over there: they may substitute them—some of those
laundresses are the most shameless hussies. Twenty-two pairs
of socks. I'll tell you what! Put your wallet in the toe of
a sock. You won't need any money till you get to Petersburg, and if, which God forbid, someone starts rummag-
ing in your luggage they won't find it. I'll put the letter
for your uncle there too. Won't he be glad to see you!
Seventeen years and not a single line—that's no joke! Here
are the scarves and there are the handkerchiefs. Sonechka
still has half a dozen to mark. Don't lose your handkerchiefs, ducky, they're wonderful—batiste and cotton!
I bought it at Mikheyev's for two rubles twenty-five a
yard. Well, that's all the linen. Now for the suits. Where's
Yevsei? Why doesn't he come? Yevsei!"

Yevsei sauntered lazily into the room.

"Did you call me, Madam?" he asked, still more lazily.

"Call you?" repeated Anna Pavlovna angrily. "Why don't
you come and watch me pack? If you should need anything on the way you'll turn everything upside down.
Can't tear yourself away from your beloved—what a treasure forsooth! The day is long—you'll have plenty of time.
Is that how you mean to look after your master there?
Mind you do what I say! Look here—this is the best
frock-coat—see where I'm putting it? And you, Sashenka,
take care of it—don't put it on every day, the cloth costs
16 rubles a yard. Put it on when you have to call on

important people, but mind where you sit down, don't be like your aunt, who never seems to be able to find an empty chair or sofa, but manages to flop down just where there's a hat or something. The other day she sat right in a saucer of jam—such a disgrace! When you go to see ordinary people, put on this blue coat. Now for the waistcoats. One, two, three, four. Two pairs of trousers. Ah, me! You have enough clothes to last you three years. Oh dear, how tired I am! After all, I've been at it the whole morning. You can go, Yevsei! Let's talk of something else, Sashenka. The guests will be here soon, and we shall have other things to think about."

She sank onto the sofa and made him sit beside her.

"Well, Sasha," she said after a short pause. "You are now departing for foreign parts..."

"Petersburg is not foreign parts, Mamma!"

"Wait a minute—listen to what I'm going to say. God alone knows whom you will meet there, what you will see, both good and evil. May our Heavenly Father strengthen you! Whatever you do, my dear, do not forget Him, remember that you can never be saved, wherever you are, without faith. Even if you attain high rank over there, and go up in the world—we're as good as anyone, you know, your father was a nobleman and a major—you must always humble yourself before the Lord. Pray in happiness and in grief, do not be like the peasant in the proverb, who only crosses himself when the thunder crashes. Some people never so much as peep into the church while they are in luck, but when misfortune comes they go and light candles at a ruble apiece and start giving alms left and right. That's a great sin. And by the way, talking about alms! Don't waste money on beggars heedlessly, don't give a lot at a time! Why spoil them? You make no impression on them, whatever you give! They'll squander it on drink, and only laugh at you. I know your soft heart—you'll probably start giving ten-kopek pieces all round. But you mustn't do that—the Lord will supply. Will you go regularly to church? Will you go on Sundays?"

She sighed.

Alexander said nothing. He remembered that while he had been at the university he had not been a particularly ardent church-goer. And in the country he had only accompanied his mother to church to please her. He was ashamed to lie. He said nothing. His mother understood his silence and sighed again.

"Well, I won't try to force you," she continued. "You are a young man—you can't be expected to be so eager to visit the church as we old people. Perhaps your work will keep you too busy, or you'll sit up late in nice company and oversleep. God will have mercy on your youth! Don't fret. You have a mother. She will not sleep late. So long as there is a drop of blood left in my veins, so long as all my tears have not dried up, and God forgives me my sins, I will crawl to the door of the church, if I have not the strength to walk. I will give my last breath, my last tear for you, my dear one. The Lord will hear my prayers and you'll have health and rank, awards and blessings, earthly and divine. Surely our merciful Father will not deny the pleas of a poor old woman! I ask nothing for myself. Let Him deprive me of everything—my health, my life, my sight—so long as He gives you every joy, every happiness, every good thing..."

She could not go on for the tears streaming from her eyes.

Alexander leaped to his feet.

"Mamma!" he exclaimed.

"Sit down, sit down!" she replied, hastily dabbing at her eyes. "I have a great deal more to say. What was I going to say? It's gone out of my head. See what my memory is like nowadays! Oh, yes—observe fast days, my dear, that is very important. Never mind Wednesdays and Fridays, God will let you off those, but do observe Lent, for God's sake! Mikhail Mikhailovich, now—he's considered a clever man, but look at him! He gorges himself be it meat days or fast days, even in Holy Week. It's enough to make one's hair stand on end! He gives to the poor, of course, but the Lord will never accept his charities. They say he once gave ten rubles to an old man, who turned aside and spat when he took it. Everyone bows before him, and says all sorts of nice things to his face, but behind his back they cross themselves when they speak of him, as if he were Satan himself."

Alexander listened, not without impatience, and kept looking out of the window at the distant road.

She paused for a moment.

"Above all, mind your health," she went on. "Should you fall seriously ill—which God forbid!—let me know. I will rally all my strength and come to you. Who will look after you there? They'll more likely try to rob the sick. Don't go out in the streets at night—keep away from rough-looking people. Take care of your money. Oh, and mind you save some for a rainy day! Spend with discretion. All good and all evil come from the accursed stuff. Do not squander it, do not indulge in unnecessary whims. You will receive two thousand five hundred rubles a year from me regularly. Two thousand five hundred rubles are not to be sneezed at! Don't go in for luxuries of any sort, but don't deprive yourself unnecessarily. If you feel like eating something nice, do not stint yourself. Do not give yourself up to drink—oh, it is man's chief enemy! And," here she lowered her voice, "beware of women! I know them! There are shameless hussies who will throw themselves into your arms when they see such a fine young man."

She gazed at her son with love.

"That'll do, Mamma! What about breakfast?" he said with something like annoyance.

"In a minute—just one more word. Do not hanker after other men's wives," she said, hastening to her end. "That is a great sin. It says in the Bible: 'Thou shalt not covet thy neighbour's wife!' And if some woman or other talks to you about marriage, in the name of God, don't you think of it! They'll be ready enough, the moment they see you have some money and a handsome face. Of course, if your chief, or some great and rich nobleman should take a fancy to you and wish you to marry his daughter—that's a different matter—I wouldn't say no, but you must write to me at once. I'll get to Petersburg by hook or by crook, to see they don't palm off just anyone on you, merely for the sake of getting rid of her—some old maid, a bad lot probably! They will all be greedy for such a husband! But if you fall in love with some good girl of your own accord, and the girl is the right sort, well," she let her voice drop still lower here, "you needn't mind Sonechka, you know." (The good old soul was ready to act against her conscience, so fond she was of her boy.) "Indeed, Marya Karpovna should know better than to look

so high—as if her daughter were your equal! A mere coun-
try-bred lass! Girls of a much higher station who would be
honoured..."

"Sonechka! Oh, no, Mamma, I will never forget Sonechka!" said Alexander.

"All right, all right, my dear! I didn't mean it! Work,
come back home, and then we'll see what the Lord sends.
There'll always be a choice. If you don't forget her—all the
better. And you won't..."

She seemed to be going to say something, but changed
her mind, and then, bending over, asked, close to his ear:

"And you won't forget ... your mother?"

"Now really, Mamma!" he interrupted her. "Tell them
to bring some food quickly—an omelette or something.
Forget you! How could you think such a thing? May God
punish me..."

"Stop, Sasha!" she said hastily. "Don't bring curses
down on your head! No, no! Whatever happens, if you
should commit such a sin, let me be the only one to suffer!
You're young, you're just beginning to live, you will find
friends, you will marry—a young wife will take the place
of your mother and everything. No! May God bless you as
I bless you!"

She kissed his forehead, thereby bringing her sermon to
an end.

"Why don't they come?" she said. "Marya Karpovna,
Anton Ivanich, the priest—none of them have come!
Surely service is over! Ah, there's someone coming! An-
ton Ivanich, I think—so it is! Speak of the devil..."

Everyone knows who Anton Ivanich is. He is the Wan-
dering Jew. Always and everywhere he has existed, from
time immemorial, and no one ever saw the last of him. He
was present at Greek banquets and Roman feasts, he par-
took, of course, of the fatted calf slaughtered by the happy father in honour of the return of the prodigal son.

Here in Russia, he moves under various guises. He of
whom we are now speaking is the owner of twenty souls,
mortgaged up to the hilt; he lives in a house little better
than a hut, or rather in some strange edifice that looks
like a barn, with an entrance, obstructed by a heap of logs,
somewhere at the back, close to the fence. For twenty
years he has been declaring that he will start building a

new house come spring. He had no one to keep house for him. Not a single person of his acquaintance has ever been invited to dinner or supper at his place, or even to tea, but there is no one in whose house he has not dined or supped fifty times a year.

At one time Anton Ivanich used to go about in wide breeches and a full-skirted coat, now he wears a frock-coat and trousers on week-days, and on Sundays a dress-coat of a most extraordinary cut. He is so comfortably fat because he has no sorrows, cares or troubles, though he claims that all his life he has had to bear the griefs and cares of others. It is, however, well known that no one ever wasted away from the griefs and cares of others. That's only human nature.

Nobody really needs Anton Ivanich, but not a single event is celebrated without him—whether it is a wedding or a funeral. He may be seen at all banquets and evening parties and attends all family councils—no one ever takes a step without consulting him. It might be supposed that he is extremely useful, that he fulfils some important commission in one place, gives good advice in another, carries through some bargain in a third—but nothing of the sort! Nobody ever entrusts him with a commission; he can do nothing, he knows nothing—neither how to help somebody in a lawsuit, to act as an intermediary, or to conciliate persons at odds with one another.

But there are certain errands he does undertake, such as conveying a lady's regards to a gentleman, which he never fails to do, and, while he is about it, partaking of lunch; informing someone that a certain document has been received, though what document he is never told; taking a tub of honey or a handful of seed somewhere, with strict injunctions not to spill any; reminding someone of someone else's name-day. Anton Ivanich's services are also requested when it might be awkward to send a servant. "We can't send Petrushka," it is argued. "He's sure to make a mess of it. Better ask Anton Ivanich to go." Or: "It wouldn't do to send a servant—so-and-so might be offended—better send Anton Ivanich."

How astonished people would be if he failed to appear at some dinner or party!

"Where's Anton Ivanich?" everyone would be sure to

ask in amazement. "What's the matter with him? Why isn't he here?"

And the dinner would be a failure. Someone would have to be sent to find out what the matter was, whether he was ill, or had gone away. And if he were ill, you might conclude from the kindly attentions showered upon him that he was a near and dear relative.

Anton Ivanich bowed over Anna Pavlovna's hand. "Good day, Anna Pavlovna! Nip for new!"

"New, Anton Ivanich?" echoed Anna Pavlovna, examining herself all over.

"The little bridge to your gate. I see it's just been put down. I noticed the boards didn't jump up and down under the wheels of my cart, and I saw at once it was new."

It was his habit when greeting acquaintances always to congratulate them on something—the beginning of Lent, of spring, or of autumn. If frost set in after the thaw, he congratulated his friends on the frost, if thaw set in after the frost—on the thaw.

There was nothing of this sort just now, but Anton Ivanich always found something.

"Alexandra Vasilyevna, Matryona Mikhailovna and Pyotr Sergeich send you their greetings," he said.

"Thank you so much, Anton Ivanich. Are all their children well?"

"Yes, thank God. I bring you the blessing of the Lord— the priest is just coming. Have you heard, Madam, about Semyon Arkhipich?"

"What?" exclaimed Anna Pavlovna in alarm.

"He has passed away."

"You don't say so! When was it?"

"Yesterday morning. They let me know the same evening. One of their lads came riding for me. I went at once, and didn't sleep all night. They're all in tears—I had to console them and give orders—nobody could do anything but cry, except me."

"Dear God!" cried Anna Pavlovna, shaking her head. "This life of ours... But how did it happen? Only last week he sent us greetings through you."

"Yes, Madam. Oh well, he's been ill a long time, he was a very old man. It's a miracle he held out so long."

"Old? He was only a year older than my late husband.

Well, God rest his soul," said Anna Pavlovna, crossing herself. "Poor Fedosya Petrovna—left with all those children on her hands! Dreadful! Five of them and almost all girls! When will the funeral be?"

"Tomorrow."

"You see each has his own sorrow, Anton Ivanich—here am I saying good-bye to my son."

"It can't be helped, Anna Pavlovna, we are all human. The holy scriptures tell us to endure."

"You mustn't be angry with me for troubling you. I need you to help me to bear my grief, for you feel for us just like one of the family."

"Why, Anna Pavlovna—of course I do, my dear. How many people have we like you? You don't know your own worth! I've more cares than I can cope with—there are now my own building plans too. I spent the whole of yesterday morning haggling with the contractor, and we still don't seem to be able to come to terms. 'But I must go to her,' I said to myself. 'What will she do all alone, without me? She's not so young any more—she'll lose her head.' "

"God bless you for not forgetting us, Anton Ivanich. Yes, I'm not myself at all. My head feels so strange, I hardly know what I'm doing. My throat is quite parched from crying. Won't you have something to eat? You must be tired and hungry, I'm sure."

"Thank you kindly. I did have a little something to eat and drink on the way, at Pyotr Sergeich's. But no matter. The priest will be here soon, he can say grace. Oh, there he is now!"

The priest entered the room. After him came Marya Karpovna and her daughter—a plump, rosy damsel, with a smile on her face and eyes red from weeping. Sonechka's eyes, and the expression of her face plainly said: "I will love simply, without any nonsense, I will look after my husband like a nurse, obey him in everything, and never try to be cleverer than he is. For who could be cleverer than a husband? It would be a sin! I will see to the housekeeping diligently. I will bear him half-a-dozen children, I will nurse them myself, look after them, and stitch their clothes with my own hands." Her fresh-coloured, plump cheeks and ample bosom confirmed the promise as to the children. But the tears in her eyes and her mournful smile lent her an appeal of a less prosy nature.

First of all the service had to be read, and Anton Ivanich summoned the household, lit a candle, took the book from the priest, and handed it to the clerk when the priest had done with it. After this he poured some holy water into a vial which he put in his pocket, with the words: "That's for Agafya Nikitishna!" All sat down to the table. No one but Anton Ivanich and the priest touched the food, of course, but Anton Ivanich did full justice to the Homeric repast. Anna Pavlovna could only cry and wipe her tears furtively away.

"Come, now, my dear Anna Pavlovna, don't cry!" said Anton Ivanich in affected distress, pouring himself a glass of cordial. "Anyone would think you were sending him to the slaughter." Then, drinking off half the contents of the glass, he said, smacking his lips with an expression of extreme satisfaction: "Excellent cordial! And the bouquet! You won't find another like that in the whole gubernia!"

"It's been infusing two years," said Anna Pavlovna between her sobs. "I've only just had ... a bottle ... uncorked ... for you."

"You ought to be ashamed of yourself, Anna Pavlovna," resumed Anton Ivanich.

"Put yourself in my place, Anton Ivanich—my only son, and he is leaving me! Who will be there to bury me when I die?"

"And what about us? Who am I? A stranger, forsooth? And why are you in such a hurry to die? You're more likely to get married! How I should enjoy dancing at your wedding! No more crying, now!"

"I can't help it, Anton Ivanich, really I can't. I don't know where all the tears come from!"

"As if you could keep a fine young fellow like that cooped up! Give him his freedom, he'll reel his wings, and you just see the wonders he'll do! He'll go up and up in the world, you'll see."

"May your words come true! You've hardly had any pie—take some more!"

"Thank you—I'll just finish this first. Your health, Alexander Fyodorich! Happy journey! Come back soon! And get married! What are you blushing for, Sophia Vasilyevna?"

"Nothing—I only..."

"Oh, youth, youth! Hee-hee-hee!"

"Nobody can be unhappy when you are there, Anton Ivanich," said Anna Pavlovna. "You're such a comfort! God give you health. Have a little more of this cordial!"

"I will, Anna Pavlovna, I will! One must drink when one comes to say farewell!"

The meal came to an end. The coachman had long ago harnessed the horses to the carriage, and brought it round to the porch. Servants kept running up one at a time. One carried a trunk, another a bundle, yet another a sack, and then they came back for some more. They swarmed round the carriage like flies round a pot of treacle, each thrusting his hands into it.

"That's the best place for the trunk," said one. "And the box of provisions can go here."

"And where are they to put their feet?" asked another. "Better put the trunk longways, the box can go sideways."

"If you put the trunk longways, the feather mattress will slip—better put it across! What else? Have you packed the boots?"

"I don't know. Who did the packing?"

"It wasn't me! Go and see if they're not upstairs somewhere."

"Go yourself!"

"Why can't you go? You can see I'm busy."

"Here—don't forget this!" shouted a maid thrusting a hand with a bundle in it among the heads.

"Give it here!"

"And put this in the trunk—we forgot it!" said another maid, standing on the step of the carriage and handing over a brush and comb.

"How d'you think we can do that now?" a stout footman shouted back at her. "Go away! Can't you see the trunk is right underneath!"

"Mistress's orders! You can throw them away for all I care, you lazy devils!"

"Give it here then, and be quick about it! It can be stuck into the pocket."

The wheel-horse tossed its head incessantly, the bell on the shaft-bow ringing out stridently every time, like a reminder of parting, but the side-horses stood with heads drooping thoughtfully, as if they realized to the full the delights of the journey before them, every now and then shaking their tails or stretching out their lower lips towards the wheel-horse. At last the fatal moment arrived. Another prayer was said.

"Sit down, everyone!"* commanded Anton Ivanich. "Take a seat, Alexander Fyodorich! And you sit down too, Yevsei! Sit down, can't you!" and he let himself perched on a chair for a moment. "Well—God be with you!"

Here Anna Pavlovna burst out weeping and hung on Alexander's neck.

"Farewell, farewell, my dear one!" she sobbed. "Shall I ever see you again?"

And then all was chaos. Suddenly the sound of another bell was heard and a light carriage drawn by three horses dashed into the yard. A young man covered with dust sprang out of it, ran into the room, and hugged Alexander.

"Pospelov!" "Aduyev!" they cried in unison, embracing one another.

"Where have you sprung from? How did you get here?"

"From home! I galloped day and night to say good-bye to you."

"You are a true friend!" exclaimed Alexander fervently, tears starting to his eyes. "Drove over a hundred versts to say good-bye! Oh, friendship does exist in the world! For ever, isn't it?" And he clutched once more at his friend, pressing his hand warmly.

"Till the grave!" replied the other, squeezing Alexander's hand still more violently and clutching him.

"Write to me!"

"I will, and you must write too!"

Anna Pavlovna could not make enough of Pospelov. The departure was delayed another half an hour. At last they were ready to set off. Sophia and Alexander rushed into one another's arms as they walked through the dark porch.

"Sasha! Dear Sasha!" "Sonechka!" they murmured,

*It was the custom in Russia for all present to sit down for a few moments before taking leave of a traveller.—*Tr.*

but the words died away in a kiss.

"You won't forget me there?" she asked tearfully.

"Oh, how little you know me! I shall return, believe me, and no other shall..."

"Here, take this ... it's a lock of my hair and a ring."

He placed the one and the other hastily in his pocket.

Anna Pavlovna led the way with her son and Pospelov, then came Marya Karpovna and her daughter, and last came the priest and Anton Ivanich. The carriage followed a little way behind. The coachman could hardly hold back his horses. The servants surrounded Yevsei at the gate.

"Good-bye, Yevsei Ivanich, good-bye, old fellow, don't forget us!" came from all sides.

"Good-bye, brothers, good-bye! Don't forget me!"

"Good-bye, Yevsei, good-bye, my precious one!" said Yevsei's mother, embracing him. "Here's an amulet for you—it comes with my blessing! Guard your faith, Yevsei, mind you don't go over to the heathens there! I'll put my curse on you if you do! Don't drink, don't steal; serve your master truly and faithfully. Good-bye, good-bye!"

She covered her face with her apron and turned away.

"Good-bye, Mother," said Yevsei in his lazy drawl.

A girl of about twelve years rushed up to him.

"Say good-bye to your sister," said a woman in the crowd.

"You here, too?" said Yevsei, kissing her. "Well, good-bye, good-bye! Get back to the house, you with your bare feet!"

Last of all came Agrafena, who had stood apart from the rest. Her face was a sickly green.

"Good-bye, Agrafena Ivanovna!" said Yevsei, in a shrill drawl, as he stretched out his arms towards her.

She allowed him to embrace her but did not respond to the embrace, except with a twitching of her features.

"Here—take it!" she said, producing from under her apron a small bag and thrusting it at him. "You'll be gadding about with the Petersburg wenches, I suppose," she added darting a sidelong glance at him. This glance expressed all her grief and all her jealousy.

"Me?" cried Yevsei. "May the Lord strike me dead, may my eyeballs burst! May I sink through the ground if I..."

"All right, all right!" muttered Agrafena sceptically. "I know you!"

"Oh, I almost forgot," said Yevsei and brought a greasy pack of cards out of his pocket. "A keepsake for you, Agrafena Ivanovna! You won't be able to get any here." She held out her hand.

"Give them to me, Yevsei Ivanich!" cried Proshka from the midst of the crowd.

"To you! I'd sooner burn them than give them to you!" And he put the cards back in his pocket.

"Come on, give them to me, you blockhead!" said Agrafena.

"No, Agrafena Ivanovna—say what you like, I shan't give them to you! You'll use them to play with him. Good-bye!"

Without a backward glance he waved his hand and trudged after the carriage, looking sturdy enough to pick up Alexander, coachman, carriage, horses and all, and carry them on his shoulders.

"Wretch!" cried Agrafena following him with her eyes and drying her streaming tears on the hem of her kerchief.

They halted at the copse. While Anna Pavlovna sobbed and took leave of her son, Anton Ivanich, after patting one of the horses on the neck, seized it by the nostrils and shook its head from side to side, evidently much to the horse's displeasure, for it bared its teeth and snorted.

"The girth of the wheel-horse has worked loose," he told the coachman. "Can't you see the pad is awry?"

The coachman glanced at the pad, but seeing that it was in its right place he did not move from the box-seat, and merely set the breeching to rights a trifle with the end of the whip.

"Time to go—God be with you!" said Anton Ivanich. "Come, Anna Pavlovna—enough of tormenting yourself! And you, Alexander Fyodorich—get in! You've got to be at Shishkovo before nightfall. Good-bye, good-bye, God send you happiness, high rank, decorations, the best of everything, all good things and a fortune! Well then, God speed! Be off, and mind you keep the horses well in hand going downhill," he added, addressing the coachman.

Alexander, his cheeks wet with tears, got into the carriage, and Yevsei approached the mistress, bowed low before her and kissed her hand. She gave him a five-ruble note.

"Behave yourself, Yevsei, and remember—if you serve your master well, I'll marry you to Agrafena. If not..."

She could not go on. Yevsei clambered on to the box-seat. The coachman, whom the prolonged delays had wearied terribly, suddenly seemed to come to life. He pulled down his hat, settled himself comfortably on the seat, and lifted the reins. The horses started at a light canter. The coachman whipped up the sidehorses in turn, they bounded forward, straining their necks, and the *troika* dashed along the road to the forest. The crowd that had turned out to see the travellers off remained behind in a cloud of dust, silent and motionless, until the carriage had quite disappeared from sight.

Anton Ivanich was the first to recover.

"Now everybody can go home," he said.

Alexander had gazed over the back of the carriage until he could no longer see anyone, and then flung himself face downward on the cushioned seat.

"Don't desert me in my misery," said Anna Pavlovna to Anton Ivanich. "Stay and have dinner with me!"

"Certainly, Madam! I'll have supper, too, if you like."

"You might as well stay the night."

"How can I? Tomorrow's the funeral."

"So it is! Well, you know best then. Give Fedosya Petrovna my love, tell her I am sincerely distressed by her sorrow, and would go to see her myself, if God had not, tell her, sent me a sorrow of my own—if I had not just said good-bye to my son."

"I'll tell her. I'll be sure to tell her."

"Sashenka, my darling!" she whispered, looking round. "He's gone, he's disappeared from sight!"

Anna Pavlovna sat silent the whole day, neither dining nor supping. But Anton Ivanich talked, dined, and supped.

She could only say, from time to time: "Where is he now, my darling?"

"He must be at Neplyuevo now. Oh no, what am I saying? He's not at Neplyuevo, he's only approaching it. He'll stop there for tea," Anton Ivanich replied.

"No, he never takes anything at this time."

And so Anna Pavlovna travelled with Alexander in her mind. When, according to her reckonings, he must have

arrived at Petersburg, she fell to praying, to telling fortunes by the cards, and to talking about Alexander to
Marya Karpovna.

And he?

We shall meet him next in Petersburg.

II

Pyotr Ivanovich Aduyev, our hero's uncle, had, like
his nephew, gone to Petersburg at the age of twenty, sent
there by his elder brother, Alexander's father. And there
he had lived for seventeen years without a break. After
his brother's death he stopped writing to his relatives, and
Anna Pavlovna had had no news of him since the time of
his selling his small estate, which was situated not far from
her own village.

In Petersburg he passed for a moneyed man, and there
may have been sufficient grounds for this opinion. He was
attached to some important personage to carry out special
commissions, and had been awarded several orders. He lived
in one of the better streets, rented an excellent appart-
ment, kept three menservants and as many horses. He was
not an old man, he was at the age described as "the prime
of life"—between thirty-five and forty. But he did not
like to mention his age, and that not on account of petty
vanity, but in accordance with some well thought-out
calculations, as if he wished to insure his life at a higher
premium. However that may be, no vain desire to please
the fair sex could be discerned in his manner of concealing
his age.

He was a tall, well-built man; his features were large and
regular; his face was of a smooth olive hue, his carriage
was good and his manners reserved but agreeable. A *bel
homme*, as such men are usually called.

His expression, too, was reserved, showing self-control
and a determination to prevent his face from being the
mirror of his soul, which, in his opinion, would have been
inconvenient both for himself and others. It was thus that
he appeared in society. But it would have been erroneous
to describe him as wooden-faced. He was merely tranquil.
Sometimes, however, traces of fatigue could be discerned

in his countenance—no doubt from over-work. He was regarded as an active and practical man. He was always scrupulously well-dressed, even to the point of dandyism, but never over-dressed, and always with taste. His linen was of the best quality, his hands were white, the nails long and rosy.

One morning, after he had awoken and rung for his valet, the latter brought him three letters with his morning tea, and informed him that a young gentleman calling himself Alexander Fyodorich Aduyev, and claiming that Pyotr Ivanich was his uncle, had been, and had promised to come again about twelve o'clock.

Pyotr Ivanich received this information with his usual calm, but with a stir of interest, raising his brows as he listened.

"Good. You can go," he said to the valet.

He picked up a letter but stopped in the act of opening it, as if lost in thought.

"A nephew from the country—a pleasant surprise!" he muttered. "And I hoped they had quite forgotten about me over there. Well, I shan't stand on ceremony with him. I'll shake him off."

He rang once more.

"Tell that gentleman when he comes that I had to leave for the factory as soon as I got up and shall be back in three months."

"Yes, sir," said the valet. "And what shall I do with the presents?"

"What presents?"

"His servant brought them—country presents from the mistress, he said."

"Presents?"

"Yes. A tub of honey, a sack of dried raspberries..."

Pyotr Ivanich shrugged his shoulders.

"Two lengths of linen, some jam."

"I can imagine what the linen is like!"

"The linen is good, and the jam is made with syrup."

"Very well. Now go. I'll have a look at them presently."

He picked up one of the letters, opened it and ran his eyes over the page. It looked for all the world like an ancient Slavonic charter, and there was not a single punctuation mark. Aduyev began reading half-aloud.

"Dear Sir, Pyotr Ivanich,

"Having been close friend with your late father and often played with you when you were a child and having often partaken of bread and salt in your house, which emboldens me to feel assured of your goodness and efforts on my behalf in the hope that you have not forgotten old Vasily Tikhonich and all of us here gratefully remember you and your parents and pray for you..."

"Of all the ... who's it from?" wondered Pyotr Ivanich, glancing at the signature. "Vasily Zayezhalov! Bless me if I remember him! What does he want of me?"

And he went on reading.

"Do not refuse my humble request! Being in Petersburg is not the same as it is for us here in the country, you are at home there, you know all about everything, I expect. An accursed lawsuit has been imposed upon me, and I have been struggling with it for nearly seven years. Do you remember the little wood two versts from my village? The Board made a mistake in the title deed, and my enemy Medvedev has taken advantage of it—the clause is wrong, he says, and that's that. Medvedev's the one who was always fishing in your waters without permission. Your late father chased him away and held him up to shame and always meant to complain of this impertinence to the Governor, but he was too kind-hearted—God rest his soul!—to do it, though such a scoundrel should not have been spared. Help me, Pyotr Ivanich, my good sir! The case has come up before the Senate. I do not know what department it is, or who will handle it, but I am sure they would tell you immediately. Please go to the secretaries and senators, get them on my side, tell them I am the victim of a misunderstanding, an error in the title deed. They will do anything for you, I'm sure. And while you are about it you might as well take me out patents for three ranks and send them to me. And I have another very urgent request to make, Pyotr Ivanich—do take pity on an innocent sufferer and help me with advice and with action! There is a certain councillor in the Gubernia administration—Drozhzhov by name—he has a heart of pure gold! He would die rather than let a friend down. I know no other house in the town like his—the moment I arrive I go straight to him, and stay with him for weeks on end—I must never even dream of staying anywhere else—and he dines and wines me, and we play boston till late in the night. And a man like that has been done out of a promotion and now they are nagging him to send in his resignation! Go and see all the grand people, dear friend, tell them what sort of a man Afanasy Ivanich is. Whatever he undertakes is a success. Tell them the information about him is untrue, it was falsified by the Governor's secretary—they'll listen to you—and send me an answer by return of post. And go and see my old colleague Kostyakov. I heard from a man passing through these parts—Studenitsin, one of your Petersburg people, perhaps you know him—that he lives in Peski. Any boy will show you his house. Write by return of post, don't delay, telling me if he is alive and well, what he is doing, if he remembers me. Make his acquaintance, become friends with him. He's a splendid man—open-hearted, jolly.

"I end this letter with one more small request..."

Without reading the letter to the end Aduyev slowly tore it in four, throwing the pieces into a waste paper-basket under the desk. Then he stretched and yawned.

He selected another letter and began reading it half-aloud, as before.

"Dear Brother, Honoured Sir, Pyotr Ivanich."

"What sister is this!" exclaimed Aduyev, glancing at the signature. "Marya Gorbatova." He stared at the ceiling, trying to remember.

"Now what's this? Something familiar ... oh, yes! My brother married a Gorbatova. It must be her sister, the one who ... oh, I remember!"

He frowned and resumed his reading.

"Though fate has parted us, for ever, perhaps, and there is a gulf between us ... the years have passed..."

He skipped a few lines and went on reading further.

"I shall remember till my last breath how we walked round our lake together and, you, imperilling your life and health, went into the water up to your knees to get me a big yellow flower growing in the reeds, and how the juice from its stem stained our hands and you brought water in your cap so that we could wash them. How we laughed! How happy I was then! That flower lies between the pages of a book to this day..."

Aduyev stopped reading. Evidently this circumstance displeased him highly. He shook his head incredulously.

"And have you still got that ribbon," he went on reading, "that you stole from my chest-of-drawers, despite all my cries and entreaties..."

"*I* steal a ribbon?" he cried, frowning heavily. He skipped a few more lines and read on:

"And I have vowed to remain unmarried all my days, and feel quite happy. No one can forbid me to remember those blissful days..."

"Aha! An old maid!" said Pyotr Ivanich to himself. "No wonder she still has yellow flowers in her head! What next?"

"Are you married, dear brother? And if so, to whom? Who is the one who adorns with her person the path of your life? Tell me her name! I will love her like a sister, and in my dreams will join her image with yours, I will pray for you both. And if you are not married, then tell me why—write frankly. I will guard your secrets in my bosom, and they will only be wrested from me together with my heart. Do not delay. I burn with impatience to read your ineffable lines..."

"Oh no, you won't—there won't be any ineffable lines," Pyotr Ivanich told himself.

"I did not know," he read, "that our dear Sasha had suddenly taken it into his head to visit the metropolis—lucky man! He will see grand houses and shops, enjoy all manner of luxury, and press to his bosom his adored uncle—while I shed tears and remember happier days. If I had known of his departure I would have sat day and night embroidering a cushion for you—a moor with two dogs. You cannot imagine how often I have wept, glancing at the design. What can be more sacred than friendship and faithfulness? I now have only this one thought, to which I devote my days, but there is no good wool here, and so I humbly beg you, my dearest brother, to send me the very best English wool to match the pattern enclosed in this letter, as soon as you can, bought at the best shop. But how I do run on! A terrible idea halts my pen. Perhaps you have quite forgotten us, after all why should you remember a poor sufferer, who has withdrawn from society and weeps bitter tears. But no! I cannot believe you could be a monster like other men. No! My heart tells me that amidst the luxury and pleasures of the metropolis you still cherish your former feelings for all of us. This thought is balm for my aching heart. Forgive me, I cannot go on, my hand shakes so...

"Yours till the grave,

"MARYA GORBATOVA.

"P.S. Have you got any nice books, brother? Send me some, if you don't need them yourself. I would remember you on every page, and weep, or you might buy some new ones in a shop, if they're not too expensive. They say Mr. Zagoskin and Mr. Marlinsky have written some very nice novels—any of these would do. And I read in the newspaper about something called *On Prejudices*, by Mr. Puzini—do send it, I can't bear prejudices!"

When he got to the end Aduyev's first impulse was to throw this letter away too, but he refrained.

"No," he told himself. "I'll keep it. There are people who like letters of this sort. Regular collections are made. I may have a chance to oblige someone."

He threw it into a beaded basket hanging on the wall, and passed on to the third letter.

"My dear brother-in-law, Pyotr Ivanich," he read.

"Do you remember how we saw you off seventeen years ago? And now God has called upon me to send my own child off with my blessing on a long journey. Look at him, dear friend, and remember the dear departed, our precious Fyodor Ivanich. Sashenka is the image of him. God alone knows what my heart has gone through, in letting him go to strange parts. I send my dear one straight to you. I told him not to put up anywhere, only with you."

Aduyev shook his head again.

"Silly old woman!" he growled and went on reading.

"In his inexperience he would probably have put up at an inn, but I know how this would grieve his uncle, and told him to go straight to you. Oh, what a happy meeting you will have! Do not deny him your advice, my dear brother-in-law, and take him under your wing. I hand him straight over to you."

Again Pyotr Ivanich came to a stop.

"He has no one but you," he read. "Look after him, don't spoil him, but don't be too severe, either. There will always be people to criticize him, that's what strangers are for, but only one's own folk can be lovingly kind. And he's such an affectionate boy. You only have to see him, and you'll never want to part with him. And tell his chief, when he starts in the civil service, to look after my Sashenka and, above all, to treat him kindly. He's very sensitive, you know. Guard him from wine and cards. I suppose you'll be sleeping in the same room—Sashenka has a habit of sleeping on his back, and that makes him groan and toss, poor child. You must wake him gently and make the sign of the cross over him, and it will pass at once. In the summer you must cover his mouth with a handkerchief. It falls open in his sleep, and the accursed flies get in towards the morning. And please help him if he should need money."

Aduyev frowned, but his face cleared again when he read on:

"I will send whatever is required, I have given him one thousand rubles to keep by him, don't let him spend it on trifles, and see he doesn't fall into the hands of some wheedling rascal, there must be plenty of swindlers and rogues in the capital. And, last of all, forgive me, dear brother-in-law, I have almost forgotten how to write.

"Respectfully, your sister-in-law,
"A. ADUYEVA.

"P.S. I send you our country gifts—raspberries from my own garden, white honey, as pure as tears, sheer lawn for two dozen shirts, and some home-made jam. All this comes with my best wishes. When there's no more left I will send some more. Look after Yevsei, too. He is obedient and does not drink, but he may get spoilt in the capital; if so, whip him."

Pyotr Ivanich slowly replaced the letter on the table, extracted a cigar still more slowly, and, after rolling it between his hands, began to smoke. He meditated long on the trick, as he called it in his own mind, which his sister-in-law had played on him. He made a searching mental analysis of the situation, and the steps he himself ought to take.

He split it all up under the following headings: he did not know his nephew and, therefore, could not love him, and so his heart dictated no obligations whatever to him, and any decision must be based on the laws of reason and justice. His brother had married and known the pleasures of conjugal life, but why should he, Pyotr Ivanich, who had enjoyed none of the privileges of marriage, burden himself with the care of his brother's son? There was no earthly reason why he should.

On the other hand, the situation might be summed up as follows: a mother sends her son straight to him, to his care, without knowing whether or not he desires to undertake such a burden, without even knowing whether he is alive and in a position to do anything for his nephew. This was, of course, foolish, but since the thing has been done and the nephew was in Petersburg, with no one to help him and no friends, even without letters of introduction to anyone, young, completely inexperienced ... would he be justified in leaving him to his fate, casting him into the multitude, without advice or instructions? And if any evil should befall him, would not Pyotr Ivanich have to answer for it to his own conscience?

Here Aduyev could not but remember how his late brother and that same Anna Pavlovna had seen him off, seventeen years previously. They certainly could not have done anything for him in Petersburg, and he had made his way himself ... but he remembered her tears on parting with him, how she had blessed him, like a mother, her caresses, her pies, and her parting words: "When Sashenka grows up"—Sashenka was then a child of three—"perhaps you will be kind to him, brother." At this stage in his meditations Pyotr Ivanich rose and strode hastily into the hall.

"Vasily!" he cried. "When my nephew calls, show him in. And go and find out if the room upstairs is still to let, and if it is, tell them I will take it. Oh—the presents! What shall we do with them?"

"The storekeeper saw them being taken upstairs, and asked me if we would care to sell him the honey. 'I'll give a

good price,' he said, and he would take the raspberries, too."

"Excellent! Let him have them! Well, and what about
the lawn? Will it do for chair covers? Then put it away,
and the jam, too—it can be eaten, it must be good."

Pyotr Ivanich was just going to start shaving when Alexander Fyodorich arrived. He would have fallen on his
uncle's neck, but Pyotr Ivanich, pressing the youth's tender palm in his powerful fist, kept him at a certain distance, as if to take a good look at him, but in reality to
check his effusions and keep them within the limits of a
handshake.

"Your mother is right," he said. "You are the living
image of my late brother. I would have known you anywhere. But you are better-looking. Well, I won't stand on
ceremony with you—I'll go on shaving, and you sit there,
opposite me, so that I can see you. And let us have a talk."

With these words Pyotr Ivanich went about his business
as if there were nobody there, soaping his jaws and bulging
out each cheek in turn with his tongue. Alexander was
embarrassed by such a reception, and did not know how to
begin the conversation. He attributed the coldness of his
uncle to the fact that he had not come straight to his
house.

"Well, how is your mother? In good health? She must
be getting on in years, I suppose," asked the uncle, making faces at himself in the mirror.

"Mamma is well, thank God. She sends you greetings
and my aunt Marya Pavlovna does, too," said Alexander
timidly. "My aunt told me to give you a kiss from her."
He rose and approached his uncle, with the intention of
kissing him on the cheek, the head, the shoulder, or anywhere he could.

"Your aunt is old enough to know better, but I see she
is just as great a fool as she was twenty years ago."

The perplexed Alexander retreated to his place.

"Have you had her letter, Uncle?" he asked.

"Yes, I have."

"Vasily Tikhonich Zayezhalov," said Alexander Fyodorich, "earnestly begs you to look into his case, and..."

"Yes, I've had a letter from him, too. Do you still have
asses like that in the country?"

Alexander did not know what to think—so confounded was he by such a characterisation.

"Forgive me, Uncle," he began, almost in trepidation.

"What for?"

"Forgive me for putting up at the coaching inn and not coming straight to you. I did not know where you lived."

"Why apologize? You did very well. Goodness knows what your Mamma meant! How could you have come to me without knowing if I had anywhere to put you up? I have, as you see, a bachelor establishment, just enough for one—reception-room, drawing-room, dining-room, sitting-room, study, dressing-room and washing-room—not a room to spare. I would be in your way, and you would be in mine. But I have found a room for you in this house."

"Oh, Uncle!" cried Alexander. "How can I thank you for your kindness?"

And again he sprang up with the intention of proving his gratitude by word and deed.

"Not so fast, don't touch me!" said his uncle. "The razor is very sharp, you'll cut yourself and me, too, if you're not careful."

Alexander realized that try as he might he would not be able on this day to embrace and press to his bosom his adored uncle, and postponed the operation for another time.

"It's a cheerful room," continued Pyotr Ivanich. "True, the windows look out on a wall, but surely you won't be sitting at the window all day. When you're at home you'll be busy, you won't have any time to be gaping out of the window. And not expensive—only forty rubles a month. There's a place in the hall for your servant. You must learn to live alone from the very beginning, without a nurse. You can start your own little household, meals and tea, in a word, your own nook, your own *chez soi*, as the French say. You can receive anyone you like there. Of course when I dine at home you will always be welcome, and on other days—young men here mostly dine at an inn, but I would advise you to send out for dinner. It's quieter at home and you don't risk rubbing shoulders with God knows whom. Do you agree with me?"

"I am very grateful to you, Uncle."

"No occasion for gratitude. We're kinsmen, aren't we?

I am only doing my duty. Well, I must dress and go out, I have my work, and my factory."

"I didn't know you had a factory, Uncle."

"Glass and porcelain. But it's not only mine. I have two partners."

"Is it doing well?"

"Not bad. We sell mostly at fairs in remote provinces. We've done very well in the last couple of years. If things go like that for another five years we shall be all right. One of my partners is not very reliable, however—a spendthrift, but I know how to keep him in hand. Well, good-bye! Have a look at the town, stroll about, dine somewhere, and come to me for tea this evening. I shall be at home, and we can have a real talk. Vasily! Show the gentleman his room and help him to settle in."

"So that's how it is in Petersburg," said Alexander to himself, alone in his new dwelling. "If one's own uncle is like that, what will strangers be like?"

Young Aduyev paced his room in profound meditation. And Yevsei talked to himself as he set the room to rights.

"What kind of a life is it here?" he growled. "They say the stove is only heated once a month in Pyotr Ivanich's kitchen, people mostly dine out. Oh, Lord! Fine folk, I must say! And they call themselves Petersburgers. At home even the dogs eat from their own bowls."

Alexander seemed to share Yevsei's opinion, though he said nothing. He went to the window, from which he had a view of chimneys, roofs, and brick walls, black with soot ... and he compared all this with what, only two weeks ago, he had seen from the window of his house in the country. He felt disheartened.

He went out—in the street he found aimless bustle, everyone hastening somewhere, absorbed in his own business, scarcely looking up at the passers-by, and then only to avoid jostling one another. He remembered the gubernia town where the most casual meetings in the street were, in some way or other, interesting. Ivan Ivanich goes to see Pyotr Petrovich, and the whole town knows why. Marya Martynovna comes out of church, Afanasy Savich goes fishing. A policeman rides at breakneck speed from the Governor's house to the doctor's, and everyone knows that Her Excellency has brought forth an infant, although, according to the cronies and grannies, no one ought to have known anything about it. Everyone asks: is it a boy or a girl? The ladies get out their best bonnets. And there comes Matvei Matveich, stepping out of his house with his stout stick at six o'clock in the evening, and everyone knows that he is taking his evening constitutional, without which his digestion would not work, and that he will not fail to stop at the window of the old councillor who, as is also well known, takes tea at that hour. A greeting and a few words are exchanged with every person you meet, and even if you do not greet a person, you know exactly who he is, where he is going, and what for, and in his glance you can read: and I know who you are and where you are going, and what for. If it *should* happen that strangers, who have never before met, come across one another in the street, the faces of both become living question-marks. They halt and look back once or twice, and when they get home they describe the dress and gait of the unknown individual, and many are the surmises as to who the stranger might be, where he came from, and what he had come for. But here in Petersburg, people push one another out of the way with their angry glares, as if they were all sworn foes.

At first Alexander glanced with the curiosity of a country dweller into the faces of every passer-by and every decently dressed person, taking each one for some minister of state, foreign envoy, or famous writer. "Could it be he?" he wondered. "Is it that one?" But he soon got tired of this, for he met ministers, writers and diplomats at every step.

When he looked at the houses he felt still more disheartened. The sight of these monotonous stony edifices, standing like vast tombstones in an unbroken chain, plunged him into gloom. "When the street comes to an end," he told himself, "there will be space for the eye to roam—a hill, some trees, a tumble-down fence," but no!—there was nothing but the same stone walls of exactly similar houses, each with its four rows of windows. And when this street came to an end, another, just like it, began. Whether you looked to the right or to the left, houses, houses, houses, stone upon stone, over and over again, closed in on you like an army of giants. No space for the eye to rest on

... you were hemmed in on all sides—and human thought
and feeling seemed to be hemmed in, too.

The provincial visitor's first impressions of Petersburg
are gloomy. Everything seems strange and mournful to
him; no one takes any notice of him; he is lost in the great
city; neither the novelty, the variety, nor the crowd can
distract him. His provincial vanity is at war with everything
he sees here, and has not seen at home. He ponders over it
all, and transfers himself mentally to his native town. How
pleasant everything looks there! One house has a peaked
roof and a front garden planted with acacias. Here is a
little pent-house on the roof—a shelter for pigeons. The
merchant Izyumin is a great pigeon-fancier, that's why he
built a dove-cote on the roof for them; he stands on the
roof every morning and every evening, in nightcap and robe,
waving a stick, to which a rag is attached, and whistl-
ing to urge his pigeons to fly higher. The next house is
like a lantern—it has windows on all four sides and a flat
roof, a very old house; it looks as if it were just about to
fall down or burn up by spontaneous combustion; the
boards have acquired a light grey shade. Nervous work
living in a house like that—but people do live there. The
owner does occasionally take a look at the bulging ceiling,
and shakes his head, wondering aloud if it will hold till
spring. Then he says, "Let's hope it will," and goes on as
before, fearing more for his purse than for his safety. Next
door is the quaint concave façade of the apothecary's
house, with two wings like sentry-boxes; and beside it
is a house hidden among trees. And now comes one which
has turned its back on the street, and here is an endless
fence, and the trees behind it are loaded with apples—a
temptation for young boys. The houses keep at a respectful distance from the churches, which are surrounded by
dense grass and tombstones. Anyone can see that an office is an office: no one approaches it except on business.
But here, in the capital, an office is not to be distinguished
from ordinary houses, and there is even—just fancy!—a
shop in the same building. At home, as soon as you have
walked through a few streets you begin to sense the pure
air, you walk past wettle fences, vegetable plots, and presently you come to wheat-fields. And the quiet, the stillness, the monotony! In the streets, in the faces of peo-

ple, the same blessed quiet. And everyone lives openly, with no attempt at concealment. No one is cramped for space. The very cocks and hens strut about the streets at their own sweet will, the goats and cows nibble the grass, and the little boys fly kites.

But here—oh, how bleak it is! And the provincial sighs for the fence across the street from his house, for the dusty, dirty street, the shaky bridge, the sign hanging over the door of the wine shop. He hates to admit that St. Isaac's Cathedral is grander and taller than the church in his home town, that the hall in the Club of the Nobility is bigger than the hall at home. He maintains an angry silence when such comparisons are made in his hearing, sometimes, however, venturing to remark that a certain cloth or wine is cheaper and better in his home town, and that people there would not waste a glance at rarities from over the sea, such as these huge prawns and shells and red fish. "Buy fancy cloth and useless trifles from foreigners, if you like," he says. "They swindle you, and you are grateful to them!" And how delighted the provincial is when he discovers that the caviare, the pears or the bread-rolls are better in his native town. "Call that a pear?" he says. "Where I come from even the *servants* wouldn't eat it."

But when he enters one of these houses with a letter of introduction, his disenchantment is still greater. He had expected to be received with open arms, everybody vying with one another to find him a seat, to press refreshments on him ... they will skilfully elicit—he thinks—what his favourite dish is, and he will be so overcome by all this attention that he will end by throwing ceremony aside, embracing host and hostess, as if they had known one another for twenty years. Everyone will drink home-made wine, perhaps sing in chorus...

But not a bit of it! They hardly glance at him, they grimace, say they are busy. If he asks to be received on business they name an hour when people neither dine nor sup, and they may never have heard about elevenses—not a snack, not a drink. The host backs away from the caller's embrace, and regards him somewhat suspiciously. From the next room comes the sound of spoons clattering, glasses ringing—the caller expects an invitation, but instead he is told by various subtle hints that it is time for him to go.

Everywhere locked doors, everywhere door-bells—and isn't that a wretched thing? And faces are so cold and inhospitable. At home, you just walk boldly in. If the family has had dinner already, they will lay the table for the guest all over again. The samovar is always on the table, morning and evening, and there are no door-bells even in the shops. All and sundry are met with embraces and kisses. There, a neighbour really is a neighbour. People live on the most cordial, intimate terms. A relation really is a relation there. He would die for his own kin ... ah me!

Alexander reached Admiralty Square, and stopped short in admiration. He stood in front of the Bronze Horseman a whole hour, in ecstatic meditation,—not, like the unfortunate Yevgeny in Pushkin's poem, with bitter upbraidings in his soul. He gazed at the Neva and at the buildings on either side of it, and his eyes glowed. He felt suddenly ashamed of his devotion to the shaky bridges, the little front gardens, the broken-down fences. His mood changed to one of elation. The bustle, the crowd—everything acquired a new significance in his eyes. Once more the hopes, crushed under the weight of his first, melancholy impressions, revived. The new life opened its arms to him, luring him towards the unknown. His heart beat violently. He dreamed of lofty toil, of noble aspirations, and strode proudly along Nevsky Prospekt, telling himself that he was a citizen of a new world. His head in the clouds, he returned home.

At eleven o'clock that evening his uncle invited him to drink tea.

"I've just come from the theatre," he said, from the sofa where he was lying.

"What a pity you didn't tell me, Uncle—I would have gone with you."

"I was in the stalls, where would you have sat—on my lap?" rejoined Pyotr Ivanich. "You can go by yourself tomorrow!"

"It's so sad all by oneself in the crowd, Uncle. There's no one to exchange impressions with."

"And no reason to do so. You must learn to feel and think—in a word, to live—alone. The time will come when you will need the ability. And before you go to the theatre you'll have to get yourself some decent clothes."

Alexander looked down at his coat, astonished at his uncle's words.

"What's wrong with my clothes?" he asked himself. "Blue coat, blue trousers..." "I have a lot of clothes, Uncle," he said. "Königstein made them—he makes the Governor's clothes."

"Can't be helped—they won't do. I'll take you to my own tailor in a day or two. But that's a small matter. There are more important things to discuss. Tell me—what made you come here?"

"I came here—to live."

"To live? If by that you mean to eat, drink and sleep, it wasn't worth while coming so far. You will not eat or sleep as well as you did in the country. But if you had any other ideas, kindly tell me."

"To enjoy life was what I meant to say," added Alexander, blushing hotly. "I got tired of living in the country—the same thing over and over again."

"Ah-ha! So that's it! And do you intend to rent a first-floor apartment on Nevsky Prospekt, to keep a carriage, to acquire a wide range of acquaintances, and have a regular at-home day?"

"All that would be very expensive," said Alexander naively.

"Your mother writes that she has given you a thousand rubles," said Pyotr Ivanich. "That's not enough. An acquaintance of mine arrived recently—he had become tired of the country, too, and wanted to enjoy life. But he brought with him fifty thousand rubles, and will receive as much every year. He really will enjoy life in Petersburg, whereas you—will not. That's not what you came for."

"You seem to imply, Uncle, that I don't know what I came for."

"That's about the truth of the matter, or rather, there is some truth in it. And that's no good, either. Surely, before deciding to come you must have put to yourself the question: What am I going for? It would have been as well if you had."

"My answer was ready before I asked myself that question," replied Alexander, not without pride.

"Then why don't you tell me? Well, what was the answer?"

"I was drawn here by an irrepressible desire, by a thirst for noble activities. I was devoured by the desire to elucidate, to fulfil..."

Pyotr Ivanich raised himself a little on the sofa, took the cigar out of his mouth and listened attentively.

"...To fulfil those hopes which surged..."

"You don't write poetry, do you?" asked Pyotr Ivanich suddenly.

"Yes, and prose, Uncle! Shall I bring some to show you?"

"No, no! Later on. I just asked."

"Why?"

"Oh, the way you speak..."

"Don't you like the way I speak?"

"I don't say that. It's very fine no doubt, only rather odd."

"Our teacher of aesthetics used to speak like that and he was considered the most eloquent of all the professors," said Alexander, somewhat taken aback.

"What did he talk about?"

"About his subject."

"Ah!"

"How ought I to speak, Uncle?"

"More simply, like everybody else, and not like a professor of aesthetics. But this can't be explained all at once; you'll see for yourself by and by. As far as I remember university lectures and can interpret your words, you wish to say that you came here to make a career and a fortune. Is that it?"

"Yes, Uncle, a career..."

"And a fortune," added Pyotr Ivanich. "What's a career without a fortune? A good idea—but you shouldn't have come."

"Why not? It isn't your own experience that makes you say that, I hope," said Alexander looking round the room.

"Well said! It's true I have a comfortable apartment and my affairs go well enough. But, as far as I can see, there is a great difference between you and me."

"I should not dream of comparing myself to you."

"That's not the point. You may be ten times cleverer and better than I am, but it seems to me that your nature is not one to submit to new ways. And as for the ways prevalent in the country—upon my word! You, for instance,

have always been the spoiled darling of your mother—
how could you endure what I have had to endure? You're
probably a dreamer, and there's no time for dreaming here.
People of our sort come here to get things done."

"Perhaps I would be able to accomplish something, if
you did not refuse me your advice and the fruits of your
experience."

"I'm afraid to advise you. I cannot answer for you and
your country ways. If nothing came of it you might reproach me, but I don't mind telling you my opinion, if
you like. You can heed it or not, just as you choose. But
no! I have no hope of success. You have your own outlook
on life. How can I change it? You are all for love, for
friendship, for the delights of life, for happiness. People
over there think life consists in nothing else—all ah's and
oh's. They shed tears, moan, say pretty things, but they
do nothing. How am I to break you of all that? It's not
so easy."

"I will endeavour to adapt myself to modern ways,
Uncle. Only today, gazing at these vast edifices, at the ships
which bring gifts from distant lands to us, I meditated on
the achievements of modern man, I understood the agitation of this crowd, its rational activities, and felt ready
to merge myself with it."

During this monologue Pyotr Ivanich's eyebrows shot
up higher and higher, and he gazed attentively at his
nephew. Alexander broke off.

"A simple enough matter," said his uncle. "But look
what they get into their heads—'this crowd with its rational activities'! You should have stayed at home, indeed
you should have! You could have lived out your days there
in perfect contentment. You would have been the clev-
erest of all, there, passing for an author and an eloquent
individual, believing in eternal, unchangeable love and
friendship, in kinship, and in happiness. You would have
married and your life would have flowed on smoothly
into old age, and you really would have been happy in
your own way; but you will never be happy as they understand happiness here. All your conceptions would have
to be reversed."

"But, Uncle—are not love and friendship, those sacred, lofty emotions which have fallen by chance, as it

were, from heaven to the earth and its filth..."

"What's that?"

Alexander said nothing.

"Love and friendship have fallen into the filth! Now really, you can't talk such nonsense *here*!"

"Do not they exist here as much as there, I meant?"

"Love and friendship exist here, too. There's no shortage of that stuff anywhere. But they're not the same here as they are in the country. In time you will learn this for yourself. The first thing you must do is to forget these *sacred* and *divine* emotions, and regard things as they really are. It would be a great deal better, and you would speak more simply. But after all, it's none of my business. You're here, and you don't intend to go back. If you fail to find what you're looking for, don't blame me. I can only tell you what, in my opinion, is good, and what I consider bad, and you can do as you like. Who knows, perhaps it may be possible to make something of you. Oh, yes! Your mother asks me to supply you with money. Now, listen to me! Don't ask me for money. It is fatal to a good relationship between decent people. But you mustn't think I would refuse you. Oh, no! If you have no alternative, you must apply to me, of course. After all, it would be better to borrow from an uncle than from a stranger—at least you wouldn't have to pay interest. But to prevent such an emergency arising I will look for a place for you, so you can earn money. Well, good-bye! Look in tomorrow, we'll discuss ways and means."

Alexander made to go back to his room.

"I say—would you like some supper?" his uncle called after him.

"Why, yes, Uncle, I wouldn't mind."

"I haven't got anything."

Alexander said nothing. "Then why the invitation?" he thought.

"I don't eat at home, and the restaurants are all closed now," continued his uncle. "Let it be a lesson to you at the very start—get used to it. You get up and go to bed with the sun in the country, and eat and drink according to the dictates of nature. If it's cold you put on a hat with earflaps, and there you are; when it's light—that's the daytime, when it's dark, that's night. *You* can hardly keep your eyes open now, but *I* shall sit down to work—I must have my accounts ready by the end of the month. You breathe fresh air all the year round over there, but that pleasure costs money here, like everything else. Poles apart! People don't eat supper here, especially at their own expense—and not at mine either. And it'll be good for you— you won't groan and toss in your sleep so much, and I have no time to get up and make the sign of the cross over you."

"It will be quite easy to get accustomed to that, Uncle."

"All the better. And is it still the same as it used to be in the country—can you still visit friends in the night, and count on their getting supper for you at once?"

"Why, Uncle, I hope there's nothing wrong with that! The Russian's chief virtue..."

"Now, now! What's the virtue in it? You're so bored that you're glad to see any scoundrel. 'Welcome, welcome, eat as much as you like, only distract us in our idleness, help us to kill time, and let us have a look at you. At least it's something new. And we don't grudge the food—it costs us nothing whatever.' A most unpleasant virtue!"

And Alexander went to bed trying to decide what sort of a person his uncle really was. He went over the whole conversation in his memory—there was much he could not understand, and much that he did not quite believe.

"I say the wrong things," he pondered. "Love and friendship are not eternal! I wonder if my uncle is making fun of me? Can it really be that such customs prevail here? Why, it was my eloquence that Sonechka liked best of all in me! And could it be that her love is not eternal? And don't people really eat supper here?"

He lay tossing in his bed for a long time, his head full of disturbing thoughts, his empty stomach keeping him awake.

Two weeks passed.

Pyotr Ivanich grew more pleased with his nephew with every day.

"He is not at all tactless," he told one of his partners, "which is surprising in a country boy. He never forces himself on me, never comes without an invitation. And as soon as he notices that he is in the way, he goes. And he never asks for money. He's a quiet fellow. A bit eccentric—always trying to kiss me—and holds forth like a di-

vinity student, but he'll shake all that off. Thank goodness, I don't have to support him."

"Any fortune?" asked the other.

"No. About a hundred souls."

"Well! If he's clever he'll get on here. You yourself
began in a small way, and now, thank God..."

"Oh, no! Not he! He'll never achieve anything. That
silly enthusiasm will get him nowhere—forever oh-ing and
ah-ing! He'll never get used to things here. What sort of a
career can he make? He should never have come—oh, well,
it's his own business!"

Alexander considered it his duty to love his uncle, but
he could not get used to his character and cast of mind.

"My uncle seems to be a kind man," he wrote one
morning to Pospelov. "He's very clever, but he's rather a
prosaic person, always absorbed in business and accounts.
His spirit is chained to the earth and never rises to pure
contemplation, freed from all earthly considerations, of
the spiritual nature of man. For him the heavens are closely bound up with the earth, and it seems to me that our
souls will never become completely united. I thought,
when I came here, that, being my uncle, he would give
me a place in his heart, would warm me with the embrace
of friendship in the midst of the cold-hearted crowd. And
friendship, as we know, is *another providence*. But he is
himself the very embodiment of this crowd. I thought he
and I would spend our time together, would never be parted for a moment, but what did I find? Cold advice, which
he calls practical. I would rather it were unpractical but
full of warm, heartfelt sympathy. It isn't that he's proud,
but he is opposed to all sincere effusions. We neither dine
nor sup together, and never go anywhere. When he comes
home he never tells me where he has been or what he has
been doing, just as he never tells me where he is going, and
what for, who his friends are, what his likes and dislikes
are, and how he spends his time. He never gets particularly angry, nor is he ever affectionate, melancholy, or gay.
Impulses of love and friendship, aspirations towards the
beautiful, are alien to his heart. You can hold forth like a
prophet, almost as well as our great, unforgettable Ivan
Semyonich, when—do you remember?—he thundered

from the platform, and his fiery glances and words made us tremble with enthusiasm. But my uncle just listens with his eyebrows raised and looks at me queerly, or laughs in a way he has, a laugh that makes my blood freeze—and farewell, inspiration! Sometimes I seem to see Pushkin's Demon in him. He does not believe in *love* and that sort of thing, says there is no such thing as happiness, that no one ever promised it to men, and that there is nothing but everyday life, divided equally into good and evil, into pleasure, luck, health, success, tranquillity, and then displeasure, bad luck, anxiety, sickness and so on, that we must learn to regard everything simply, and not cram our heads with useless (think of it, useless!) questions as to why we were created, and what we aspire to, that all that is not our business, and that it prevents us from seeing what lies under our nose, and attending to our own business—he talks of nothing but business. It's impossible to tell whether he is doing something enjoyable, or is engaged in some prosaic business matters. He's always the same, whether sitting over accounts, or at the theatre. He does not go in for violent emotions, and seems neither to know nor to care for the beautiful. It is alien to his soul. I don't even believe he has read Pushkin..."

Pyotr Ivanich suddenly appeared in his nephew's room, and found him writing a letter.

"I've come to see how you've settled in," he said, "and to discuss business."

Alexander sprang up and hastily covered some object with his hand.

"Put it away, do, if it's a secret!" said Pyotr Ivanich. "I'll look the other way. Well—have you put it away? Something's fallen out. What is it?"

"Nothing, Uncle," began Alexander, but broke off in confusion.

"A lock of hair, if I am not mistaken. Most decidedly nothing. Well, since I've seen that, show me what is hidden in your hand."

Alexander, like a schoolboy caught doing something naughty, reluctantly opened his hand and displayed a ring.

"What's that? Where did it come from?" asked Pyotr Ivanich.

"That, Uncle, is a tangible sign of intangible relations."

"What, what? Hand it over, your tangible sign."

"It's a token of..."

"You brought it from the country, probably."

"It's from Sonechka, Uncle, a keepsake when we said farewell."

"So that's what it is! And you carried it with you over a thousand versts?"

Pyotr Ivanich shook his head.

"You should have brought another sack of dried raspberries instead. They can at least be sold to the storekeeper, but these tokens of yours..."

He glanced from the lock of hair to the ring. The hair he sniffed at, and the ring he weighed in his hand. Then he took a piece of paper from the table, wrapped up both tokens in it, made a compact ball of it all and flung it out of the window.

"Uncle!" screamed Alexander, seizing his arm, but it was too late. The ball flew over the corner of a neighbouring roof, landed on a barge on the canal below, rebounded, and fell into the water.

Alexander looked in silence at his uncle, with an expression of bitter reproach.

"Uncle!" he said.

"Well?"

"How am I to call such an act?"

"As the throwing out of the window of intangible signs and all sorts of rubbishy trifles which ought not to be kept in your room."

"Trifles! That's what you call trifles!"

"And what did you think they were? A half of your heart? I come to speak to him on business, and what do I find him doing? Sitting and thinking about all sorts of rubbish!"

"And does that interfere with business, Uncle?"

"Greatly. Time is passing and you still haven't said a word to me of your intentions—whether you wish to go into the civil service, or have chosen some other occupation—not a word! And all because your head is full of Sonechka and tokens. I suppose that's a letter to her you were writing, isn't it?"

"Well, I had just begun."

"And have you written to your mother?"

"Not yet—I was going to write to her tomorrow."

"Why tomorrow? Tomorrow for your mother, and for Sonechka, whom you are bound to forget in a month's time—today!"

"Sonechka! As if I could forget her!"

"You're bound to. If I hadn't thrown away your tokens you might perhaps have remembered her an extra month. I have done you a double service. In a few years those tokens would have reminded you of a folly which would have made you blush."

"Blush for such pure, sacred memories? That would be denying the meaning of poetry."

"What's so poetic in folly? The sort of poetry there is in your aunt's letter, I suppose. A yellow flower, a lake, some mystery. You can't think how sick it made me feel to read it! I almost blushed, and I am certainly not in the habit of blushing any more."

"Uncle, that's terrible! Does it mean you have never loved?"

"I can't stand tokens."

"But there's no more feeling in that sort of life than there is in a block of wood!" exclaimed Alexander in violent agitation. "It's vegetation, not life! To vegetate without inspiration, without tears, without life, without love..."

"And without locks of hair!" added his uncle.

"How can you mock so callously at what is the best thing on earth, Uncle? Why, it's a crime—love ... sacred trepidation!"

"I know your sacred love—at your age you think of nothing but locks of hair, slippers, garters; if you so much as touch a hand—sacred, elevated love runs through your whole being, and if you had your own way you'd... Your love, unfortunately, is still to come. Nobody escapes it, but serious business may escape from you if you do not take it up."

"And is not love a serious business?"

"No. It's a pleasing distraction, and one shouldn't give up too much time to it, or everything will go wrong. That's why I fear for you."

Pyotr Ivanich shook his head.

"I have almost found you a place. You want to work, don't you?"

"Oh, Uncle, how glad I am!"

Alexander sprang up and imprinted a kiss on his uncle's cheek.

"So he grabbed his chance after all!" said his uncle, wiping his cheek. "How did I let myself get caught unawares? Now listen to me. Tell me what you know, and what you feel yourself capable of."

"I know divinity, civil, criminal, natural and public law, diplomacy, political economy, philosophy, aesthetics, archaeology..."

"Stop! Stop! Can you write Russian decently? That's what's chiefly wanted nowadays."

"What a strange question, Uncle! Can I write Russian?" exclaimed Alexander, running over to the chest-of-drawers and taking from it a heap of papers, his uncle in the meantime picking up a letter from the table and beginning to read it.

Alexander came back to the table with his papers, and saw his uncle reading his letter. The papers fell from his grasp.

"What's that you're reading, Uncle?" he asked in alarm.

"I found a letter lying here—to a friend, I suppose. Sorry—I only wanted to see what your writing was like."

"And have you read it?"

"Almost—there are only two lines left, let me finish it. What's the matter? There can't be any secrets in it, or you wouldn't have left it lying about like that."

"What must you think of me now!"

"I think you write fairly well—correctly and smoothly."

"So you haven't read it?" asked Alexander eagerly.

"I seem to have read it all," said Pyotr Ivanich, running his eyes over the two pages. "You begin by describing Petersburg, your impressions, and then myself."

"Oh, Lord!" cried Alexander, covering his face with his hands.

"What's the matter with you?"

"And you can say that calmly? You are not angry, you don't hate me?"

"Not at all! Why should I hate you?"

"Say it again—calm me!"

"Of course I'm not angry!"

"I simply can't believe it! Prove it to me, Uncle."

"What d'you want me to do?"

"Embrace me!"

"Sorry! I can't do that."

"Why not?"

"Because there would be no reason, or rather no sense in it, or, to use the words of your professor, my consciousness does not impel me to it. If you were a woman, now, it would be different. There one acts without reason, moved by quite different impulses."

"Feelings strive for release, Uncle, demand impulsive acts, effusions..."

"They do not seek release or demand anything in my case. If they did I would restrain them—and I would advise you to do the same."

"But why?"

"So that afterwards, when you come to know the person whom you have embraced better, you should not blush for your embrace."

"And has it never happened to you, Uncle, that you repelled a person, and later regretted it?"

"It has. And therefore I never repel anyone."

"Not even me—for such an act? You won't call me a monster?"

"According to you, everyone who writes nonsense must be a monster. I'm afraid there'd be a great many monsters if this were so."

"But to read such home truths about oneself—and from your own nephew!"

"You think you have written the truth?"

"Oh, Uncle! Of course I was mistaken—I will alter it. Forgive me!"

"Shall I dictate you the truth?"

"Please do!"

"Sit down, then, and write."

Alexander drew a sheet of note-paper towards him and picked up his pen, and Pyotr Ivanich, glancing at the letter he had just read, dictated:

"Dear Friend—got that?"

"Yes."

"I will refrain from describing Petersburg and the impression it made on me."

"On me," repeated Alexander, writing.

"Petersburg has been described long ago, and what has not been described must be seen for oneself. My impressions are worth nothing. There is no point in wasting time and paper on them. I will describe my uncle instead, for this refers to me personally."

"Uncle!" interjected Alexander.

"Well, you wrote that I am kind and clever—perhaps I am, perhaps I'm not. Better let's take the middle course. Write! My uncle is neither stupid nor bad-tempered, and wishes me well..."

"Uncle! I am capable of appreciating it, I feel it!" exclaimed Alexander, reaching over to kiss him.

"...Although he is not forever throwing his arms round my neck," said Pyotr Ivanich, continuing to dictate.

Alexander, unable to get at him, hastily sat down again.

"...And wishes me well because he has neither cause nor desire to wish me ill, and because my mother, who once treated him kindly, asked him to look after me. He says he does not love me—and with good reason: it is impossible to love anyone after knowing him only a fortnight, and I don't love him yet, though I say I do."

"How can you!" exclaimed Alexander.

"Go on writing! But we are getting used to one another. He says it is possible to do without love altogether. He does not sit with his arms round me from morning till night, because this would be quite unnecessary. Besides he has no time for it.

" '...opposed to sincere effusions,' that can stay, that's good. Have you got that?"

"Yes."

"Well, what else is there here? 'Prosaic soul ... demon...' Go on!"

While Alexander wrote, Pyotr Ivanich picked up a bit of paper from the desk, twisted it into a spill, set light to it, and lit his cigar, after which he threw the paper down and stamped on it.

"My uncle is neither a demon nor an angel, but a man like everyone else," he dictated, "but he's not quite like you and me. He thinks and feels on earthly terms, believing that, since we dwell upon the earth, we ought not to fly up into the heavens, where so far no one has invited us, but should occupy ourselves with human affairs, to which we are called. And therefore he takes all earthly affairs and also life itself for what they are, and not for what we should like them to be. He believes in the existence of good and of evil, the beautiful and the hideous. He believes also in love and friendship, but he does not think they have fallen from heaven into filth, supposing rather, that they were created at the same time as human beings and for human beings, and must be understood in this sense, and that we should examine things closely in their true light, and not soar away, God knows where. He admits the possibility of attachments between honourable men, which, from frequent contact and habit, may grow into friendship. But he considers, also, that during separation habit loses its power and people forget one another, and that this is by no means a crime. He therefore assures me that I will forget you, and you, me. This seems very strange to me, and to you also probably, but he advises us to get accustomed to the idea, in order not to make fools of ourselves. He has a similar opinion of love, with slight modification—he does not believe in constant, eternal love any more than he believes in hobgoblins, and advises us not to, either. He advises me, by the way, to devote as little thought to this as possible, and I advise you to do the same. He says love will come of itself, without being summoned. He says life does not consist in love alone, but that, like everything else, there is a time for it, and it is foolish to spend ages dreaming of nothing but love. Those who seek it and cannot do without it for a moment, live by the dictates of the heart, and even lower instincts, at the expense of the mind. My uncle likes to keep busy, and advises me to cultivate the habit also, which advice I hand on to you. We belong to society, he says, which is in need of us. And while doing business, he does not forget his own interests. Business brings in money, and money—comforts, of which he is very fond. Besides, he may have certain intentions, owing to which I shall probably not be his heir. My uncle is not always thinking of his work and his factory, he knows quite a few poets by heart, not just Pushkin..."

"You, Uncle!" exclaimed Alexander in surprise.

"Yes. You'll find it out for yourself one day. Go on:

he reads in two languages everything new that comes out
of any note regarding all branches of human knowledge;
he loves art, has a fine collection of paintings of the Flemish
school—that is his taste—frequently visits the theatre, but
does not fuss, or gush and sigh, for he considers this puerile and believes that we must control our impulses, refrain from imposing our impressions on others, because no
one has the slightest use for them. He does not use extravagant language, which he advises me not to do either,
and I advise you. Good-bye, write to me as seldom as possible, and do not waste your time. Your friend, *et cetera.*
And now, the month and the date."

"How can I send such a letter?" asked Alexander.
" 'Write as seldom as possible!'—and this to one who travelled over a hundred versts for the sole purpose of saying
a last farewell! 'I advise you to do this, that, and the other.'
He's just as clever as I am, he graduated second at the university."

"Never mind—send it. Perhaps it'll make him a bit
wiser. It will give rise to all sorts of new ideas in his mind.
You may have graduated from the university, but your
real schooling is only just beginning."

"I can't bring myself to send it, Uncle."

"I never interfere in other people's affairs, but you asked
me yourself to do something for you. I am trying to get
you onto the right path and make your first steps easier,
and you resist me stubbornly. Well, just as you like—I'm
only telling you my opinion, I'm not forcing you. I'm not
your nurse."

"Forgive me, Uncle. I am ready to obey you," said
Alexander and sealed up the letter with no more ado.

He then looked round for the other letter—to Sophia.
It was neither on the table, under the table, nor in the
drawer.

"What are you looking for?" his uncle asked.

"I'm looking for the other letter—to Sophia."

His uncle joined in the search.

"Where can it be?" he said. "I didn't throw it out of
the window—'pon my word I didn't!"

"Uncle! What have you done? You lit your cigar with
it!" said Alexander mournfully, gathering up the scorched
fragments of his letter.

"Did I?" exclaimed his uncle. "How could I have done that? And I never even noticed. Fancy burning such a treasure! And yet—d'you know what? In one respect it's all for the best."

"Really, Uncle, I can't see in what respect it could be for the best," said Alexander despairingly.

"It is—really, it is. You won't have time to write to her by this post, and by the time the next goes you'll probably have changed your mind, you'll be busy with your work. You'll have other things to think of, and thus you will have committed one folly less."

"But what will she think of me?"

"Whatever she likes. And I believe it will be good for her, too. You don't mean to marry her, do you? She will think you have forgotten her, and will forget you in her turn, and will have less to blush for when she meets her future husband, and assures him that she has never loved anyone but him."

"You're an extraordinary man, Uncle! Constancy does not exist for you, promises are not sacred. Life is so beautiful, so full of delights and pleasures. Like a smooth, enchanting lake..."

"In which grow yellow flowers, of course," interrupted his uncle.

"Like a lake," continued Alexander, "life is full of something mysterious and alluring, concealing so much..."

"Slime, my friend."

"Why must you dig up the slime, Uncle? Why destroy all the joys, hopes, blessings? Why always look on the dark side?"

"I look on the real side—and advise you to do the same, then you won't make a fool of yourself. Your attitude to life is all very well in the country, where people know nothing about it, and they're not even people—they're angels. Zayezhalov is a saint, your aunt is a lofty, sensitive soul. Sophia is just as big a fool as your aunt, and probably they are both..."

"Go on, Uncle!" exclaimed the infuriated Alexander.

"...both dreamers like you, no doubt. Always sniffing round after eternal friendship and love. For the hundredth time I tell you—you should never have come here."

"No, she's not the kind to assure her future husband

that she has never loved anyone!" said Alexander, almost as if speaking to himself.

"Still thinking of that?"

"On the contrary, I am sure she will show him, with noble frankness, my letters and..."

"Tokens," put in Pyotr Ivanich.

"Yes, and the tokens of our relations. And she will say to him: 'This was he who first touched my heart-strings. This is the name to which they first responded.'"

Pyotr Ivanich's eyebrows shot up, and his eyes opened wide. Alexander fell silent.

"Well, have you stopped harping on your strings? All I can say, dear boy, is that your Sophia will be a ninny if she does anything of the sort. I trust she has a mother, or somebody who can stop her."

"And you can call this, the most sacred impulse of the soul, this noble effusion of the heart, folly, Uncle? What am I to think of you?"

"Whatever you like. She would make her fiancé suspect God knows what. Why, the marriage might be broken off—and what for? Just because you once picked yellow flowers together! That's not the way to go about things! Well, since you can write good Russian, we'll go to the office tomorrow. I have mentioned you to one of my former colleagues there, the head of a department. He says there's a vacancy. There's no time to lose. What's that bundle of papers?"

"My university notes. Allow me to read you a few pages from Ivan Semyonich's lecture on Greek art."

He was already hastily turning over the pages.

"Oh, spare me, please!" cried Pyotr Ivanich, wrinkling up his features. "And what's that?"

"Oh, that's my thesis! I should like to show it to my future chief. There's one project in particular, worked out by me."

"Oh! Oh! One of those projects which had been carried out a thousand years ago, or which can never and should never be carried out."

"Why, Uncle! It was shown to a very prominent person, a great advocate of education. He actually invited the rector and myself to dinner because of it. And here's the beginning of another."

"Have two dinners with me, only don't finish any more projects!"

"But why not?"

"Because you won't write anything worth while, and time will be wasted."

"What? After all the lectures I've attended!"

"They'll come in handy in time, but now you must observe, read, learn, and do what you're told."

"How is the chief to know what I can do?"

"He'll know at once. He's a dab at that. And what post would you like to occupy?"

"I don't know, Uncle, what to..."

"There are ministers," said Pyotr Ivanich, "deputy ministers, directors, vice-directors, heads of departments, head clerks, their assistants, clerks with special duties. Isn't that a wide enough choice for you?"

Alexander pondered. He felt at a loss, confronted by such a wide choice.

"I might as well start as head clerk," he said.

"You might!" agreed Pyotr Ivanich.

"I could get used to the work, Uncle, and in a month or two I might become the head of a department."

Pyotr Ivanich pricked up his ears.

"Of course, of course!" he said. "And in another three months you could become a director, and a year after—let us say—a minister. Would that suit you?"

Alexander flushed, but said nothing.

"Didn't the head of the department tell you what the vacancy was?" he asked after a pause.

"No," replied his uncle. "He didn't say what it was, and anyhow we'd better leave it to him. You see how hard you find it to make a choice, and he knows what would be best. Don't tell him about your difficulty in choosing, and not a word about your projects, either. He might be offended at your not trusting him, and shout you down. He's a hard man. And I would not advise you to speak to the Petersburg *belles* about tangible tokens—they wouldn't understand you. How could they? It would be above their heads. I could hardly understand you myself, and they would only grimace."

While his uncle was speaking, Alexander kept turning a bundle of papers over and over in his hands.

"What's that you're holding?"

Alexander had been awaiting this question with impatience.

"It's ... I've been wanting to show you for a long time ... some verses. You asked me about them once."

"I don't seem to remember. I don't think I asked you."

"You see, Uncle, I regard work in an office as a very prosaic occupation, in which the soul has no part, and the soul thirsts to express itself, to share with its fellowmen the feelings and ideas with which it overflows..."

"Well, and what about it?" asked his uncle impatiently.

"I feel that creative work is my vocation."

"You wish to do something over and above office work—is that how your words must be interpreted? Well, highly laudable. What do you want to go in for—literature?"

"Yes, Uncle. I wanted to ask you if you could help me to get something published."

"And are you sure you have talent? Without it you will merely be an unskilled labourer in the field of art, and what's the good of that? If you have talent—that's another matter. It would be worth while working. You can do a lot of good. That's capital—worth a great deal more than your hundred souls."

"Do you measure that by money, too?"

"How else? The more people read what you write, the more money you will be paid."

"And fame? Fame is the true reward of the songster."

"Fame is tired of mothering songsters. There are too many candidates. In the old days fame, like a woman, made up to everyone, but now—you may have noticed—she seems to have vanished, to have hidden herself. Notoriety exists, but somehow one doesn't hear a word about fame. Or can it be that she has invented a new way of showing herself—those who write best get the most money, and those who don't write well mustn't mind getting nothing for their pains. At least, good writers have a good life nowadays, they don't freeze and die of starvation in attics even if people don't run after them in the street any more and point at them as if they were court jesters. People have discovered that a poet is no heavenly denizen but a human being who looks, walks, thinks and commits follies just like the rest of us. So why gape at him?"

"Like the rest of us—oh, Uncle! How can you say that? A poet bears a special imprint—a higher power dwells in his bosom."

"Just as it sometimes does in others—in a mathematician, a watchmaker, and in us factory owners. Newton, Gutenberg, Watt were just as much endowed with higher powers as Shakespeare, Dante and the rest. If I ever manage to improve our Pargolovo clay by some means so that it can be made to produce better porcelain than Saxonian or Sèvres ware, don't you think this would prove the presence of higher powers in me?"

"You confound art with crafts, Uncle."

"God forbid! Art is one thing, and crafts is another, but the creative principle may dwell in both, or in neither. If it does not, the craftsman is called a craftsman and not an artist, and the poet is not a poet, but a mere poetaster. Didn't they tell you that in the university? What *did* you learn there?"

Pyotr Ivanich was quite vexed with himself for having condescended to explain such a commonly accepted truth.

"Too much like sincere effusions," he told himself. Aloud he said, "Show me what you have there. Poetry?"

He took the bundle and ran his eyes over the first page:

> *Whence come these grievous meditations*
> *Which float in an uncalled-for crowd?*
> *Which slay desires and aspirations...*

"Give me a light, Alexander."

After lighting a cigar he resumed his reading:

> *And in deep gloom our hearts enshroud?*
> *Why on a sudden do dark sorrows*
> *Immerse the soul in heavy sleep?*
> *What undeterminable horrors*
> *All unawares upon us creep?*

"The same thing spun out to eight lines—well diluted!" remarked Pyotr Ivanich, and read on:

> *Which of us mortal men can know*
> *Why suddenly the dew-like tears*
> *Appear upon the paling brow?*

"What's this? Sweat appears on the brow, but I never saw *tears* there."

> *A sign that unknown evil nears,*
> *Beneath the silence of the skies*
> *Some dread and awful meaning lies.*

" 'Dread' and 'awful' mean the same thing."

> *I watched the sky—a pallid sphere,*
> *The moon sails past, in silence bound,*

"Ah, the inevitable moon! No getting along without it! If you have daydream and maiden, you are lost—I give you up."

> *I watch the sky—a pallid sphere,*
> *The moon sails past, in silence bound,*
> *And something seems to say that here*
> *The fatal mystery is found.*

"Not bad! Give me a light again, my cigar's out. Where was I? Oh, yes:

> *The grimly silent stars that dot*
> *The mystical nocturnal height*
> *Seem joining in an evil plot*
> *And glitter with deceitful light.*
> *Although to some the restful night*
> *Their souls with calm may seem to fill,*
> *The sleeping world is full of spite,*
> *All in the Universe bodes ill.*
> *That gnawing sorrow bears no name..."*

Pyotr Ivanich yawned portentously, and continued:

> *But grief may disappear like flame,*
> *That burns a while, then fades and dies,*
> *Subsiding never more to rise.*

He now began gabbling, almost to himself:

And then, perchance, another sprite
Makes its abode within our minds,
And then a feeling of delight
Its way into our spirit finds.

"Neither good nor bad," he said, when he had come to the end. "After all, some people began worse. Go on, write, work at it, if that's what you like. Perhaps you will show talent. Then we shall see."

Alexander was saddened. He had expected quite a different appraisal. He found, however, a slight consolation in regarding his uncle as a cold, almost soulless being.

"And here's a translation from Schiller," he said.

"Enough. I see it is. So you know languages, too?"

"I know French, German, and a little English."

"Congratulations—why didn't you tell me before? You may be made into something, after all. You told me about political economy, philosophy, archaeology, and God knows what else, and never said a word about the most important thing of all—that's misplaced modesty. I'll find you literary work immediately."

"Will you, Uncle? I shall be most grateful to you! Let me embrace you!"

"Wait till I've found you something."

"Won't you show some of my works to my future chief, to give him an idea of what I can do?"

"No, no! If necessary you can show them to him yourself, but perhaps it won't be necessary. Will you make me a present of your projects and other writings?"

"Will I? Why, of course, Uncle!" exclaimed Alexander, flattered by his uncle's request. "Shall I make a list of all of them in chronological order?"

"No, don't trouble. Thanks for the gift. Yevsei! Give these papers to Vasily!"

"Why to Vasily? Let him take them to your study."

"He was asking me for some paper to line trunks with or something the other day."

"Uncle!" exclaimed Alexander in horror, snatching back the bundle of papers.

"But you gave them to me, it's none of your business

what use I make of your present."

"Nothing is sacred to you, nothing!" groaned Alexander, pressing the papers to his breast with both hands.

"Listen to me, Alexander," said Pyotr Ivanich, tearing them from his nephew's grasp, "this will save you from embarrassment later on, and you will thank me."

Alexander let go of the bundle.

"Here you are, Yevsei, take them away!" said Pyotr Ivanich. "Well, now it's nice and tidy in your room— no more rubbish in it. It will depend on yourself whether it becomes filled with a lot of litter, or with something useful. Let us now drive to the factory for a breath of fresh air, and see how the work is going."

The next morning Pyotr Ivanich took his nephew to the office, and while he chatted with his friend, the head of the department, Alexander acquainted himself with this world, so new to him. He was still dreaming about his projects and wondering what state problem he would be given to solve, but in the meantime he stood there looking around him.

"It's just like my uncle's factory!" was the conclusion he finally came to. "There, one man picks up a lump of clay, flings it into the maw of the machine, turns it a few times, until out comes a cone, an oval, or a disc, then passes it on to the next man, who dries it over the fire and hands it to a third who gilds it, after which a fourth draws the design on it, and there emerges a cup, a vase, or a saucer. And here—in comes a petitioner, bowing low with a pitiful smile as he hands in his paper, one man takes it, gives it a slight touch with his pen and hands it to another, who throws it on top of a thousand other papers, where, however, it is not lost; with a number and date stamped on it it passes unhurt through a score of hands, proliferating and producing more of its kind. A third man picks it up and opens some cupboard, glances into a book or at another paper, utters a few cabalistic words to a fourth, whose pen immediately starts squeaking busily. When his pen has finished squeaking, the fourth man hands on the parent document, with yet another infant affixed to it, to a fifth man, whose pen also squeaks industriously, and another paper is born, and the paper goes on and on, and never gets lost—its originators may die, but it will go on living for another hundred years. Even after it has long been covered with the dust of ages it may still be disturbed and consulted. And day by day, hour by hour, today, tomorrow, for ever and ever, the bureaucratic machine goes on working smoothly, never resting, as if there were no such thing as human beings—only wheels and cogs.

"Where is the mind that animates and sets this paper factory in motion?" wondered Alexander. "Is it in books, in the papers themselves, or in the heads of these people?"

And the faces! You do not see such faces in the street, their owners do not seem to show themselves in the daylight. It is here, apparently, that they are born and bred, growing up with their posts, and dying at them. Alexander took a good look at the department chief. Like a thundering Jupiter he had only to open his mouth for some Mercury, his breast adorned with a glittering copper disc, to come running up immediately. He had only to hold out his hand with some paper in it, and a dozen hands were stretched out to receive it.

"Ivan Ivanich!" he said.

Ivan Ivanich sprang from his seat at a desk, hastened up to Jupiter, and stood before him at attention. Alexander was seized with trepidation, though he could not have said why.

"Give me a pinch of snuff."

With eager servility Ivan Ivanich held out the open snuff-box in both his hands.

"Oh, and give that one a test!" said the chief, pointing to Aduyev.

"So that's who is to give me a test!" thought Alexander, looking at the rusty figure of Ivan Ivanich whose coat sleeves were worn to a sheen. "Can it be that such a man solves state problems?"

"Have you a good hand?" asked Ivan Ivanich.

"Hand?"

"Yes—handwriting. Be so good as to copy out this paper."

Alexander, though astonished at the demand, did as he was asked. Ivan Ivanich screwed up his features when he saw what Alexander had written.

"He writes badly," he reported to the head of the department, who also glanced at the paper.

"Yes—no good! Can't make a fair copy. Let him do second copies for a start, and when he gets used to that you can put him on filling in forms. Perhaps he'll do—he's had a university education."

Very soon Aduyev, too, had become a cog in the machine. He wrote, wrote endlessly, and could no longer understand how anything else could be done of a morning. The memory of his projects now only brought a blush to his cheeks.

"You were right about that, Uncle," he said to himself. "Ruthlessly right. Can it be you were right about everything else? Can it be that I have been mistaken in my inspired thoughts, in my passionate belief in love, friendship, people, and in myself? What is the meaning of life then?"

He bent over his paper, and his pen squeaked still more loudly, while tears gleamed on his eyelashes.

"Fortune positively smiles on you," Pyotr Ivanich told his nephew. "When I started, I had to work a whole year without a salary, and you begin straight away at senior rates. That comes to seven hundred and fifty rubles, and bonuses will bring it up to a thousand. A very good start! The head of the department speaks well of you, but says you are absent-minded—sometimes you forget to put in commas, sometimes you leave out the contents of a document. You must pull yourself together. The great thing is to attend to what is going on around you, and not let your mind wander goodness knows where."

Pyotr Ivanich pointed upwards. From now on he became even kinder to his nephew.

"What a wonderful man our head clerk is, Uncle!" said Alexander one day.

"What makes you think so?"

"We have become very friendly. Such an elevated soul, such pure, noble ideas! And the assistant, too—he seems to be a man of iron will and firm character."

"You became friends already?"

"Oh, yes!"

"Has the head clerk invited you to his Thursday evenings?"

"Most pressingly! Every Thursday. He seems to have taken a fancy to me."

"And has the assistant asked you for a loan?"

"Yes, Uncle—a mere trifle. I gave him twenty-five rubles that I had on me. He asked me for another fifty."

"Oh, you gave him some! Ah!" said Pyotr Ivanich in vexation. "It's partly my fault for not warning you. I didn't know you were simpleton enough to lend money after a fortnight's acquaintance. Can't be helped—we'll go shares. You can consider I owe you twelve rubles fifty."

"But, Uncle, surely he'll return it?"

"Not he! I worked there. He has owed me a hundred rubles ever since I worked there. He borrows from everyone. Next time he asks you, tell him I asked him to remember his debt to me and he'll leave you alone. And mind you don't go to the head clerk's house!"

"Why not, Uncle?"

"He's a gambler. He'll draw you into a game with a couple of fellows like himself, and between them they'll clean you out."

"A gambler?" repeated Alexander in amazement. "Is it possible? He seemed to be so addicted to sincere effusions."

"And while talking to him, you can let it slip out that I have taken charge of all your money, and then you'll see how fond he is of sincere effusions and whether he'll ever invite you to his home again on a Thursday."

Alexander fell into deep thought. His uncle shook his head.

"Did you really think you were surrounded by angels?" he said. " 'Sincere effusions! Taken a fancy to you!' Apparently it never occurred to you before to wonder if there weren't any scoundrels among them. You should never have come here! Really you shouldn't have!"

One day, just after Alexander had waked up, Yevsei handed him a large envelope and a note from his uncle.

"Here's some literary work for you at last," he wrote. "I met a journalist friend yesterday, and he gave me something for you to try your hand at."

Alexander's hands shook with excitement as he opened the envelope. It contained a manuscript in German.

"What's this?" he said. "Prose? What's it about?"

He read the pencilled inscription at the top:

"*The Soil*, an article for the agricultural department. Kindly translate as quickly as possible."

He studied the article long and thoughtfully, then, sighing, he slowly picked up his pen and began to translate. Two days later the article was finished and dispatched.

"Splendid! Splendid!" his uncle told him a few days later. "The editor is delighted, though he considers your style is not austere enough. But you can't expect everything straight away. He would like to make your acquaintance. Call on him tomorrow, in the evening, about seven—he has another article for you."

"On the same subject, Uncle?"

"No—something else. He told me what, but I've forgotten. Oh, yes—on *potatoes*! Really, Alexander, I think you were born with a silver spoon in your mouth. I begin to hope that something may come of you, after all—perhaps I shall one day stop telling you that you should not have come here. A month has hardly passed, and everything seems to be coming your way. A thousand rubles' salary, an editor offering you twenty-five rubles a sheet—that comes to two thousand two hundred rubles. *I* didn't begin like that," he said, knitting his brows slightly. "Write to your mother that you have found work, and how. I'll also write to her and tell her that, remembering her kindness to me, I have done all I could for you."

"My mother will be ... very grateful to you, Uncle, and I am too," said Alexander, sighing, but he no longer tried to embrace his uncle.

III

Over two years passed by. Who could have recognized our country bumpkin in this smartly dressed young man with the elegant manners? He has changed greatly and grown to manhood. The soft lines of his youthful face, the transparent delicacy of his skin, the down on his chin—all, all have disappeared, as have also his bashful timidity and the awkward grace of his movements. His features have matured, forming a countenance which displays character. The lilies and roses have vanished beneath a light tan. The down on his cheeks has been replaced by small whiskers. His light, springy gait has become firm and even. Some bass notes have been added to his voice. The sketch has developed into a finished portrait. The youth has become a man. Assurance and courage shine from his eyes—not the courage which makes itself heard a mile away, regards everything with arrogance, and says to all and sundry, by glance and manner: "Look, beware, do not touch, do not tread on my foot—or else ... I'll make short work of you!" The manifestation of the courage I am speaking of, far from repelling, attracts. It shows itself in a striving towards good, towards success, in a desire to overcome all obstacles in its way. The ecstatic expression of Alexander's face has been modified by a tinge of thoughtfulness, the first dawnings of doubt, and perhaps the only result of his uncle's lessons and of the merciless analysis to which the latter subjected everything that went on in Alexander's heart. At last Alexander has learned tact, that is, he has acquired the ability to handle people. He no longer rushes eagerly at everyone he meets, especially since, despite his uncle's warnings, he has allowed himself to be rooked at cards a couple of times by the friend with a tendency to *sincere effusions*, and lent the man of iron will and firm character quite a lot of money. Other persons and occurrences have done much to help strengthen his character. Here he has noticed that people poke fun on the sly at his youthful raptures, and call him a romantic. There, he is being ignored, as practically nothing is to be gained from him. He does not give dinners, does not keep a carriage, does not play cards for high stakes.

At first Alexander's heart ached and mourned after each crash of his rosy dreams against reality. It never occurred to him to ask himself: what great thing have I done to distinguish myself from the crowd? What are my merits and why should I be noticed? And yet his vanity suffered.

Little by little he began to admit to himself that apparently there are thorns as well as roses in life, and that the thorns sometimes inflict pain, though not so severe as his uncle had foretold. And at last he started learning self-control, ceased giving way so frequently to impulse and emotion, and checked his tendency towards high-flown language, at least in front of strangers.

But he was by no means able as yet, much to the distress of Pyotr Ivanich, to break up into component parts all which moves and stirs the soul of man. He would not as yet admit that all the mysteries and secrets of the heart could be brought to the light of day.

In the morning Pyotr Ivanich gave him a sound lesson. Alexander listened, sometimes feeling abashed and sometimes plunged in profound meditation, and in the evening went off to some party or other and returned in a doze. For three days he went about as in a dream, and his uncle's doctrines were consigned to the devil. The magic and excitement of a ball, the blaring of the band, the naked shoulders, the fiery glances, the smiling rosy lips kept him awake all night. The memory of a waist on which his hand had rested, a languid glance which had followed him as he went away, the hot breath he had felt on his cheek during a waltz, the low words exchanged at a window to the accompaniment of the lusty mazurka, eyes sparkling, and the lips uttering heaven knows what—all passed before him in succession. His heart beat violently, and he hugged his pillow in feverish perturbation, tossing and turning in his bed.

"Where is love? It is love I thirst for—love!" he cried. "Will it come soon? When will those divine moments, those sweet sufferings, that blissful trepidation, those tears, begin?" And all the rest of it.

He appeared before his uncle the next morning.

"Oh, what a party that was at the Zaraiskys' last night, Uncle!" he said, and fell to dreaming over the memories of the ball.

"Good, was it?"

"Divine!"

"Was the supper decent?"

"I didn't have any."

"What? At your age not to have supper when you can! I see you are getting accustomed to the way of life here in earnest, almost too much so. And was everything done in style? Dresses, lighting?"

"Indeed it was!"

"And the guests—were they a nice set of people?"

"Very, very nice! Such eyes, such shoulders!"

"Shoulders? Whose?"

"Weren't you asking about them?"

"About whom?"

"Why—the young ladies."

"No, I wasn't. But never mind—were there many pretty ones?"

"Ever so many—the only pity is that they are all so alike. Whatever one of them says and does in certain circumstances you may be sure the next one will say and do, like a lesson learned by heart. There was one ... not exactly like the rest ... there's no independence or character in them that you'd notice. Movements, glances—all the same! You never hear an original idea, or catch a glimmer of feeling—everything is covered with the same gloss. It seems that nothing can break through that gloss. Can it be that feeling will be suppressed forever, that it will never display itself to anyone? Will their stays always stifle the sigh of love and the cry of an anguished heart? Will emotion never be given freedom?"

"Everything will be disclosed to their husbands, and if everyone were to think aloud as you do, probably many girls would remain spinsters all their lives. There are silly little fools who reveal prematurely what should be concealed and suppressed—and what do they get for it but tears? There's no profit in it."

"Profit here, too, Uncle?"

"As everywhere else, my boy. Those who do not think of profit are incalculable fools. A clear-cut statement of fact."

"To suppress in one's bosom one's noblest impulses and emotions!"

"Oh, you will never suppress anything, I know that! You are ready—in the street, at the theatre, anywhere— to fall sobbing on a friend's neck."

"And why not, Uncle? People would only say: there's a man with strong feelings, a man who feels thus is capable of all that is lofty and noble, and is incapable of..."

"Incapable of calculating, that is to say, thinking. A fine figure—a man with strong feelings and vast passions! There are all sorts of temperaments, aren't there? Enthusing, exalted natures! People like that least resemble real men and that's nothing to boast about. You should ask if he can control his emotions; if so, he's a man."

"According to you emotions need controlling as if they were steam," remarked Alexander. "Sometimes a little may be released, sometimes it must be shut off, the valve must be opened or closed..."

"Yes, not for nothing has Nature given man this valve—it is reason, and you do not always make use of it, sad to say, but for all that you're a decent chap."

"It's depressing to listen to you, Uncle. Better introduce me to that lady who has just come to Petersburg."

"Who? Lyubetskaya? Was she there last night?"

"Yes, and she talked about you a great deal, enquired about her case."

"Oh, yes. By the way..."

Pyotr Ivanich took a paper out of a drawer.

"Take her this and tell her that only yesterday I managed to get it almost by force from the Chamber. Explain the matter to her thoroughly. You heard me talking to the official about it, didn't you?"

"Yes, yes. I'll explain it to her, don't worry."

Alexander seized the document with both his hands and put it in his pocket. Pyotr Ivanich looked at him.

"What makes you want to know her? I don't think she's particularly good-looking—she has a wart at the side of her nose."

"A wart? I don't remember. How did you come to notice it, Uncle?"

"Right at the side of her nose—as if one could help noticing it. What is it you want with her?"

"She's so kind and worthy."

"So you didn't notice the wart on her nose, but you have discovered that she is kind and worthy? Funny! Wait a minute, though! She has a daughter, a little brunette. Ah! Now I understand! So that's why you didn't notice the wart on her nose."

They both laughed.

"And I can't understand, Uncle," said Alexander, "how you could notice the wart on her nose before you noticed her daughter."

"Give me back that paper. You'll probably pour out all your emotions and quite forget to close the valve, and make a mess of things."

"No, I won't, Uncle. And I don't mean to give you back the paper, whatever you say. I'll go at once."

And he left the room.

So far things had been running their course. At his office his superiors had noticed Alexander's ability and had given him a good post. Ivan Ivanich began offering his snuff-box respectfully to him, foreseeing that, like many other upstarts, Alexander would overtake him, lord it over him, get promoted to head of department, and then vice-director, like that chap, or even director, like that other chap, both of whom had begun their careers under him and learnt the ropes from him. "And I've got to slave for them," he added. At the editorial office of the magazine Alexander had also become an important personage. He selected the material, translated articles, and corrected those of others, even sending in contributions embodying his own views on the theory of agriculture. In his own opinion he had more than enough money, but his uncle was still not content. And he did not only work for money. He had not given up the joyful thought of another, loftier vocation. His youthful ardour sufficed for everything. He stole time from sleep and office work and wrote poems, novels, historical essays and biographies. His uncle no longer lined his trunks with Alexander's writings, but read them in silence, after which he whistled, or declared: "Better than the one you showed me last time." Some of his articles appeared under a pen name and Alexander listened with a happily fluttering heart to the approving judgements of his friends, of whom he had any number, at the office, in teashops, and in private houses. His fondest dream—next to the dream of love—was coming true. The future offered him much brilliance, great triumphs. It seemed as if no ordinary lot awaited him, when suddenly...

Several months flashed past. Alexander was scarcely seen anywhere, he seemed to have disappeared. He visited his uncle less frequently. The latter thought he was busy, and let him alone. But one day the editor of the magazine, happening to meet Pyotr Ivanich, complained that Alexander was not handing in his work on time. The uncle promised to speak to his nephew at the earliest opportunity. An opportunity arose two or three days later. One morning Alexander rushed like a madman into his uncle's room. He was in a flurry of happy excitement.

"Good morning, Uncle! Oh, how glad I am to see you!" he said, and would have embraced Pyotr Ivanich if the latter had not retreated behind the table.

"Good morning, Alexander! Where have you been all this time?"

"I've been—busy, Uncle. I've been making compilations from German economists."

"Oh! So the editor was lying! The other day he told me you weren't doing anything—isn't that just like a journalist? I'll tell him what I think of him next time we meet."

"Don't say anything to him," interrupted Alexander. "I haven't sent in my work yet, that's what he meant."

"Why, what's the matter with you? You have such a triumphant look. Have they made you an assessor, or given you a cross?"

Alexander shook his head.

"Money, then?"

"No."

"Then what makes you look so triumphant? If it's not that, then don't get in my way, but sit down and write to Moscow, to the merchant Dubasov, to send the rest of the money as soon as possible. Read his letter—where is it? Oh, here it is!"

Both were silent a few moments, and then both began writing.

"I've finished," said Alexander a few minutes later.

"Very quick—well done! Let me see. What's this? You've addressed it to me. 'Honoured Sir, Pyotr Ivanich!' His name is Timofei Nikonich. You've written 520 rubles—it's 5,200! What's the matter with you, Alexander?" Pyotr Ivanich laid down his pen and stared at his nephew. Alexander blushed.

"Don't you notice anything in my face?" he asked.

"You do look rather silly now you mention it. Wait a minute! Are you in love?" asked Pyotr Ivanich.

Alexander made no reply.

"Have I guessed right?"

Alexander, with a smile of triumph and a radiant glance, nodded affirmation.

"So that's it! I should have guessed at once. So that's what's made you lazy, that's why you are never seen anywhere! And all those Zaraiskys and Skachins come pestering me: 'What's happened to Alexander Fyodorich, where is he?' And all the time he's in the seventh heaven!"

Pyotr Ivanich resumed his writing.

"It's Nadya Lyubetskaya," said Alexander.

"I didn't ask," said his uncle. "Whoever it is, it's folly. Which Lyubetskaya? The one with the wart on her nose?"

"Oh, Uncle!" Alexander interrupted him in vexation. "What wart?"

"Right on her nose. D'you mean to say you haven't yet noticed it?"

"You're mixing everything up. It's her mother who has a wart on her nose, I think."

"It's all the same."

"All the same! Nadya! She's an angel! Can it be you have not noticed her? To have seen her, and not to remember her..."

"What's so wonderful about her? What is there to notice? You say she hasn't got a wart on her nose."

"Must you keep harping on that wart? For shame, Uncle—surely nobody could say she was like those worldly, conventional puppets! Just take a look at her face—what profound, quiet thought dwells there! This is a thinking, not just a feeling girl ... by no means a shallow girl."

His uncle's pen began to squeak over the paper, but Alexander continued.

"You will never hear from her lips the usual trivial commonplaces. What brilliancy of mind shines through her remarks! What fire in her emotions! How thoroughly she understands life! You poison it with your sceptical views, but Nadya reconciles me to it."

Alexander paused, quite absorbed in his dreams of Nadya. Then he started off again:

"And when she lifts her eyes you see at once what a passionate, tender heart she has. And her voice, her voice! How melodious, how seductive! And when this voice utters words of love—what earthly bliss could be higher! Uncle! How beautiful life is! How happy I am!"

Tears came into his eyes; he rushed to his uncle and hugged him convulsively.

"Alexander!" cried Pyotr Ivanich, springing to his feet. "Close that valve of yours immediately! All the steam

is escaping! You are mad! Look what you've done! Committed two follies in a single moment—ruffled my hair and
made me drop a blot on my letter. I thought you had
quite given up those habits. You haven't been like this
for a long time. Look at yourself in the mirror, pray do.
Did you ever see such a stupid countenance? And yet
you're not really stupid."

"Ha, ha, ha! I'm happy, Uncle."

"That's obvious."

"Pride shines in my glance, doesn't it? I know it does.
I gaze at the crowd as only a hero, a poet and a lover,
happy in the consciousness of mutual love, could gaze."

"And as only a madman or someone still worse could...
Well—what am I to do about this letter?"

"Let me scrape the blot off—it won't show," said
Alexander.

He rushed up to the table and, with the same nervous energy, began scraping and rubbing till he made a
hole in the paper. The table shook from all these movements, and knocked against the whatnot. On the whatnot
was a bust of Sophocles or Aeschylus—in Italian alabas-
ter. The venerable tragedian rocked backwards and forwards several times on his unsteady pedestal, fell off the
shelf, and was broken into smithereens.

"Your third folly, Alexander," said Pyotr Ivanich,
gathering up the fragments. "That cost fifty rubles."

"I'll pay, Uncle, oh, I'll pay, only don't abuse my
impulse! It was pure and noble. I am happy, happy!
Heavens, how beautiful life is!"

His uncle grimaced and shook his head.

"When will you learn wisdom, Alexander? What rubbish
you do talk!"

All this time he was regarding the broken bust ruefully.

"'I'll pay,' he says, 'I'll pay.' And that would be the
fourth folly. I see you are burning to tell me of your
happiness. Very well, then. Since an uncle is obliged to
participate in every folly perpetrated by his nephews, so
let it be. I will give you a quarter of an hour. Sit still, don't
commit a fifth folly, but tell me all about it, and then,
after this new folly, go. I have no more time to spare.
Well—so you are happy, and what about it? Hurry up and
tell me!"

"Such things cannot be put into words," remarked Alexander with a modest smile.

"I tried to help you, but I see you are still intent on beginning with the usual preamble. In that case your tale would take at least an hour. And I have no time. The post will not wait. Come now, I'd better do the telling myself."

"You—that would be amusing!"

"Highly amusing—listen, then! Yesterday you had a private interview with your beauty..."

"How did you know?" interrupted Alexander eagerly. "Are you having me shadowed?"

"Of course I am—I engage paid spies for no other purpose! What makes you think I am so interested in what you do? What is it to me?"

These words were accompanied by an icy glance.

"Then how did you know?" asked Alexander, coming nearer to his uncle.

"Sit down, sit down, for God's sake, and keep away from the table, or you'll be breaking something else. It's all written on your face, I can read it from here. Well, so you made a declaration," he continued.

Alexander reddened, but said nothing. Evidently his uncle had hit the nail on the head again.

"You were both very foolish in the accepted fashion," said Pyotr Ivanich.

His nephew made an impatient gesture.

"It all began with trifles when you found yourselves alone," said Pyotr Ivanich. "The pattern of her embroidery, say. You asked who it was for? She replied 'for Mamma or my aunt,' or something of the sort, and you were both trembling as if you had an ague..."

"You guessed wrong this time, Uncle. We didn't begin with the pattern of her embroidery, we were in the garden," said Alexander, and checked himself.

"Well then, with a flower or something," said Pyotr Ivanich. "It may even have been a yellow one, but never mind. Whatever your glance fell on, any excuse for talking, anything to loosen your tongue. You asked her if she liked this flower, she said, 'Yes.' 'And why?' you asked her. 'I just do,' she replied, and you both fell silent, because you wanted to say something quite different, and the conversation flagged. Then you looked at one another, smiled, blushed."

"Oh, Uncle, Uncle!" cried Alexander, highly embarrassed.

"Then," continued his uncle inexorably, "you began telling her that a new world had opened before you. At this she looked up suddenly, as if it were a most surprising piece of news. You, I suppose, were taken aback, and lost your thread, and then began saying almost inarticulately that only now you had begun to understand the value of life, that you had seen her before too—what's her name—Marya?"

"Nadya."

"That you had seen her in your dreams, that something told you you'd meet, that mutual liking had brought you together, and that now, you would dedicate to her alone all the poetry and prose you wrote... And I can just imagine how you waved your hands about ... probably knocked something over, broke something."

"Uncle! You must have been eavesdropping!" shrieked Alexander, almost beside himself.

"Yes, I was hiding behind a bush. I have nothing else to do but run after you and listen to all sorts of rubbish."

"But how do you know all this?" asked the astonished Alexander.

"It's simple. From the time of Adam and Eve everyone has gone through the same thing, with slight variations. When you know the characters of the *dramatis personae* you know the variations. This surprises you—and you a writer! For three days now you will go about leaping and jumping like a madman, and falling on everybody's neck—only not on mine, for mercy's sake! I would advise you to lock yourself into your own room for this period, and there let all the steam escape, and play all your tricks on Yevsei, so that nobody sees. Then you will think things over, and try for something more—a kiss, for example."

"A kiss from Nadya! Oh, what a lofty, divine reward!" wailed Alexander in ecstasy.

"Divine?"

"And do you consider it earthly?"

"Undoubtedly—the effect of electricity. Lovers are simply a pair of Leyden jars. They are both heavily charged, the kisses release the electricity, and when it is all exhausted, farewell love!—the cooling process begins."

"Uncle!"

"Well? And what did you think?"

"What an attitude! What ideas!"

"Oh, yes, I forgot—there are still 'tangible tokens' to be exchanged between you. You'll be bringing all sorts of rubbish home again, and mope over them and gaze at them, and forget all about your work."

Here Alexander clapped his hand to his pocket.

"What—already? You will do what people have been doing since the creation of the world."

"That means you did the same yourself, Uncle."

"Why, yes, only you are doing it still more foolishly."

"More foolishly! Do you call it folly that I love more profoundly, more intensely than you did, Uncle, that I do not mock at feeling, do not jest at it, do not trifle with it callously like you, do not tear down the veils from sacred mysteries?"

"You will love as others do, neither more profoundly nor more intensely. Like others, you will tear down the veils from mysteries. But with the difference that you will believe love is eternal and immutable, and will think of nothing but love—and that is where you are foolish. You are preparing more sorrow for yourself than is absolutely necessary."

"What you say is appalling, Uncle! How many times have I sworn to myself that I would conceal from you the workings of my heart!"

"And why didn't you? Why did you come and bother me?"

"But, Uncle, you are the only family I have here. With whom should I share this overwhelming emotion? And you ruthlessly plunge your surgeon's blade into the most secret mazes of my heart."

"I do not do it for my own pleasure. You asked my advice. How many follies have I saved you from!"

"No, Uncle—I would rather appear eternally foolish in your eyes than adopt such an attitude to life and human beings. That would be too painful, too sad for me. I do not want life on such terms. I won't have it—do you hear me?"

"I hear you. But what am I to do? I can't deprive you of life."

"Despite all your predictions, I shall be happy," said Alexander. "I shall love once and for ever!"

"And I foresee that you will break a lot more things on my table. But never mind! Love all you want. Nobody hinders you, young people have always been known to occupy themselves most diligently with love, but then not to the extent of neglecting work. Love is one thing and business is another."

"But I am making extracts from the German."

"Nonsense! You're doing nothing of the kind! You're simply indulging in 'blissful dreams', and the editor will refuse to have anything to do with you."

"Let him. I am not in need. How could I think of contemptible lucre, when..."

"Oh—contemptible lucre! Contemptible! Why don't you build a hut in the mountains, live on bread and water, and declare:

> *A wretched hovel shared with thee,*
> *To me a paradise would be.*

Only when you have no more 'filthy lucre', don't come begging to me—I shan't give you any."

"I don't think I have often troubled you on this score."

"So far, thank God, you haven't, but it might happen, if you throw up your work. Love demands money, too—for dressing up and various other purposes. Oh, love at twenty! It's such a worthless emotion, oh how worthless it is—simply no good at all!"

"And when is it any good, Uncle? At forty?"

"I know nothing about love at forty—but love at thirty-nine..."

"Like your own?"

"Say, like my own."

"That is to say—no love!"

"How do you know?"

"As if you could love!"

"Why not? Am I not human, or am I eighty? But when I love, it is rationally, I do not knock things over or break anything."

"Rational love! A fine love when a man knows exactly

what he's about," remarked Alexander scornfully. "A love that never causes one to forget oneself for a moment."

"In violent, animal love," Pyotr Ivanich interrupted, "a man does not know what he is about, but in rational love, he does. Otherwise it is not love."

"What is it then?"

"Just foulness, as you would say."

"You ... in love," said Alexander, gazing incredulously at his uncle. "Ha, ha, ha!"

Pyotr Ivanich went on writing in silence.

"And with whom, Uncle?" asked Alexander.

"Do you want to know?"

"I do."

"With my betrothed."

"Your betrothed!" repeated Alexander, scarcely able to bring the words out; and, springing up, he approached his uncle.

"Not too near, Alexander, close your valve!" said Pyotr Ivanich, noting the wide-open eyes of his nephew and hastily moving various small objects—small busts, statuettes, a clock and the ink-pot—towards himself.

"Do you mean you are going to get married?" asked Alexander in a tone of astonishment.

"I do."

"And you are so calm! Writing business letters to Moscow, talking about abstract matters, going to your factory and still able to discuss love with such infernal coldness!"

"Infernal coldness—that's new! It's supposed to be hot in the nether regions. But why do you look at me like that?"

"You—are going to get married!"

"What is there so extraordinary about that?" asked Pyotr Ivanich, laying down his pen.

"Getting married! And without telling me a word!"

"Forgive me, I forgot to ask your permission."

"Not that, Uncle, but I ought to have been told. My own uncle is going to get married, and I know nothing about it, nobody tells me."

"Well, now I've told you."

"But only because the subject happened to come up," said Alexander. "I should have been the first to hear of your happiness. You know how I love you and share..."

"I avoid all sharing on principle, especially with reference to marriage."

"Listen, Uncle," said Alexander impetuously. "Perhaps ... but no, I cannot conceal anything from you. It's not my way, I will tell you all..."

"Oh, Alexander, I'm too busy—if it's a new story, couldn't it wait till tomorrow?"

"I only wanted to say that perhaps I, too, am near the same happiness."

"What?" exclaimed Pyotr Ivanich, pricking up his ears. "This promises to be interesting."

"Interesting, is it? Then I will tease you—I won't tell!"

Pyotr Ivanich picked up an envelope with the utmost indifference, put his letter into it, and began sealing it.

"Perhaps I, too, will get married," Alexander said, close to his uncle's ear.

Pyotr Ivanich stopped sealing his letter and looked at him very gravely.

"Close the valve, Alexander!" he said.

"Joke away, Uncle, but I am in earnest. I am going to ask Mamma's permission."

"You—marry?"

"Why not?"

"At your age!"

"I'm twenty-three."

"And time to get married, you think. At that age only peasants marry, when they need a woman to do the housework."

"But if I am in love with a girl and in a position to marry, do you consider I should not..."

"I would by no means advise you to marry a woman you are in love with."

"Uncle! That's new! I never heard that before!"

"There are plenty of things you have never heard yet."

"I always thought marriage without love was wrong."

"Marriage is one thing, and love is something else," said Pyotr Ivanich.

"So one should marry for money?"

"Not for money, but taking money into consideration among other things. Man is so made that he needs the company of woman. One begins by thinking about getting married, and then proceeds to look about and select the right woman."

"Look about! Select!" said Alexander in astonishment.

"Yes, select. That is why I would not advise you to marry while you are in love. Love passes, you know—that's a commonplace."

"It is a gross lie and a scurrilous libel."

"Oh, there's no persuading you just now! You will see for yourself in time, but for the present remember my words: love, I repeat, passes, and then the woman who was once your ideal of perfection turns out, perhaps, to be far from perfect, and it will be too late to do anything about it. Love screens from you the lack of qualities necessary in a wife. Whereas when you set out to make your own selection, you can coolly weigh the claims of this or that woman to the qualities you would like to see in your wife. That is the main consideration. And having discovered such a woman, your feelings for her will undoubtedly last, for she will answer to your requirements. Hence there will grow between you an intimacy which later develops into..."

"Love?" asked Alexander.

"Let us say, habit."

"To marry without feeling, without the poetry of love, without passion, coldly reasoning! And why?"

"And you would marry without reasoning, without asking yourself why? Just as you came here without asking yourself why?"

"So you are going to marry for money?" said Alexander.

"Taking money into consideration."

"It's the same thing."

"No. To marry for money would mean to marry for money alone. That would be base. But to marry without taking everything into consideration would be folly. And as for you, you ought not to be thinking of marrying at all yet."

"When ought I to marry, then? When I am old? Why should I follow absurd examples?"

"Including my own? Thanks."

"I don't mean you, Uncle—I mean in general. You hear of a wedding, and you go to take a look—and what do you see? A lovely, delicate creature, hardly more than a child, only waiting for the magic touch of love to unfold into a luscious flower, and here she has been abruptly wrenched away from her dolls, her nurse, her childish pastimes, from dances—and thank God if that is all, for often no one troubles to look into her heart, which, it may be, already belongs to another. She is dressed up in gauze and lace and adorned out with flowers and, despite her tears and pallor, dragged to the altar, and set beside—whom? Beside an elderly man, most likely unattractive, who has already used up the vigour of youth. Either he casts glances of lascivious desire at her, or inspects her coldly from top to toe, as if thinking: 'You're very pretty, but I suppose you're full of whims and fancies—love and roses—I'll soon put a stop to all that nonsense. None of your sighing and dreaming, behave yourself, now!' Or, worst of all, he dreams of her fortune. The very youngest of these is at least thirty. He often has a bald pate, but then he has been decorated with a cross, or even, perhaps, a star. And they say to her: 'This is the man to whom all the treasures of your youth, the first stirrings of your heart, your love, your glances, your words, your virginal caresses, your whole life shall belong.' And all around crowd the young and handsome men who are a match for her, and one of whom should be standing beside the bride. They devour the poor victim with their eyes, as if telling themselves: 'When we have lost our youth, our health, when we have gone bald, we too will marry and get ourselves a charming blossom like this one.' It's terrible!"

"Alexander, Alexander, it won't do!" exclaimed Pyotr Ivanich. "You've been writing for two years about soil, potatoes and other important things which demand an austere, concise style, and you still rant. For God's sake, don't yield to ecstasy, or if you are overcome by its fumes at least hold your tongue till they clear away, for you will never say or do anything sensible in that state—nothing but absurdity."

"But, Uncle, is not the poet's thought born of ecstasy?"

"I don't know where it's born. I only know it comes ready-made from the head, that is to say, after having been through the process of cerebration, and only then is it any good." Pyotr Ivanich paused, and then went on: "And to whom, in your opinion, should these exquisite creatures be given in marriage?"

"To those they love, to those who have not yet lost the sparkle of youth and beauty, whose mind and heart are still very much alive, in whose eyes the brightness has not yet been extinguished, on whose cheeks the blood has not yet cooled, and whose freshness—the sign of health—has not vanished. To those who are able, with a hand that has not shrivelled up from old age, to lead their beloved along the path of life, to bestow upon her a heart full of love, capable of understanding and sharing her feelings, when the laws of nature..."

"Enough. What you mean is fine fellows like yourself. If we lived amidst fields and forests—yes, but here if a fellow like yourself gets married you'll see what a lot of good will come of it! The first year he will be mad with bliss, and then he will begin hanging about the wings of the theatre, or, since those laws of nature of which you speak demand change and novelty, he will make his wife's maid her rival—very nice, isn't it? And the wife, seeing what her husband is up to, will suddenly develop a passion for finery and masquerades, and will make him a... And when there's no money, it's still worse. 'We've nothing to eat,' he'll say."

Pyotr Ivanich pulled a sour face.

He continued: " 'I'm a married man,' he'll say. 'I have three children—help me, I have nothing to eat, I'm poor...' Poor! How utterly loathsome! But I trust you will fall neither into the one nor the other category."

"I shall fall into the category of happy husbands, Uncle, and Nadya into that of happy wives. I have no desire to marry the way most people do. 'My youth has gone,' is the burden of their song. 'I'm tired of living alone, it's time to get married.' I'm not that sort."

"You're talking nonsense, my dear boy."

"Why do you say that?"

"Because you're just like all men, and them I know well. Come on then, tell me why you want to get married."

"Why? Nadenka—my wife!" exclaimed Alexander, covering his face with his hands.

"Well? You see you don't know yourself."

"Oh! The very thought sends cold thrills down my back. You don't know how I love her, Uncle! I love as no one has ever loved before—with all my soul—I am all hers!"

"I would rather you swore, Alexander, or, if there's no help for it, embraced me, than kept on repeating that idiotic phrase. I wonder you can bring yourself to say the words—'as no one has ever loved before!' " Pyotr Ivanich shrugged his shoulders.

"Why—don't you believe it's possible?"

"After all, taking this love of yours into consideration I really begin to think it is—for nothing could be more idiotic."

"But she says we must wait a year, that we are too young, we must test our feelings ... a whole year ... and then..."

"A year! Why didn't you say so at once?" Pyotr Ivanich interrupted. "Was it she who suggested it? What a clever girl she must be! How old is she?"

"Eighteen."

"And you're twenty-three! Well, old chap, she's a thousand times cleverer than you. She knows what's what, I can see that. She'll play with you, flirt with you, have a good time, and then ... why, some of these lasses are really very clever. You won't get married. I thought you were in a terrific hurry to bring it off, and in secret too. At your age these follies are committed so quickly that one has no time to interfere. But a whole year! She'll make a fool of you long before that."

"Nadya make a fool of me! Nadya—a coquette, an ordinary lass! My Nadya! For shame, Uncle! Whom have you been living with all your life, whom have you had dealings with, whom have you loved, if you can harbour such dark thoughts?"

"I have lived among human beings, and loved a woman."

"She deceive me! That angel, that embodiment of sincerity, a woman such as God never created before—all purity and light!"

"But for all that a woman—and she will most probably deceive you."

"You'll be saying that I will deceive her, too, next."

"With time you will—you, too."

"I! Think what you like of those you do not know—but me! Aren't you ashamed of thinking so basely of me? What do you take me for?"

"For a human being."

"All people are not the same. Know then that I have given her my solemn promise to love her all my life. I am ready to confirm it with a vow."

"I know, I know! A decent man never doubts the sincerity of his vow to a woman, but later he changes, cools off—how it happens he does not know himself. It is not done intentionally, there is nothing base there, nothing blameworthy—but nature does not allow us to love for ever. The believers in eternal, unchangeable love behave just the same as those who do not believe, but they either do not see this, or do not wish to admit it. We, forsooth, are above all that, we are not men, we are saints—snuff and nonsense!"

"But surely, there are lovers-spouses—who love each other eternally, and live together their whole life?"

"Eternally! The man whose love lasts a fortnight is called a fly-by-night, but two or three years—that's eternity. Analyse the substance of love and you will see for yourself that it cannot be eternal. The vivacity, ardour and feverishness of this emotion prevent it from being long-lived. 'Lovers-spouses, live their whole lives together,' to be sure. But do they really love one another all their lives? Are we to suppose that their first feelings of love bind them for ever? That they seek each other continually, that they gaze at one another, never wearying of it? What happens to all those little services, the continual solicitude, the craving to be together, the tears, the raptures, and all that nonsense? The coldness and apathy of husbands have become a byword. 'Their love has turned to friendship,' people say pompously. So it isn't love any more—it's friendship. What sort of friendship is this? Husbands and wives are bound by common interests, circumstances, a shared life, and so they go on living together. If they are not they part, love someone else— some sooner, some later—and this is called unfaithfulness. And if they stay together, they go on from habit, which, I would whisper in your ear, is a great deal stronger than love. Not for nothing has it been called second nature. Otherwise people would never cease to suffer when parted, or when the beloved object dies—but you see they do console themselves. All this harping on eternal love! No sound reasoning, just loud talk."

"And aren't you afraid for yourself, Uncle? According to this, your bride will—forgive me—deceive you too?"

"I don't think so."

"What complacency!"

"Not complacency—just sane calculations!"

"Calculations again!"

"Well, reasoning if you prefer it."

"Supposing she were to fall in love with somebody else!"

"We mustn't let it come to that. But if such a misfortune were to occur, there are ways of moderating it."

"Are there really? Is it in your power..."

"Definitely."

"Then all cuckolded husbands would do so," said Alexander. "If there were a way."

"Not all husbands are alike, my dear boy. Some are perfectly indifferent to their wives, pay no attention to what is going on round them, and do not wish to see anything. Others, for the sake of their pride, would like to do the same but they simply can't. They don't know how to go about it."

"What would you do?"

"That's my secret. It's no use talking to you. You're in a fever."

"I'm happy now and I thank God! And what is in store for me I have no desire to know."

"The first half of your sentence is so wise that a man not in love could have said it. It shows the ability to enjoy the present moment. But the second—forgive me—is no good at all. 'I have no desire to know what is in store for me,' in other words, 'I do not wish to realize that there was a yesterday and there is a today. I do not wish to think, to consider, I will not prepare for this exigency, nor avert that one, I will yield to chance.' I ask you!"

"And what is your way, Uncle? Do you think that when the moment of bliss comes one should take a magnifying glass and examine it?"

"No, a minimizing glass, so as not to go suddenly off your head with joy, and rush into everyone's arms."

"Or, say, there is a moment of sadness," continued Alexander. "Must it also be looked at through your minimizing glass?"

"No, a magnifying glass should be used for sorrow. It is easier to bear when you imagine it twice as great as it really is."

"But why," continued Alexander, in vexation, "should I nip each joy in the bud by frigid reasoning, instead of savouring it? Why should I think—she will deceive me, it will pass? Why should I torture myself in advance, before anything has happened?"

"Ah, but when it does happen," interrupted his uncle, "you will be able to say to yourself—sorrow too will pass, just as it has passed many times before for me, and for others, too. I don't think there is any harm in that, and it is worth thinking about. Then you will not torture yourself when you see the fickleness of life's fortunes. You will be calm and tranquil, in so far as man can be."

"So that's the secret of your calmness!" mused Alexander.

Pyotr Ivanich went on writing in silence.

"But what a life!" Alexander burst out again. "Never to succumb to the moment's bliss, always to be thinking, thinking... No, I feel this is not right. I want to live without your cold analysis, not wondering whether misfortune or peril lie in wait for me. What does it matter? Why should I think about it beforehand and poison my happiness?"

"I've just told you why—but you keep harping on the same string. Do not compel me to make invidious comparisons. This is why: because, when you have foreseen a danger or an obstacle or a disaster, it will be easier to cope with it or to bear it when it comes. You will not go mad or die. And when happiness comes, you will not leap about and break marble busts—is that clear? You are told: this is the beginning—try to imagine from it what the end will be; but you shut your eyes, and shake your head, as if you had seen a bogey, and go on living like a child. According to you one should live from day to day, taking things as they come, and measuring life by dinners, balls, love and constancy. Everybody is longing for the golden age. Didn't I tell you that, while your ideas were very well for country life, with your woman and half a dozen children, there is work to be done here, in this town. And it requires that you should always be thinking, always remembering what you did yesterday, what you are doing today, in order to know what must be done to-morrow; in other words, you must be constantly testing yourself and your actions. In that way something real may be achieved. But your way— Oh, what's the good of talking to you now? You're delirious. Oh, oh! It's nearly one. Not another word, Alexander. Go away, I won't listen to you! Come to dinner with me tomorrow—there'll be some people."

"Friends of yours?"

"Yes—Konev, Smirnov, Fyodorov—you know them. And a few others."

"Konev, Smirnov, Fyodorov. They're all people with whom you have business."

"Oh, yes—they're all very useful people."

"And are these the people you call your friends? Come to think of it I can't remember ever seeing you greet any-one with particular enthusiasm."

"I've told you over and over again that I call those my friends whom I meet the oftenest, and who contribute either to my advantage or to my enjoyment. For heav-en's sake—why feed people for nothing?"

"And I thought that in view of your forthcoming mar-riage you were giving a farewell dinner for your true friends, for those you really love, with whom you would recall, over a goblet of wine, your jolly young days, and, perhaps, on parting, would press warmly to your bosom."

"In those words of yours there is everything that does not and should not exist in real life. With what enthusiasm your aunt would have thrown her arms round you! True friends, when you might say simply—friends. A goblet, when people really drink out of wine-glasses, and embrace on parting, when there is no question of parting. Ugh, Alexander!"

"And do you not regret parting with your friends, or at least the prospect of seeing them less frequently?" asked Alexander.

"Not a bit. I have never been so intimate with anyone as to have regrets, and I advise you to follow my example."

"But perhaps they're not like you. Perhaps they are sorry to lose in you a dear friend, a companion."

"That's their worry, not mine. I have lost many friends

in this way, and you see I have not died of it. So you'll come tomorrow?"

"Tomorrow, Uncle, I'm..."

"What?"

"Invited to the country."

"To the Lyubetskys', I suppose."

"Yes."

"I see. Well, just as you like. Don't neglect your work, Alexander. I shall tell the editor what you are up to."

"Oh, Uncle, really! I swear I'll finish the extracts from the German economists..."

"Begin them first. Remember, now—don't come asking for filthy lucre once you become hopelessly swamped in 'rosy dreams'."

IV

Alexander's life was divided into two halves. The mornings were devoted to his work. He rummaged among dusty files, gathered a multitude of facts which had nothing to do with himself, calculated on paper millions of money not belonging to him. But sometimes his brain refused to think for others, his pen slipped out of his fingers, and he was overcome by those "rosy dreams" which vexed Pyotr Ivanich so much.

At such moments Alexander would throw himself back in his chair and mentally soar to blissful regions, where there were neither paper nor ink, neither strange faces nor official uniforms, where peace, sweetness and coolness prevailed, where flowers emanated their fragrance in an elegantly furnished drawing-room from which came the sounds of a piano, where a parrot hopped about in its cage, while in the garden outside, the branches of birch-trees and lilac bushes swayed in the gentle breeze. And the queen of all this was she...

In the morning, though seated in his office, Alexander was present in spirit on the island where the Lyubetskys' villa was situated, and in the evening he was there in the flesh, with his whole being. Let us cast an indiscreet glance at his bliss.

It was a hot day, one of those days which occur so sel-

dom in Petersburg. The sun shone beneficently on the
fields, but scorched the Petersburg streets, its rays baking
the pavement and, reflected back from the cobble stones,
baking the pedestrians too. Men and women walked slowly and languidly, and dogs—with their tongues lolling. The
town was like one of those fabulous cities in which, at
the wave of a magician's wand, everything has turned to
stone. No carriages rattled over the cobble stones. Awnings
hung over windows like lowered eyelids. The road gleamed
like a parquet floor. The pavements burned the soles of
people's feet. All was drowsy tedium.

The pedestrian, wiping the sweat from his face, sought
the shade. A mail-coach, slowly conveying six passengers
out of town, scarcely stirred the dust beneath its wheels.
At four o'clock the clerks emerged from their offices and
trudged home.

Alexander, dashing out as if the roof had fallen in, looked
at his watch. Too late to get there in time for dinner!
He darted into a restaurant.

"What can I have? Quick!"

"Soup *julienne* and *à la reine,* sauce *à la provençale,*
à la maître d'hôtel, roast turkey, game, a soufflé for dessert."

"Give me soup *à la provençale, julienne* sauce, roast
soufflé and dessert, and be quick about it!"

The waiter stared at him.

"What's the matter?" asked Alexander impatiently.
The waiter disappeared and brought the first thing
that came into his head. Alexander was perfectly satisfied. Without waiting for the last course he ran to the Neva. A boat and two boatmen were waiting for him.

An hour later, coming in sight of the promised land, he
rose in the boat and peered into the distance. At first his
eyes were dimmed by fear and anxiety, gradually changing
to doubt. But suddenly his features were irradiated by a
joyful light, like a ray of sunshine. He had made out a familiar dress at the gate—and now he was recognized, a
handkerchief was waved. He was expected, perhaps had
been for a long time. The very soles of his feet tingled
with impatience.

"Oh, if it were possible to walk on the water!" thought
Alexander. "All sorts of idiotic inventions are made, why

does no one invent a way of doing that?"

The boatmen wielded the oars slowly, with the regularity of machinery. Sweat poured in copious streams down their sunburnt faces. What did they care that Alexander's heart throbbed violently in his bosom, that with his eyes fixed on a single point, he twice put first one, then the other foot over the side of the boat? It was all the same to them, they rowed on as stolidly as ever, now and again wiping their hot faces on their sleeves.

"Quicker!" he cried. "Fifty kopeks for vodka!"

Oh, how they bent over the oars now and bounced up and down in their seats! Exhaustion was quite forgotten. What unexpected strength they displayed! The oars danced over the water. At every stroke the boat glided forward about ten yards; a dozen strokes of the oars, and the boat, describing a semi-circle over the water, approached the bank with a graceful movement and smoothly came to rest. Alexander and Nadya smiled at each other from afar, never taking their eyes off each other's faces. Alexander plunged one foot in the water and stepped ashore. Nadya laughed.

"Careful, sir! Wait till I give you a hand," said one of the boatmen, when Alexander was already on dry land.

"Wait for me here," he told them and ran up to Nadya.

She had been smiling at him tenderly from the distance. With every stroke of the oars, which brought the boat ever nearer, her heart beat more and more excitedly.

"Nadezhda Alexandrovna!" he said, scarcely able to breathe for joy.

"Alexander Fyodorich!" she said in reply.

Impulsively both rushed forward, but stopped suddenly and stood looking at each other with a smile, their eyes moist, unable to utter a word. Several minutes passed thus.

Pyotr Ivanich can hardly be blamed for not having noticed Nadya at once. She was not a beauty, and did not attract attention at first glance.

But once you examined her features more closely you found yourself unable to look away. Her face was seldom in repose for two minutes together. The thoughts and varying emotions passing through her excessively impressionable mind pursued one another continually, and the different shades of feeling blended into a marvellous play, lending her face a new and unexpected expression every minute. The eyes would suddenly flash like lightning, now darting a burning glance, now hiding beneath the long lashes. Next her face would seem lifeless and still, like the face of a marble statue. After this you expected another penetrating ray, but nothing of the sort! The lids would be slowly raised, and you would be bathed in a mild radiance, as if the moon were slowly emerging from behind a cloud. Your heart would not fail to respond to this glance with a gentle throb. The same was true of her movements. There was much grace in them, but it was not the grace of a sylph. There was that wildness and abruptness in this grace that nature bestows on all, but which art then erases, instead of merely toning them down and the last vestiges are gone. These vestiges still showed in Nadya's movements. She might be sitting in a picturesque pose, when suddenly, moved by God knows what inner stirrings, this picturesque pose would be disrupted by some utterly unexpected and equally entrancing gesture. Her conversation would take similarly unexpected turns—some veracious observation would be followed by a dreamy remark, then a harsh judgement, a childish prank, or a subtle affectation. Everything she did or said betrayed an ardent mind, a wilful, restless heart. And Alexander was not the only one who was smitten by her charms. Pyotr Ivanich alone might escape—and there are not many like him.

"You were waiting for me? Oh, Lord, how happy I am!" said Alexander.

"Waiting for you? Me? Nothing of the sort," replied Nadya, with a toss of her head. "I'm always in the garden, you know that."

"Are you angry with me?" he asked timidly.

"Whatever for? What an idea!"

"Then give me your hand."

She gave him her hand, but snatched it away the minute he touched it—and then a sudden change came over her. Her smile disappeared, something like vexation showed in her face.

"Why, are you drinking milk now?" he asked.

Nadya had a cup and a rusk in her hands.

"I'm having dinner," she replied.

"Dinner, at six o'clock, and just milk?"

"You, of course, couldn't look at milk after one of your uncle's grand dinners. But we live in the country—our ways are humble."

She bit off a few crumbs from the rusk with her front teeth and sipped the milk, with a charming grimace.

"I did not dine with my uncle, I refused his invitation yesterday," said Alexander.

"For shame! How can you tell such fibs? Where have you been all this time then?"

"I was at the office till four..."

"And now it's six. Don't tell me, admit you were tempted by the dinner and the pleasant company. I suppose you had a wonderful time!"

"Upon my word I did not go to my uncle's!" said Alexander in eager expostulation. "How could I have got to you so early if I had?"

"Oh, it seems early to you? You'd think nothing of coming two hours later," said Nadya, turning from him with a swift pirouette and walking up the path to the house. Alexander followed her.

"Don't come near me!" she said, waving him back. "I can't bear the sight of you."

"Stop teasing, Nadezhda Alexandrovna!"

"I'm not teasing at all. Tell me where you were all this time!"

"I left the office at four," began Alexander, "and it took me an hour to get here."

"In that case you would have been here by five, and it's six now. What did you do for a whole hour? See what stories you tell!"

"I had a quick meal at a restaurant."

"A quick meal! Only an hour!" she said. "Poor dear! You must be famished! Won't you have some milk?"

"Oh, give me that cup!" said Alexander, stretching out his hand.

But she suddenly came to a standstill, turned the cup upside down and, paying not the slightest attention to Alexander, curiously watched the last drops from the cup running into the sand.

"You are pitiless," he said. "How can you torture me so?"

"Do look, Alexander Fyodorich!" Nadya interrupted him, absorbed in her occupation. "Will I be able to pour a drop on that little beetle crawling along the path? Oh, I did! Poor little thing! It will die!" And she picked the beetle up solicitously, placing it on the palm of her hand and breathing on it.

"You take a great interest in that beetle," he said in a tone of vexation.

"Poor little thing! Look at it, it will die," said Nadya mournfully. "What have I done?"

She carried the beetle in the palm of her hand for some time, but when it stirred and began to crawl back and forth on her hand, Nadya shuddered, flung it on the ground and trampled on it, saying, "Nasty thing!"

"Well, where have you been?" she asked again.

"I told you..."

"Oh, yes! At your uncle's! Were there many people? Was there champagne? You smell of champagne even at a distance."

"But I wasn't at my uncle's!" Alexander cried in despair. "Who told you I was?"

"You told me yourself."

"Why, I suppose they're only just sitting down to dinner now. You don't know those dinners—as if they could be over in an hour!"

"You had two hours for dinner, from four to six."

"And what time did I have for the journey, then?"

She made no reply, but reached for a branch of acacia, and then ran on along the path.

Alexander followed her.

"Where are you going?" he asked.

"Where d'you suppose? To Mamma, of course."

"But why? Perhaps we'll be in her way."

"Oh no, we won't!"

Marya Mikhailovna, Nadya's mother, was one of those good-natured, simple mammas who admire everything their children do. Marya Mikhailovna would, let us say, order the carriage.

"Where are you going, *Maman*?" asks Nadya.

"Just for a drive—it's such lovely weather," says her Mamma.

"Oh, but Alexander Fyodorich said he would come."

And the carriage is sent away.

Another time Marya Mikhailovna sits sighing and taking snuff as the needles click over the endless muffler she is knitting, or she may be deep in some French novel.

"*Maman*, why aren't you getting dressed?" asks Nadya sternly.

"What for?"

"We're going out, aren't we?"

"Going out?"

"Yes. Alexander Fyodorich is coming for us. Surely you haven't forgotten!"

"Why, I know nothing about it."

"What d'you mean?" exclaims Nadya, displeased.

Then the mother would put away her knitting and her book and go and dress. Nadya enjoyed complete freedom, disposing of herself and her mamma and her time and occupations at her own sweet will. And yet she was an affectionate, even a tender daughter, though she could not be called obedient, for it was not she who obeyed her mother, but her mother who obeyed her.

"Go to *Maman*," said Nadya when they got to the door of the drawing-room.

"And you?"

"I'll come afterwards."

"Then I will, too."

"No, you go first."

Alexander went in, but immediately came back on tiptoe.

"She's dozing in her chair," he whispered.

"Never mind, we'll go in. *Maman, Maman!*"

"Eh?"

"Alexander Fyodorich has come."

"Eh?"

"Monsieur Aduyev has come to see you."

"Eh?"

"See how soundly she sleeps! Don't wake her!" pleaded Alexander.

"But I will! *Maman!*"

"Eh?"

"Wake up, now! Alexander Fyodorich is here."

"Where's Alexander Fyodorich?" said Marya Mikhailovna, looking straight at him and adjusting her cap, which had slipped to one side. "Oh! It's you, Alexander Fyodorich! Do come in! I was sitting here and fell asleep. I don't know why, perhaps we're going to have bad weather. And my corn's shooting, that means rain. I dozed, and dreamed that Ignaty was announcing visitors, but I couldn't make out who they were. And then Nadya called out, and I woke up at once. I'm a light sleeper—the tiniest creak and I open my eyes. Sit down, Alexander Fyodorich, how are you?"

"Quite well, thank you."

"And how is Pyotr Ivanich?"

"He's quite well, too, thank you."

"Why doesn't he ever come to see us? I was thinking only yesterday—he might just drop in. But no—he's very busy, I suppose."

"Very," said Alexander.

"And we haven't seen *you* for several days, either," continued Marya Mikhailovna. "As soon as I woke up to-day I asked, 'What's Nadya doing?' 'She's still asleep,' they told me. Well, let her sleep, I said. She's out all day in the garden, the weather's fine, she gets tired. At her age one sleeps soundly, at my age it's different—you wouldn't believe it, I suffer from insomnia! It quite depresses me—must be nerves or something, goodness knows what! The maid brought me my coffee—I always have coffee in bed, and while I was drinking it I thought to myself, 'How is it we see nothing of Alexander Fyodorich? I hope he isn't ill.' Then I got up—and if it wasn't eleven o'clock already! Fancy! The servants never tell me! I went to Nadya's room, and she was still asleep. I woke her. 'Time to get up, dearie—nearly twelve o'clock, what's the matter with you?' I'm after her all day, like a nurse. I sent away the governess on purpose, so as not to have strangers around. Trust your child to a stranger, and God knows what might happen! No! I brought her up myself, I'm very strict with her, I never let her leave my side, and I must own that Nadya is a good girl—she never keeps a single thought from me. I know her through and through. Then the chef came and I spent an hour talking to him. Then I read *Mémoires du Diable*—I love that Soulier. He writes so beautifully. Then my neighbour Marya Ivanovna called with her husband and the morning passed before I knew where I was, and suddenly I noticed it was four o'clock—time for dinner. Oh, yes—why didn't you come to dinner? We waited for you till five."

"Till five?" repeated Alexander. "I simply couldn't, Marya Mikhailovna—I was kept at the office. Never wait for me if I'm not here by four, I beg you."

"That's what I said, but Nadya kept saying, 'Just a little longer'!"

"Me? *Maman*, how can you! Didn't I say, 'Let's have dinner, Mamma,' and you kept saying, 'No, we'll wait, Alexander Fyodorich hasn't been here for a long time, he's sure to come to dinner.' "

"Listen to her, listen to her!" said Marya Mikhailovna, shaking her head. "What a shameless little baggage! Putting her own words into my mouth!"

Nadya turned away to the flowers and began teasing the parrot.

"I said, 'Well, Alexander Fyodorich won't come now,' " continued Marya Mikhailovna. " 'It's half past four.' But she kept on, 'No, *Maman*, we must wait, he's sure to come.' At a quarter to five, I said, 'Say what you will, Nadya, Alexander Fyodorich must have gone out to dinner somewhere, and he isn't coming, and I'm hungry.' But no—'Wait a little, wait till five.' And she fairly starved me. What, Miss, can you deny it?"

"Polly, Polly!" came from among the flowers. "Where did you have dinner today—at Nunky's?"

"What's that? Hiding?" went on the mother. "I suppose you're ashamed to show yourself in the daylight."

"Not a bit," retorted Nadya, emerging from among the flowers and seating herself at the window.

"And she wouldn't even sit down to table," said Marya Mikhailovna. "Asked for a cup of milk and went out into the garden. And she never had a bite of dinner. What? Look me in the eyes, Miss!"

Alexander heard this narrative in astonishment. He glanced towards Nadya, but she had turned her back on him and stood plucking at an ivy leaf.

"Nadezhda Alexandrovna," he said. "Am I really so fortunate? Did you really think of me?"

"Don't come near me!" she cried out, vexed to find her cunning exposed. "Mamma's only joking, and you believe her."

"And where are the strawberries you put away for Alexander Fyodorich?" questioned her mother.

"Strawberries?"

"Yes, strawberries."

"You ate them at dinner," said Nadya.

"Me? Aren't you ashamed of yourself—you put them away and didn't give me any. 'Alexander Fyodorich is coming,' you said. 'I'll give you some when he comes.' What d'you say to that?"

Alexander directed a glance of arch tenderness at Nadya. She blushed.

"She pulled out the stumps herself, Alexander Fyodorich," added her mother.

"Why do you tell such stories, *Maman*? I pulled the stumps out of two or three and ate them myself, Vasilissa did the others."

"Don't you believe her, Alexander Fyodorich—Vasilissa was sent to town early in the morning. Why pretend? I'm sure Alexander Fyodorich would rather you had done them than Vasilissa!"

Nadya smiled, then disappeared once more among the flowers, and came back with a plateful of strawberries. She held it out to Alexander. He kissed her hand and received the plate as if it were a marshal's baton.

"You don't deserve any. Keeping us waiting so long," said Nadya. "I was two hours at the gate, and fancy— I could see someone coming and thought it was you and waved my handkerchief, and it was a stranger, some officer. And he had the cheek to wave back."

Visitors came and went during the evening. Dusk fell. Again the three of them—mother, daughter and Alexander—were alone. And then this trio, too, was gradually broken up. Nadya went out into the garden. Marya Mikhailovna and Alexander were left to perform their halting duet. For a long time she chanted to him of her doings of yesterday and today, and of what she would do tomorrow. He began to suffer agonies of boredom and anxiety. Evening was approaching and he had not yet been able to say a word to Nadya in private. He was rescued by the chef. That benefactor entered the room to ask the mistress what they would like for supper, and Alexander was barely able to control his impatience, which was even greater than it had been in the boat. During the discussion of rissoles and yoghurt Alexander planned a skilful retreat. He employed all manner of manoeuvres to get away from Marya Mikhailovna's chair. First he went to the window and looked out, his feet almost carrying him to the open door. Then slowly, he moved towards the piano, struck the keys here and there, picked up some music from the stand with feverish fingers, looked at it and put it back. He actually had the self-control to sniff at a flower or two and wake the parrot. Then his impatience reached the breaking point. There was the open door beside him, but it would not have been quite the thing to escape through it—he must stand for a minute or two and go out casually. But the chef had already retreated two steps, one last word and he would be gone, and then Madame Lyubetskaya would certainly start talking to him again. Alexander could bear it no longer, he slipped through the doorway as sinuously as a snake, leapt down from the top step of the porch and was at the end of the garden path in a couple of bounds—on the bank, next to Nadya.

"So you remembered me at last," she said, with a good-humoured rebuke.

"If you only knew what I've been going through!" replied Alexander. "And you did not come to my rescue!"

Nadya showed him the book in her hand.

"This is what I would have called you within another minute, if you hadn't come," she said. "Sit down, Mamma won't come now. She's afraid of the damp. I've got such a lot of things to tell you—oh!"

"And so have I—oh!"

And then they told each other nothing, or practically nothing—just a few things they had already said a score of times before. The usual dreams, the sky, the stars, their mutual sympathy, their happiness. The conversation was mostly carried on in the language of glances, smiles and ejaculations. The book lay on the grass.

Night fell—but is there really such a thing as night in Petersburg in the summer? It is no night, some other name must be found—something like half-light. It was beautifully quiet. The Neva seemed to be slumbering; every now and then, as if in its sleep, a wavelet lapped gently against

the shore, and again all was hushed. A belated breeze springing up somewhere ruffled the drowsy waters, but could
not wake them, merely rippling their surface and fan-
ning Nadya and Alexander with its cool breath, or bringing them from afar the sound of singing—and again all was
silent, the Neva as motionless as a sleeper whom a slight
noise has caused to open his eyes for a moment, only to
close them again immediately, his heavy eyelids still more
firmly sealed. Then the sound of distant thunder seemed to
come from beyond the bridge, followed by the barking
of a dog left to guard the stake-nets a little way away,
and again all was quiet. The trees formed a dark vaulted
roof, their branches swaying noiselessly. Lights twinkled
in the summer cottages along the banks.

What enchantment is borne on the warm air at such
times? What is the secret which haunts flowers, trees and
grass, and fills the soul with inexplicable longing? Why is
it that thoughts and feelings quite different from those
born amidst noise and crowds come to us? And what an
atmosphere for love is created by this sleep of nature,
this half-light, these silent trees, fragrant blossoms, this
solitude! How irresistibly the mind is attuned to dreams,
the heart to those rare sensations which appear, in the
light of everyday, regular, austere life, such useless, inap-
propriate, absurd futilities. Useless they may be, and yet it
is only in such moments that the soul attains a vague
glimpse of possible happiness so eagerly sought at other
times, and not found.

Alexander and Nadya went closer to the river and leaned
over the garden railings. Nadya gazed long and thoughtfully at the Neva, into the distance, and Alexander gazed
at Nadya. Their souls were brimming with joy, their hearts
felt a pang at once, sweet and painful, but their tongues
were still.

And then Alexander touched her waist gently. As gently she pushed his hand away with her elbow. He tried again,
and this time she pushed his hand away still more gently,
never taking her eyes off the river. At his third venture
she did not push his hand away at all.

He took her hand—she did not withdraw it. He pressed
the hand and it responded to his pressure. They stood in
silence—but with what feelings!

"Nadya," he said softly.

She said nothing.

Alexander bent over her with a beating heart. She could feel his hot breath on her cheek, she started, she turned away, and—did not retreat in noble indignation, did not cry out. She was no longer able to pretend, to retreat. The magic of love silenced the voice of reason, and when Alexander pressed his lips to hers, she responded to his kiss, almost imperceptibly, it is true, but she did respond.

"Most improper!" severe mammas will exclaim. "Alone in the garden, without her mother, kissing with a young man!" Well—it can't be helped! It may have been improper, but she did respond to his kiss.

"Oh, how can a mortal know such happiness!" said Alexander to himself, bending to her lips again, this time leaving his lips on hers for several seconds.

She stood there pale, motionless, tears glistening on her eyelashes, her breast heaving violently.

"It's a dream!" whispered Alexander.

Nadya suddenly started—the moment of oblivion had passed.

"You forget yourself!" she exclaimed and stepped hastily away from him. "I'll tell Mamma!"

Alexander fell from the clouds.

"Nadezhda Alexandrovna! Do not spoil my bliss by reproaches! Do not be like..."

She looked at him, burst out into loud merry laughter, and came back to the railings, her head and her hand resting trustingly on his shoulder.

"And do you love me so much?" she asked, wiping away a tear which was rolling down her cheek.

Alexander moved his shoulders imperceptibly in a gesture of inexpressible eloquence. Pyotr Ivanich would have called the expression of his face idiotic, and perhaps it was, but how much bliss there was in this idiotic expression!

They gazed at the water, the sky, the distance again, as if nothing had happened. But they were afraid to look at each other, and when their glances did at last meet, they smiled and immediately turned away again.

"Can there really be sorrow in the world?" said Nadya after a pause.

"They say there is," replied Alexander musingly. "But I can't believe it."

"What sorrow can there be?"

"My uncle would say—poverty."

"Poverty! But don't the poor feel just what we now feel? Then they're not poor any more!"

"My uncle says they have no time for that sort of thing—they have to eat and drink."

"Ugh! Eat! It's not true what your uncle says—one can be happy without food. I went without dinner today, and look how happy I am."

He laughed.

"Why, for such a moment I would give all I have to the poor—all!" continued Nadya. "Let the poor come! Oh, why can't I give everyone some happiness to console and gladden them?"

"Angel! Angel!" uttered Alexander rapturously, pressing her hand.

"You're hurting me!" cried Nadya, wrinkling her forehead, and pulling away her hand.

But he seized the hand again and began pressing fiery kisses on it.

"How I will thank God," she went on, "today, tomorrow, my whole life—for such an evening! How happy I am! And you?"

And then she was plunged in sudden thought. A look of anxiety came into her eyes.

"Listen!" she said. "They say nothing ever repeats itself. Does it mean that this moment will never repeat itself either?"

"No, no!" replied Alexander. "It's not true! It will repeat itself! There will be still better moments! Yes, I feel there will be..."

She shook her head incredulously. And his uncle's lessons came into his head, so that he broke off suddenly.

"No," he told himself. "No, it cannot be! My uncle never knew such happiness, that's why he's so stern and mistrustful of others. Poor thing! I pity his cold, hard heart! It has never known the intoxication of love, that's the reason for his jaundiced view of life. May the Lord forgive him! If he could see my bliss, not even he would dare to touch it, or to insult it with impure doubts. I pity him."

"No, no, Nadya, we will be happy," he continued, aloud. "Look round you! Doesn't everything here rejoice at the sight of our love? God himself will bless it. How joyfully we shall go through life hand in hand. How *proud*, how *great* we shall be in *our mutual love*!"

"Oh, don't keep looking ahead," she interrupted him. "Don't prophesy! Somehow it frightens me when you talk like that. I'm sad even now."

"What is there to be afraid of? Surely we have the right to believe in ourselves?"

"No, no!" she said, shaking her head.

He looked at her and grew thoughtful.

"Why not?" he said. "After all, what could destroy this world of happiness of ours? What is it to anyone what we do? We will always be alone, we will keep others at a distance—what have we to do with them? And what have they to do with us? Nobody will think about us, we shall be forgotten, and then we shall not be disturbed by rumours of sorrow and misfortune, just as, here in this garden, no sound disturbs the solemn silence..."

"Nadya! Alexander Fyodorich!" came suddenly from the porch. "Where are you?"

"D'you hear?" said Nadya in prophetic tones. "It is a hint from fate—this moment will never be repeated. I feel it."

She seized his hand, pressing it, and, casting a glance at him that was strange and sad, suddenly plunged into the gloom of the alley.

"Alexander Fyodorich!" came from the porch again. "The yoghurt's been on the table ever so long."

He shrugged his shoulders and went into the house.

"After a moment of ineffable bliss comes yoghurt!" he said to Nadya. "Can the whole of life really be like this?"

"So long as it's not worse!" she replied cheerfully. "And the yoghurt's delicious, especially when one hasn't had dinner."

She was elated by her happiness. Her cheeks burned, her eyes blazed with an unusual brilliance. What a nice hostess she was, how gaily she chattered! Not a trace of the momentary sadness remained. It was all swallowed up in joy.

The dawn had already covered half of the sky when

Alexander took his seat in the boat. The boatmen, in expectation of the promised reward, spat on the palms of
their hands and began bouncing up and down in their seats
as before, working the oars with all their might.

"Not so fast," said Alexander. "Another fifty kopeks
for vodka!"

They looked at him and then at one another. One
scratched his chest, the other his back, and they began
moving the oars almost unnoticeably, scarcely touching
the water. The boat floated like a swan.

"And my uncle would like to persuade me that happiness is a mirage, that nothing is to be wholly believed in,
that life... He ought to be ashamed of himself! It's too bad!
Why should he want to deceive me so cruelly? No—this
is life, just as I had imagined it, as it should be, as it is and
as it will be. Otherwise there is no life."

A fresh morning breeze blew gently from the north.
Alexander started slightly, both from the breeze and from
his memories, then he yawned and, wrapping his cloak
round him, gave himself up to daydreams.

V

Alexander had attained the summit of his happiness.
There was nothing left for him to desire. His work, his
journalistic labours, all were forgotten, abandoned.
He was passed over at the office, but he scarcely noticed
it, and then only because his uncle reminded him of it.
Pyotr Ivanich advised him to stop wasting time over trifles, but at the word "trifles" Alexander shrugged his
shoulders, smiled pityingly and said nothing. His uncle,
seeing that his advice was unavailing, also shrugged his
shoulders, smiled pityingly and said nothing. But he could
not help remarking:

"Have it your own way, but mind you don't come asking for filthy lucre!"

"Don't worry, Uncle!" replied Alexander. "Shortage
of money is a misfortune, but I don't need much, and I
have enough."

"Then I can only congratulate you," retorted Pyotr
Ivanich.

Alexander obviously avoided him. He had lost all faith in his uncle's dismal forecasts but feared his cold attitude to love in general, and his insulting hints at his nephew's feelings for Nadya in particular.

He could not bear to listen to his uncle's analysis of his love, upon which he calmly brought to bear the laws that applied to everyone else, thus profaning what Alexander regarded as lofty and sacred. He concealed his ecstasy, his belief in a future of rose-coloured happiness, sensing that the roses would shed their petals and turn into ashes the moment his uncle's analysis touched them. And at first his uncle avoided him too, expecting Alexander to squander all he had in his idleness, and then come to him for money and sponge on him.

There was something solemn and mysterious in Alexander's gait, glance, and whole manner. He regarded others as a capitalist at the Exchange regards petty speculators, with modest dignity, saying to himself: "Sorry creatures! Which of you has a treasure like mine? Which of you can feel as I do? Which has such fortitude of soul?" and so on and so on.

He was convinced that he was the only person in the world who loved and was loved so intensely.

And it was not only his uncle whom he avoided, but the *mob* as he said. He either worshipped at the shrine of his divinity, or sat alone in his study, drunk with bliss, analyzing it, splitting it up into infinitesimally small atoms. This he called *creating a world of his own*, and, seated there in his solitude, he really did create for himself a sort of world, in which he lived most of the time, going only seldom and unwillingly to his office, which he dubbed a *bitter necessity*, a *necessary evil*, or *dismal prose*. He had a variety of names for it. To his editor and his friends he did not go at all.

To converse with his ego was for him the highest pleasure. "Only when alone with himself," he wrote in a story he worked on now and then, "can a man see himself as in a mirror. Only then does he learn to believe in human greatness and dignity. How splendid he is in this converse with his spiritual forces! Like a general he reviews them critically, draws them up according to a soundly thought-out plan, and, at their head, dashes forward, acts, creates.

How pitiful, on the contrary, is he who cannot and fears to be alone with himself, who avoids his own company, and is ever seeking that of others, alien to him in mind and spirit..." To look at, Alexander might have been believed a thinker discovering new laws for the structure of the world or the life of humanity—but he was only a man in love.

See him in his high-backed armchair! Before him is a sheet of paper on which a few stanzas are scribbled. Now he bends over the sheet of paper to make some correction, or to add a few lines, now he throws himself back in his chair to think. On his lips flickers a smile—it is obvious that he has only just removed them from the brimming chalice of happiness. His eyes close luxuriously, like a dozing cat's, or suddenly flash with the fire of inner emotion.

All is quiet. Nothing is to be heard but the hum of carriages far away in the busy street, and now and then Yevsei, tired of cleaning boots, muttering aloud:

"I mustn't forget—I owe a kopek for vinegar and ten kopeks for cabbage, I must pay it back tomorrow, or else the shopkeeper won't give me credit another time, the cur! Weighing out his bread, as if it were a famine year—it's a disgrace! Lord, but I'm tired! I'll just finish cleaning this boot and have a nap. They're asleep long ago at Grachi, I suppose—not like here! Oh, Lord, when shall I see it again?"

Here he sighed gustily, breathed on the boot and once again began flourishing his brush. He considered this his main, if not only, duty, and judged a servant or any other man by his ability to clean boots. He cleaned them himself with a kind of passion.

"Stop it, Yevsei! You won't let me work with your nonsense!" shouted Alexander.

"Nonsense!" Yevsei growled. "Nonsense! It's you who waste time on nonsense—I do real work. Look how dirty you made your boots, it's all I can do to get them clean!"

He placed the boot on the table, gazing lovingly at the mirror-like surface of the leather.

"See if you find anyone else to clean them like that!" he said. "Nonsense indeed!"

Alexander plunged deeper and deeper into his dreams of Nadya, which gradually merged into dreams of writing poetry.

There was nothing on his desk. Everything reminiscent of his former occupations, of office work, or journalism, was piled under the desk, on cupboard shelves, or under the bed.

"The very sight of *that filth*," he said, "frightens off creative thought and it flies away like a nightingale from a copse at the sudden creaking of ungreased cart-wheels in the road."

The dawn often found him working at some elegy. All the time not spent at the Lyubetskys' was devoted to poetry. He would write a poem and read it to Nadya. She would copy it on a pretty sheet of paper and learn it by heart, and he knew the *poet's highest bliss—to hear his creation from beloved lips*.

"You are my Muse," he told her. "Be the vestal virgin of that sacred flame which burns in my breast! If you neglect it it will be extinguished forever."

He sent his poems under pen names to the papers. They were published, for they were not bad, not lacking in verve here and there, permeated with ardent feeling and they scanned smoothly enough.

Nadya gloried in his love and called him, "My poet."

"Yes, yours, yours for ever!" he said. Glory awaited him with a smile, and it was Nadya, he thought, who would weave the wreath for him, interspersing the laurel leaves with myrtle, and then—"Life, life, how beautiful thou art!" he exclaimed. "And my uncle? Why does he try to disturb the peace of my soul? Is he not a demon sent me by fate? Why does he poison my happiness with his gall? Is it not envy, because his own heart knows not such pure joys, or is it, perhaps, a dark desire to injure ... I must flee from him! He will slay my loving soul, infect it with his own hatred, he will corrupt it."

And he fled from his uncle, did not see him for weeks on end, for months. And if, when they met, the conversation drifted to feelings, Alexander maintained a scornful silence, or listened like one whose convictions are not to be shaken by any arguments whatever. He considered his own convictions infallible, his own opinions and feelings incontrovertible, and was determined henceforth to be guided by them alone, saying that he was no longer a boy, and that there was no reason *why only the opinions of others should be sacred,* and the like.

But his uncle always appeared the same. He never asked his nephew anything and either did not notice or chose to ignore his behaviour. Seeing that Alexander stuck to his resolutions, that he went on living as before and did not ask for money, Pyotr Ivanich was as affectionate as ever and even reproached him playfully for coming to see him so seldom.

"My wife is angry with you," he said. "She looks upon you as a relative. We always dine at home—do come!"

That was all. But Alexander did not often go, he had no time. Morning at the office, from afternoon to nightfall at the Lyubetskys'—there was only the night left, and at night he retired into his own self-created world and continued to create. And after all, one must sleep a little, too.

He was not quite so successful with prose. He wrote a comedy, two stories, an essay and a book of travels. His activity was remarkable, his pen fairly scorched the paper. At first he showed his uncle the comedy and one of the stories, asking him if he thought them any good. His uncle glanced through a few pages at random, and sent them back, with an inscription at the top: "They would do for papering partitions."

Alexander was furious, and sent the manuscripts to a magazine, which, however, returned them both. Only in two places the pencilled comment in the margins of the comedy was: "Not bad," and that was all. For the rest the remarks were: "weak", "false", "immature", "feeble", "undeveloped", etc., and at the end were the words: "On the whole, the author shows ignorance of the human heart ... excessive fervour, unnatural, stilted, no real characters ... the hero is a freak ... no such people exist ... not fit for publication. Still, the author seems to be not without talent, he must work."

"No such people exist!" said the saddened and astonished Alexander. "How can that be? Why, the hero is myself! Surely I don't have to portray the banal characters to be met at every step, to think and feel like the crowd, to do what everyone else does! Wretched people out of everyday petty tragedies and comedies bear no marks of distinction—is art to sink to this?"

He sought confirmation of the purity of his artistic doctrine by evoking the shade of Byron and referring to Goethe and Schiller. He could imagine no other hero for a play or a novel but a corsair, a great poet, an artist, who must act and feel as he did himself.

He laid the scene of one of his stories in America. The background was extremely exotic—American landscape, mountains, and amidst them all an exile who had carried off his beloved. The whole world had forgotten them. They admired themselves and the scenery, and when tidings of pardon came and they could return to their native land, they refused to go. And twenty years after, some European traveller on a hunting expedition escorted by Red Indians found a hut on a hill-top, and in it a skeleton. This European had once been the rival of the hero. How good Alexander had thought this story, with what enthusiasm he had read it aloud to Nadya on winter evenings! How eagerly she had listened to him! How could such a story have been rejected?

He never said a word to Nadya of this failure. He swallowed the bitter pill in silence and consigned it to oblivion. "Well, what about your story?" she asked. "Has it been published?" "No," said he. "It won't do. There's too much in it that seems wild and strange to the common run of people."

If he had only known how truly he had spoken, though all-unconscious of any other interpretation that might have been given to his words.

The very idea of work seemed strange to him. "What is talent for?" he asked. "It's the mediocre toiler who works. Talent creates, with ease and freedom." But recalling that his articles on agriculture, and even his verses, had at first been nothing special, had gradually improved and attracted the attention of the public, he fell to thinking and realized the absurdity of his conclusions, and with a sigh he postponed the writing of prose till another time, when his heart should beat less wildly, his thoughts should resume some kind of order, and then, he vowed, then he would work at it properly.

Day followed day, days of unbroken pleasure for Alexander. He was happy when he could kiss the tip of Nadya's finger, sit opposite her for two hours in a picturesque attitude without taking his eyes off her face, stirred to his very soul, heaving sighs, or declaiming verses suitable to the occasion.

It would be only fair to say that she sometimes responded to his sighs and his verses with yawns. And no wonder—her heart was engaged, but her mind remained idle. Alexander took no trouble to provide it with food. The year, appointed by Nadya for probation, was drawing to an end. She was again at the same summer villa with her mother. Alexander reminded her of her promise, asked permission to speak to her mother. Nadya wanted to put it off till they went back to town, but Alexander insisted.

One evening, on parting with him, she told Alexander he might speak to her mother the next day.

Alexander did not sleep all night and did not go to work. The thought of the morrow went round and round in his head; he kept thinking of what to say to Marya Mikhailovna, and composed a speech of some sort, but the moment he remembered that it was to be not a speech but a proposal, he fell to dreaming, and forgot it all. And he arrived at the summer villa in the evening quite unprepared. But nothing was required, after all. When Nadya met him as usual in the garden, there was a shade of thoughtfulness in her eyes, she did not smile and seemed rather absent-minded.

"You mustn't speak to Mamma today," she said. "That horrid count is with her."

"Count? What count?"

"As if you didn't know what count! Count Novinsky, of course, our neighbour. That's his house over there—you have often admired his garden."

"Count Novinsky! Here!" said Alexander in astonishment. "What for?"

"I don't really know myself," replied Nadya. "I was sitting here reading the book you gave me and Mamma was out, she went to Marya Ivanovna. It had begun to rain and I had just gone into the house, when a carriage drove up to the porch, blue with white trimmings, the one that was always passing us, you admired it, don't you remember? I saw Mamma step out of it with some man. They came in. Mamma said, 'And this is my daughter, Count—allow me to introduce her.' He bowed and I bowed. I felt embarrassed, I blushed, and ran to my room. But I heard Mamma—how could she!—say, 'Excuse me, Count—she's terribly shy.' Then I guessed it must be our neighbour Count Novinsky. He probably brought Maman from Marya Ivanovna's in his carriage on account of the rain."

"Is he ... very old?" asked Alexander.

"Old? Not a bit. Why, he's young and handsome."

"So you were quick enough to see that he was handsome," said Alexander peevishly.

"I like that! How long does it take to look? I even spoke to him. Oh, he's ever so polite—he asked me what I did, talked about music, asked me to sing something, but I didn't, I can hardly sing at all. This winter I really must get Maman to engage a good singing master for me. The count says singing is all the rage now."

All this was said with remarkable animation.

"I thought you would have something else to do this winter, Nadezhda Alexandrovna," remarked Alexander.

"What?"

"What?" repeated Alexander reproachfully.

"Oh—that! Did you come by boat?"

He looked at her in silence. She turned away and went into the house.

Alexander entered the drawing-room not quite at his ease. Who was this count? How ought he to behave in front of him? What would his manners be? Proud? Slighting? The count rose immediately and bowed politely. Alexander responded with an awkward bow. The hostess introduced them. Somehow Alexander did not like the count, who was, however, a fine-looking man—tall, slender, fair-haired, with large expressive eyes and a pleasant smile. His manners were simple, elegant and suave. Such a man could win the favour of anyone, but he did not win Alexander's.

Although Marya Mikhailovna asked him to sit down near her, Alexander took a seat in the corner of the room and picked up a book, which was most ill-bred, awkward and unsuitable. Nadya stood by her mother's chair looking

with interest at the count, and listening to what he said
and how he said it. He was something new for her.

Alexander was unable to conceal his dislike of the count.
But the count did not seem to have noticed his rudeness—
he was extremely polite, turning to Alexander as he spoke,
and trying to draw him into the conversation. All in vain—
Alexander either said nothing at all or answered in mono-
syllables.

When Madame Lyubetskaya chanced to mention his
name the count asked if he was not related to Pyotr Ivanich.

"He's my uncle," replied Alexander brusquely.

"I often meet him in society," said the count.

"No doubt. That's nothing to wonder at," replied
Alexander, shrugging his shoulders.

The count suppressed a smile, biting his underlip ever so
slightly. Nadya exchanged glances with her mother, and
blushed, lowering her eyes.

"Your uncle is a pleasant, clever man," remarked the
count in a tone of light irony.

Alexander made no reply.

Unable to restrain herself, Nadya went up to Alexander
and under cover of the conversation between the count
and her mother, whispered in his ear, "You ought to be
ashamed. The count is so kind to you, and you..."

"Kind!" repeated Alexander angrily and almost audib-
ly. "I have no need of his kindness, don't use that
word."

Nadya retreated from him hastily and looked long and
steadily at him from a little distance, her eyes wide open,
then she again took up her position behind her mother's
chair and no longer paid any attention to Alexander.

But Alexander kept waiting for the count to go so that
he could at last speak to Nadya's mother. But ten o'clock
struck and then eleven, and the count, far from leaving,
went on and on talking.

All the subjects around which the conversation usually revolves at the beginning of an acquaintance, had been
exhausted. The count began to talk in a humorous vein.
He did it very well—there was not a trace of anything forced,
no pretension to wit in his jokes, only a peculiarly
amusing way of relating, not so much an anecdote, as

some fact or incident which was new to his hearers or, with an unexpected word, turning a serious thing into something comic.

Both mother and daughter surrendered completely to the enchantment of his humorous stories, and Alexander himself could not help smiling behind his book more than once. But inwardly he was fuming.

The count discussed everything with equal skill and tact— be it music, people, or foreign lands. The talk turned to men and women—he criticized men, including himself, artfully praised women in general, and paid his hostesses a few compliments.

Alexander remembered his literary work, his verses. "This is where I could best him," he told himself. The talk turned on literature; the mother and daughter mentioned that Alexander was a writer.

"Now he'll sing small," thought Alexander.

But not a bit of it. The count spoke of literature as if he had never occupied himself with anything else. He made a few remarks, casual but just, about modern Russian and French celebrities. To crown it all, it transpired that he was friends with the best Russian writers, and had made the acquaintance of certain French writers when in Paris. Of some he spoke with respect, others he described with a slight touch of caricature. He said he did not know Alexander's poetry, had never heard of it.

Nadya looked a bit queerly at Alexander as if asking: "What, my friend? You haven't gone very far..."

Alexander was abashed. His rude and insolent expression gave place to one of dejection. He was like a cock with a wet tail, trying to shelter from the rain under an awning.

The sound of clinking glasses and spoons came from the dining-room, where the table was being laid, and still the count sat on. All hope was gone. He actually accepted Madame Lyubetskaya's invitation to stay and have some yoghurt for supper.

"Fancy a count eating yoghurt," whispered Alexander, glancing venomously at him.

The count supped with appetite, joking all the time, evidently feeling quite at home.

"Never been in the house before, and eats for three,

the shameless wretch!'' Alexander whispered in Nadya's ear.

"He's hungry,'' she replied in all simplicity.

At last the count went away, but it was now too late for a serious talk. Alexander picked up his hat and fled. Nadya ran after him and managed to soothe him.

"Tomorrow, then?'' said Alexander.

"We won't be at home tomorrow.''

"Well—the day after.''

They parted.

Alexander arrived earlier than usual on the appointed day. Unfamiliar sounds reached him from the house while he was still in the garden. What was it—could it be a 'cello? As he drew nearer he made out the sounds of a man's voice—and what a voice! Resonant, fresh, it seemed to be making straight for a woman's heart. It reached the heart of Alexander too, but in a different manner—his heart sank and ached with anguish, envy, hatred, and a vague but heavy foreboding. Alexander entered the house through the servants' hall.

"Who's that singing?'' he asked the footman.

"Count Novinsky.''

"Has he been here long?''

"Since six.''

"Tell Miss Nadezhda quietly that I came, and will call later.''

"Yes, sir.''

Alexander turned on his heel and set off to roam around the villas scattered about, scarcely noticing where he was going. Two hours later he returned to the house.

"Still here?'' he asked.

"Yes, sir. And I think the count is staying to supper. The mistress ordered roast partridge.''

"Did you tell Miss Nadezhda I called?''

"Yes, sir.''

"And what did she say?''

"She didn't say anything.''

Alexander went home and did not put in an appearance for two days. God knows what were his thoughts and feelings during that time. At last he went again.

When he caught sight of the house he stood up in the boat, screening his eyes with his hand and gazing ahead.

There was the blue dress flitting between the trees—the dress that sat so well on Nadya; how blue suited her! She always wore that dress when she wanted Alexander to admire her specially. A weight was lifted from his heart.

"Oh, she wants to console me for her temporary, involuntary neglect," he told himself. "It was my fault, not hers. My behaviour was unpardonable. It could only put people against me. A stranger, a new acquaintance... It was only natural that, as the hostess, she— Ah, there she comes from the narrow path behind that bush, she's going to the railings, she'll stand and wait there."

Sure enough she came out into the broad alley ... but who was that with her?

"The count!" exclaimed Alexander ruefully, hardly able to believe his eyes.

"Eh?" said one of the boatmen.

"Alone in the garden with him," whispered Alexander. "Just as she used to be with me."

Nadya and the count went up to the gate and, without a glance towards the river, turned and strolled back along the alley. He was leaning over her, talking in a low voice. She walked beside him with her head bent.

Alexander stood for some time in the boat with his mouth open, motionless, his hands stretched towards the bank, and then, letting them fall, sat down again. The boatmen went on rowing.

"Where are you going?" Alexander shouted at them furiously. "Back!"

"You want us to go back?" one of them asked, gaping and staring at him.

"Back, I said. You're not deaf, are you?"

"And we're not to go over there?"

The other boatman began silently and rapidly pulling at one oar, then struck out with both, and the boat was propelled in the opposite direction. Alexander pulled his hat down almost to his shoulders and plunged into anguished thought.

After this he did not go to the Lyubetskys' for a whole fortnight.

Two weeks—what a long time for a man in love! But he waited all the time—surely they would send someone to inquire what was keeping him away. He might be ill. They

had always done so before, if he was indisposed or in a
bad temper. Nadya would begin with an official inquiry
in her mother's name, and afterwards write on in her own
name. The sweet reproaches, the tender anxiety! The
impatience!

"I shan't yield at once, not this time," Alexander told
himself. "I'll torture her a little. I'll teach her how to go
gallivanting with a strange man. The reconciliation won't
be so easy."

And he conceived a ruthless scheme for vengeance, he
dreamed of her remorse, and of his generous forgiveness
and the sermon he would preach her. But no servant came
from the Lyubetskys, no remorseful notes were sent by
Nadya. He seemed no longer to exist for them.

He grew thin and pale. Jealousy is the most agonizing of diseases, especially when it is founded on
groundless suspicions. When proofs are forthcoming it is
the end of jealousy, and, for the greater part, of love itself; then at least the lover knows what to do, but till then
it's sheer torture. And Alexander experienced it to the
full.

At last he made up his mind to go there in the morning,
hoping to find Nadya alone and having it out with her.

He arrived. There was nobody in the garden, in the great
hall, or in the drawing-room. He went through the house
and opened the back door...

What a sight met his eyes! In the yard two grooms in
the count's livery were holding saddle horses. On one of
these the count and a servant were helping Nadya to
mount; the other was being held in readiness for the count
himself. On the steps of the porch stood Marya Mikhailovna. She was watching the scene with evident anxiety, her
brow wrinkled.

"Sit firmly, Nadya," she said. "Look after her, Count, for
God's sake. I'm so nervous about her. Hold on to the horse's
ear, Nadya—look what a devil it is, spinning like a top."

"It's all right, *Maman*," said Nadya gaily. "I know
how to ride. Look!"

She lashed the horse with her whip, so that it plunged
forward, straining at the reins.

"Oh, oh! Hold it back!" cried Marya Mikhailovna, with
a helpless gesture. "Stop—it'll kill you."

But Nadya jerked the reins and the horse stood still. "Look how it obeys me!" said Nadya and stroked the horse's neck.

Nobody noticed Alexander. Pale and silent he gazed at Nadya who, as if to mock him, had never been so beautiful. How the riding-habit and that hat with the green veil became her! How graceful the lines of her body! Her face seemed to be suffused with shy pride and the joyous glow of new sensations. Blushes came and went on her cheeks, so happy she was. The horse gave a light bound, forcing the slender rider to bend gracefully, and then lean backwards. Her figure swayed in the saddle like the stalk of a flower stirred by the breeze. Then the groom brought up the count's horse.

"Shall we go through the copse again, Count?" asked Nadya.

"Again!" thought Alexander.

"That would be very nice," replied the count.

The horses started.

"Nadezhda Alexandrovna!" cried Alexander wildly, to his own surprise.

Everyone came to a standstill as if turned to stone, and gazed in astonishment at Alexander. This lasted almost a minute.

"Oh, it's Alexander Fyodorich," said the mother, who was the first to regain her presence of mind. The count bowed civilly. Nadya flung her veil off her face, turned and looked at him in terror, her mouth half-open, and then turned away quickly, whipping up her horse, which disappeared through the gate in a couple of bounds; the count followed close behind her.

"Not so fast, for God's sake!" the mother cried after them. "Hold on to its ear. Dear God! Oh, my Lord! She'll fall—I know she will. What's taken possession of her?"

And it was all over. There was nothing to be heard but the sound of hooves, nothing to be seen but a column of dust rising from the road. Alexander remained alone with Madame Lyubetskaya. He looked at her in silence, as if asking, "What does it all mean?" And she did not keep him waiting for an answer.

"They've gone," she said, "Oh, well, youth must have its fling, and you and I can have a talk, Alexander Fyodorich. How is it there's been no sign from you for the last two weeks? Don't you love us any more?"

"I've been ill, Marya Mikhailovna," he replied morosely.

"Anyone can see that—you're so pale and thin. Sit down at once and have a rest—shall I order some soft-boiled eggs? It's a long time till dinner."

"Thanks—I don't want anything."

"Why not? They'd be ready in a minute, they're lovely eggs. A Finnish peasant brought them today."

"No, thank you."

"What's the matter with you? I kept waiting and waiting and wondering what it meant—you don't come yourself, and you don't bring us any French novels. Don't you remember promising us something—*Peau de Chagrin* or something of the sort? I waited and waited, but no. Alexander Fyodorich doesn't love us any more, I said to myself, he doesn't really."

"I'm afraid it's you who don't love me any more, Marya Mikhailovna."

"It's a sin to talk like that, Alexander Fyodorich! I love you like my own son. I don't know about Nadya—she's still a child, what does she understand? How can she appreciate people? I tell her every day, 'How is it we never see Alexander Fyodorich, why doesn't he come?' And I kept expecting you. Believe it or not, I never sat down to dinner till five o'clock every day. I kept thinking: he'll be here any minute. Nadya herself sometimes said, 'Who are you waiting for, Mamma? I'm hungry and I think the count is too.'"

"And does the count come here very often?" asked Alexander.

"Almost every day, and sometimes twice a day. He's so kind, he's become so fond of us. And so Nadya says, 'I'm hungry, and that's all. Time to sit down to dinner.' 'And supposing Alexander Fyodorich comes?' 'He won't,' she says. 'I bet you anything he won't. It's no good waiting.'"

These words of Madame Lyubetskaya were like a knife in Alexander's heart.

"Is that what she said?" he asked, forcing a smile.

"Yes, those were her very words, that's just how she hurried me. I'm very strict, even if I do look so good-na-

tured. I scolded her: 'Sometimes you wait for him till
five without dinner, another time you don't want to wait
for him at all. Silly girl! That's not nice. Alexander Fyodorich is our old friend, he is fond of us, and his uncle, Pyotr
Ivanich, has shown us much kindness. It's not nice to neglect him. He may get angry and stop coming to see us.' "

"And what did she say?" asked Alexander.

"Oh, nothing. You know how lively she is—she jumps up
and sings, or runs up to me, saying, 'He'll come if he wants
to.' Such a giddy thing! And I thought: he'll come. And
another day passes—and you don't come. So I say again,
'I wonder if Alexander Fyodorich is all right, Nadya?'
'I don't know, Mamma,' she says, 'how am I to know?'
'Let's send and find out how he is!' We kept saying we'd
send but we never did. I forgot, I relied on her and she's
no more reliable than the wind. And now she's all for
this horse-riding. She saw the count through the window
on horseback once, and kept on and on at me, 'I want to
ride!' I did all I could to stop her but no—'I want to!'
Madcap! We didn't ride when I was a girl. That's not how
we were brought up at all. But nowadays—oh, horror!—
ladies have actually begun to smoke! There's a young widow living over the way there—she sits on the balcony all
day smoking cigarettes. People walk by, drive past, and
she doesn't care a bit. Why, in my young days if a gentleman so much as smelled of tobacco in the drawing-
room..."

"And has this been going on long?" asked Alexander.

"I don't know—they say it became the fashion five or
six years ago—it all comes from the French."

"No, I mean—has Nadezhda Alexandrovna been riding
long?"

"About ten days. The count's so kind, so obliging.
What wouldn't he do for us? How he spoils her! Look at all
these flowers—all from his garden. Sometimes I feel quite
ashamed. 'Why do you spoil her so, Count? There'll be no
holding her soon.' And I scold her. Marya Ivanovna and I,
yes and Nadya, too, were at his stables. I always keep watch
over her myself, you know—after all, nobody can look after a daughter as a mother does! I brought her up myself
and I may say without boasting—there aren't many such
daughters. And Nadya learned in front of us. Then we had

lunch in his garden and now they go riding every day. And what a fine house he has! We went over it—such taste, such luxury!"

"Every day!" said Alexander, half to himself.

"Well, why shouldn't she enjoy herself? I was young myself once..."

"And do they stay out long?"

"Three hours or so. Come now, what's been the matter with you?"

"I don't know. I have a kind of pain in my chest," he said, pressing his hand to his heart.

"Don't you do anything for it?"

"No."

"Oh, you young people! It's all nothing, it'll pass, but the day comes when it's too late! Is it an aching pain, or a stabbing pain?"

"Aching and stabbing," said Alexander abstractedly.

"That's a chill. For mercy's sake don't neglect it, it might get worse, it might develop into pneumonia! And you take no medicine! I'll tell you what—take some opodeldoc and rub your chest hard with it every night, rub till the skin gets red, and don't drink tea, drink herbs—I'll give you a recipe."

Nadya came back pale with fatigue. She flung herself on the sofa, almost breathless.

"Look at her," said Marya Mikhailovna, laying her hand on the girl's forehead. "She's so tired she can hardly breathe. Drink some water and go and change and loosen your stays. Nothing good will come of this riding."

Alexander and the count stayed all day. The count was invariably courteous and attentive to Alexander, invited him to come and see his garden, to share the rides, offered him a horse.

"I can't ride," said Alexander coldly.

"You can't?" said Nadya. "Oh, it's such fun! We'll go out again tomorrow, won't we, Count?"

The count bowed.

"That'll do, Nadya," said her mother. "Don't pester the count, child."

There was, however, nothing to point to the existence of any special relations between the count and Nadya. He was equally courteous to mother and daughter, sought

no opportunity to be alone with Nadya, did not follow
her into the garden, looked at her just as he looked at her
mother. The ease with which she treated him, her daily
rides with him might be put down to the wildness and
unsteadiness of her character, perhaps to her innocence, her
lack of breeding, and ignorance of the ways of society; as for
her mother, it was all perhaps weakness and lack of foresight.

The courtesy of the count and his daily visits might be
attributed to the nearness of the two houses, and the cordial welcome he always received at the Lyubetskys'.

To the unbiased eye the matter seemed natural enough.
But Alexander looked through a magnifying glass and saw
much that the unbiased eye did not.

He asked himself why Nadya had changed towards him?
She no longer waited for him in the garden, she met him
with alarm instead of with a smile, and had of late begun
to be much more particular about her clothes. No more
familiarity in her manners. She was more careful of what
she did, as if she had grown wiser. Every now and then
there was something secretive in her eyes and in her words.
Where were the sweet whims, the wildness, the pranks, the
playfulness? They had all vanished. She had become grave,
thoughtful, silent. It was as if she had something on her
mind. Now she was just like all other girls—hypocritical
like them, telling lies as they did, anxiously inquiring after one's health ... always obliging, outwardly courteous—
to him, to Alexander ... and to whom else? Oh, God!
And his heart sank.

"All this means something," he kept assuring himself.
"There's more to it than meets the eye. I will find out
what it is at all costs, and then woe to—

> *I will not let the foul seducer*
> *With his ungodly, wicked art*
> *Pervert that innocent young heart.*
> *That such a villain should endeavour*
> *Exerting all his poisoned power*
> *To blight a half-unfolded flower,*
> *To mar its loveliness forever..."*

And that very day, when the count had gone, Alexander
tried to find a moment to speak to Nadya in private. What

didn't he try? He picked up the book with which she had formerly called him away from her mother, held it up for her to see and went towards the river-bank, thinking she would come running after him. But he waited and waited, and she did not come. He went back to the house. She was sitting reading and did not look up when he came in. He sat down beside her. She did not raise her eyes, and after a moment asked him in rapid casual tones if he was writing anything, if anything new of his had come out. Not a word about the past.

He began talking to her mother. Nadya went into the garden. Her mother left the room and Alexander, too, rushed into the garden. Catching sight of him, Nadya got up from the bench and went, not to meet him, but walked slowly along the alley circling the garden, towards the house, as if to avoid him. He hastened his steps, and she did, too.

"Nadezhda Alexandrovna," he called to her from the distance. "I should like to speak to you."

"Come into the house—it's damp here," she replied.

When she got back she again sat down beside her mother. Alexander felt he was going to faint.

"And since when have you begun to be afraid of damp?" he asked spitefully.

"The evenings are so dark and cold now," she answered, yawning.

"We'll be going back to town soon," said her mother. "Alexander Fyodorich, would you be so kind as to go to our flat and remind the landlord to mend two locks on the door, and repair the shutter in Nadya's bedroom? He promised to, but he's sure to forget. They're all the same—all they think about is money."

Alexander rose to take his leave.

"Mind, don't stay away so long this time!" said Marya Mikhailovna.

Nadya said nothing.

At the door he turned towards her. She took a few steps towards him. His heart leaped.

"At last!" he thought.

"Are you coming tomorrow?" she asked coldly, but her eyes were fixed on him with eager curiosity.

"I don't know. Why?"

"I just asked. Are you?"

"D'you want me to?"

"Are you coming tomorrow?" she repeated in the same cold tones, but with a shade of impatience.

"No," he replied irately.

"And the day after?"

"No, I won't come for a whole week, two perhaps ... a long time." And fixing a searching glance on her he tried to read in her eyes the impression produced by his reply.

She said nothing, but dropped her eyes as he answered, and what was in them—were they dimmed by sadness, or did a flash of joy light them up for a moment?—it was impossible to read anything on that beautiful marble countenance.

Alexander squeezed his hat in his hand and went out.

"Don't forget to rub your chest with opodeldoc!" Marya Mikhailovna called after him.

And again Alexander was faced with a problem—to discover what Nadya's question had meant. What was concealed beneath it—the desire to see him, or the fear of seeing him?

"It's agony! Agony!" he exclaimed despairingly.

Poor Alexander could not hold out—three days later he went there again. Nadya was standing at the gate when his boat approached. His heart leapt, but as he got nearer the bank she turned, pretending not to see him, and after taking a few uncertain steps along the path as if she were merely out for a stroll, returned to the house.

He found her with her mother. There were a few visitors from town there, as well as their neighbour Marya Ivanovna, and the inevitable count. Alexander's sufferings were unendurable. Another day passed in empty trivial conversation. How tired he was of the visitors! They chatted serenely about all sorts of trifles, arguing, joking, and laughing incessantly.

"They can laugh," thought Alexander, "when ... Nadya ... has changed to me. It's nothing to them! Wretched empty souls—anything amuses them!"

Nadya went into the garden; the count did not follow her. Of late he and Nadya seemed to avoid one another in Alexander's presence. He sometimes found them in the garden or in a room, alone, but they soon parted, and so long as he was there did not come together again. A new and terrible discovery for Alexander—a sign that they were in connivance.

The guests left. The count left, too. Nadya, who was in the garden, did not know this and did not hasten back to the house. Alexander left Marya Mikhailovna unceremoniously and went into the garden. Nadya was standing with her back to him holding on to the railings with one hand, with her head propped on the other, as on that unforgettable evening. She neither saw him nor heard his approach.

How his heart beat as he crept up to her on tiptoe!

He almost stopped breathing.

"Nadezhda Alexandrovna," he said, his voice almost inaudible from agitation.

She started as if a pistol had gone off near her, turned, and retreated a step from him.

"Look—what's that smoke?" she said, in evident embarrassment, pointing eagerly at the opposite side of the river. "Is it a fire, or a furnace in the factory?"

He looked at her in silence.

"I thought it was a fire, really I did. Why do you look at me like that, don't you believe me?"

She paused.

"You, too!" he began. "Just like the rest! Who could have thought it—two months ago?"

"What d'you mean? I don't understand you," she said, and made as if to go.

"Wait, Nadezhda Alexandrovna, I can no longer bear this torture."

"What torture? Really I don't know."

"Don't pretend! Tell me—can this be you? Are you the same as you used to be?"

"I'm the same as ever," she said sturdily.

"What? You haven't changed to me?"

"No. I think I'm as nice to you as I always was, I'm always glad to see you."

"Just as glad! Then why do you always run away from me?"

"Me run away? What will you say next? I am standing at the railings, and you say—I'm running away!"

She gave a forced laugh.

"Nadezhda Alexandrovna, stop this hypocrisy," Alexander continued.

"Hypocrisy? Why d'you keep nagging at me?"

"Can this be you? My God! Six weeks ago, in this very place…"

"What's that smoke over there I should like to know."

"Awful! Awful!" said Alexander.

"Well, what have I done to you? You've stopped coming to us—that's your business … no one wants to keep you against your will," began Nadya.

"Always pretending! As if you did not know why I stopped coming!"

Looking aside, she shook her head.

"And the count?" he brought out at last in tones which were almost threatening.

"What count?"

She made a face and tried to look as if she had never heard of the count.

"Well," he said, looking her straight in the eyes, "will you tell me you are indifferent to him?"

"You must be mad!" she replied, retreating from him.

"You're not far wrong," he pursued. "My reason is failing with every day. How could you behave so insidiously, so ungratefully to one who loved you more than the world, who forgot all for your sake, all … who expected soon to be made happy for life, and you…"

"Well, what about me?" she said, retreating still further from him.

"What about you?" he countered, infuriated by her coolness. "Have you forgotten? I will remind you that here, on this very spot, you swore a thousand times to belong to me. 'God hears these vows,' you said. Yes. He did hear them. You will have to blush before this sky, before these trees, before every blade of grass … everything that witnessed our happiness. Every grain of sand here speaks of our love. Look, look around you! You are a perjurer!"

She gazed at him in horror. His eyes flashed, his lips turned white.

"How unkind you are!" she said timidly. "What are you so angry about? I haven't refused you, you haven't spoken to *Maman* yet … how do you know?"

"Speak—after all you have done?"

"What have I done? I don't know."

"Allow me to tell you then! What is the meaning of these rendezvous with the count, these rides?"

"Ought I to have run away from him every time *Maman* went out of the room? And the rides mean—that I like riding ... it's such fun. When you gallop—oh, what a darling horse that Lucy is! Did you see her? She knows me already!"

"And the change in your behaviour to me?" he went on. "Why is the count at your house every day, from morning till night?"

"Oh, Lord, how do I know? How absurd you are! *Maman* likes him."

"It's not true. Your *Maman* likes what you like. All those presents—the music, the albums, the flowers—are they all for *Maman*?"

"Yes. *Maman* loves flowers. She bought some yesterday from the gardener."

"And what are you always whispering to him about?" went on Alexander, not heeding her words. "See! You turn pale, you yourself know that you are at fault. To destroy a man's happiness, to forget, to end everything so quickly, so easily ... hypocrisy, ingratitude, lies, treachery ... yes, treachery! How could you sink so low? The rich count, the society lion, only has to bend a favourable eye on you, and you melt, prostrate yourself before this tawdry sun. Where's your shame? The count must not come here any more," he said breathlessly. "D'you hear me? Give him up, break off all relations with him, let him forget the way to your house! I won't have it!"

He seized her hand in his fury.

"*Maman! Maman!* Come here!" cried Nadya in a piercing voice, tearing herself from his grasp and rushing headlong towards the house.

He sat down on the bench and clutched his head in his hands.

She ran into the house, pale, terrified, and sank into a chair.

"What's the matter? Why did you shout?" asked her mother, who had come out to meet her, in alarm.

"Alexander Fyodorich is—unwell," she brought out with difficulty.

"But why were you so frightened?"

"He's so terrible... *Maman*, don't let him come to me, for God's sake!"

"How you frightened me, you crazy thing! Well, what if he is ill? I know he has a pain in his chest. What's so terrible about that? It's not consumption. Rub the chest with opodeldoc and it'll go. I suppose he didn't obey me, didn't rub his chest."

Alexander came to his senses. His fever passed but his tortures were redoubled. He had cleared up none of his doubts, and only frightened Nadya, and now of course he would never get an answer out of her. He had not managed the affair well. As a lover will, he suddenly asked himself: "Supposing she is not to blame? Perhaps she really does not care for the count! Her foolish mother invites him every day, and what can she do? As a man of the world, he is polite. Nadya is a pretty girl. He may want to make her fall in love with him, but it by no means follows that she is in love with him. Perhaps it's the flowers and the rides, the innocent amusement she likes, and not the count himself. Even admitting that there is a little coquetry in all this, after all isn't it pardonable? Older people than she do all sorts of things."

He relaxed and a ray of hope shone in his soul. All lovers are the same—blind and over-discerning by turns. And then it is so delightful to acquit the beloved.

"But why has she changed in her behaviour to me?" he asked himself suddenly, and again went pale. "Why does she avoid me, does not speak to me, seems to be ashamed? Why was she all dressed up yesterday—when they were not expecting visitors? No one came but the count. Why did she ask if the ballet season would soon begin?" Quite a simple question, but Alexander remembered that the count had promised quite casually to get a box for every performance, whatever the difficulty, so it meant he would be with them. "Why did she leave the garden yesterday? Why didn't she go into the garden? Why did she ask this, why did she not ask that?"

And once more he was plunged in painful doubt, once more he suffered agonies, and came to the conclusion that Nadya had never loved him at all.

"My God, my God," he cried in despair. "How hard,

how bitter life is! Grant me deathly tranquillity, that slumber of the soul..."

Fifteen minutes later he went into the house, dejected and apprehensive.

"Good-bye, Nadezhda Alexandrovna," he said timidly.

"Good-bye," she said abruptly, not raising her eyes.

"When may I come again?"

"Whenever you like. Oh, yes, but we shall be going back to town next week. We'll let you know."

He took his leave. Over two weeks passed. Everyone had gone back to town. The aristocratic salons scintillated again. The official lit the bracket lamps in his drawing-room, bought half a pood of tallow candles, set out two card tables, in expectation of a visit from Stepan Ivanich and Ivan Stepanich, and told his wife that their at-home day would be Tuesday.

Alexander still received no invitation from the Lyubetskys'. Once he met their chef and their housemaid. The housemaid, seeing him, ran away; evidently she was acting in the spirit of her young mistress. The chef stopped.

"Have you forgotten us, Sir?" he asked. "We've been back over a week."

"Perhaps you're not settled down yet, not receiving?"

"Oh, yes, we are, Sir. Everybody's called excepting you. The mistress is always wondering why you don't come. His Excellency calls every day—such a kind gentleman! I took a little notebook to him from the young mistress the other day, and he gave me a handsome tip."

"You fool, you!" said Alexander, and rushed away so he could not hear more.

That evening he passed the Lyubetskys' house. The lights were all on. At the front door was a carriage.

"Whose carriage is it?" he asked.

"Count Novinsky's."

The next day and the next the same thing happened. But at last he went to call. The mother received him cordially, with reproaches for his absence, scolding him for not rubbing his chest with opodeldoc. Nadya was calm, the count courteous. The conversation flagged.

He called two or three times again. In vain he gazed expressively at Nadya; she seemed not to notice his glances, and oh! how she used to notice them before!

Sometimes when he stood talking to Marya Mikhailovna, Nadya would get behind her mother's chair and make faces at him, trying to make him laugh.

He was plunged in intolerable melancholy. All he thought about was how to throw off this cross he had himself undertaken to bear. All he wanted was to get an explanation.

"Whatever the answer," he told himself. "Anything to turn doubt into certainty."

He pondered long how to tackle the situation, and at last, having come to a decision, went to the Lyubetskys'. Everything was in his favour. There was no carriage at the door. He went quietly through the ball-room and stood for a moment at the door of the drawing-room, to pull himself together. Nadya was at the piano, playing. On the other side of the room her mother was seated on a sofa, knitting a scarf. Nadya, hearing footsteps in the ball-room, went on playing more quietly, her head bent forward. She awaited the appearance of the visitor with a smile. The visitor appeared, and the smile instantly vanished, replaced by a look of terror. She changed countenance slightly and got up. This was not the visitor she was expecting.

Alexander bowed silently and passed like a shadow towards the mother. He walked quietly, without his previous confidence, with a drooping head. Nadya sat down and went on playing, looking over her shoulder anxiously every now and then.

Half an hour later something took her mother from the room. Alexander went up to Nadya. She rose as if to go.

"Nadezhda Alexandrovna," he said disconsolately. "Wait, give me five minutes, no more!"

"I won't listen to you!" she said, and again made as if to go. "Last time you were so..."

"I was wrong then. I will be quite different now, I promise you. You will not hear a single reproach. Do not refuse to hear me, it may be for the last time. There must be an explanation—you did say I could ask your mother for your hand, you know. After this, so much has happened that ... in a word—I must repeat my question. Sit down and go on playing. Then your mother would not hear. It isn't the first time, you know."

She obeyed him mechanically. Blushing slightly she

struck a few chords and fixed her eyes on him in anxious anticipation.

"Where are you, Alexander Fyodorich?" asked the mother, who had gone back to her place.

"I wanted to speak to Nadezhda Alexandrovna about ... literature," he replied.

"Go on then, do. It's really quite a long time since you've had a talk."

"Only give me a brief sincere answer to one question," he began in low tones. "And our explanation will be over. Don't you love me any more?"

"Quelle idée," she replied in some confusion. "You know how much *Maman* and I have always valued your friendship ... how glad we always were to see you."

Alexander looked at her, thinking: "Can this be the mischievous, open-hearted child, the artlessly playful girl I knew? How quickly she has learned to dissemble! How swiftly her feminine instincts have developed! Can it be that those dainty whims were only the seeds of hypocrisy and cunning? See how rapidly that girl has become a woman, without the help of my uncle's methods! And it's all the count's school, and all in a mere two or three months. Oh, Uncle, Uncle! Here too you were mercilessly right!"

"Now listen," he said in a voice that made the little hypocrite drop her mask in a trice. "Never mind *Maman*—just for a moment be the old Nadya, who used to love me a little ... and answer frankly—I must know, I must, by God!"

She said nothing, but changed the music and peered hard at it as she began playing a difficult passage.

"Very well, I will put the question differently," went on Alexander. "Tell me, has not someone, someone who shall be nameless, has not someone taken my place in your heart?"

She snuffed the candle, fidgeting long with the wick, but said nothing.

"Answer me, Nadezhda Alexandrovna—one word will relieve my agony, and save you from an unpleasant explanation."

"Stop, for God's sake! What am I to say to you? I have nothing to say," she replied, turning away.

Another man would have been content with this reply, and realized that there was nothing for him to do. He would have understood all, from the inarticulate distress written on her face and apparent in all her movements. But Alexander was not satisfied. Like an executioner he tortured his victim, and inspired by wild, desperate desire, forced himself to drink the cup to the dregs.

"Come!" he said. "Put an end to this torture! Doubts, black doubts, disturb my mind, tear at my heart. I'm worn out! I feel as if my heart will burst under the strain! I have no way of confirming my suspicions. You must come to a decision, otherwise I shall never know rest."

He looked at her expectantly. She said nothing.

"Have mercy on me!" he began again. "Look at me—am I like myself? People are shocked, they don't recognize me. Everyone pities me, you alone..."

And indeed—his eyes shone with a wild light. He was thin, pale, beads of sweat stood on his brow.

She glanced at him furtively and something like pity flickered in her glance. She actually took his hand, but dropped it immediately with a sigh, and maintained her silence.

"Well?" he asked.

"Oh, leave me in peace!" she said miserably. "You're tormenting me with your questions."

"I implore you, for God's sake!" he said. "End everything with a single word! What's the good of all this secrecy? A grain of foolish hope will remain with me and I shall not desist, I shall appear before you daily, pale, distressed... I shall make you miserable. Shut the door on me, I shall roam beneath your windows, meet you at the theatre, in the street, everywhere, like a ghost, like a *memento mori*. This may all be very foolish, ridiculous. Some may find it funny, but to me it is painful. You don't know what passion means, what it can drive one to. God grant you never may! What's the good? Wouldn't it be better to say it straight out?"

"But what is it you want to know?" said Nadya, throwing herself back in her chair. "I'm all confused ... my mind is in a fog."

She pressed her hand feverishly to her forehead, and immediately removed it.

"I ask you—has anyone taken my place in your heart? One word—*yes*, or *no*—will settle everything. Surely that won't take long to say."

She tried to speak but could not and, lowering her eyes, began striking a key with her finger again and again. It was obvious that a violent struggle was going on within her. "Oh!" she at last uttered grievously. Alexander mopped his brow with his handkerchief.

"Yes, or no?" he repeated, holding his breath.

A few seconds passed.

"Yes, or no?"

"Yes," whispered Nadya almost inaudibly, and bent low over the keyboard, striking loud chords as if in a kind of trance. The "Yes" was scarcely more distinct than a sigh, but it deafened Alexander. His heart seemed to be torn from its roots, his knees gave way. He sank on to a chair beside the piano, and said nothing.

Nadya glanced at him in alarm. He was staring at her blankly.

"Alexander Fyodorich!" suddenly called the mother from her room. "Which ear is buzzing?"

He did not answer.

"*Maman* is speaking to you," said Nadya.

"Eh?"

"Which ear is buzzing?" cried out the mother. "Quick!"

"Both," said Alexander sombrely.

"Oh, you—the left, of course! I've been guessing whether the count will come today."

"The count," repeated Alexander.

"Forgive me!" said Nadya in imploring tones, rushing up to him. "I don't understand myself. Everything just happened, against my will. I don't know how... I couldn't deceive you."

"I will keep my word, Nadezhda Alexandrovna," he said, "I will not make you a single reproach. Thank you for your frankness. You have done much, very much, to-day. It was hard for me to hear that 'Yes' ... but still harder for you to say it. Farewell—you will not see me any more. That will be a reward for your sincerity. But the count, the count!"

He set his teeth and moved towards the door.

Then he came back and said, "But where will all this

lead you? The count will not marry you. What are his intentions?"

"I don't know," said Nadya, shaking her head sorrowfully.

"Oh, God, how blind you are!" exclaimed Alexander, in horror.

"His intentions cannot be evil," she said in a weak voice.

"Beware, Nadezhda Alexandrovna!"

He took her hand, kissed it, and went unsteadily out of the room. He was a pitiable sight. Nadya remained motionless in her place.

"Why don't you play, Nadya?" asked her mother a few minutes later.

Nadya sighed, as if awakened from a deep sleep.

"One minute, *Maman*!" she replied and, her head pensively on one side, began irresolutely picking out a few notes. Her fingers trembled. She was obviously suffering from remorse and from the doubt aroused in her by the word "Beware!" When the count arrived she was taciturn and dull. There was something forced in her manner. Under the pretext of a headache she went early to her room. And that night life appeared a bitter thing to her.

Hardly had Alexander got to the bottom of the stairs when his powers deserted him. He sat down on the last step, covered his eyes with his handkerchief and broke out into loud tearless sobs. Just then the yardman was passing by. He stood still, listening.

"Marfa, come here!" he cried, going to the door of the lodge. "Come here, listen! There's someone bellowing like a bull. I thought it was our Arapka broken her chain, but no, it's not Arapka."

"No, that's not Arapka," said Marfa, listening. "What can it be?"

"Go and get the lantern—it's hanging behind the stove."
Marfa brought the lantern.

"Still bellowing?" she asked.

"Yes, yes! Can it be some thief has got in?"

"Who's there?" cried the yardman.
No answer.

"Who's there?" echoed Marfa.

But the sobbing continued. As the two of them came to

the porch, Alexander rushed off and away.

"Why, it's a gentleman!" cried Marfa, looking after him. "And you thought it was a thief! You couldn't think of anything cleverer to say! As if a thief would cry in a strange porch!"

"Then he must be drunk."

"Better and better!" said Marfa. "You judge everyone by yourself. All drunks don't bellow like you."

"Well, what's the matter with him then—he isn't hungry, is he?" said the yardman crossly.

"What!" said Marfa, looking at him unable to find an answer. "Who can say—perhaps he's dropped something—some money..."

They both squatted down and began, by the light of the lantern, groping all over the floor of the porch.

"Dropped something!" growled the yardman, holding the lamp low. "How could he drop anything here? The steps are clean, made of stone, you could see a needle on them—dropped something indeed! He'd have heard if anything dropped. It would rattle on the stones. He'd have picked it up, wouldn't he? Where could he have dropped something here? There isn't anywhere! Dropped! Dropped, indeed! Not the sort to drop anything, he isn't! No—that sort is more likely to find a way of putting things in his own pocket! Dropped! I know them, the rogues! Dropped, indeed! Where could he have dropped anything?"

And they groped on the floor for a long time, looking for the lost money.

"Nothing there," said the yardman at last with a sigh, and blew out the light, nipping the wick between his two fingers and wiping them on his sheepskin coat.

VI

That same night, at about twelve o'clock, when Pyotr Ivanich, holding a candlestick and a book in one hand, and with the other holding up the skirts of his dressing-gown, was going from his study to his bedroom, his manservant told him that Alexander Fyodorich wished to see him.

Pyotr Ivanich knitted his brows, thought for a moment, and then said quietly:

"Ask him into the study, I'll be there in a minute."

"Hullo, Alexander!" he cried, going back to his study. "Haven't seen you for a long time! Every day we kept thinking you would come, and all of a sudden you turn up at night. Why so late? And what's the matter with you? You look awful!"

Alexander, without a word of reply, collapsed into a chair. Pyotr Ivanich surveyed him with curiosity.

Alexander heaved a sigh.

"Are you all right?" asked Pyotr Ivanich solicitously.

"Yes, thank you," Alexander replied in a feeble voice. "I move, eat, drink, so I must be well."

"It's no joking matter—you ought to see a doctor."

"Lots of people have given me that advice, but no doctors or opodeldoc can help me. My illness is not physical."

"What's the matter with you? You haven't been gambling or losing money, have you?" asked Pyotr Ivanich eagerly.

"You can't imagine a grief that has nothing to do with money," said Alexander, trying to smile.

"What sort of grief can that be if it isn't worth a brass farthing, like some of your griefs?"

"The sort of grief I am now in. Do you know what my present grief is?"

"Grief? Everything's all right in your home—I know that from the letters to which your mother treats me every month. Nothing can be worse at the office than it already is. You've been passed over for your junior—that's really too bad! You say you're well, you haven't lost money or been gambling ... these are the only important things, one could cope with anything else; next comes a lot of rubbish, love, I suppose."

"Yes, love. But do you know what has happened? When you do, perhaps you won't take it so lightly, but will be horrified."

"Tell me, then. I haven't been horrified for a long time," said his uncle, sitting down. "But it isn't so hard to guess, either. You've probably been cheated."

Alexander jumped up, seemed to be about to speak, but sat down again without a word.

"Aha! So it's true? You see! I told you so, but you said: 'Oh no, that could never be!' "

"How could I have imagined such a thing?" Alexander said. "After all that..."

"You should not have imagined, you should have foreseen, that is, known—that's more like it—and acted accordingly."

"You can reason so calmly, Uncle, when I..." said Alexander.

"What is it to me?"

"Oh, I forgot. You wouldn't care if the whole town was burned down or sank through the earth."

"But what about my factory?"

"You joke, but I am suffering in earnest. I'm so miserable, I'm like a sick man."

"And have you really grown so thin from love? Why, that's outrageous! No! You have been ill and now you are beginning to recover, and high time. This folly has been going on for more than eighteen months—that's no joke. A little more and I should have begun to believe in constancy and eternal love."

"Uncle," said Alexander. "Have pity on me! I'm going through hell."

"And what d'you want me to do about it?"

Alexander drew up his chair to the desk and his uncle started moving the ink-pot, paper-weight and other objects out of his nephew's way.

"Comes here at night," he muttered. "Going through hell—he's sure to break something or other again."

"I shall find no consolation from you," began Alexander. "Nor do I demand any. I only ask your help, as my uncle, my relative... I seem silly to you, don't I?"

"Yes, if you weren't so pitiful."

"So you do pity me?"

"Very much. I'm not made of stone, am I? A good chap, clever, well brought-up, and he comes to grief for no earthly reason—and what for? For a lot of rubbish."

"Prove that you pity me."

"How? You say you don't need money."

"Money, money! Oh, if my misfortune were nothing but lack of money I would bless my fate."

"Don't say that," said Pyotr Ivanich gravely. "You're young—you would curse, not bless your fate. I myself have cursed my fate more than once."

"Hear me out patiently."

"Will it take long, Alexander?" asked his uncle.

"Yes, I need all your attention. Why?"

"Well, you see, I'd like to have some supper. I was going to go to bed without, but if we are to sit here long, then let's have supper and drink a bottle of wine, and you can tell me all about it the while."

"And you can eat supper?" exclaimed Alexander in astonishment.

"I most certainly can. Can't you?"

"I? Have supper? You won't be able to swallow a bite yourself when you hear that this is a matter of life and death."

"Life and death?" repeated his uncle. "Well, of course, that's extremely important, but let's just try—I think we'll manage to swallow a bite."

He rang the bell.

"Ask what there is for supper," he said to the servant who answered his summons. "And tell them to get out a bottle of Lafitte, with the green seal."

The servant retired.

"Uncle! You're not in the right mood to hear the sad tale of my grief," said Alexander, picking up his hat. "I'd better come tomorrow."

"No, no!" Pyotr Ivanich said quickly, seizing his nephew by the hand. "I'm always in the same mood. If you come tomorrow, you'll find me at breakfast, or still worse, engaged. Better get it over now. Supper won't spoil anything. I shall listen and understand even better. On an empty stomach, you know, it's not so easy."

Supper was brought in.

"Come on, now, Alexander!" said Pyotr Ivanich.

"I can't eat anything, Uncle," said Alexander impatiently and shrugged his shoulders as he watched his uncle busying himself about the supper table.

"At least have a glass of wine—the wine's not bad."

Alexander shook his head.

"Well, take a cigar and tell me, and I'll listen with both my ears," said Pyotr Ivanich, and began eating with relish.

"You know Count Novinsky, don't you?" began Alexander, after a pause.

"Count Platon?"

"Yes."

"He's a friend of mine—well?"

"I congratulate you on having such a scoundrelly friend!"

Pyotr Ivanich suddenly stopped chewing and looked at his nephew in astonishment.

"Well, well!" he exclaimed. "And do you know him?"

"I know him very well."

"Have you known him long?"

"Three months."

"How's that? I've known him for five years and always considered him a decent man; everyone has a good word for him, ask whom you will, and here you demolish him all of a sudden!"

"How long is it since you began sticking up for people, Uncle? You used always to..."

"I have always stuck up for decent people. And how long is it since you began abusing people, instead of calling them all angels as you used to?"

"That was before I knew them, but now—Oh, human beings, pitiable breed, deserving of tears and laughter! I admit that I am utterly in the wrong for not having listened to you when you advised me to beware of everyone."

"And I still advise you to. There's no harm in being on the alert. If a man turns out a ruffian, you will not have been taken in, and if he turns out to be a decent person, you will be pleasantly disappointed."

"Show me some decent people," said Alexander scornfully.

"Well, there's you and me—aren't we decent people? The count, since you mention him, is a decent man, too. And there are plenty more. Everyone has something bad about him. But not everyone is altogether bad."

"Everyone, everyone!" said Alexander firmly.

"What about yourself?"

"Me? I at least shall have saved a heart which, though broken, is free of baseness, a tortured soul, but one that cannot be reproached with falseness, hypocrisy, treachery, I shall not become infected..."

"Well, we'll see. But what has the count done to you?"

"What has he done? He has stolen my all."

"Speak more plainly. The word *all* may cover God knows what—money perhaps. He wouldn't do that."

"That which is dearer to me than all the treasures in the world," said Alexander.

"And what may that be?"

"All—happiness, life!"

"But you're alive."

"Unfortunately I am. But such a life is worse than death."

"Tell me straight out what has happened."

"Something awful," said Alexander. "God, oh God!"

"Aha! I suppose he's stolen your beauty from you, that ... what's her name? Yes, he's a dab at that. You'll find it hard to compete with him. The lady-killer!" said Pyotr Ivanich, popping a piece of turkey into his mouth.

"He shall pay dear for his skill," said Alexander, flushing up. "I will not yield without a fight. Death shall determine which of us is to possess Nadya. I will crush this cheap rake. He shall not live, shall not enjoy his stolen treasure. I will sweep him off the face of the earth."

Pyotr Ivanich laughed.

"Oh, the provinces!" he said. "*A propos* the count, Alexander—did he say whether he had received any porcelain from abroad? He sent for a consignment in the spring. I shoul like to have a look at it."

"We're not talking of porcelain, Uncle. Didn't you hear what I said?" Alexander interrupted him fiercely.

His uncle grunted, gnawing at a bone.

"And what have you to say to it?"

"Oh, nothing. I'm listening to you."

"For once in your life listen attentively. I have come to you on a serious matter. I want to regain my composure, to find the answers to a million agonizing questions which are harassing me ... I am at my wits' end ... I don't know what I am doing—help me!"

"I am quite at your service. Only tell me what you want. I'm even ready with money—so long as it's not for some trifle."

"Trifle. It is hardly a trifle when perhaps in a few hours' time I shall no longer be alive, or I shall have become a murderer ... and you laugh, you eat your supper calmly."

"I beg your pardon. You've had supper yourself, I suppose, and you don't want to let me eat."

"I haven't had a bite for two days."

"So it really is something important!"

"Tell me one thing—will you do me the greatest favour?"

"What?"

"Will you be my second?"

"The cutlets are quite cold," said Pyotr Ivanich irately, pushing the dish away from him.

"Uncle, you can joke!"

"I ask you, how can I listen to such nonsense with a straight face? Asking me to be your second!"

"And you won't?"

"Of course I won't!"

"Never mind. Another will be found, some stranger who will help me to avenge the deadly injury I have received. I will only ask you to speak to the count, to find out the conditions."

"I couldn't do that. I couldn't bring myself to suggest such folly to him."

"Then, farewell," said Alexander, taking up his hat.

"What—going? Won't you have a glass of wine?"

Alexander started to go, but sank into a chair near the door in profound dejection.

"To whom can I go, where can I seek sympathy?" he said softly.

"Listen to me, Alexander," said Pyotr Ivanich, wiping his lips with his napkin, and moving his chair nearer his nephew. "I see I shall really have to talk to you seriously. Let's talk then. You came to me for help. I will help you, but not in the way you imagine, and on condition that you obey me. Don't ask anyone to be your second— no good will come of it. You are making a mountain out of a molehill, the story will get about everywhere, you will become a laughing-stock, or, worse still, you will get into trouble. Nobody will agree to be your second, and even if you do find some madman, the count will not fight. I know him."

"Not fight! Then there is not a drop of honour in his nature," said Alexander angrily. "I did not know he was as base as all that."

"He is not base, only wise."

"And in your opinion I am foolish."

"N-no—you're in love," drawled out Pyotr Ivanich.

"If you intend to point out to me the folly of duelling, Uncle, then I warn you it will be a waste of time. I shall remain firm."

"I do not. It has long been proved that it is foolish, on principle, to fight duels. But people do fight, there are always plenty of fools, and there's no making them see reason. I only want to point out that you, in particular, ought not to fight."

"I should like to see how you're going to convince me of that!"

"Then listen. Tell me—with whom are you more angry— with the count, or with her—what's her name—Anyuta, isn't it?"

"Him I detest, her I despise," said Alexander.

"Let's begin with the count. Say he accepts your challenge, say even that you find some fool of a second— what then? The count will kill you as easily as swatting a fly, and afterwards everyone will laugh at you. A fine revenge! That's not what you want, you know. What you want is to annihilate the count."

"Who knows which of us will kill the other?" said Alexander.

"He's sure to kill you. As far as I know you can't shoot at all. And according to the rules he would have the first shot."

"The decision will lie with Heaven."

"Well, say what you like—Heaven will decide in the count's favour. They say the count can hit the same spot several times running at fifteen paces, and you think he'll miss you on purpose! Even admitting that Heaven allows such awkwardness and injustice, and you chance to kill him—what then? Would that give you back the girl's love? No, she would loathe you, and you would be sentenced to twenty-five years of soldiering. And—most important of all—the next day you would be ready to tear your hair with remorse, and lose all feeling for your beloved."

Alexander shrugged scornfully.

"Since you know all about it, Uncle," he said, "tell me

what I am to do in my position."

"Nothing. Leave things as they are. Everything's spoilt anyhow."

"Leave my happiness in his hands, leave him the proud possessor! What terrors could deter me! You do not know my torments. You have never loved if you hope to restrain me by such cold moralizing. Milk flows in your veins, not blood."

"Stop talking nonsense! As if there weren't scores of girls like your Marya or Sophia, or whatever she's called."

"Her name is Nadezhda."

"Nadezhda, is it? And which one is Sophia?"

"Sophia is in the country," replied Alexander grudgingly.

"You see," went on his uncle. "Sophia, there, Nadezhda, here, Marya somewhere else. The heart is a very deep well—it takes a long time to get to the bottom of it. It goes on loving till old age."

"No, the heart only loves once."

"You are just repeating what you have heard others say. The heart loves as long as its strength is not all expended. It has a life of its own, and, like the other parts of a human body, has its youth and its old age. If one love is unlucky, it merely quietens down and waits in silence for the next. And if that one does not come off, if the lovers are parted, the power to love remains in abeyance till the third, or the fourth time, until, at last, the heart puts all its force into some one happy encounter, to which there are no obstacles, after which it slowly and gradually cools down. Some people are lucky in love the first time, and these are the ones who exclaim that one only loves once. While a man is not old and has his health..."

"You keep talking about youth, Uncle, in other words about physical love."

"I speak about youth because senile love is a mistake, an ugliness. And what is physical love? There is no such thing, or it is not love, just as there is no such thing as purely ideal love. In love, body and soul take equal parts. Otherwise love is not complete. We are neither spirits nor beasts. You say yourself, 'milk runs in the veins, not blood'. So you see, on the one hand, we have blood in the veins—that's physical, and on the other, vanity, habit,

that's spiritual. And there's love for you! What was I saying—ah, yes—you'll be sentenced to soldiering. Besides,
after all this fuss your young lady won't let you go near
her. You would simply have injured her and yourself—
can't you see that? I trust this side of the question has
been sufficiently investigated. Now..."

Pyotr Ivanich poured himself out some wine and drank.
"That blockhead!" he said. "The Lafitte's cold."

Alexander was silent, his head bowed.

"Now tell me," went on his uncle, warming the glass
of wine between the palms of his hands. "What makes you
wish to sweep the count off the face of the earth?"

"I told you what. Has he not destroyed my happiness?
He came bursting in, like a wild beast..."

"Into the sheep-fold," interrupted his uncle.

"...And stole everything," continued Alexander.

"He did not steal, he just came and took what he wanted. Was he obliged to inquire whether your beauteous
maiden was free or not? I cannot understand the folly
which, I admit, most lovers have perpetrated since the
beginning of creation—being angry with the rival. What
could be more idiotic—*sweep him off the face of the
earth*! What for? Simply because she liked him. As if it
were his fault and as if matters would be improved by
punishing him. And your—what's her name—Katenka,
isn't it?—did she resist him? Did she make any effort to
avoid the peril? She yielded of her own free will, ceased
to love you, so there's nothing more to be said. What's
done cannot be undone. And it would be sheer egoism to
insist on your rights. There's some sense in demanding
faithfulness from a *wife*—an obligation has been taken on,
the well-being of a whole family often depends on this.
But even then one cannot demand that she must never
love anyone ... one can only demand that she should—you
know. And didn't you hand her over to the count yourself? Did you try to win her back?"

"That's just what I want to do!" said Alexander, jumping up. "And you want to restrain my noble impulse."

"To win her back with a club in your hand!" his uncle
broke in. "We don't live in the Kirghiz steppe. The civi-
lized world knows other weapons. You should have taken
it up in time and quite differently, have fought another

sort of duel with the count, in the presence of your beloved."

Alexander stared at his uncle in astonishment.

"What sort of duel?" he asked.

"I'll tell you in a minute. How have you behaved so
far?"

With innumerable digressions, presenting all sorts of
mitigating circumstances, quibbling and faltering, Alexander told him the whole story.

"You see? You're to blame all round," declared Pyotr
Ivanich, who had been listening to him with an expression of distaste. "How many follies you have committed!
Oh, Alexander, you should never have left home. Was
it worth while coming for this? You could have carried on
just the same at home, with your auntie, on the shores of
the lake. Oh, how could you be such a baby, making scenes,
flying into a rage... Ugh! Who behaves like this nowadays? What if your—what's her name, Julia?—tells the
count everything? But no, there's no danger of that,
thank God! She's probably clever enough, when he asked
about you, to have told him..."

"Told him what?" asked Alexander quickly.

"That she was making a fool of you, that you are in
love with her, that you've been a nuisance, a nasty bore...
They always do, you know."

"You think she ... said ... that?" asked Alexander,
turning pale.

"Undoubtedly. Surely you don't imagine she would
tell him how you picked yellow blossoms in the garden
together? What a simpleton you are!"

"But what sort of duel should I have fought with the
count?" asked Alexander impatiently.

"I'll tell you. You should not have been rude to him,
or avoided him and made faces at him; on the contrary,
you should have replied to his courtesies by being twice
as courteous, three times, ten times... And you shouldn't
have irritated your, what's her name, Nadezhda (got it
right, this time, didn't I?) with reproaches, you should
have yielded to her whims, pretended to have noticed nothing, to have no suspicions whatever, to consider such a
thing as deception an impossibility. You should not have
let them become so intimate, you should have cleverly

interfered with their tête-à-têtes, have gone everywhere with them, even when they went for rides, and, skilfully, quite casually, have thrown down the gauntlet to your rival in her presence, rallying all the forces of your mind, all your wit and cunning, and then, you know—exposing and striking at your rival's weak spots without appearing to mean anything, good-naturedly, even reluctantly, gradually stripping him of the trappings a young man dons to show off before a pretty girl. You should have noticed what it was that impressed and dazzled her in him most of all, and then attacked these very points, belittling them, making them appear commonplace, showing that the new hero was nothing special, and had donned his bright feathers to strut before her. And all this should have been done with coolness, patience, ability—that is the true duel in our age. But you are not capable of it."

With this Pyotr Ivanich drained his glass and immediately refilled it.

"Contemptible subterfuges! To try to win a woman's heart by ruses," said Alexander indignantly.

"And is it better to try winning it with a club? It may be possible by wiles to retain someone's affection—but I don't think it can be done by force. I can understand the desire to get rid of a rival. It is quite natural to make efforts to keep the woman one loves, to anticipate or prevent danger. But to beat the rival because he has inspired affection would be equivalent to hitting the object you have bruised yourself against, as children do. Say what you like, but the count has done nothing wrong. As far as I can see you know nothing about the mysteries of love and that is why your love affairs and your stories are so bad."

"Love affairs," exclaimed Alexander, tossing his head contemptuously. "And can there be anything pleasing or enduring about love inspired by cunning?"

"I don't know whether it's pleasing, it depends on how you feel, I don't care about that. As you know, I have not a very high opinion of love. I could live quite well without it. But that it is more enduring—that's true enough. You must use finesse in handling the heart. It's a delicate instrument—if you don't know which chord to touch in it, it may come out with God knows what music. Inspire love however you like, but retain it by using your brain.

Cunning is a function of the brain, and there is nothing despicable in it. You should not humiliate your rival or try to slander him—by this means you put your lady against you. All you have to do is to strip him of the trappings with which he dazzles your lady-love, to show him to her as just an ordinary mortal and no hero... It seems to me legitimate to defend one's property with noble artifices. These are not despised in warfare. You wanted to get married—a fine husband you'd be, making your wife scenes and shaking a club in a rival's face—you'd simply be a fool."

Pyotr Ivanich tapped his forehead with his finger.

"Your Varenka was a hundred times cleverer than you when she suggested waiting a year."

"But could I have used cunning, even if I knew how? Not loving her as I do. There are people who can pretend to cool off, who stay away on purpose for several days—and that works. But I cannot do this! To pretend and calculate, when the very sight of her takes my breath away and makes my knees shake, when I am ready to undergo any tortures just for the sake of seeing her. No, you can say what you like but there is more ecstasy for me in loving with all my soul, even though it means suffering, than in being loved without loving myself, or in half-loving as an amusement, according to some ignoble system, playing with a woman as if she were a lap-dog, and then rejecting her."

Pyotr Ivanich shrugged his shoulders.

"Very well, then, suffer, if it gives you pleasure," he said. "Oh, the provinces! Oh, Asia! You ought to live in the East. They still tell women whom to love there, and if they disobey, drown them. But here," he continued, as if talking to himself, "if you want to be happy with a woman, not in your way, like a madman, but rationally, a great deal is needed. You must know how to transform a girl into a woman according to a well thought-out plan, methodically. If you want her to understand and fulfil her vocation, you must surround her with a magic circle, not too narrow, so that she does not notice or overstep the limits, you must skilfully take possession not only of her heart—that's nothing, it's an uncertain, not lasting possession—but of her mind, her will, subordinate her tastes and morals to your own, so that she sees through your eyes, thinks with your mind..."

"In other words, make her a doll or a submissive slave to her husband," interrupted Alexander.

"No, why? Go about it in such a way that neither her feminine nature nor her qualities change. Leave her freedom of action in her own sphere, but see that your penetrating mind follows her movements, her sighs, her acts, that every stirring of agitation, every impulse, every vestige of emotion always and everywhere meets the outwardly indifferent, but ever vigilant eye of the husband. Let there be permanent control without the slightest tyranny. Skilfully, unnoticed by her, lead her along the desired path. Oh, a woman must go through a wise and difficult school—and that school is a wise, experienced man— that's the whole point."

He coughed meaningly and gulped down his wine.

"Then," he continued, "the husband can sleep peacefully even when his wife is not at his side, or sit free of care in his study when she sleeps."

"Aha! So that's the famous secret of conjugal happiness!" said Alexander. "To fasten to oneself by guile the mind, heart and will of a woman, and to rejoice in this, to glory in it—this is happiness! And supposing she notices?"

"Why glory in it?" asked his uncle. "That is not required."

"Judging by the fact that you are sitting free of care in your study, Uncle," said Alexander, "while my aunt sleeps, I conclude that this man..."

"Sh! Be quiet," said his uncle, with a wave of his hand. "It's a good thing my wife's asleep, or, you know..."

Just then the door of the study opened softly, but no one appeared.

"And the wife," said a woman's voice from the hall, "should never show that she is aware of her husband's magnificent schooling, but should have her own little system, and not chatter about it over a bottle of wine."

The two Aduyevs rushed to the door, but rapid footsteps and the rustle of skirts were heard in the hall—and then all was still.

Uncle and nephew looked at one another.

"Well, Uncle?" said the nephew, after a pause.

"Well? Never mind!" said Pyotr Ivanich knitting his brows. "I shouldn't have boasted. Learn, Alexander, and do not marry, or if you do, marry a fool. You'll never manage a clever woman. It takes subtlety."

He thought for a time and suddenly smote his brow.

"Why didn't I guess she would know about your late visit?" he said in vexation. "And that a woman never sleeps when there's a secret between two men in the next room, that she's sure either to send her maid or come herself? Idiotic not to have foreseen it, it's all you and that accursed Lafitte! Giving myself away! Such a lesson from a woman of twenty!"

"Are you afraid, Uncle?"

"Afraid? Not a bit. I've made a mistake—I mustn't lose my head, I must find a way out."

He once more fell to thinking.

"She was boasting," he said after a pause. "What kind of system can she have? She can't have any system! She's too young. She only said so out of spite. But she's caught sight of the magic circle now, and she'll become wily too. Oh, I know what a woman's nature is! But we'll see."

He smiled triumphantly, and the wrinkles on his forehead disappeared.

"I shall have to go about things differently," he said. "The old method won't do. Now I shall have to..."

He broke off suddenly, glancing anxiously towards the door.

"Well, all that's to come," he said. "Now let's take up your affairs, Alexander. What were we talking about? Oh, yes, you said you wanted to kill your ... what's her name?"

"I despise her too deeply for that," said Alexander, sighing heavily.

"You see? You're already half-cured. But is it true? I think you're still angry. Well, never mind, go on despising her—it's the best thing you can do in your condition. I was going to suggest something, but I won't."

"Oh do, for God's sake, do!" said Alexander. "There isn't a spark of reason left in me. I am suffering, I'm going out of my mind ... lend me some of your cold reason. Say anything that may ease and soothe my wounded heart!"

"If I do, you'll rush back to her again."

"What an idea! After that..."

"People go back after worse things. Do you give me your word of honour you won't?"

"I'll swear to it if you like."

"No, your word of honour—that'll be safer."

"My word of honour."

"Very well, then—we have decided that the count is not to blame."

"Well, and what then?"

"Well, and what has your ... what's her name, done?"

"Nadya?" cried Alexander in astonishment. "Nadya has done nothing?"

"Of course not! What has she done?—tell me that! You have no reason to despise her."

"She has done nothing? No, Uncle, that's going a little too far. Say, the count ... after all ... he didn't know ... although even then... But she? Then who is to blame? Am I?"

"That's more like it. But in fact no one is to blame. Tell me what you despise her for."

"For a base act."

"What act exactly?"

"She repayed lofty, boundless passion with ingratitude."

"What's there to be grateful for? Was it for her sake, to please her, that you fell in love? You wanted to do her a service, did you? In that case you would have done better to have fallen in love with her mamma."

Alexander stared at him and could find nothing to say.

"You should not have let her see the whole force of your feelings. Women grow cool when men tell them all. You should have studied her disposition and acted accordingly, not have lain at her feet like a lap-dog. How can one ignore the character of a partner with whom one has business? You ought to have discovered at the start that nothing more was to be expected of her. She played out her romance with you to the end and she'll do just the same with the count and, perhaps, with someone else. Nothing more is to be expected of her. This is the limit of her abilities. It is not in her. And you imagined God knows what."

"Why did she fall in love with another?" interrupted Alexander sadly.

"So that's what she's guilty of! A clever question! Oh, you savage! And why did you fall in love with her? Come on now, fall out of love this minute!"

"Does it depend on myself?"

"And did it depend on her to fall in love with the count? You say impulses should never be suppressed, but when it affects yourself, you immediately ask, 'Why did she fall in love with another?' 'Why did this one die, that one go out of his mind?' How can such questions be answered? Love has to come to an end some time or other—it can't go on for ever."

"It can, it can! I feel the strength of my own heart—I would have loved with an eternal love!"

"Yes, and if anyone were to love you in real earnest, you'd take to your heels! You're all like that—I know you!"

"Even if her love came to an end," said Alexander, "why did it have to be like that?"

"What does it matter how? You were loved, you were happy—and that's all."

"Giving herself to another!" said Alexander, turning pale.

"Would you have had her love another on the sly, while assuring you of her love? Come now! Tell me, what she ought to have done, and in what way she has been to blame!"

"Oh, I'll have my revenge on her!" said Alexander.

"You are ungrateful," pursued Pyotr Ivanich. "That's a bad thing! However a woman treats you, whether she deceives you, cools towards you, behaves, as the poets say, with *guile*—you may blame nature, indulge, if you will, in philosophical meditations, execrate the world, life, whatever you like, but never, by word or deed, hurt a woman! The only weapon to be used against a woman is indulgence, at the worst—forgetfulness. A decent man will not permit himself any other. Remember how you bored everyone with your happiness a year and a half ago, how you didn't know what to do with yourself for joy! Eighteen months of uninterrupted happiness. Say what you like, you are ungrateful!"

"Oh, Uncle, there was nothing in the world so sacred to me as love! Without love, life is not worth living!"

"Oh," interrupted Pyotr Ivanich irately. "You make me sick."

"I would have worshipped Nadenka," went on Alexander. "I would not have envied the happiness of anyone in the world. I dreamed of spending my whole life with Nadenka—and now... Where is the vast, noble passion of which I dreamed? It has been turned into a silly Lilliputian comedy of sighs, scenes, jealousy, lies, hypocrisy. Oh God, oh God!"

"Why did you imagine things that do not exist? Didn't I tell you that all this time you wanted to lead an imaginary life? According to you, a man's only occupation is to be a lover, a husband, a father—you will hear of nothing else. But as well as all this a man is a citizen, he has a position in society, work to do—whether he be a writer, a landed proprietor, a soldier, an official, an industrialist ... and with you all this is overshadowed by love and friendship ... what an Arcadia you live in! You've crammed yourself with novels, listened to your auntie in the country, and brought all these theories here. And now you've invented—'noble passion'."

"Yes, noble!"

"Enough, I beg you! Are there really any noble passions?"

"What do you mean?"

"Well—are there? Does not passion mean that some feeling or infatuation, or affection or that sort of thing has reached a point when reason no longer functions? And where's the nobility in that, I ask you? It's plain madness. And why do you only look on one side of the medal? I am now speaking of love. Look on the other side and you will see that love is not a bad thing. Remember the happy moments when you bored me to tears..."

"Oh, don't remind me, don't remind me!" said Alexander, waving his hands frantically. "It's all very well for you to reason like this, you are sure of the woman you love! I should like to see what you would do in my place!"

"Me? I would seek distraction—at the factory. Come with me tomorrow."

"You and I will never agree," said Alexander sadly. "Your view of life does not console me, it repels me. I am sad, there is a chill at my heart. Up till now love saved me from that chill. Now love has gone, and there is grief in my heart. I am afraid, miserable..."

"Get down to work."

"You're quite right, Uncle. You and your like can reason thus. You are cold by nature, your soul is incapable of emotion..."

"And you fancy you have a mighty soul! Yesterday in the seventh heaven, and cast down at the least little thing... You can't bear grief with fortitude."

"Steam, steam," said Alexander faintly, in feeble self-defence. "You think and feel and speak exactly like an engine rolling over the rails—smoothly, evenly, calmly."

"Well, and that's not so bad. Better than going off the tracks, bumping into a rut, as you have just done, and not being able to get up again. Steam, steam! Steam, you see, does credit to man! In this invention lies the principle which makes human beings of you and me. Even animals can die of grief. There have been cases of dogs dying on the grave of their masters, or dropping dead from joy after a long separation. What's the virtue in that? And you considered yourself a being of a higher order, an extraordinary person..."

Pyotr Ivanich glanced at his nephew and suddenly broke off.

"What? Surely you're not crying?" he said and his face darkened, that is to say, he went red.

Alexander said nothing. His uncle's last arguments had quite cut the ground from beneath his feet. He had nothing with which to oppose them, he was still held in thrall by his misery. He remembered his lost happiness, and that now another man... And tears streamed freely down his cheeks.

"Now, now! You ought to be ashamed of yourself," said Pyotr Ivanich. "And you a man! For God's sake, go somewhere else and cry!"

"Uncle! Remember the years of your youth!" sobbed Alexander. "Did you really endure the most bitter insult which fate can deal to a human being calmly and coolly? To have lived such a full life for a year and a half, and suddenly—all gone! Nothing left! After all that sincerity—cunning, secrecy, coldness! Oh God, could there be any greater torment! It's easy enough to say of another—you have been deceived. But to feel this? How she changed! How she began dressing herself up for the count! Sometimes when I came she would turn pale, could hardly speak, she lied... Oh, no, no..."

Here his tears flowed more violently than ever.

"If I could console myself," he continued, "by the thought that I had lost her owing to circumstances, that she had acted under compulsion ... that she had died—even *that* would be easier to bear ... but no, no ... another man! It's appalling, intolerable! And no way of getting her from the thief! You have deprived me of my weapons. What am I to do? Teach me! I am choking, I am in pain ... misery, anguish! I shall die, I shall shoot myself!"

He leaned his elbow on the desk, put his head in his hands, and sobbed loudly.

Pyotr Ivanich was completely taken aback. He walked up and down the room once or twice, then stopped in front of Alexander and stood there, scratching the back of his head, not knowing what to do.

"Have some wine, Alexander," he said as tenderly as he knew how. "Perhaps it'll..."

The only sign that Alexander had heard him was a violent convulsion of his head and shoulders, and he went on sobbing. Pyotr Ivanich frowned, waved his hand in a gesture of despair and went out of the room.

"What am I to do with Alexander?" he said to his wife. "He's sitting there bawling, I can't stay in the room! He's simply worn me out!"

"And you went away and left him?" she asked. "Poor boy! I'll go to him."

"There's nothing you can do—it's his nature. Just like his aunt—she was just such a cry-baby. I kept on arguing with him."

"Is that all you did?"

"And I convinced him. He agreed with me."

"No doubt you did! You're very clever and ... cunning," she added.

"And thank God for that! It's all that's required, I should think."

"That's what you think, but he's crying."

"It's not my fault, I did everything I could to comfort him."

"What did you do?"

"A great deal. I talked for a whole hour—my throat's positively parched. All about the theory of love—I expounded it all to him, I offered him money ... supper ... I tried to get him to take some wine..."

"And he went on crying?"

"Simply bawling! It got worse and worse."

"Amazing! Let me go to him! I'll see what I can do, and in the meantime you can think over your new method."

"What's that?"

But she had slipped out of the room like a shadow.

Alexander was still sitting there with his head in his hands. Someone touched him on the shoulder. He raised his head. Before him stood a young and beautiful woman in a dressing-gown and a cap *à la Finnoise*...

"Ma tante!" he exclaimed.

She sat beside him, gazed at him steadily as only women know how to gaze, then gently wiped his eyes with her handkerchief and kissed his forehead. He pressed his lips to her hand. They talked long.

An hour later he went out, thoughtful but smiling, and slept peacefully for the first time after many sleepless nights. She went back to her room with red eyes. Pyotr Ivanich had long been snoring.

Part Two

I

About a year passed since the scenes and events described in the last chapter.

Alexander gradually progressed from gloomy despair to cold dejection. He no longer heaped curses, with the appropriate grinding of the teeth, upon the count and Nadenka, but merely branded them with his profound contempt.

Lizaveta Alexandrovna, his uncle's wife, consoled him with all the tenderness of a friend and a sister. He surrendered himself willingly to her sweet guardianship. Such natures as his love to place their will at the disposal of another. They cannot get on without a nursemaid.

At last his passion died down, his true grief passed, but he could not bear to part with it. He kept it up by force, or rather, he created for himself an artificial grief, played with it, arrayed himself in it, wallowed in it.

He had come to love the role of a martyr. He was quiet, dignified, abstracted, as behove a man who had, as he put it, received a *blow from the hand of fate*. He spoke of elevated sufferings, of sacred, lofty feelings crushed and trampled in the mud—and by whom? "By a mere girl," he would add, "a heartless coquette, and by a contemptible *debauché*, a tinsel society lion! Can it be that fate has sent me into the world in order that all that is highest in me should be sacrificed to a nonentity?"

Such affectation would not have been pardoned in a man by another man, or in a woman by another woman—

and the affected one would have swiftly been brought down to earth—but young people of opposite sexes will forgive one another anything.

Lizaveta Alexandrovna listened indulgently to his jeremiads and consoled him as best she could. They by no means disgusted her, perhaps partly because she found in her nephew a kind of fellow-feeling, heard, beneath his amorous complaints, a voice not quite alien to her own sufferings.

She listened eagerly to the groans of his heart and responded to them with scarcely discernible sighs of her own and with tears which no one saw. She even found comforting words to say, attuning them to her nephew's sentimental, affected rantings. But Alexander would not hear of consolation.

"Don't tell me, *ma tante*!" he protested. "I do not wish to disgrace the sacred name of love by giving that name to my relations with that..." Here he made a scornful grimace and was about to say like Pyotr Ivanich—"what's her name?"

"And yet," he said, with ever-deepening scorn, "she is to be forgiven! I was too much above both her and the count and all that wretched, trivial set. No wonder I remained an enigma to her!"

And after these words the scornful expression stayed for a long time on his countenance.

"My uncle says I ought to be grateful to Nadenka," he continued. "For what? What was the mark of that love? Nothing but vulgarity, nothing but commonplaces! Was there ever the slightest sign of anything rising above the ordinary sphere of daily cares? Was the slightest hint of heroism or self-sacrifice to be seen in this love? No, it almost all went on with the mother's authority. Did she ever deviate from the laws of society, of duty for my sake by so much as an inch? Never! And this is love! A young girl, and unable to infuse poetry into this feeling!"

"What sort of love would you demand from a woman?" asked Lizaveta Alexandrovna.

"Oh!" replied Alexander. "I would demand the first place in her heart! A beloved woman should not notice, should scarcely see other men; they should all—all but me—appear intolerable to her. I should be higher, handsomer"—here he drew himself up—"better, nobler than all. Every moment not spent with me should be for her a lost moment. In my eyes, in my conversation she should find her happiness, and know no other."

Lizaveta Alexandrovna tried to conceal a smile. Alexander did not notice this.

"She should be ready to sacrifice all contemptible advantages, all calculations for me," he went on with flashing eyes. "She should throw off the despotic yoke of mother or husband, fly with me to the ends of the world, if necessary, bear cheerfully all deprivations, scornfully laugh at death itself—that is love! And that..."

"And how would you reward her for that love?" asked his aunt.

"I?" said Alexander, lifting his eyes to heaven. "Oh, I would devote my whole life to her, I would lie at her feet! To look into her eyes would be the highest bliss for me! Her every word would be law for me. I would sing her beauty, our love, nature,

> *She would inspire my tongue to speak*
> *The language of Petrarch and love...*

But haven't I shown Nadenka how I can love?"

"So you don't believe in love if it is not expressed exactly as you would like? Strong feelings hide themselves, you know."

"Do you seek to convince me, *ma tante*, that feelings like my uncle's, for instance, hide themselves?"

Lizaveta Alexandrovna suddenly blushed. She could not help inwardly agreeing with her nephew that there was something suspicious about feelings which did not show themselves at all, that perhaps they did not exist, that if they did they would come to the surface, that there should be an inexplicable charm in the very atmosphere of love.

Here she mentally reviewed the whole period of her married life and became lost in thought. Her nephew's indiscreet hint had stirred a secret which she had buried very deep in her heart, and confronted her with the question: was she happy?

She had no right to complain. All the outward conditions of happiness as striven for by the crowd, were hers, like items in a programme. Prosperity, even luxury in the present, security in the future—everything to free her from the trivial carking cares which gnaw at the hearts and wither the bosoms of so many poor souls.

Her husband had always worked indefatigably, and still did so. But what was the principal aim of his labours? Was he working for a common human aim, fulfilling the task set him by life, or merely for sordid aims, just to attain importance in the eyes of men, to attain official and financial status, to be free of need and the pressure of circumstances? God alone knew! He did not like talking about lofty aims—he called it ranting; and he always said, drily and simply, that men must be doers.

Lizaveta Alexandrovna reached the sad conclusion that she herself, and his love for her, were not the only aims of his strivings and efforts. He had worked before his marriage, before meeting his wife. He never spoke to her of love, or asked her about hers. He turned off her questions in this respect with a jest, a witticism, or by affecting drowsiness. He had begun to speak of their wedding very soon after meeting her, as if implying that love was to be taken for granted, that there was no need to talk about it.

He hated all cheap effects, which was all very well of course, but then he did nor care for sincere manifestations of feeling either, and did not believe that others might feel a need for them. And though he could have inspired her with deep passion by a single glance or word, he gave her no sign, he did not want it. Her love did not even flatter his vanity.

She had tried arousing his jealousy, thinking that then his love would be bound to show itself. But nothing of the sort occurred. The moment he observed that she seemed to like some young man in society, he hastened to invite him to the house, showered him with compliments, could not praise him enough, and never seemed to be afraid to leave him alone with his wife.

Lizaveta Alexandrovna sometimes deceived herself, imagining that Pyotr Ivanich was perhaps exercising strategy, that this was the secret of his mysterious system—always to keep her in a state of uncertainty, thus keeping her love alive. But her husband's very next discussion of love disillusioned her.

If he had been rude, rough, callous, slow-witted, one of those husbands whose name is legion, whom it is so innocent, so necessary, so delightful to deceive, for their good and one's own, who seem to have been created in order that a woman should look around for someone who is their direct opposite, things might have been different.

Then, perhaps, she would have acted as the majority of women in such cases act. But Pyotr Ivanich was a man of intelligence and tact such as are seldom met with. He was subtle, penetrating, skilful. He understood all the stirrings of the heart, all the spiritual tempests, but he only *understood* them, nothing more. The whole code of love was in his mind—not in his heart. In all his arguments it was clear that he was speaking of what he had heard and knew, but not of what he felt. He talked about passions, but would not acknowledge their power over himself, even laughed at them, considering them misguided, distorted flights from reality, something like illnesses, for the cure of which, in time, remedies would be discovered.

Lizaveta Alexandrovna felt his mental superiority to all the people around him, and this tortured her. "If only he weren't so clever," she thought, "I would be saved..." He worshipped worthy aims, that was clear, and required of his wife that she also should not lead a life of dreaming.

"But, my God," thought Lizaveta Alexandrovna, "did he really only marry to have a housekeeper, to give his house the completeness and dignity of a home, to have more weight in society? A hostess, a wife in the crudest sense of the word. Cannot he, with his mind, see that even in the most worthy aims it is love that counts with women? Family obligations—these are her cares. But can they be fulfilled without love? Even nannies and wet-nurses make idols out of their charges—and a wife, a mother! Oh, I am ready to purchase feeling at the price of torment, I am ready to bear all the sufferings inseparable from passion, if only I can live a full life, feel with my whole being, and not just vegetate!"

She glanced at the luxurious furniture, the expensive bibelots scattered about her boudoir—and all this comfort, with which other women are surrounded by their loving husbands, seemed to her a cold mockery of true happiness. She was the witness of two extremes—in the nephew and in the uncle. One was ecstatic almost to madness, the other, cold almost to hardness.

"How little either of them, indeed the majority of men, understands true feeling! And how well I understand it!" she thought. "And what's the good of anything? What's it all for? Oh, if only..."

She closed her eyes and rested thus a few minutes, then opened them, looked round, sighed heavily, and once more assumed her usual tranquil poise. Poor woman! Nobody knew of all this, nobody saw it. These unseen, intangible, nameless sufferings, without wounds, bloodshed, screened from sight not by rags, but by silks and satins, might have been counted a sin in her. But she concealed her sorrow with heroic self-sacrifice, and even found the strength to console others.

Alexander soon ceased speaking of lofty sufferings and misunderstood, unwanted love. He proceeded to a more common theme. He complained of the tedium of life, of emptiness in his heart, of weary grief.

> *I have outlived my sufferings...*
> *And wearied of my dreams...*

"And now I am pursued by a black demon," he kept saying. "It accompanies me everywhere, *ma tante*—at night, during a friendly chat, while sipping from the convivial goblet, and in the moment of profoundest thought."

Several weeks passed in this manner. Another fortnight, and it seemed as if the queer fellow would recover completely and perhaps become quite a decent, that is, simple and ordinary person, like everyone else. But no! The peculiarities of his strange disposition found occasion to show themselves in everything.

One day he came to his aunt in a fit of disgust with the entire human race. Every word was a stab, every argument an epigram directed against those whom he should have respected. No one was spared. Lizaveta Alexandrovna and Pyotr Ivanich came in for their share. She tried to discover the cause.

"You want to know," he began softly, solemnly, "what is *agitating, infuriating* me? Then listen! As you know, I had a friend whom I have not seen for several years, but for whom I have always kept a warm place in my heart. My uncle, when I first came here, made me write him a strange letter, expounding his favourite rules and way of thinking. But I tore it up and sent another, so it could not have been this which has made my friend change. After this letter, our correspondence ceased and I lost sight of my friend. And now what do you think has happened? Three days ago as I was walking along Nevsky Prospekt, I suddenly came across him. I was stunned, sparks ran through my veins and tears came into my eyes. I held out my hands to him, too happy to say a single word, I could hardly breathe. He took one of my hands and shook it. 'How d'you do, Aduyev,' he said, as if we had only parted the day before. 'Have you been here long?' He was surprised that we had never met before, asked me carelessly what I was doing, where I worked, saw fit to inform me that he had a splendid post, that he was satisfied with his work, his chiefs and his colleagues, and ... with everybody and with his own life ... then he said he had not time, he was hurrying off to a dinner—d'you hear me, *ma tante*? He meets a friend after a long separation, and cannot put off a dinner!"

"But perhaps they were waiting for him," remarked his aunt. "Etiquette would not allow..."

"Etiquette and friendship! You too, *ma tante*, but never mind that—I will tell you something still better! He thrust a paper with his address on it into my hand, saying he would expect me the next evening—and vanished. I stood staring after him, and it was a long time before I could recover my equanimity. My childhood companion, the friend of my youth! But I told myself he might have meant to put off everything till the evening and then to devote the time to frank, heart-to-heart talk. 'So be it,' I thought. 'I'll go.' I went. He had nine or ten guests. He stretched out his hand to me more cordially than the day before, it is true, but immediately invited me, without a word, to sit down to a game of cards. I said I didn't play, and sat down alone on a sofa, supposing he would leave the game and come to me. 'You don't play?' he said in astonishment. 'Then what do you do?' What a question! Well, I waited an hour, two hours, and he never came near me. I lost my patience. He offered me first a cigar, then a pipe, regretted that I did not play, that I was bored, tried to amuse me—and how do you think? By constantly turning to me and telling me how he was getting on in the game! At last, unable to stand it any longer, I went up to him and asked him if he intended to spare any time for me that evening. I was overwrought, and my voice trembled. This seemed to surprise him. He looked at me strangely. 'All right,' he said. 'Just let me finish the rubber.' At this I seized my hat and made for the door, but he noticed and stopped me. 'The rubber will soon be over,' he said. 'We'll have supper in a minute.' At last they finished. He sat down beside me, yawning. And that is how our friendly talk began. 'Did you want to tell me anything?' he asked. It was said in such a dull, unfeeling voice that I only looked at him with a mournful smile and said nothing. Then he suddenly became animated and showered me with questions, 'What's the matter with you?' 'Are you in want of anything?' 'Can I help you in the way of work?' and so on. I shook my head and told him it was not about work that I wanted to talk to him, not about material advantages, but about something nearer to my heart: the golden days of childhood, our games, our pranks... And fancy—he didn't even let me finish speaking! 'The same old dreamer!' he said, and suddenly changed the subject, as if he considered all this mere trifles, and began gravely asking me about my affairs, my hopes for the future, my career—just like my uncle! I was astonished, I could not believe anyone's heart could have become so hard. I made one last attempt, dwelt on his question about my affairs, and began telling him how I had been treated. 'Only listen to what *people* have done to me,' I began. 'What?' he interrupted me in alarm. 'D'you mean to say you've been robbed?' He thought I was talking about my servants! He's like my uncle, he recognizes no other grief. To think that a man should become so callous. 'Yes,' I said, 'people have robbed my soul.' Then I began telling him about my love, my torments, the emptiness in my soul. I warmed up as I spoke, and it seemed to me that the tale of my sorrow would melt ice, that his eyes would be wet with tears. And suddenly he burst out laughing. I saw he was holding his handkerchief in his hand; while I was relating my story, he had kept trying not to laugh, but he could not restrain himself any longer. I broke off, horror-struck.

" 'Enough, enough,' he said. 'Have a drink of vodka and we'll have supper. Waiter—vodka! Come on, come on ... ha-ha-ha... There's some excellent roast ... ha-ha-ha ... roastbeef...'

"He took my arm but I tore it away and fled from this monster. That's what people are like, *ma tante*," concluded Alexander, and departed with a desperate gesture.

Lizaveta Alexandrovna felt sorry for Alexander. She pitied his ardent but misguided heart. She saw that with another sort of upbringing and correct views of life he could have been happy himself and made another happy. But now he was the victim of his own blindness and the anguished errors of his heart. He made life a torture for himself. How could she show his heart the right path? Where was the compass to set him right? She felt that only a gentle, friendly hand could nurse this sick flower back to health.

She had once been able to tone down the restless impulses of her nephew's heart, but that had been in regard to love. She had known then how to treat an injured heart. Like a skilful diplomat she had criticized Nadenka with all her might, holding up her treachery in the worst possible light, belittling her in Alexander's eyes, and then managed to prove to him that she was not worthy of his love. In this way she had removed from his heart the excruciating pain, substituting for it a tranquil, if not quite just, feeling of scorn. Pyotr Ivanich had on the contrary endeavoured to justify Nadenka and had thus not merely failed to console Alexander but had rubbed salt in his wounds, by forcing him to admit that he had been passed over for a man in every way superior to himself.

But friendship was another matter. Lizaveta Alexandrovna could see that Alexander's friend was wrong in the eyes of Alexander, and right in the eyes of the crowd. But try and prove that to Alexander! She did not dare attempt it herself, so she went to her husband for advice, supposing, not without reason, that he would find plenty of arguments against friendship.

"Pyotr Ivanich," she said ingratiatingly, "I have a favour to ask you."

"What is it?"

"Guess!"

"Out with it! You know I never refuse any of your requests. I suppose it's something about the summer cottage in Peterhof. But it's a bit early, isn't it?"

"It isn't that," said Lizaveta Alexandrovna.

"What then? You said you were afraid of our horses, and would like quieter ones."

"Not that."

"Then it's about the new furniture."

She shook her head.

"Sorry, then I don't know," said Pyotr Ivanich. "Here you are, better take this lottery ticket and spend it as you like. It's yesterday's draw."

He began feeling for his wallet.

"Never mind, don't trouble, put the money back!" said Lizaveta Alexandrovna. "What I want won't cost you a kopek."

"To refuse money when you're offered it," said Pyotr Ivanich, putting his wallet back. "Incomprehensible! What is it that you want, then?"

"Only a little good will..."

"As much as you like."

"You see—Alexander came to see me the other day."

"Oh, I begin to smell trouble!" groaned Pyotr Ivanich. "Well?"

"He's so depressed," went on Lizaveta Alexandrovna. "I'm afraid all this will lead him to..."

"What's the matter now? Disappointed in love again?"

"No, in friendship."

"Friendship? He's going from bad to worse! In friendship—that's interesting! Tell me about it."

"It's like this."

And Lizaveta Alexandrovna told him all she had heard from her nephew. Pyotr Ivanich shrugged his shoulders.

"And what do you want me to do? You see the kind of fellow he is."

"You could show him sympathy, ask him to open his heart to you..."

"No, no! You do that, please!"

"Speak to him—you know, kindly, not the way you always do. Don't laugh at his feelings."

"Would you rather I cried?"

"It would do no harm."

"And what good will it do him?"

"A great deal—and not him alone," remarked Lizaveta Alexandrovna under her breath.

"What's that?" asked Pyotr Ivanich.

She said nothing.

"Oh, that Alexander! He's a dead weight on me."

"Why do you say that?"

"And you ask me why? I've been bothering with him six years. Now he cries and must be consoled. Now I have to answer his mother's letters."

"You poor thing—what a burden! What hard work! To get a letter once a month from an old woman which you throw away without opening, or to have to talk to your own nephew! Why, it distracts you from your whist! Oh, men, men! So long as there's a good dinner, gold seal Lafitte, and a rubber of whist, nothing else matters to you! And if to this be added an opportunity for displaying your importance and wisdom—you are happy."

"Just as you are of an occasion to flirt," remarked Pyotr Ivanich. "To each his own, my dear! What more is needed?"

"What more? And the heart? That is never spoken of."

"I like that!"

"We are much too superior to bother about trifles like that. We decide human destinies. We only want to know what a man has in his pocket and what Order he wears, nothing else interests us. And you would like everyone to be like that. One sensitive being appears among them, capable of loving and making others love him!"

"He certainly showed how he made that, what's her name—Verochka, isn't it?—love him," remarked Pyotr Ivanich.

"And you can compare him with such a person! It's sheer irony of fate! A sensitive tender nature always seems to get linked up with some cold-hearted creature. Poor Alexander! His mind is not so highly developed as his heart, and so he is to blame in the eyes of those whose minds outstrip their feelings, who strive to attain everything through reason."

"You will agree, however, that this is the most important thing—otherwise..."

"I don't agree, I shall never agree. It may be the most important thing at your factory, but you forget that human beings have feelings."

"They have five senses," said Pyotr Ivanich. "I learned that with my A.B.C."

"Vexatious! Tragic!" whispered Lizaveta Alexandrovna.

"Well, don't be cross! I'll do whatever you say—but tell me how to do it," said Pyotr Ivanich.

"You can give him a little lesson."

"Scold him? Certainly. That's precisely what I'm good at."

"You and your scoldings! Explain to him, very kindly, what can be demanded and expected from friends nowadays. Tell him his friend is not so much to blame as he thinks. I don't have to teach you. You're so clever—you have so many wiles," added Lizaveta Alexandrovna.

Her last words caused Pyotr Ivanich to frown slightly.

"Haven't the two of you had about enough of sincere effusions?" he said irately. "Whispering, whispering, and still haven't had it all out about friendship and love! Now you want to involve me..."

"It'll be the last time," said Lizaveta Alexandrovna. "I hope he'll settle down after this."

Pyotr Ivanich shook his head dubiously.

"Has he enough money?" he asked. "Perhaps he hasn't, and that's why..."

"You think of nothing but money! He would give all his money for one kind word from his friend."

"That would be just like him! He gave one of the clerks in his office money once and all for sincere effusions... There's the doorbell ... perhaps it's Alexander. What am I to do? Say it again: scold him, and what else? Give him money?"

"Don't scold him! You'll only make matters worse. I asked you to talk to him about friendship, to be kind and sympathetic to him."

Alexander bowed silently, and ate a big dinner in silence, making pellets of bread between the courses and scowling from beneath his brows at the bottles and decanters. After dinner he picked up his hat.

"Where are you off to?" asked Pyotr Ivanich. "Stay with us a little."

Alexander obeyed in silence. Pyotr Ivanich, after thinking out a way of approaching the matter as tenderly and skilfully as possible, suddenly burst out, in a rapid stream:

"I heard your friend has treated you in rather a dastardly manner, Alexander."

At these unexpected words Alexander jerked his head as if stung, and cast a glance full of reproach at his aunt. She had not expected such a crude approach to the matter, and at first she bent low over her embroidery, then raised her head and looked at her husband as reproachfully. But he was under the dual protection of digestion and drowsiness and so these glances simply glanced off him.

Alexander responded with an almost inaudible sigh.

"Really now," went on Pyotr Ivanich, "do you call that a friend? You haven't met for five years and he has become so cold that he does not half-strangle his friend with his embraces when you do meet. But he does invite you to his house, he wants to treat you to a game of cards, to food and drink... And then—treacherous man!—noticing your sour expression, begins asking you about your affairs, your circumstances, your needs! What contemptible inquisitiveness! And then—crowning baseness!—he dares to offer his services, his help—perhaps even money! No sincere effusions! Appalling, appalling! Show me this monster, bring him to dinner on Friday! What stakes does he play for?"

"I don't know," said Alexander angrily. "Laugh, Uncle! You are right! I alone am to blame. To believe in people, to seek sympathy—in whom? To cast pearls—before whom? All around is baseness, cravenness, pettiness, and I still retain my youthful belief in the good, in valour, in constancy..."

Pyotr Ivanich's head began to nod more and more frequently and regularly.

"Pyotr Ivanich," whispered Lizaveta Alexandrovna, tugging at his coat sleeve. "Are you asleep?"

"Asleep?" said Pyotr Ivanich, waking up. "I heard everything—'valour, constancy'... I wasn't asleep."

"Leave him alone, *ma tante,*" said Alexander. "If he doesn't get a nap he'll have indigestion and God knows what would happen then! Man may be the ruler of the earth, but he is also the slave of his digestion."

He tried to produce a bitter smile, but only succeeded in making a rueful grimace.

"Tell me what you wanted from your friend!" asked Pyotr Ivanich. "A sacrifice of some sort? Did you want him to fall into a frenzy, or throw himself out of the window? What's your idea of friendship?"

"I no longer demand sacrifices, believe me! Thanks to my experience of human nature I have descended to a miserable theory of friendship, and love. See—I have always carried these lines about, they seemed to me the truest definition of these two feelings as I used to understand them, and as they ought to be, but now I see they are lies, a slander on human beings, that they display a pitiful ignorance of their hearts. People are not capable of such feelings. Away with these perfidious words!"

He took his pocket-book out and extracted from it two tiny slips of paper covered with scribbles.

"What's that?" asked his uncle. "Let me see!"

"They're not worth it," said Alexander, preparing to tear up the papers.

"Read it, read it!" insisted Lizaveta Alexandrovna.

"This is how two of the latest French novelists define true friendship and love, and I used to agree with them, thinking I should meet such people in my way through life and find in them— Oh, well..."

He made a scornful gesture and began reading.

" 'To love, not with that false, timid friendship which exists in our gilded salons, that cannot withstand a handful of gold, that fears an ambiguous word, but with that powerful amity that gives blood for blood, that shows itself in battle and in bloodshed, beneath the thunder of cannon, the howling of the tempest, when friends kiss with powder-blackened lips, and put their bleeding arms round one another. And if Pilades is mortally wounded, Orestes, bidding him a manly farewell, puts an end to his sufferings with a thrust of his dagger, swears a terrible oath to avenge his friend and keeps his vow, then dries his tears and calms down.' "

Pyotr Ivanich's low, even laugh was heard.

"Who are you laughing at, Uncle?" asked Alexander.

"At the writer, if he is not joking, and if he really means it, and then at you if that is really your idea of friendship."

"Is it so very funny?" asked Lizaveta Alexandrovna.

"Very, very funny! Sorry—it's at once funny and pathetic. But Alexander himself agreed it was, and allowed me to laugh. He said just now that such friendship is all lies and a libel on human beings. This is quite an important step forward."

"It is lies because people are incapable of rising to the understanding of friendship as it ought to be..."

"If people are incapable of it, then it ought not to be," said Pyotr Ivanich.

"But there have been examples."

"They are exceptions, and exceptions are hardly ever any good. 'Bloody embraces, terrible oaths, dagger thrust...' "

And again he burst out laughing.

"Well, read about love, now," he said. "My sleepiness has quite passed."

"If it gives you an occasion to laugh some more—with pleasure," said Alexander, and began reading the following:

" 'To love means to belong to oneself no longer, to cease living for oneself, to enter into another's being, to concentrate all human feelings—hope, fear, grief, pleasure—on one object. To love means to live in infinity...' "

"What rubbish!" interrupted Pyotr Ivanich. "Just a conglomeration of words!"

"No, it's beautiful, I like it," interposed Lizaveta Alexandrovna. "Go on, Alexander!"

" 'To know no limit to feeling, to devote oneself to one being,' " continued Alexander. " 'To live, to think only for this being's happiness, to find greatness in humiliation, enjoyment in sorrow and sorrow in enjoyment, to yield to all sorts of conflicting emotions, in addition to those of love and hate. To love means to live in an ideal world.' "

At this Pyotr Ivanich shook his head.

" 'In an ideal world,' " continued Alexander, " 'sur-

passing in brilliance and majesty all that we know of
brilliance and majesty—in this world the sky will appear
clearer, nature more luxuriant. Life and time will be divided into two parts—presence and absence, into two seasons—
spring and winter. The first part will be equivalent to
spring, the second to winter, since however beautiful the
flowers, however clear the heavenly azure, in the absence
of the beloved the beauty of the one and the other is
darkened. In the whole world we shall see only one being
and in that being we shall see the whole Universe... Finally,
to love means to gather every glance from the beloved
being, as the Bedouin gathers every drop of dew for the
refreshment of his heat-blistered lips. To be swarming with
ideas in the absence of the beloved, and in his presence to
be unable to express a single one; to vie with one another
in making sacrifices.' "

"Enough, for God's sake, enough!" interrupted Pyotr
Ivanich. "I have no patience. You said you would tear
them up! Do so as quickly as you can—that's the way!"
Pyotr Ivanich actually rose from his chair and began pacing the floor. "Can there really have been a time when
people thought and did all that in perfect seriousness?"
he said. "Can it be that what they write of knights and
shepherdesses was not just idle nonsense? How can anyone
want to strike these wretched chords of the human soul,
to analyze these feelings so minutely ... love! To attrib-
ute so much importance to it!"

He shrugged his shoulders.

"Why drift so far away, Uncle," said Alexander. "I am
aware of this force of love in myself, and am proud of it.
I am only unhappy because I have never met anyone worthy
of such love and as richly endowed with such a power
of love."

"The power of love," repeated Pyotr Ivanich. "It's
the same as saying the power of weakness!"

"That's beyond you, Pyotr Ivanich," remarked Lizaveta Alexandrovna. "And you won't admit of the existence of such love in others."

"And you—do you mean to say you believe in it?"
said Pyotr Ivanich, going up to her. "But no, you must be
joking! He's still a child and understands neither himself
nor others, but it would be unpardonable in you. Could

you really respect a man if he were to love you like that? Do people really love like that?"

Lizaveta Alexandrovna laid down her work.

"How do they love, then?" she asked softly, taking his hands and drawing him towards her.

Pyotr Ivanich gently released his hands and pointed surreptitiously at Alexander, who was standing at the window with his back to them, every now and then resuming his pacing backwards and forwards.

"Come now!" he said. "As if you didn't know how people love!"

"Love," she echoed pensively and slowly took up her work.

For a quarter of an hour there was silence in the room. Pyotr Ivanich was the first to break it.

"What work are you engaged upon now?" he asked his nephew.

"Me? Nothing."

"That's not much. Well, at least you read, I suppose."

"Yes."

"And what, may I ask?"

"Krylov's *Fables*."

"A good book. But is that all?"

"At present, all. Oh, heavens—what portraits, how true to life!"

"You seem to be angry with the human race. Is it love for that ... what's her name?.. that has made you like this?"

"Oh, I've forgotten all that folly! The other day I happened to pass by the places where I was so happy and suffered so, and I was sure the remembrance would make my heart burst."

"Well, and did it burst?"

"I saw the house and the garden and the railings, and my heart was not even wrung."

"There you are then—I told you so! What makes you hate people so?"

"What? Their baseness, their shallowness... My God! When you think of the wickedness going on in a place where nature has been so generous..."

"What's that to you? Do you want to reform people?"

"What is it to me, you ask? Don't I get bespattered with

the mud in which others wallow? You know what befell me—after that how can I help detesting, despising people?"

"And what happened to you?"

"In love—deception, in friendship—cold forgetfulness. Besides, it makes one sick to see people, to have to live with them! All their thoughts, words, deeds—all built upon sand! Today they all strive for one aim, hurrying, knocking one another over, committing base acts, flattering, humiliating themselves, scheming, and tomorrow they have forgotten all about it and are hot for something else. Today they are in transports over something, tomorrow they vilify it. Today they are ardent, tender, tomorrow—cold. The more you see of it the more terrible and repulsive life seems! And people..."

Pyotr Ivanich, who had sat down in an easy chair, was beginning to doze again.

"Pyotr Ivanich," said Lizaveta Alexandrovna, nudging him gently.

"Spleen, spleen! You should do something," said Pyotr Ivanich, rubbing his eyes. "Then you'd stop ranting against people. There's no sense in it. What's wrong with your friends? They're all decent people."

"You can't name a single one who isn't exactly like one of the beasts in Krylov's fables."

"The Khozarovs, for instance."

"A whole family of beasts," broke in Alexander. "One showers me with flattery to my face, can't do too much for me, and behind my back—I know what he says about me! Another will shed tears of sympathy for your injury today, and tomorrow he will weep with the person who injured you. Today he will laugh with you at someone, and tomorrow he will laugh at you with someone. Disgusting!"

"Well, and the Lunins?"

"They're a nice lot, too! He's like the ass the nightingale flew away from to the other end of the world. And she looks just like a good-natured vixen."

"What have you to say about the Sonins?"

"Nothing good! Sonin is always ready with good advice when a disaster is over, but try to turn to him in need ... then he'll let you go home without supper, as the fox did with the wolf. Remember how servile he was to you when he hoped to get a post through your aid. Well, you should hear what he says about you now."

"And Volochkov—don't you like him, either?"

"A contemptible beast—and bad-tempered to boot."
Alexander even spat.

"Well, you certainly have pulled everyone to pieces,"
said Pyotr Ivanich.

"What have I to expect from people?" continued Alexander.

"Everything—friendship, love, promotion, money... Well,
complete your gallery with our portraits. What kind of
animals are my wife and I?"

Alexander made no reply, but an expression of subtle,
scarcely discernible irony crossed his features. He smiled.
Neither the irony nor the smile was lost upon Pyotr Ivanich. He glanced at his wife, who lowered her eyes.

"And you yourself—what kind of an animal are you!"
asked Pyotr Ivanich.

"I have never done anyone any harm," declared Alexander in dignified accents. "In my relations with others
I have done all. I—I have a soft heart. I opened wide my
arms to others, and what have they done to me?"

"Listen to him—isn't he absurd," said Pyotr Ivanich,
turning to his wife.

"You find everything absurd," she replied.

"I have never demanded of people," continued Alexander, "either good deeds, generosity, or sacrifice ...
all I demanded was that which I had every right to expect."

"And you consider yourself in the right? You have
come scatheless through the fire. Wait a minute, I'll show
you up."

Lizaveta Alexandrovna heard the note of severity in
her husband's voice, and was alarmed.

"Pyotr Ivanich," she whispered. "Don't!"

"Let him hear the truth! I won't be long. Be so kind
as to tell me, Alexander, when you were trouncing all your
acquaintances just now, some as rascals, some as fools,
did not your conscience prick you?"

"Why should it, Uncle?"

"Because you have for several years received a cordial welcome from these animals. Admittedly, these people have used wiles, they have, as you say, schemed in regard to people they hoped to get something from. But they had nothing to expect from you—what made them invite you and be kind to you? It's not nice, Alexander," added Pyotr Ivanich gravely. "For that alone another man would hold his tongue, even if he discovered some bad things about them."

Alexander flushed.

"I put their kindness down to your recommendation," he said, rather meekly, without any arrogance now. "And then being in society..."

"Very well, let us take your more intimate relationships. I've tried hard to convince you, with what success I don't know, that you have been unjust to your—what's her name?—Sashenka, is it? For a year and a half you were treated as one of the family in their house. You stayed there from morning till night, and were even loved by that *contemptible girl*, as you now call her. That hardly deserves contempt, one would think."

"Why did she deceive me then?"

"You mean, falling in love with another man? We've been through all that, haven't we? Do you really believe that if she had gone on loving you, you would not have got tired of her?"

"I? Never!"

"I see you don't understand a thing. We will go on. You say you have no friends, and I thought you had three."

"Three!" exclaimed Alexander. "There was one, and he..."

"Three," insisted Pyotr Ivanich. "The first, in order of time, is that *one*. Another man, not having met you for several years, would have turned away from you on meeting, but he invited you to his house and when you arrived with your sour face he asked you sympathetically if you were in need of anything, offered you his services, his help, and I am sure would have given you money. And in our times this is the stumbling-block in many friendships. You must bring him to me. I see he's a decent man, though you call him dastardly."

Alexander was standing, his head bowed.

"And who do you consider your second friend is?" continued Pyotr Ivanich.

"Who?" said Alexander in astonishment. "Why—nobody."

"Aren't you ashamed!" cried Pyotr Ivanich. "What d'you say to that, Liza? And he doesn't even blush! And what do you consider me, may I ask?"

"You're ... a relation."

"Imposing title! I thought I was something more. That's bad, Alexander. That's a trait which would be described, even in copy-book maxims, as *base*, and I don't think you'll even find it in Krylov."

"But you have always repulsed me," said Alexander shyly, not raising his eyes.

"Yes, when you wanted to hug me."

"You laughed at me, at my feelings."

"And why did I?" asked Pyotr Ivanich.

"You watched my every step."

"Aha! You've said it. 'Watched.' Where will you find another such tutor? Why did I take all this trouble? I might even refer to a few other things, but that would be like a vulgar reproach."

"Uncle!" said Alexander, approaching him with open arms.

"Go back to your place. I haven't done yet," said Pyotr Ivanich coldly. "Your third and best friend, I hope, you will name yourself."

Alexander looked at him again as if asking, "Where is he?" Pyotr Ivanich pointed to his wife.

"There she is."

"Pyotr Ivanich," interrupted Lizaveta Alexandrovna. "Don't try and be subtle, I beg you."

"Don't you interfere!"

"I appreciate my aunt's friendship," murmured Alexander inarticulately.

"No, you don't. If you did, you would not have looked at the ceiling, you would have pointed to her. If you appreciated her friendship, you would, from respect for her qualities, have hesitated to despise people. She alone would have redeemed the defects of others in your eyes. Who dried your tears and mingled her tears with yours? Who showed sympathy for all your nonsense—and *what* sympathy? Who but a mother would have taken all your affairs to heart, as she did—I don't think even a mother could! If you had felt this you would not have smiled ironically just now, you would have seen that this is no fox, no wolf, but a woman who loves you like a sister."

"Oh, *ma tante*!" said Alexander, abashed and completely overcome by this reproach. "Surely you cannot think I don't appreciate all this and don't consider you a brilliant exception to the crowd! Heavens, I swear..."

"I believe you, Alexander," she replied. "Take no notice of Pyotr Ivanich. He is making a mountain out of a molehill. He's glad of an opportunity to show off. Stop it, Pyotr Ivanich, for heaven's sake!"

"I'll be done in a minute—*one last word*. You say you have done all that your duty to others demands."

Alexander could no longer speak, and did not raise his eyes.

"Come now, tell me—do you love your mother?"

Alexander was suddenly roused.

"What a question!" he said. "Whom could I love so well? I adore her, I would give my life for her!"

"Good. Then, apparently, you are aware that she lives and breathes for you alone, that all your joys and sorrows are her joys and sorrows. She no longer measures time by months and weeks, but by the news she gets from you and about you. Tell me, how long is it since you wrote to her?"

Alexander started.

"About three ... weeks," he muttered.

"No. It's four months. What do you think of that? Come now, what sort of an animal are you? Perhaps you can't give it a name because it's not in Krylov?"

"Has anything happened?" asked Alexander, alarmed.

"The old lady is ill with grief."

"Oh, is she? My God, my God!"

"It's not true," said Lizaveta Alexandrovna, and ran to the escritoire, from which she took a letter and handed it to Alexander. "She's not ill, but she misses you sorely."

"You spoil him, Liza," said Pyotr Ivanich.

"And you're really too severe. Circumstances distracted Alexander temporarily..."

"To forget one's mother for a silly girl! Fine circumstances!"

"That'll do, for goodness' sake!" she said firmly, and pointed to her nephew.

Alexander had finished reading his mother's letter and was hiding his face behind it.

"Don't try to stop my uncle, *ma tante*! Let him thunder out his reproaches! I deserve worse. I'm a monster!" he said, his face working desperately.

"Never mind, Alexander," said Pyotr Ivanich. "There are many such monsters. You were carried away by a folly and for a time forgot your mother—that's natural. Love for one's mother is a tranquil emotion. You are all she has in the world—and so it's natural for her to grieve. You don't deserve the extreme penalty for that. I will say, in the words of your favourite author:

> *Instead of calling others ugly creatures*
> *You'd better have a look at your own features!*

and advise you to be indulgent to the failings of others. That's a law we must all observe, if we would go on living. That's all. Well, I'll take a nap now."

"Are you angry with me, Uncle?" said Alexander in a voice of profound sorrow.

"What makes you think that? Why should I upset myself? I never dreamed of being angry. I only wanted to play the part of the bear in Krylov's 'Monkey and the Mirror'. Did I do it well? Eh, Liza?"

He tried to give her a kiss as he passed, but she turned away.

"I think I obeyed your orders precisely," he added. "What's the matter? Oh, yes, I forgot one thing—what's the state of your heart, Alexander?"

Alexander said nothing.

"You don't need any money?" asked Pyotr Ivanich. "No, Uncle."

"Never asks for any!" said Pyotr Ivanich, closing the door behind him.

"What will my uncle think of me?" asked Alexander after a pause.

"The same as before," replied Lizaveta Alexandrovna. "Do you really think he spoke with feeling, from his heart?"

"And didn't he?"

"Not he! I assure you he only wanted to make an impression. Look how methodically he expounded his theories! How he ranged all the arguments against you in regu-

lar order! First the weaker ones, and last the strongest.
First he found out the reason for your unfavourable opinion of people ... and then ... all system! He's forgotten
it all now, I suppose."

"What a mind! What a knowledge of life and people,
what self-control!"

"Yes, a splendid mind and too much self-control,"
said Lizaveta Alexandrovna, "but..."

"And you, *ma tante*, will you stop respecting me? Believe me, only the shocks I have undergone could have
distracted me. Dear God! Poor Mamma!"

Lizaveta Alexandrovna held out her hand to him.

"I shall never cease respecting your good heart, Alexander," she said. "It is feeling that leads you into error, and
so I always pardon your errors."

"Oh, *ma tante*, you are an ideal woman."

"Simply a woman."

His uncle's harangue had made a great impression on
Alexander. He fell into anguished meditation, seated at his
aunt's side. The tranquillity she had with such skill
and labour implanted in his heart seemed suddenly to
have deserted him. She waited in vain for some angry out-
burst, tried to challenge him to a spiteful remark, and
dropped the most pointed witticisms at the expense of
Pyotr Ivanich. Alexander was deaf to all her endeavours,
had nothing to say for himself. He seemed to have been
doused with cold water.

"What's the matter with you? What makes you like
this?" his aunt asked.

"Oh, *ma tante*, I feel sick at heart! My uncle has made
me see myself as I am—he has made a devastating analysis."

"Take no notice of him! He is not always right, you
know!"

"Oh, don't try and comfort me! I am now hateful
in my own eyes! I have despised and detested others, and
now I despise and detest myself! You can get away from
people, but where can you hide from yourself? Everything
is so trivial—all these comforts, the emptiness of life,
other people, myself..."

"It's all Pyotr Ivanich!" said Lizaveta Alexandrovna,
sighing profoundly. "He's enough to drive anybody to despair!"

"There is only one comfort left to me, and that a negative one—I have deceived no one, have been fickle or faithless neither in love nor in friendship."

"Nobody has known how to appreciate you," said his aunt. "But believe me a heart will be found capable of doing so. I assure you it will. You are still so young—forget all this, do something! You have talent—write! Are you writing anything now?"

"No."

"Write!"

"I'm afraid, *ma tante*."

"Take no notice of Pyotr Ivanich! Talk to him about politics, agriculture, about anything you like but poetry. What he says about that will never be worth hearing. The public will appreciate you, see if they don't. Promise me you will write."

"Very well."

"Will you begin soon?"

"As soon as I can. My only hope lies in that now."

Pyotr Ivanich, having had his nap, came back to them, fully dressed, with his hat in his hand. He, too, advised Alexander to busy himself with his work at the office, and at the agricultural department of the magazine.

"I will try, Uncle," said Alexander. "But I have just promised my aunt, here..."

Lizaveta Alexandrovna made him a sign to be quiet, but Pyotr Ivanich had noticed.

"What? What have you promised her?"

"To bring me some new music," she put in.

"No, that's not it. What was it, Alexander?"

"To write a novel or something."

"Haven't you given up the idea of fiction yet?" exclaimed Pyotr Ivanich, flicking a speck of dust from his coat. "You shouldn't try and lead him astray, Liza."

"I have no right to give it up," said Alexander.

"What prevents you?"

"Why should I wilfully and ungratefully reject the honourable vocation to which I am called? One bright hope in life remains to me, and you would have me destroy it, too! If I destroy that which has been granted me from above, I destroy my very self."

"Well, and what wonderful thing has been granted you—

tell me that, please!"

"It's not a thing I can explain to you, Uncle, if you don't understand it yourself. Has anything but a comb ever made your hair stand on end, Uncle?"

"No!" said Pyotr Ivanich.

"There you are, then! Have passions ever raged within you, has your imagination ever been fired, creating within you exquisite visions begging to be brought to life? Has your heart ever throbbed in a special way?"

"Crazy, crazy! Well, what follows?" exclaimed Pyotr Ivanich.

"It follows that to one who has not experienced this it is impossible to explain why, haunted by some restless spirit which repeats, day and night, in dreams, and in waking hours, 'Write, write!' one feels the compulsion to write."

"But you can't write."

"Enough, Pyotr Ivanich! You can't write yourself, so why try and stop others?" said Lizaveta Alexandrovna.

"Forgive me, Uncle, if I say that you are no judge of this."

"Who is, then? Is she?"

Pyotr Ivanich pointed to his wife.

"She doesn't mean it, and you believe her," he added.

"Why, you yourself advised me to write, when I first came here, to test my powers."

"Well, and you did, and nothing came of it. Now you should give it up."

"Do you mean to say you have never found a single sensible idea or one good line of poetry in my work?"

"Certainly I have. You're no fool—as if one could fail to find a single bright idea among such a lot of writing by a clever man! But that's not talent, you know, it's just brains."

"Oh!" exclaimed Lizaveta Alexandrovna, moving impatiently in her chair.

"As for heart-throbs, trepidation, raptures and all that— who has not known them?"

"First and foremost you yourself, I believe," remarked his wife.

"There you are! Have you forgotten how I admired...?"

"Admired what? I don't seem to remember."

"Everyone experiences all those things," pursued Pyotr Ivanich, turning to his nephew. "Who is there that is unmoved by the stillness, the darkness of night, or, let us say, by the rustling of leaves in a grove, by a garden, pools, the sea? If artists were the only ones who felt all this, there would be nobody to appreciate them. But to reflect all these sensations in one's work is quite another matter. That requires talent, and I don't think you have any. Talent can't be concealed—it shines from every line, from every stroke of the brush."

"Pyotr Ivanich, it's time for you to be going," said Lizaveta Alexandrovna.

"In a minute!"

"You want to shine," he continued, "and you have the opportunity. The editor praises your work, he says your articles on agriculture are excellently written, that there are ideas in them. Everything shows, he says, that they are the work of a trained mind, and no mere craftsman. I was pleased. Well, I thought, all the Aduyevs have brains! You see, I have my vanity, too! You could both distinguish yourself at your office, and win fame as a writer."

"A nice kind of fame—as a writer on soil!"

"To each his own—some are destined to soar in heavenly regions, others to dig the soil and wrest from it its treasures. I can't see why a modest vocation should be despised. It, too, has a poetry of its own. Why shouldn't you work your way up, amass money by your own labours, marry well, as most people do? What more do you want, I should like to know? Your duty done, your life spent in honourable industry—that's what I call happiness! Look at me—I'm a councillor of state by rank, an industrialist by trade—and if you were to offer me instead the calling of a great poet, I wouldn't accept it, by God, I wouldn't!"

"Pyotr Ivanich, you'll be late, really you will," interrupted Lizaveta Alexandrovna. "It's almost ten."

"Yes, it's high time I was off. Well, good-bye! People will imagine they are extraordinary, for no reason at all!" grumbled Pyotr Ivanich, as he left.

II

When he got back to his own rooms Alexander sat down in an easy chair to think. He went over the whole conversation with his uncle and aunt in his mind, and took himself sternly to task.

How was it that, at his age, undulging in hatred and contempt for others, analyzing and criticizing their worthlessness, triviality, failures, picking each and every one of his acquaintances to pieces, he had forgotten to subject himself to the same analysis? How blind he had been! And his uncle had lectured him as if he were a schoolboy, exposed all his failings, and in front of a woman, too.

How his uncle must have gained in his wife's eyes today! That didn't matter, of course, it was as it should be. But it was at Alexander's expense that he had gained. His uncle had shown himself incontestably the superior, in every way.

"After that," he mused, "where is the advantage of youth, freshness, ardour of mind and heart, when an older man, with nothing but a certain amount of experience, a man with a callous heart and no spiritual energy, is able at every step, casually, merely *en passant*, as it were, to humiliate a younger one? When would they be able to fight on equal terms and when would the balance be on his side? On his side, it might be thought, were talent and exuberant spiritual forces ... and yet his uncle was a giant compared to him! With what assurance he argued, how easily he disposed of every objection, achieving his aim with jests and yawns, laughing at emotion, at the heartfelt effusions of friendship and love, in a word, at everything which the elderly are supposed to envy the young!"

Going over all this in his mind, Alexander blushed with shame. He took a vow to keep a strict watch over himself, and seize the first opportunity for crushing his uncle, for demonstrating that no amount of experience can take the place of that which has been *implanted from above*, that, preach as Pyotr Ivanich might, from this moment not a single one of his cold, methodical predictions would come true! Alexander would find his own path, and follow it with firm, measured and by no means timid steps. He was no longer the Alexander of three years ago. He had seen into the innermost recesses of his own heart, observed the play of passions, discovered the secret of life, not, of course, without sufferings, against which, however, he had hardened himself once and for all. His future was clear to him, he was up in arms, a man, not a child any more! He had only to step boldly forward, and his uncle would see this, and, in his turn, would play the part of a mere apprentice, in comparison with Alexander, the experienced master. He would discover to his astonishment that there is another life, that there are other distinctions, that there is another kind of happiness besides the wretched career which he had chosen for himself, and which—out of jealousy perhaps—he was trying to impose on Alexander. One more noble effort, and the struggle would be over.

Alexander cheered up. Once more he began to create a world of his own, and a rather more sober one than the first had been. His aunt encouraged him in this, but secretly—when Pyotr Ivanich was asleep, or was away at his factory, or the English Club.

She questioned Alexander about his occupations. And what pleasure this gave him! He told her the plan of his writings, and sometimes, on the pretext of asking for advice, sought her approval.

She often argued, but still more often agreed with him.

Alexander clung to his work as a man clings to his last hope. "Beyond that," he said to his aunt, "there is nothing left for me any more. Nothing but the bare steppe, waterless, treeless, nothing but gloom and emptiness. What would life be then? I might as well be in my grave." And he worked with a will.

Sometimes the memory of his lost love came back to him, and, deeply stirred, he would take up his pen and write a pathetic elegy. Another time, his spleen would well up, bringing with it the hatred and contempt for human beings which had been raging in the depths of his heart, and lo and behold, powerful verse would be born of the impulse! At the same time he was planning and working on a novel. He expended much thought, emotion and toil on this, and about six months of his life. At last the novel was ready, revised, and a fair copy made. His aunt went into raptures over it.

The scene of this novel was no longer laid in America, but in some Tambov village. The characters were ordinary people—gossips, liars, monsters of all sorts in frock-coats, traitresses in corsets and pretty hats. It was all perfectly correct and appropriate.

"I think this might be shown to my uncle, *ma tante*."

"Yes, yes, of course!" she replied. "And yet—wouldn't it be better to have it published first, without showing him? He's always against that sort of thing, he's sure to say something. You know he regards it as mere child's play."

"Oh no, I think I'll show it to him," said Alexander. "After your judgement and what I myself feel about it, I fear nobody's opinion. Besides, I want him to see..."

So they showed it to Pyotr Ivanich. He frowned slightly and shook his head.

"What's this? Have you both been at it?" he asked. "It seems rather a lot. And what small writing! Why do people want to write, I don't know."

"Don't shake your head!" said his wife. "First listen! Read it to us, Alexander! But you must really listen, don't go to sleep, and then tell us what you think of it. It's easy to pick faults if you want to find them. Do be indulgent!"

"No, not indulgent, just fair!" said Alexander.

"There seems to be nothing for it—go ahead!" said Pyotr Ivanich with a sigh, "but I'll only listen on condition, in the first place, that you don't read it after dinner, for then I can't be sure I won't go to sleep. Don't take it to heart, Alexander! Anything read to me after dinner, always puts me to sleep. And in the second place, that if it's anything sensible I'll tell you my opinion, but if not I will just hold my tongue, and you can think what you like."

Alexander began reading. Pyotr Ivanich, who did not once doze off, never took his eyes off Alexander, hardly ever blinking, and twice he nodded approvingly.

"You see!" said his wife under her breath. "I told you!"

He nodded to her, too.

The reading went on for two evenings. The first evening, when Alexander stopped, Pyotr Ivanich, to his wife's astonishment, told them how the story would go on.

"How did you know?" she asked.

"It wasn't very hard. The idea isn't new—it's been used hundreds of times. There's really no need to go on, but we'll see how he develops it."

When, the following evening, Alexander came to the end of the last page, Pyotr Ivanich rang the bell. The servant came into the room.

"Get my clothes ready," he said. "Excuse me for interrupting you, Alexander, I'm in a hurry. I shall be late for whist at the club."

Alexander finished reading. Pyotr Ivanich beat a hasty retreat.

"Well, good-bye," he said to his wife and Alexander. "I won't come in here again before going."

"Wait a minute!" cried his wife. "Why don't you say anything about the novel?"

"It was not in the agreement," he replied, and turned to go.

"Sheer obstinacy!" she said. "Oh, he's very stubborn, I know him! Take no notice, Alexander!"

"It's hostility," Alexander told himself. "He wants to drag me down, get me into his own sphere. After all he's a clever official, an industrialist, and nothing more. And I'm a poet."

"You're impossible, Pyotr Ivanich," his wife began, almost in tears. "You might say just *something* at least! I saw you nod, so you must have liked it. You're simply too obstinate to admit it! How can we admit we liked the novel? We're too clever for that! You did think it good!"

"I nodded because this novel shows that Alexander is clever, but it was not clever of him to write it."

"Come now, Uncle, that sort of judgement..."

"Now listen! You won't believe *me*, so it's no good my arguing. We better find an arbitrator. I'll tell you what I'll do to put an end to all this between us, once and for all! I'll say I'm the author of the novel and send it to a friend of mine who works for a magazine. Let's see what he says! You know him, and will probably trust his judgement. He's a man of experience."

"All right—we'll see!"

Pyotr Ivanich sat down at his desk and rapidly scribbled off a few lines, after which he handed the note to Alexander.

"I have turned author in my old age," he had written. "There it is: I want fame, I want to profit in this line too— a crazy whim, I suppose! And so I have produced the enclosed novel. Look it over and if it's worth anything, have it published in your magazine, for money, naturally. You know I don't care to work for nothing. You are astonished, perhaps you won't believe me, but I give you permission to use my name, so you see I can't be lying."

Assured of a favourable opinion of the novel, Alexander waited patiently for a reply. He was quite glad his uncle had mentioned payment in his note.

"Very clever of him," he thought. "Mamma complains that she is getting low prices for her wheat, she probably won't be sending me any money for a time. A thousand or two would come in very handy just now."

Three weeks passed and there was no reply. At last one morning a large parcel and a letter were brought to Pyotr Ivanich.

"Aha! They've sent it back," he said, looking slyly at his wife.

But he would neither open the parcel nor show the letter to her, beg as she might. That same evening, before going to his club, he went to see his nephew.

The door was not locked. He went in. Yevsei was stretched out across the floor, snoring. The wick of the night-light was dropping. He looked into the next room— all was darkness.

"Life in the provinces!" growled Pyotr Ivanich.

He roused Yevsei, showing him the door and the wick, and threatening him with his stick. In the farthest room Alexander was seated with his arms on his desk, and his head on his arms; he, too, was asleep. A piece of paper lay before him. Pyotr Ivanich glanced at it—verses.

He picked up the paper and read the following:

> *The spring of youth cannot forever last,*
> *The fleeting hours of love will ne'er return,*
> *Long dead is love and buried in the past,*
> *No more will my fond heart with passion burn.*
> *And now upon the long forsaken altar*
> *An idol stands, erected by myself.*
> *I worship it ... but...*

"And fell asleep himself. Go on, worship, dear boy! Persevere!" said Pyotr Ivanich aloud. "Your own verses, and look how they put you to sleep! What do you need anybody else's judgement for? You've condemned yourself."

"Oh!" said Alexander, stretching. "Still fulminating against my work? Tell me frankly, Uncle, what makes you persecute talent so unremittingly, when you cannot but admit..."

"Envy, Alexander, envy! Judge for yourself: you will achieve fame, honour, perhaps even immortality and I shall remain an obscure man, compelled to be content with the name of a useful drudge. And I'm an Aduyev, too. Say what you like, it hurts. What am I? I have lived out my days quietly, in obscurity, simply doing my duty, and actually proud of it—even happy! What a wretched lot, isn't it? When I die, that is to say, when I no longer feel or know anything, *travelling minstrels will not mention me, remote ages, posterity, the world will not resound with my name*, will not know that there was once a councillor of state named Pyotr Ivanich Aduyev, and I shall not be able to console myself with this thought in my grave, even if I and my grave should survive to posterity. How different is your case: when, *extending your thunderous wings, you soar beneath the clouds,* my only consolation will be that I have contributed *my drop of honey* to the mass of human labour, as your favourite author says."

"Never mind him—why do you call him my favourite author? He merely mocks at his neighbour."

"Mocks, does he? Is it not since you found your own portrait in Krylov that you have cooled towards him? *A propos!* Are you aware that your future fame, your immortality is in my pocket? Of course I'd rather it was your money—more tangible..."

"My fame?"

"Well—the answer to my note."

"Oh! Give it to me at once, for the love of God. What does he write?"

"I haven't read it—read it yourself, read it aloud."

"How could you restrain your impatience?"

"What's it to me?"

"What? Aren't I your nephew? Didn't you want to

know? What indifference! It's sheer egoism, Uncle!"

"Perhaps. I won't deny it. But after all, I know what's in it. Read."

Alexander started reading aloud and Pyotr Ivanich tapped his boots with his cane as he listened. This is what was in the letter:

"What kind of a hoax is it, Pyotr Ivanich? *You* write a novel! Who's going to believe that? And you thought you could take in an old hand like me! Even if, which God forbid, it were true, if you diverted your pen from lines which are, in the literal sense of the word, so dear, every one being worth its weight in gold, and, abandoning your esteemed accounts, had written the novel lying before me, even then I would say to you that the delicate products of your factory are infinitely more solid than this creation."

Alexander's voice suddenly wavered.

"But I reject these injurious suspicions of you," he continued in low, uncertain tones.

"Louder, Alexander, I can't hear," said Pyotr Ivanich.

Alexander continued in the same low voice:

"Since you must be interested in the author of this novel you would probably like to know my opinion. Here it is. The author must be a young man. He is no fool, but for some obscure reason he is angry with the whole world. He writes so savagely, so bitterly. No doubt a disappointed man. Oh, Lord, when will we get rid of people like that! It's too bad that, owing to a false attitude to life, so much talent perishes among us in empty, sterile dreaming, in vain efforts to accomplish that for which the writer has no vocation."

Alexander stopped and caught his breath. Pyotr Ivanich lit a cigar and blew a smoke ring. As usual, his face expressed perfect composure. Alexander went on reading in hollow, scarcely audible tones:

"Vanity, dreaminess, the precocious development of emotional tendencies and mental sloth, with the inevitable result—idleness—such are the causes of this evil! Science, toil, practical work—only these are capable of bringing our sick, idle young men to their senses."

"He could have said the same thing in three lines," said Pyotr Ivanich, glancing at his watch, "and he has written a regular dissertation in a friendly letter. What a pedant!

Do you wish to read further, Alexander? Don't go on—it's a bore. I have something to say to you."

"No, Uncle, let me drain the cup to the dregs!"

"Go on then, and much good may it do you!"

"This deplorable channelling of spiritual forces," read Alexander, "is displayed in every line of the novel you have sent me. Tell your *protégé* that in the first place a writer only writes something worthwhile when he is not carried away by self-absorption and prejudice. He must cast a calm, clear glance at life and humanity, otherwise he will express nothing but his own *ego*, which nobody cares a rap about. This defect is the outstanding feature of the novel. The next and most important condition, and you'd better not tell the author this, to spare his youth and his vanity as an author—the most troublesome of vanities—talent is required and there is not a scrap of talent here. The style is quite correct and irreproachable throughout, the author even knows how to spell," Alexander was hardly able to go on reading.

"Why didn't he say that at first," said Pyotr Ivanich, "instead of all this long harangue? You and I are perfectly capable of finding out all the rest without his aid."

Alexander was utterly shattered. In silence, like a man stunned by an unexpected blow, he stared blankly at the wall. Pyotr Ivanich took the letter from his hands and read out the postscript: "If you really want this novel to come out in our magazine I'll publish it, as a favour to you, in the summer months, when people don't read much, but there can be no question of payment."

"Well, Alexander, how do you feel?" asked Pyotr Ivanich.

"Better than might be expected," replied Alexander with an effort. "I feel like a man who has been deceived in everything."

"Say rather, a man who has been deceiving himself, and desired to deceive others too."

Alexander did not hear this remark.

"Has it all been a dream—has this, too, betrayed me?" he whispered. "Bitter loss! I ought to be used to disappointment! But why, I should like to know, was this unconquerable impulse to create implanted in me?"

"That's just it! The impulse was implanted, but the

power to create seems to have been forgotten," said Pyotr
Ivanich. "I told you so."

Alexander replied with a sigh, deep in thought. Then he
began violently pulling out all the drawers in his desk and
extracting from them various notebooks, sheets and scraps
of paper, which he hurled furiously into the fireplace.

"Don't forget these," said Pyotr Ivanich, pushing towards him the unfinished verses lying on the table.

"Away with them!" cried Alexander desperately, flinging the paper into the fireplace.

"Is that all? Have a good look," said Pyotr Ivanich,
casting a glance around him. "Make a good job of it while
you're about it. What's that bundle of papers on the top
of the wardrobe?"

"In it goes, too," said Alexander and reached up for it.
"It's articles on agriculture."

"Don't burn those. Give them to me," said Pyotr
Ivanich, holding out his hand. "That's not nonsense!"

But Alexander did not heed him.

"No," he said furiously. "If noble creative work in the
sphere of the beautiful is no longer for me, at least I won't
go in for drudgery. Here, fate shall not break me!"

And the bundle flew into the fireplace.

"Too bad!" said Pyotr Ivanich, at the same time rum-
maging with his stick in the basket under the table, to see
if nothing more remained to be cast into the flames.

"And what shall we do with the novel, Alexander? I
have it at home."

"You don't need it for papering a partition by any
chance?"

"No, not now. Shall we send for it? Yevsei! Asleep
again! My overcoat will be stolen under your very nose,
see if it isn't! Quickly go to my rooms and ask Vasily to
give you the thick exercise-book lying on the desk in
my study, and bring it here."

Alexander sat looking at the flames, his chin in his
hand. The exercise-book was brought. Alexander seemed
to hesitate when his eyes fell on the fruits of his six
months' toil. Pyotr Ivanich observed this.

"Get it here, Alexander!" he said. "And let's talk about
something else."

"In with it!" cried Alexander, flinging the exercise-book into the flames.

They both watched it burn—Pyotr Ivanich with obvious satisfaction, Alexander mournfully, almost tearfully. The top page stirred and rose as if an invisible hand were turning it, the edges curled, it turned black, then warped and suddenly burst into flame. After it the next few pages took fire, and then suddenly several rose slightly and burned all together; the page underneath them was still white, but a few seconds later it also began to turn black at the edges.

Alexander, however, had had time to read: "Chapter III." He remembered what was in this chapter and he felt regret for it. Getting up he seized the tongs to rescue the remains of his work. "Perhaps, still..." hope whispered to him.

"Wait, let me do it with my stick!" said Pyotr Ivanich. "You'll burn you hands with the tongs."

He pushed the exercise-book to the back of the grate, right on the glowing embers. Alexander stopped uncertainly. The exercise-book was very thick and did not yield at once to the action of the flames. First dense smoke rolled up from it; a tongue of flame occasionally made its way to the top and licked the cover, leaving a black patch and disappearing again. It could still have been saved. Alexander was just stretching out his hand towards it when at that very moment a flash lit up the chairs, the face of Pyotr Ivanich, the desk. The whole book burst into flames which a moment later died down, leaving in their stead a heap of black ashes, over which tongues of fire writhed here and there like snakes. Alexander threw down the tongs.

"All over!" he said.

"All over!" echoed Pyotr Ivanich.

"Ugh!" said Alexander. "I'm free!"

"This is the second time I have helped you to clean up your room," said Pyotr Ivanich. "I hope, this time..."

"No bringing back the past, Uncle!"

"Amen to that!" said his uncle, placing a hand on Alexander's shoulder. "Well, Alexander, I advise you to lose no time! Write to Ivan Ivanich at once to send you some work on the subject of agriculture. After all these follies, if you start straight away, you'll do something good. He's always asking me, 'What's become of your nephew?' "

Alexander shook his head mournfully.

"I couldn't," he said. "No, I couldn't! It's all over!"

"Then what do you intend to do now?"

"To do?" he repeated and seemed to be lost in thought. "For the present—nothing."

"One can only do nothing in the provinces. Here one must... Or else why did you come? It's incomprehensible. Well, enough of that for the present! I have a request to make of you."

Alexander slowly raised his head and cast an interrogatory glance at his uncle.

"You know my partner Surkov, don't you?" said Pyotr Ivanich, moving his chair nearer Alexander.

Alexander nodded.

"You met him at dinner at my house once or twice, but I don't suppose you realize the sort of a bird he is? He's a good chap, but empty-headed. His main weakness is women. He is, unfortunately, as you have seen, not bad-looking, that is to say, rosy, glossy, tall, always curled and scented, dressed up to the nines. And he imagines all women are in love with him—he's a regular fop. But that's not the point—I wouldn't mind that. The trouble is that—as soon as he goes in for some new love affair he starts throwing money about. He squanders it on surprises, gifts, and such like. He begins showing off, buys a new carriage, new horses ... sheer extravagance. He paid court to my wife, too. I actually stopped sending my servant for theatre tickets—Surkov was sure to bring them. If you wanted to change your horses, procure some rarity, elbow your way through the crowd, go and view a summer villa, you could leave it to him, he was a perfect treasure. Such a useful man, you couldn't hire one like him for all the money in the world! Pity to lose him! I took care not to meddle, but my wife got sick of him, so I had to send him packing. When he starts on a fling the interest on his capital isn't enough for him, and he begins asking me for money. When I refuse he mentions his capital. 'What's the use of your factory to me? I never have any loose cash in my pockets.' If he were to take up with some... But no—he's for ever seeking liaisons in society. 'What I need,' he says, 'is a noble affair. I can't live without love.' Isn't he an ass?

Nearly forty, and can't live without love!"

Alexander thought of himself and smiled mournfully.

"He's a liar," continued Pyotr Ivanich. "I have found out what he is really after. He only wants to be able to boast, for people to say he is having an affair with so-and-so, to be seen in the box of so-and-so, or tête-à-tête on the balcony of a country house with so-and-so late at night, or driving with her in some lonely place, or riding with her. And yet it turns out these noble affairs—the devil take them!—cost a great deal more than ignoble ones. And that's why the idiot is always in trouble."

"What are you leading up to, Uncle?" asked Alexander. "I don't see where I come in here."

"You will see in a minute. Not long ago Julia Pavlovna Tafayeva, a young widow, came back from abroad. She's very good-looking. Her husband was a friend of Surkov and myself. Tafayev died abroad. Well, have you guessed?"

"Yes—Surkov is in love with the widow."

"Quite right. He's gone quite crazy. And what next?"

"That I don't know."

"What a slow-witted fellow you are! Then listen: Surkov has intimated to me several times that he will soon be in need of money. I guessed at once what that meant, but I could not make out which way the wind was blowing. I tried to find out what he needed money for. He hemmed and hawed and at last said he wanted to furnish an apartment on Liteinaya Street. I tried to think what there was about Liteinaya Street and then I remembered that Tafayeva lives there, right opposite the house he has chosen. He has already given a deposit. A catastrophe is imminent ... unless you come to the rescue. Now have you guessed?"

Alexander raised his head slightly, let his glance travel over the walls and ceiling, and then blinked several times and turned his glance upon his uncle, but said not a word.

Pyotr Ivanich looked at him, smiling. There was nothing he enjoyed so much as discovering mental lapses or lack of ingenuity in others, and letting them see that he had done so.

"What's the matter with you, Alexander? And you a novelist!" he said.

"I've guessed, Uncle."

"Thank heavens!"

"Surkov is asking for money. You haven't any and you want me..."

Pyotr Ivanich laughed. Alexander looked at his uncle in surprise without finishing the sentence.

"That's not it!" said Pyotr Ivanich. "As if I'm ever without money! Ask me for some, and you'll see! No, this is what it is. Tafayeva asked him to remind me of my acquaintance with her husband. I called on her. She asked me to come again. I said I would and promised to bring you. Now you understand, I hope."

"Me?" repeated Alexander, gazing wide-eyed at his uncle. "Oh, yes, of course, now I understand," he added hurriedly, stumbling over the last word.

"And what is it you have understood?" asked Pyotr Ivanich.

"I'll be hanged if I know! Wait a bit—perhaps she has an interesting circle of acquaintances and you want me to find distraction ... seeing how miserable I am."

"Wonderful idea! As if I would take you about to people's houses just for that! After this it would only remain for me to put a handkerchief over your mouth against the flies when you are asleep. No, that's not it at all! This is what it is—make Tafayeva fall in love with you!"

Alexander raised his eyebrows and looked at his uncle.

"You're joking, Uncle! It's absurd!" he said.

"Real absurdities you perform very seriously, but a simple, natural matter you call absurd. What's absurd about it? Think how absurd love itself is—the pounding of the pulses, the play of vanity ... but what's the good of talking to you? You still believe in a destined object of love, in the affinity of souls."

"No, I no longer believe in anything whatever. But how can one love, or win another's love, to order?"

"*One can*, it's you who cannot. Don't be afraid—I shall not impose such a difficult task upon you. Here is all you have to do. Pay court to Tafayeva, be attentive, don't leave Surkov alone with her ... quite casually you know ... drive him mad! Get in his way—when he says one word—say two; when he states an opinion—contradict him flatly. Get him into a fix whenever you can, show him up at every step..."

"What for?"

"You still don't understand? In order, my dear fellow, that he should first be driven to distraction by jealousy and vexation, and then grow cool. The one soon follows the other with him. He is ridiculously vain. Then he won't need an apartment, his capital will remain untouched, the affairs of the factory will go on smoothly. Now do you understand? I've already played this game with him five times. When I was young and a bachelor, I acted for myself, or if unable to do so, got a friend to act for me."

"But I don't know her," objected Alexander.

"That's why I want to take you to her next Wednesday. On Wednesdays some of her old friends gather round her."

"But if she responds to Surkov's love, you will agree that my attentions will infuriate her as well as him."

"Nonsense! A decent woman, once having seen through a fool, will have nothing to do with him, especially before witnesses—her vanity won't allow her to. And if another, cleverer and better-looking, appears at his side, she will be ashamed and throw him over at once. It is for that I have selected you."

Alexander bowed.

"Surkov is not dangerous," continued his uncle. "But Tafayeva receives very few visitors, and in her little circle he may pass for a celebrity and a sage. Outward appearances have a great effect on women. Surkov knows how to make himself pleasant, and so they put up with him. Perhaps she flirts with him, and he thinks... Even clever women like it when follies are committed for them, especially expensive ones. But it is generally someone else they love, not the one who commits the follies. Surkov is not the only one who fails to understand this—give him a lesson."

"But Surkov probably goes there on other days, too. Say I get in his way on Wednesdays—how will it be on the other days of the week?"

"Must I teach you everything? Flatter her, pretend to be a little in love—the next time she'll invite you for some other day, Thursday or Friday. Redouble your attentions, and then I will start working on her, I'll hint that you are really ... you know what! As far as I can make out she's ... susceptible ... probably has weak nerves. I think she, too, has nothing against true sympathy ... and effusions."

"But it's impossible," said Alexander thoughtfully. "If I were still capable of falling in love, but I'm not ... nothing will come of it."

"On the contrary! If you were to fall in love you would be unable to pretend, she would see through you at once and start playing you against each other. As it is, all you have to do is to infuriate Surkov. I know him like my own five fingers. As soon as he sees that he is out of luck he will stop wasting his money for nothing and that's all I want. Look here, Alexander, this means a great deal to me! If you bring it off—remember those two vases you liked at the factory? You shall have them. But you'll have to buy the pedestals yourself."

"My dear Uncle, do you really think I..."

"Why should you take trouble and lose your time for nothing? Done? Never mind—the vases are very fine. In our day and age people don't do anything for nothing. When I do something for you, offer me a present—I'll accept it."

"It's a strange task," said Alexander uncertainly.

"I hope you will not refuse to undertake it for my sake. I am ready to do all I can for you. When you need money come to me. Wednesday, then! This affair will only last a month—two at the most. I'll let you know when you're not required any more and you can give it up."

"Very well, Uncle, I'm willing. But it's very strange. I won't answer for my success—if I were still capable of love it would be different ... but I'm not."

"And a good thing too, or you'd spoil the whole business! I guarantee the success of it. Good-bye!"

He went, but Alexander sat long at the fireside, watching the beloved ashes.

When Pyotr Ivanich got home his wife asked:

"How is Alexander, and what about his novel? Will he go on writing?"

"No, I have cured him forever."

He told her the contents of the letter he had received with the novel and how they had burned everything.

"You are ruthless, Pyotr Ivanich," said Lizaveta Alexandrovna, "or else you don't know how to carry out properly anything you undertake."

"You did a fine thing urging him to waste so much paper! D'you imagine he has talent?"

"No."

Pyotr Ivanich gazed at her in astonishment.

"Then why did you..."

"You still don't understand, you haven't guessed?"

He said nothing, involuntarily remembering his own words to Alexander.

"What is there to understand? It's all so clear," he said, gazing at her.

"Tell me what it means then?"

"You ... you ... wanted to give him a lesson ... but differently, more gently, in your own way."

"Such a clever man and he can't understand! Why was he so gay, so healthy, almost happy of late? Because he had hope. And I supported him in this hope. Well, is it clear now?"

"So you were humouring him all the time?"

"I think it was pardonable. And what have you done? You don't feel the slightest pity for him—you have taken away his last hope."

"Nonsense! Why his last? There are many follies ahead still."

"What will he do now? He'll go about with a hang-dog air again."

"No, he won't! He won't have any time. I have given him work to do."

"What work? Another article on potatoes to translate? Can this really satisfy a young man, especially such an ardent ecstatic nature? All you think about is to provide him with mental occupation."

"No, my dear, it's nothing to do with potatoes, though it does concern my factory."

III

Wednesday came round. Some twelve or fifteen guests were assembled in the drawing-room of Julia Pavlovna. Four young ladies, two bearded foreigners whose acquaintance the hostess had made while abroad, and an officer formed one circle.

Apart from the rest, on a couch, sat an old man who looked like a retired military man, with two tufts of grey hair on his upper lip and a great many ribbons on the lapel of his coat. He was talking to an elderly man about rents and leases.

In another room an old lady and two men were playing cards. A very young girl was seated at the piano, and another, sitting beside her, was talking to a student.

The Aduyevs arrived. Few people could enter a drawing-room with such ease and dignity as Pyotr Ivanich. After him, somewhat uncertainly, came Alexander.

What a difference there was between them—one a head taller than the other, well-built, strong and healthy, with assurance in his glance and manners. The thoughts and character of Pyotr Ivanich were not to be guessed at from his glance, his movements, or his words—so skilfully was everything in him concealed by his manners and self-control. Every gesture and glance seemed to have been calculated in advance. His pale, imperturbable countenance showed that in this man passions were held in strict subservience by the mind, that his heart beat fast or subsided according to the dictates of his head.

In Alexander, on the contrary, everything betrayed a weak and delicate constitution—the changing expressions flitting over his face, a kind of languor, slowness and uncertainty in his movements, the limpid glance which showed every sensation of his heart, every thought stirring in his mind. He was of medium height, thin, and pale, but his pallor, unlike that of Pyotr Ivanich, was not natural to him, it was the result of incessant inner agitation. Unlike his uncle's, his hair did not show abundant growth on head and cheeks, but descended from his temples and to the back of his head in soft, light strands which shimmered like silk.

The uncle introduced the nephew.

"And where's my friend Surkov?" asked Pyotr Ivanich, looking round in surprise. "Has he deserted you?"

"Oh, no, I am very grateful to him," replied the hostess. "He often comes to see me. You know, except for my late husband's friends, I see hardly anyone."

"But where is he?"

"He'll be here any minute. Fancy, he promised me and my cousin faithfully to get us a box for tomorrow's performance, though everybody says it's impossible ... and he's gone for it now."

"He'll get it, I'll answer for him. He's a genius at that sort of thing. He always gets me tickets when my connections prove of no avail. Where he gets them, and what he pays for them, is his secret."

At last Surkov arrived. His clothes were spruce, and in every fold of his coat, in every detail of his toilet, his corinthian pretensions could be clearly seen, his superiority over all other fashionable men, over fashion itself. If, for example, the fashion demanded frock-coats worn open, his opened so wide that it looked like the extended wings of a bird. If turned-down collars were the rage, he ordered himself a collar that made him look, in his frock-coat, like a miscreant caught from behind, trying to struggle out of his captor's grip. He himself instructed his tailor how to make his clothes. He now appeared in the Tafayeva drawing-room with his cravat fastened to his shirt by a pin of such extravagant dimensions that it was more like a club.

"Well, did you get it?" came from all round.

Surkov was just going to reply when, catching sight of Aduyev and his nephew, he stopped short with a glance of surprise.

"He has a foreboding," said Pyotr Ivanich to his nephew softly. "Oh, he's carrying a stick—what's the meaning of that?"

"What's that for?" he asked Surkov, pointing to the stick.

"I stumbled getting out of my carriage the other day, and I'm rather lame," replied the other with a little cough.

"Rubbish!" whispered Pyotr Ivanich to Alexander. "Observe the handle—d'you see the golden lion's head? The other day he boasted to me that he paid Barbier six hundred rubles for it, and now he's showing it off. That gives you an idea of the means he employs. Fight him, drive him from his position!"

Pyotr Ivanich pointed through the window to the house opposite.

"Remember, the vases are yours," he added. "Pluck up your spirit!"

"Have you a box for tomorrow's performance?" Surkov asked Mme Tafayeva, going up to her with a triumphant air.

"No."

"Then allow me to present you with one!" he said.

The ends of the officer's moustache twitched in a slight smile. Pyotr Ivanich cast a sidelong glance at his nephew, and Julia Pavlovna blushed. She at once invited Pyotr Ivanich to the box.

"Thank you very much," he replied. "Tomorrow I am on duty in the theatre, I am taking my wife there. But allow me to present a young man as my substitute!"

He pointed to Alexander.

"I was just going to invite him, too. There are only three of us—my cousin, myself, and..."

"He will substitute for me," said Pyotr Ivanich. "And, if necessary, for that rascal!"

He pointed to Surkov and said something to Julia Pavlovna in a low tone. While he was speaking she twice stole a glance at Alexander and smiled.

"Thanks!" said Surkov, "but you should have suggested this substitute before, when there was no ticket. We'd see then how he would have substituted me."

"Oh, I am extremely obliged to you," said the hostess to Surkov eagerly. "The only reason I didn't invite you to the box is because you have a stall. You probably prefer to sit right up front, especially for the ballet."

"No, no, you are prevaricating, you don't believe that! Not for the world would I relinquish a seat beside you!"

"But the seat has already been promised."

"What? To whom?"

"To M. Renier."

She pointed to one of the bearded foreigners.

"*Oui, madame m'a fait cet honneur,*" the latter murmured hastily.

Surkov, his mouth open, looked from the foreign gentleman to Julia Pavlovna.

"I'll change with him. I'll offer him my stall," he said.

"You can try."

The bearded man disclaimed the offer with the utmost resolution.

"My profoundest thanks," said Surkov to Pyotr Ivanich, casting a sidelong glance at Alexander. "I owe this to you."

"Not at all, my dear fellow! Perhaps you'd like to come to my box? There'll only be my wife and I. You haven't seen her for a long time—you could pay her court."

Surkov turned from him in vexation. Pyotr Ivanich quietly departed. Julia seated Alexander at her side and engaged him in conversation for a whole hour. Surkov made several rather awkward attempts to butt in, but somehow always out of turn. He mentioned the ballet receiving "Yes" for an answer when it should have been "No", and vice verse. It was obvious that nobody was listening to him. Then he turned the subject to oysters, declaring that he had eaten a hundred and eighty that morning, and was not vouchsafed so much as a glance. He uttered a few more commonplaces, but seeing they gained him nothing, seezed his hat and began hovering around Julia, giving her to understand that he was displeased and intended to go. But she took no notice.

"I'm going!" he said at last with ill-concealed vexation. "Good-bye!"

"So soon?" she said calmly. "Be sure to look in at the box for a minute tomorrow."

"What hypocrisy! A minute! You know very well I would not exchange a place in paradise for a place at your side!"

"If you mean the theatrical paradise, I believe you."

He no longer wanted to go. His vexation had melted away from Julia's kindly words. But everyone had seen him take his leave, there was no help for it and he went, looking behind him like a dog anxious to follow its master, but being driven back.

Julia Pavlovna was twenty-three or twenty-four years old.

Pyotr Ivanich had guessed right—her nerves really were weak, but this did not prevent her from being an extremely pretty, intelligent and graceful woman. She was, however, shy, dreamy and sensitive, like most nervous women. Her features were delicate and refined, her glance gentle, always pensive, often melancholy, for no reason or, if you will, on account of her nerves.

Her views on the world and life were not too favourable, she had meditated over the question of her own existence and come to the conclusion that she was superfluous in this world. But she blanched if, which God forbid! anyone, ever so casually, mentioned the tomb, or death in her presence. The brighter side of life escaped her vision. In a garden or a grove, she would choose a dark, dense avenue for her walk, glancing indifferently at a smiling landscape. At the theatre she went to serious dramas, seldom to comedies, never to vaudevilles. She stopped her ears if the sounds of gay songs reached her, and she never smiled at a joke.

Sometimes her features expressed weariness, not the weariness of suffering or sickness, it was rather a kind of languor. It was clear that she was waging an inner struggle with some alluring dream, and that the struggle was draining her of strength. After these bouts she would remain silent and melancholy for a long time, and then suddenly become unaccountably gay, which was, however, quite in harmony with her nature. That which amused her would not have amused another. All nerves! But what will not these ladies call it? *Destiny, sympathy, instinctive attraction, mysterious sorrow, vague desires*—the words jostle one another, but always end up with the one word "nerves" accompanied by a sigh and a bottle of smelling salts.

"How well you understand me!" said Julia Pavlovna to Alexander, when he was taking leave of her. "No one, not even my husband, has ever really understood my nature!"

The fact was that Alexander himself was just such another as herself. What a field for him!

"Good-bye."

She gave him her hand.

"I hope you will find your way to my house without your uncle, now," she added.

The winter came. Alexander usually dined at his uncle's on Fridays. But four Fridays passed, and he did not show up, nor did he come on the other days of the week. Lizaveta Alexandrovna was quite angry. Pyotr Ivanich growled at being made to wait for dinner an unnecessary half hour.

But Alexander was not idle. He was fulfilling his uncle's instructions. Surkov had long stopped going to Tafayeva's, and spread it abroad that all was over between them, that he no longer had anything to do with her. One evening—

it was a Thursday—Alexander, returning home, found on his table two vases, and a note from his uncle. Pyotr Ivanich thanked him for his friendly efforts and invited him to come to dinner the next day, as usual. Alexander sat thinking, as if this invitation upset his plans. The next day, however, he went to Pyotr Ivanich an hour before dinner-time.

His uncle and aunt showered questions on him:

"What's the matter with you? We never see you! Have you forgotten us?"

"Well, you've done me a service!" continued Pyotr Ivanich. "Beyond all expectation! And how modest we were—'I can't, I don't know how.' He doesn't know how! I've been wanting to see you for ages, but there's no getting hold of you. Well, I'm most grateful. Did the vases arrive safely?"

"Oh, yes! But I'll send them back to you."

"Why? No, no! They're yours by all the rules of the game."

"No," said Alexander resolutely. "I will not accept this present."

"Just as you like. My wife likes them, she'll take them."

"I had no idea, Alexander," said Lizaveta Alexandrovna with a sly smile, "that you were such an adept in these affairs ... not a word to me..."

"It was Uncle's idea," replied the embarrassed Alexander. "I'm no adept at all, it was he who taught me."

"Just hark to him! He's no adept! And look how he managed the affair! I'm most grateful—most! That fool of a Surkov almost went out of his mind. I thought I should die laughing! A fortnight ago he came running to me in a pitiful state. I understood immediately what was wrong, but I didn't let on, and went on writing as if I knew nothing at all about it. 'Oh, is it you?'' I said. 'What's going on in the world?' He smiled, pretending to be perfectly calm ... but he was on the verge of tears. 'Nothing good,' he said. 'I bring you bad news.' I looked at him as if I were astonished. 'What news?' I asked. 'News of your nephew,' he said. 'What is it? What's up? Tell me at once,' I said. And suddenly his calm broke down. He began shouting, raging. I pushed my chair out of the way of his spluttering. 'You complain that he won't work, and you teach him idleness yourself.' 'I?' 'Yes, you! Who introduced him to Julia?' He's one of those men who begin calling a woman by her Christian name the very next day after making her acquaintance, you know! 'Well, and what's the harm of that?' I asked. 'The harm of that,' he replied, 'is that he's with her from morning to night.' "

Alexander blushed.

"See how he lies from spite, I thought to myself," went on Pyotr Ivanich, glancing at his nephew. "As if Alexander would stay there from morning to night! That's not what I asked him to do, is it?"

Pyotr Ivanich let his cold tranquil glance dwell on his nephew's face, but the glance seared Alexander like a flame.

"I ... do go there ... sometimes," he muttered.

"Sometimes—there's a difference," went on his uncle. "Surely not every day. I didn't ask you to do that. I knew he was lying. What's there to do there every day? You could die of boredom."

"Oh, no, she's a very clever woman ... exceedingly cultivated ... so fond of music," mumbled Alexander haltingly, rubbed his eyes, although there was nothing to rub it for, stroked his left temple, and taking out his handkerchief, wiped his lips.

Lizaveta Alexandrovna stole a furtive look at him, and then turned towards the window, smiling.

"Then you weren't bored? So much the better!" said Pyotr Ivanich. "And I was afraid I had imposed a tiresome task on you! So I said to Surkov: 'Thanks, old boy, for worrying about my nephew. I am deeply obliged to you. But aren't you exaggerating matters a little? It's not such a misfortune after all.' 'Not a misfortune?' he cried. 'He isn't doing anything—a young man should work.' 'And that's no misfortune either,' I said. 'It's nothing to you, is it?' 'Oh, isn't it?' said he. 'He's taken to using all sorts of wiles against me.' 'Ah, so *that*'s the misfortune!' I said, teasing him. 'He's put Lord knows what ideas about me into Julia's head. She's quite changed to me. I'll teach him, the milksop'—excuse me, I'm only repeating what he said—'what it means to measure his strength against me! He simply gained his end by slander. I hope you will bring him to his senses.' 'I'll scold him,' I said. 'I will cer-

tainly scold him. But is what you say true? What has he
done to annoy you?' Did you really send her flowers?"

Pyotr Ivanich again stopped speaking, as if awaiting a
reply. Alexander said nothing. Pyotr Ivanich went on:
" 'Not true?' he gasped. 'Why does he take her a bouquet of flowers every day? It's winter—what it must cost
him! I know what those bouquets mean!' 'Aha!' I said to
myself, 'blood is thicker than water. I see kinship does
mean something. You wouldn't go to all that trouble for
anyone else. But is it really every day?' I said. 'Wait, I'll
ask him! You probably invented it.' And he did, didn't he!
Surely you didn't..."

Alexander wished the earth would open and swallow
him up. But Pyotr Ivanich looked him straight in the eyes
and awaited a reply.

"Sometimes ... it is true ... I do take her..." said Alexander looking down.

"There you go again—sometimes! Not every day—that
would be needless expense. By the way, tell me how much
all this cost you! I shouldn't like you to waste your money
for me. It's quite enough that you've had so much trouble.
Send me a bill. Surkov raved on and on, you know.
'They're always out together,' he said, 'either walking, or
driving where there aren't so many people.' "

These words made Alexander wince. He stretched out
his legs, which had been tucked beneath his chair, and then
returned to his previous position.

"I shook my head incredulously," continued his uncle.
" 'As if he'd go out with her every day!' I said. 'Ask the
servants!' he said. 'I'd sooner ask him,' I said. Surely it
isn't true?"

"I do ... sometimes ... go out with her."

"But not every day! I didn't even ask you about that.
I knew he was lying. 'Well, and what of it?' I said. 'She's
a widow, she has no man in her life. Alexander is a modest
fellow, not like you, you rascal! And so she seeks his company. She must have somebody.' He wouldn't hear of it.
'You can't fool me!' he said. 'I know. Always at the theatre with her. Sometimes, I manage to get a box, with God
alone knows what trouble, and he sits in it.' At this I could
not restrain myself and burst out laughing. 'Serves you
right, you blockhead!' I thought. Alexander, Alexander—

there's a nephew for you! But I'm ashamed I made you take so much trouble for me!"

Alexander felt as if he were on the rack. Great drops of sweat poured down his forehead. He scarcely heard what his uncle was saying, and dared not so much as look either at him or at his aunt.

At last Lizaveta Alexandrovna took pity on him. She shook her head at her husband, silently reproaching him for tormenting his nephew. But Pyotr Ivanich did not relent.

"In his jealousy Surkov actually assured me," he continued, "that you were madly in love with Tafayeva. 'Sorry,' I said, 'but that is not true—after all that has happened to him he won't fall in love. He knows women too well, he despises them.' It's true, isn't it?"

Alexander nodded without raising his eyes.

Lizaveta Alexandrovna felt sorry for him.

"Pyotr Ivanich!" she said, trying to stem the tide of his speech.

"What is it?"

"A man came from the Lukyanovs in the morning with a note."

"I know. All right. What was I saying?"

"Pyotr Ivanich, you've dropped ash into my flowers again. Look—it's too bad!"

"Never mind, my dear! They say ash is good for flowers. Oh, yes—what was I saying?"

"Pyotr Ivanich—isn't it time for dinner?"

"Very well. Tell them to serve dinner. By the way, talking about dinner, that reminds me! Surkov says you dine there almost every evening, Alexander, and that's why you don't come to us on Fridays any more, and he says you spend days on end alone with her. Hang him and his lies, I'm sick of them! I drove him away at last. Of course, he was *lying*. It's Friday today, and here you are in the flesh."

Alexander crossed and uncrossed his legs, and inclined his head towards his left shoulder.

"I am most obliged to you, most! It has been the act at once of a friend and a kinsman," concluded Pyotr Ivanich. "Surkov sees that he hasn't a chance, and has retreated. 'She fancies I will break my heart for her,' he said, 'but she's wrong. I was actually going to furnish an apartment right opposite her house, and God knows what else! She little knows what happiness was in store for her. I might even have married her if she had known how to attach me. Now it's all over! Your advice was good, Pyotr Ivanich. I shall save both my money and my time.' And now the poor chap is playing Lord Byron, going about with morose looks, and he no longer asks for money. And I too say it's all over now. You've done what you set out to, Alexander, and you've done it with the skill of a master. Now I shall have peace for a long time. Don't worry about it any more! You needn't show up at her house now. I can just imagine how tedious it must be there ... do forgive me. I'll make it up to you somehow or other. When you need money, come to me. Liza—tell them to give us some good wine for dinner—we'll drink to the successful end of the affair.''

Pyotr Ivanich went out of the room. Lizaveta Alexandrovna stole a few furtive glances at Alexander and seeing that he did not say a word, went out too, to give orders to her servants.

Alexander sat on in a kind of trance, gazing at his knees. At last he raised his head and looked round—there was nobody there. He caught his breath, and looked at the clock—exactly four. He hastily picked up his hat, softly, on tiptoe, looking warily round him, made his way to the hall, took his overcoat on his arm, rushed headlong down the stairs and drove off to Julia Pavlovna's.

Surkov had not lied. Alexander was in love with Julia. He had noted the first signs of love with something like horror—as if they were symptoms of a disease. He was tortured by fear and shame. Fear of once again becoming the victim of the caprices of his own and another's heart, shame before others, first and foremost, his uncle. He would have given much to be able to conceal everything from him. It was only three months ago that he had so proudly and resolutely renounced love, had even written a rhymed epitaph on that troublesome emotion, read it to his uncle, and had openly declared his contempt for women. And here he was again at the feet of a woman! Fresh proof of his puerile impetuosity. Heavens! When would he throw off his uncle's devastating influence?

Would his life never take an unexpected turn but would it always proceed according to the prophecies of Pyotr Ivanich?

The thought reduced him to despair. He would have been glad to run away from this new love. But how could he? What a difference between his love for Nadenka and his love for Julia! The first love had been simply a regrettable error of the heart in its clamour for nourishment, and at his age the heart is so undiscriminating, it will fall upon the first object it comes across. But Julia—she was no whimsical chit, unable to understand either him, herself, or love! She was a fully developed woman, physically delicate, but with plenty of spiritual energy—for love. She was all love. She acknowledged no other conditions for happiness in life. And is it a small thing—to love? It is a gift, and Julia was a genius at it. This was the love of which he had dreamed—conscious, rational, but at the same time powerful, oblivious of everything outside its sphere.

"I do not pant from lust like an animal," he told himself, "my soul does not faint—a loftier, more significant process is going on within me. I am aware of my happiness, meditate on it, and it is more complete, if perhaps quieter. With what nobility and sincerity, quite without any affectation, did Julia yield to her feelings! She seemed to have been waiting for a man who should understand profound love—and the man appeared. Like the rightful owner he came proudly into his inherited wealth, and was humbly acknowledged. What joy, what bliss," thought Alexander on his way from his uncle to his lady, "to know that there is a being in the world who, wherever she is, whatever she does, thinks of you, concentrates all her thoughts, occupations, acts, around a single point, a single idea—the beloved! She seems to be your twin. All that she hears and sees, all that she passes by, or that passes her by, is put to the test of the impression on that other, her twin. This impression is known to them both, they have studied one another, and the impression, when tested, is accepted and confirmed in the soul, where it remains indelibly engraved. The twin renounces her own sensations if they cannot be shared or accepted by the other. She loves what he loves, hates what he hates. They live inseparably in the same thought, the same feelings. They have one organ of spiritual vision, one organ of spiritual hearing, one mind, one soul."

"What house on Liteinaya, sir?" asked the cab-driver.

Julia loved Alexander even more intensely than he loved her. She hardly realized the strength of her love, and did not try to analyze it. She was in love for the first time— that was alright, nobody can fall in love for the second time missing the first. The trouble with her was that her heart was exaggeratedly developed, moulded and prepared by novel-reading not so much for first love, as for that romantic love which is to be found in certain novels but never in life, and which is invariably ill-fated—simply because it is a practical impossibility. Julia's mind had never found healthy nourishment in her novel-reading, and had not been able to keep up with her heart. She was utterly unable to imagine quiet, simple love with no tempestuous manifestations, with no exaggerated tenderness. She would immediately have cooled to a man if he had not *fallen at her feet* at the first opportunity, if he had not made *heart-rending avowals*, if he had been such an oaf as not to *burn her to ashes in his embraces*, or had ventured to occupy himself with anything outside their love, anything as well as love, if he were not ready to drain *the cup of life* in her tears and kisses.

Out of all this came a dreaminess which created for her a special world. If anything in the ordinary world occurred not according to these special laws, her heart was outraged, she suffered. Her feminine constitution, weak in itself, was dealt a shock, and sometimes a very powerful one. Frequent agitation had exacerbated her nerves, till they were in a state of utter collapse. This is why pensiveness and unaccountable melancholy, a twilight outlook on life are to be found in so many women. This is why the system by which human beings live—well-balanced, wisely created, and based upon immutable laws—seems to them a heavy chain. This, in a word, is why reality terrifies them, forcing them to create a world of fantasy for themselves.

Who was it that had so prematurely and so unwisely undertaken the moulding of Julia's heart, leaving her mind untouched? Who but that classical triumvirate of teachers summoned by her parents to act as guardians to the youthful mind, to reveal to her the *cause and effect of everything*, to rend the veil from the past and—difficult task!—show what is beneath us, above us, within ourselves. Three nations were called upon to perform this feat. The parents themselves withdrew from her education, considering that their responsiblity was over when, relying on the recommendations of worthy friends, they had engaged Monsieur Poulet to teach her French literature and other subjects. Subsequently came Herr Schmidt, for it was the thing to study German, though, of course, there was no need to be too thorough about it; and last came the Russian tutor, Ivan Ivanich.

"But they're all so unkempt!" said Julia's mother. "They're always so badly dressed, worse than footmen! Some of them even smell of drink."

"We can't do without a Russian teacher, we can't, you know," decided her father. "Don't you worry—I'll choose a decent one."

The Frenchman was the first. Both parents made much of him. He was received as if he were a guest, and treated with the greatest respect—he was a very expensive Frenchman.

He found Julia no trouble to teach. Thanks to her governess she could chatter in French, and read and wrote it with hardly any mistakes. All Monsieur Poulet had to do was to set her to write essays. He gave her various subjects—to describe the sunrise, to define love and friendship, to write a congratulatory epistle to her parents, or to pour out her grief on separation from a girl-friend.

But from her window Julia could only see the sun setting behind the merchant Girin's house, she had never parted from a girl-friend, and as for love and friendship ... the idea of these emotions now flashed across her mind for the first time. A beginning has to be made in everything.

Having exhausted his whole repertoire, Poulet determined at last to make a beginning with that time-honoured thin pamphlet, on the title page of which is written in big letters *Cours de littérature française*. Which of us does not remember it? In two months Julia knew French literature by heart or at least the thin pamphlet, and in another three months she had forgotten it. But its pernicious influence remained. She knew who Voltaire was, and sometimes bestowed on him the authorship of *Les Martyrs*, while to Châteaubriand she attributed the *Dictionnaire philosophique*. Montaigne she called M. de Montaigne and occasionally confused him with Victor Hugo. Of Molière she knew that he wrote plays, from Racine she learned by heart the famous tirade: *A peine nous sortions des portes de Trezènes.*

In mythology she was delighted with the comedy enacted by Vulcan, Mars and Venus. She was inclined to be on Vulcan's side, till she discovered that he was lame and clumsy, and a blacksmith to boot, when she immediately went over to Mars. She liked, too, the story of Semele and Jupiter, and the description of Apollo's exile and his tricks when on the earth, accepting everything at its face value, quite unaware of any other meaning in these tales. Was the Frenchman himself aware of it—God alone knows! To her questions as to the religion of the ancients, he wrinkled up his forehead and replied pompously: *"Des bêtises! Mais cette bête de Vulcain devait avoir une drôle de mine ... écoutez,"* and then added, narrowing his eyes slightly, and patting her hand: *"Que feriez-vous à la place de Vénus?"* She did not answer, but for the first time in her life she blushed without knowing why.

The Frenchman finally perfected Julia's education by acquainting her in fact as well as in theory with the modern school of French literature. He put into her hands *Le manuscrit vert, Les sept péchés capitaux, L'âne mort,* each of which had created a sensation in its day, and innumerable other volumes then flooding France and the rest of Europe.

The poor girl embarked eagerly upon this boundless ocean. What heroes these Janines, Balzacs and Drouineaus, and the whole procession of geniuses seemed to her. What was the pitiful tale of Vulcan in comparison with their glorious images? Venus was a mere innocent in comparison with these new heroes. She devoured the works of the *école nouvelle*, and is probably doing so to this day.

While the Frenchman had gone so far, the solid German had not yet got his pupil through the grammar. With the utmost gravity he compiled tables of declensions and conjugations, invented, with many a rhyme and quirk, intricate ways for remembering case-endings.

But when he was asked to provide literature, the poor man took fright. He was shown the Frenchman's pamphlet, over which he shook his head, saying German could not be learned like this, and that extracts from all the writers were to be found in Ahler's textbook. But he was not to be let off so lightly, he was urged to acquaint Julia with all sorts of authors as Mr. Poulet had done.

At last the German promised to do so and went home deep in thought. He opened, or rather unfastened his bookcase, taking one door right off and leaning it against the wall, for the bookcase had long possessed neither hinges nor lock, and took out of it a pair of old boots, half a sugarloaf, a bottle of snuff, a carafe for vodka, a crust of black bread, a broken coffee-mill, a set of razors, a cake of soap, a shaving-brush stuck into an ointment jar, a pair of old braces, a stone for sharpening penknives and various other odd articles. At last behind all this a book appeared, a second, a third, a fourth—five in all. He clapped them against one another, so that the dust rose in clouds and settled triumphantly on the tutor's head.

The first book was Gessner's *Idylls*—"*Gut!*" said the German and read with delight the idyll of the broken jug. He opened the second—*Gothic Calendar for 1804.* He looked through it—it contained the dynasties of the European monarchs, pictures of various castles and waterfalls—"*Sehr gut!*" said the German. The third was a Bible. He put it aside, muttering piously, "*Nein!*" The fourth was Young's *Night Thoughts*; he shook his head muttering "*Nein!*" The last was Weiss, and the German smiled triumphantly. "*Da habe ich's!*" he said. When he was reminded of Schiller, Goethe and others, he shook his head, obstinately repeating, "*Nein!*"

Julia began to yawn after the German had read the first page of Weiss and then stopped listening altogether. And all she remembered of German was a few rhymes about grammar and syntax.

And the Russian teacher? He was even more conscientious than the German. He assured Julia tearfully, that a proper noun or a verb was a part of speech, and a preposition another, and at last managed to convince her of this, so that she learned by heart the definitions of all the parts of speech. She could even rattle off the prepositions, conjunctions and adverbs, and when the teacher solemnly enquired: "And what are the interjections denoting fear or astonishment?" she would immediately, without pausing for breath, declaim: "ah, oh, eh, alas, O! Well!" And her tutor was delighted.

She also knew a few truths culled from the syntax, but could never manage to apply them in practice and made grammar mistakes for the rest of her life. From history she learned that there had been a certain Alexander the Great, who had fought a great deal and been extremely brave ... and, by the way, extremely handsome ... but what else he was renowned for and what was the significance of the age in which he lived, neither she nor her teacher cared to know, indeed this is almost all there is on the subject in Kaidanov's *History*.

When literature was demanded of the Russian teacher he brought a heap of old, worn books. Here were Kantemir and Sumarokov, Lomonosov, Derzhavin, Ozerov. Her parents were astonished. They cautiously opened one book, sniffed at it and threw it aside, demanding something more modern. The teacher brought Karamzin. But who could read Karamzin after the writers of the new French school? Julia read *Poor Liza*, and a few pages from the *Travels* and returned the book.

There were plenty of intervals for the unhappy pupil between these lessons, but no pure, healthy nourishment for her mind. Her mind began to slumber, and her heart to beat an alarm. An obliging cousin stepped into the breach in the nick of time, with selections from Pushkin—*Yevgeny Onegin, The Captive of the Caucasus,* and so on. And Julia tasted the sweetness of Russian poetry. She learned *Yevgeny Onegin* by heart, and always kept the volume under her pillow.

Neither her cousin nor any other instructors were capable of showing her the significance and qualities of the poem. She took Tatyana as her model, mentally repeating to an ideal lover the burning lines of Tatyana's letter to Onegin, her heart throbbing and aching the while. Her imagination sought now an Onegin, now a hero from the masters of the new school—pale, mournful, disillusioned.

An Italian and another Frenchman completed her education, giving to her voice and movements graceful measures, in other words, teaching her to dance, to sing, to play, or at least mark time on the piano, till she should marry, but teaching her nothing about music itself. And at eighteen, with an expression permanently pensive, an interesting pallor, a slender waist, and a tiny foot, she made her début in society.

Here she attracted the notice of Tafayev, a man with all the attributes of a good match—respectable rank, a good income, a Cross pinned on his frock-coat, in a word a man with a career and a fortune. It could not be said of him that he was a nice, worthy soul and nothing more! He was by no means a man to be trifled with. He had an extremely sane judgement as to the present state of Russia, and what was lacking in her economic and industrial condition, and was considered a practical man in his own sphere.

The pale, pensive damsel, such a strange contrast to his own stolid nature, made a strong impression on him. At evening parties he would abandon the card-table and fall into unaccustomed meditation when the airy vision whirled past him. If her languid glance happened to rest on him (quite accidentally, of course) he, the brave gladiator of drawing-room conversation, would be overcome by shyness, and find himself unable to say a word to her. He got tired of this and resolved to act more decisively through the agency of certain ladies.

Inquiries as to her dowry received satisfactory replies. "We are well-matched," he reasoned to himself. "I am only forty-five, she is eighteen. Our combined fortunes are enough and to spare for two. Looks? She is quite sufficiently pretty, and I am what is called a presentable-looking man. They say she's highly educated—well, what about it? I also learned a thing or two in my day, Latin, they taught us, I remember, and Roman history. I can still remember some consul or other, what's his name, hang him! And we read about the Reformation ... and there were those lines: *beatus ille* ... how does it go on? *Puer, pueri, puero* ... no, that's not it, what the devil, I've forgotten it all! And what in God's name are we taught for, just to forget? You may say what you will, but I swear that none of those officials and clever people could say who that consul was ... or the year the first Olympian

Games were held! People are only taught because it's the thing ... so that people can see by your eyes that you've been at school. And how can you help forgetting? Nobody ever mentions all those things in society afterwards, and if they did I'm sure they'd simply be shown the door. Oh, we're a good match!"

And so the moment Julia emerged from childhood she encountered that most painful reality—an ordinary husband. He was so unlike those created by her imagination and by the poets!

Five years passed in this dull trance, as she called her loveless marriage, and now suddenly came freedom and love. She smiled, opened wide her arms to them, and surrendered to her passion much like a rider giving his galloping horse its head. He is borne forward by the powerful animal, oblivious of space. He catches his breath, houses and trees rush past him, the breeze fans his face, his breast all but bursts from the voluptuous sensation... Or else like a man in a small boat abandoning himself recklessly to the current—the sun warms him, the green shores flicker before his eyes, the playful wave caresses the stern, whispering sweet nothings, luring him on and on, showing him an endless pathway streaming before him. And he allows himself to be borne along. There is no time to look around and ask how the path will end. Will the steed hurl itself into an abyss, will the wave dash the boat against a rock? The wind sweeps thought away, the eyes are closed, the charm is irresistible ... and she, too, offered no resistance, but allowed herself to be swept off her feet... At last the poetic moment of life had arrived! She loved that sweet, tormenting trepidation of the soul, she sought agitation, and invented both torments and joys for herself. She was the slave of her love as people become the slaves of opium, and sipped eagerly at the poison.

Already unnerved by suspense, Julia stood at the window, her impatience increasing with every minute. She plucked the leaves from a rose bush, and threw them irritably on the floor. It was a moment of sheer torture. One leaf said: he comes, the next: he comes not. The entire strength of her intellect was concentrated on the solution of this profound problem. If the answer was "Yes," she smiled, if it was "No," she turned pale.

When Alexander drove up she sank wan and exhausted into a chair—so violent had been the play of her nerves! When he entered the room ... it would be impossible to describe the look with which she met him, the joy which instantly suffused all her features, as if she had not seen him for a year—whereas they had met only the day before. She pointed silently to the clock, but he had hardly begun to make excuses for himself. Believing him without hearing him out, she forgave him, forgot the pain of suspense, gave him her hand, and they sat down on the sofa and talked for a long time, then sat in silence for a long time, gazing at one another. If the servant had not reminded them, they would certainly have forgotten all about dinner.

What rapture! Never had Alexander dreamed of such completeness of *sincere, soulful effusions*! In the summer they had taken drives into the country—the crowd might be attracted by music being played somewhere, by fireworks, but they two flitted about among the trees, arm in arm. In the winter Alexander came to dinner, after which they sat side by side in front of the fire till nightfall. Sometimes they ordered horses to be harnessed to the sleigh, and, borne swiftly along the dark streets, hastened to continue the endless talk begun beside the samovar. Every object around them, every fugitive movement of thought or feeling was remarked on and shared.

Alexander dreaded nothing so much as meeting his uncle. He occasionally went to see Lizaveta Alexandrovna, but she never succeeded in provoking him to frankness. He was always nervous of being caught by his uncle and forced to be drawn into some unpleasant scene, and therefore always cut his visits short.

Was he happy? If the question were asked about someone else in the same case, the answer would have to be "Yes" and "No." In his case it was "No." With him love began in suffering. At moments when he could forget the past he believed in the possibility of happiness, in Julia, and in her love. At other times he would suddenly be seized by doubt in the midst of the most *sincere effusions*, and listen with misgivings to her passionate, ecstatic ravings. It seemed to him that before he knew where he was she would deceive him, or that some fresh *unexpected blow of fate* would suddenly destroy the exquisite world of bliss.

While tasting a moment of joy he realized that it would have to be bought at the price of suffering, and once more he would be plunged in dejection.

But the winter passed, summer came again, and love did not come to an end. Julia grew ever more attached to him. There was no deception, fate struck no *blow*. On the contrary, his glance grew clearer. He became accustomed to the idea of a constant affection. "But this love is not so passionate," he told himself once, glancing at Julia. "On the other hand it is stable, perhaps eternal. Yes, there can be no doubt of that! At last I understand thee, Fate! Thou wouldst reward me for my past torments and bring me, after long wanderings, to a quiet haven. So this is the haven of happiness!.. Julia!" he exclaimed.

She started.

"What?" she asked.

"Oh, nothing special! I just..."

"No, tell me! You meant something!"

Alexander shook his head. She insisted.

"I was thinking that, for the completion of our happiness we lack..."

"What?" she asked in trepidation.

"Oh, nothing! A strange idea came into my head."

Julia was seized with anxiety.

"Oh, do not torture me, tell me at once!" she said.

Alexander thought for a moment and began speaking in a low voice, as if to himself.

"To earn the right never for a moment to leave her, never to go back to my rooms ... to be always and everywhere at her side! To be her legitimate lord in the eyes of the world... She to call me her own, aloud, neither blushing nor turning pale ... and so on for the whole of life! And to be eternally proud of this..."

With this high-flown utterance he came, gradually, sentence by sentence, to the word—*marriage*. Julia started and melted into tears. She gave him her hand with a feeling of ineffable tenderness and gratitude, and they suddenly began talking with the utmost agitation. They decided that Alexander should speak to his aunt and ask her assistance in this important matter.

They were so happy that they did not know what to do. It was a beautiful evening. They drove outside town to a remote place and, having at last found a hillock, sat on it the whole evening gazing at the sunset, dreaming of their future life, when they would confine themselves to a small circle of acquaintances, never receive, and pay no unnecessary visits.

When they returned home they began discussing the way they would live, how they would assign the rooms, and so on. They got as far as the furnishing of the rooms. Alexander proposed to take her boudoir for his study, so as to have it next to the bedroom.

"What sort of furniture would you like in your study?" she asked.

"I should like walnut with blue velvet upholstery."

"That's very nice and practical—one should always choose dark colours for a man's study—light ones soon get spoiled by the smoke. And just here in the little passage leading from your future study to the bedroom, I'll have a pyramid of plants and flowers—won't that be lovely? I'll have an armchair put there, where I can see you in your study, and read and work."

"Soon I won't be taking leave of you like this," said Alexander on going.

She placed her hand over his mouth.

The next day Alexander went to Lizaveta Alexandrovna to reveal to her what she had long been aware of, and to ask her for advice and aid. Pyotr Ivanich was not at home.

"Why not?" she said, after listening to his confession. "You're not a boy any more. You can judge of your feelings and are free to dispose of yourself. But don't be in a hurry—get to know her really well!"

"Oh, *ma tante*, if you only knew her! Such fine qualities!"

"For example?"

"How she loves me!"

"That is, of course, an extremely important quality, but it is not all that is needed for marriage."

Here she uttered a few commonplaces about the married state, and what a wife, what a husband, should be.

"Wait a little! The autumn is coming," she added, "everyone will be returning to town. Then I'll go and see your fiancée. We'll get to know one another, and I'll go in for the matter in earnest. Don't leave her, I'm quite sure you'll be the happiest husband in the world!"

She was overjoyed.

It is a marvel how fond women are of marrying off the men of their acquaintance! Sometimes they see very well that the thing is not coming off, indeed ought not to come off at all, and yet they do everything to help matters on. All they want is to have a wedding, and after that let the newly-weds manage as best they can. God knows what makes them go to all this trouble!

Alexander asked his aunt to say nothing to Pyotr Ivanich till the very last moment.

Summer flitted by, and the dull autumn season set in. Another winter began. The meetings between Alexander and Julia were as frequent as ever.

She seemed to keep a strict account of the days, hours and minutes they were able to spend together, and was always seeking pretexts for more meetings.

"Will you be going early or late to the office?" she sometimes asked him.

"About eleven."

"Then come to me at ten, we'll have breakfast together. Perhaps you needn't go at all! Can't they get along without you?"

"Oh, but—my country ... my duty..." said Alexander.

"That's all very fine! But you can tell them you love and are loved. D'you mean to say your chief has never been in love? If he has a heart, he will understand. Or you could bring your work here—what's to prevent you from working here?"

Another time she would not let him go to the theatre, and she hardly ever allowed him to visit friends. When Lizaveta Alexandrovna came to see her, it took Julia a long time to recover from the shock of finding how young and good-looking Alexander's aunt was. She had expected to find in her the usual elderly, plain auntie, and here was a woman of twenty-six or seven, and a beauty! She made Alexander a scene and would not allow him to visit his uncle often.

But what were her jealousy and tyranny in comparison with Alexander's? Though thoroughly assured of her attachment, and aware that treachery and fickleness were not in her nature, he was nevertheless jealous. And how jealous! It was not the jealousy which springs from intense love and manifests itself in tears and groans, in wails arising from an overburdened heart, the jealousy which comes from the terror of losing happiness—it was a cold, dispassionate brand of jealousy. He tyrannized over the poor woman from love as others do not tyrannize from hate. He sometimes considered, for instance, that she did not look long or tenderly enough at him in front of her guests, and he cast savage glances around—and woe betide Julia if there happened at that moment to be some young man at her side, or even a man who was not young, or even not a man, but some woman, sometimes even an inanimate object! Insults, sarcastic remarks, dark suspicions and reproaches were showered upon her. She had to find excuses for herself then and there, and redeem her offence by all sorts of sacrifices, by complete submission—she must not speak to this one, sit in that place, go there, and she thus laid herself open to the sly smiles and whispers of knowing observers, and compromised herself by alternate blushes and pallor.

If she received an invitation, before replying she would cast a questioning glance at Alexander, and at the slightest twitching of his eyebrows she would immediately, pale and trembling, refuse it. Sometimes he gave permission, and then she would get ready, dress, be just going to get into her carriage, when he, obeying some fugitive whim, would pronounce a weighty veto and she must take off her visiting clothes and send away the carriage. Later he would probably ask her pardon, suggest going, but how could she start dressing all over again and order the carriage? So she would stay at home. He was jealous not merely of handsome men, not merely of worth or talent, but even of perfect freaks, and, finally, simply of men whose faces he did not like.

One day Julia was visited by a gentleman from her birthplace, where her kinsmen lived. He was a plain, elderly man, who talked about the harvest and about his case being considered by the Senate and Alexander, tired of listening to him, went into the next room. There was nothing to be jealous of. At last the visitor rose to go.

"I have heard," said he, "that you are at home on Wednesdays. Will you allow me to join the society of your acquaintances?"

Julia smiled and was just going to say "Delighted!" when suddenly, in a whisper louder than any shout, came the words, "Say it's impossible!"

"It's impossible!" said the trembling Julia hastily to her visitor.

But she bore it all. She was not at home to anyone, never went anywhere and stayed at home alone with Alexander.

They continued to sip the cup of their bliss systematically. When the entire store of known and ready-made pleasures was exhausted she invented fresh ones, to vary this world of theirs, which was so rich in pleasures to begin with. What an inventive gift Julia displayed! But even this came to an end. Repetitions set in. There was nothing left to desire or taste.

There was not a single place outside town which they had not visited, not a single play they had not seen in one another's company, not a single book they had not read and discussed. They had studied each other's feelings, way of thinking, virtues and failings, and now nothing was left to prevent their carrying out their design.

Sincere effusions became rarer. Sometimes they sat for hours without exchanging a word. But Julia was happy when she was silent, too.

Every now and then she would put some question to Alexander and receive a "Yes" or "No" in reply, which contented her. Or if neither was forthcoming she could just gaze steadily at him. He would smile at her and she was happy again. If he neither smiled nor replied she would fall to watching his every movement, his every glance, and interpret them in her own way, and then there would be no end to her reproaches.

They had stopped talking about the future, for this made Alexander feel a certain inexplicable embarrassment and awkwardness, and he would try to change the subject. He had begun to think, to wonder. The magic circle enclosing his love-life broke in a few places, and in the distance he glimpsed the faces of friends, all sort of frivolous pleasures, brilliant balls with a host of lovely damsels, his uncle busy and practical as always, his abandoned work...

In such a mood he was sitting beside Julia one evening. Outside a blizzard raged. The snow beat against the wind-

ow-panes and stuck in clots on the   glass. The monotonous ticking of the clock and an occasional sigh from Julia
were the only sounds in the room.

Alexander swept a glance around the room and looked
at the clock—it was ten, and he must sit there another
two hours! He yawned. His glance rested on Julia.

She was standing with her back to the fire, leaning
against the mantelpiece, her head on one side, following
all his movements with her eyes, not, however, with an
expression of suspicion and inquiry, but with one of ecstatic bliss. She seemed to be in the throes of some secret sensation, some sweet dream, and she looked weary.

She was so high-strung that even pleasurable vibrations
caused her painful exhaustion. In her, anguish and bliss
were inseparable.

Alexander responded with a cool, fidgety glance. He
crossed over to the window and began drumming on the
glass and looking out into the street.

The sounds of voices and carriage wheels reached them
from the street. Lights were burning and shadows were
flitting in all the windows. He imagined that in the most
brightly lit rooms a jolly crowd must be assembled. There,
he thought, an animated exchange of thoughts, a play
of fiery, momentary sensations, were going on. There,
life was noisy and gay. And in that room with the dimly-
lit window, some noble toiler was no doubt bending over
his useful work. And Alexander remembered that for almost
two years he had been dragging out an idle foolish existence—two years from the sum of his life's span—and all for
love! And at this thought he lashed out at love.

"And what sort of love is this?" he asked himself. "A
drowsy thing, lacking in energy! This woman surrendered
to her feelings without a struggle, without effort, offering no resistance, like a sacrificial lamb. Weak, supine
creature! Bestowing her love upon the first-comer! But for
me she would have loved Surkov in exactly the same way,
she had already begun to love him. Yes, whatever she says,
I can see that. If anyone livelier and more experienced
than I were to come along, she would yield herself to
him. It's simply immoral! Is that love? Talk about the
affinity of souls! Were ever souls so attracted as ours?
You would have thought they were fused together for

eternity, and now look! God knows what it all means, there's no making it out!" he whispered in his vexation.

"What are you doing over there? What are you thinking about?" asked Julia.

"Nothing," said he, yawning, and sat down on the sofa at some distance from her, throwing his arm round the corner of an embroidered cushion.

"Sit here—nearer!"

He neither moved nor replied.

"What's the matter with you?" she pursued, going up to him. "You're intolerable today!"

"I don't know," he said languidly. "I feel as if ... as though I..."

He did not know how to answer either her or himself. He had as yet not been able to explain to himself what was going on within him.

She sat down beside him and began talking of the future, gradually getting a little livelier. She painted a happy picture of family life, interspersing her speech with little jokes, and concluded tenderly:

"You are my husband. Look," she said, throwing out her hand with a sweeping gesture. "Soon all this will be yours. You will be the master of the house, as you are of my heart. Now I am independent, I can do what I like, go where I choose, but then, nothing can be moved without your orders. I myself will be bound by your will—but what exquisite fetters! Forge them, forge them—and soon! All my life I have dreamed of a man like you, of love like ours ... and now my dream has come true ... and happiness is near. I can scarcely believe it! Sometimes it still seems like a dream to me! Can it be that this is the reward for all my past suffering?"

Alexander could hardly bear to listen to her.

"And what if I were to stop loving you?" he asked suddenly, trying to make his voice sound facetious.

"I would tweak your ears," she replied, taking him by the ear, and then she sighed and grew pensive, all for a single jesting hint.

He said nothing.

"But what is the matter with you?" she asked with sudden eagerness. "You don't talk, you hardly hear what I say, you look from me!"

She drew nearer to him and, her hand on his shoulder, began speaking in low tones, almost in a whisper, of the same subject, but with less conviction. She reminded him of the beginning of their intimacy, the beginning of their love, its first symptoms, its first joys. She was almost breathless from her voluptuous sensations. Two red spots glowed on her pale cheeks. These gradually grew redder and redder, her eyes shone, then grew languid, the lids half-closed. Her bosom heaved. Her words were almost inaudible, and the fingers of one hand played with Alexander's silky hair. She gazed into his eyes. He moved his head gently from beneath her hand, took a comb from his pocket and carefully passed it through his hair, which she had just ruffled. She rose and gazed fixedly at him.

"What's the matter with you, Alexander?" she asked anxiously.

"Keeping on at me! As if I knew!" he thought, but did not answer her.

"Are you bored?" she asked, and there was at once a question and a doubt in her voice.

"Bored?" he thought. "That's just the word! Yes, it's this agonizing, killing boredom! This worm has been gnawing at my heart for a month now. Oh heavens, what shall I do? And she speaks of love, of marriage! How am I to bring her to her senses?"

She sat down at the piano and played some of his favourite pieces. He pursued his thoughts without listening to her.

Julia, quite discouraged, sighed, wrapped her shawl round her and flung herself into a corner of the sofa, from where she watched Alexander in an agony of distress.

He picked up his hat.

"Where are you going?" she asked in astonishment.

"Home."

"It's not eleven yet."

"I must write to Mamma. I haven't written to her for ages."

"Why, you wrote to her a few days ago."

He was silent. He could find nothing to say. He really had written to his mother and had casually mentioned it to Julia. And love never forgets a single trifle. To the eyes of love whatever concerns the beloved object is an all-important fact. The mind of a lover spins a complex web of observations, subtle considerations, memories, surmises as to all that concerns the beloved, all that goes on around him and has the least influence on him. In love, a single word, the merest hint, nay, just a glance, an imperceptible movement of the lips, are sufficient material for a surmise, from which spring all sorts of considerations, and it is a short step to some decisive conclusion that may mean heaven or hell for the lover. The logic of lovers, sometimes false, sometimes astonishingly correct, rapidly creates an edifice of surmises and suspicions, but love has the power to raze it to its foundations with still greater rapidity. Often a single smile, a tear, a couple of words are enough to lull suspicion. Nothing can escape or hoodwink the lynx-eyed watchfulness of love. The lover may suddenly take into his head a thing that would never occur to anyone else, or else fail to see what is going on under his very nose; he is as penetrating as a clairvoyant one minute, and myopic to the point of blindness the next.

Julia jumped off the sofa as agile as a cat and seized him by the hand.

"What's the meaning of this? Where are you going?" she asked.

"It's nothing, I assure you it's nothing! I simply want to have a nap. I slept badly last night, that's all!"

"Slept badly! And you told me this morning that you had slept nine hours, and that your head ached from it!"

So this was no good, either.

"Well, my head does ache," he said, somewhat embarrassed. "That's why I'm going."

"And after dinner you said your head was better."

"My God, what a memory you have! It's intolerable! Well, I just want to go home."

"Aren't you happy here? What will you do at home?"

Looking into his eyes, she shook her head dubiously. He soothed her somehow, and went.

"What if I don't go to Julia's today?" Alexander asked himself, on waking up the next morning.

He paced the room a few times.

"I won't!" he added resolutely. "Yevsei! Bring me my clothes."

And he went out for a stroll in the town.

"How jolly, how pleasant it is to walk about alone,"
he thought. "You can go where you like, stop, read a
poster, look into a shop-window, go here, there, everywhere!
It's really very nice! Freedom is a great blessing! Yes,
that's just it—freedom in the broadest, highest sense is to
be able to walk about alone!"

He tapped the pavement with his walking stick, and
greeted acquaintances cheerfully. Walking down Morskaya
Street he saw a familiar face at one window. The man
beckoned to him. He looked again. Why, it was Dumet!
And he went in, dined, stayed on till nightfall, went to the
theatre and after the theatre went out to supper. He tried
not to think of his home. He knew what awaited him there.

And in truth when he got back he found half a dozen
notes on his table and a sleepy servant in the hall. The
man had been instructed not to come back till he had
seen Alexander. The tear-stained notes were full of
reproaches and questions. The next day he had to find
excuses. He pleaded business at his office. And they
made it up somehow.

A few days later the same thing was repeated on both
sides. And after this it happened again and again. Julia
grew thin, never went out, received no one, but said not a
word, for reproaches angered Alexander.

A week or two later Alexander arranged with some
friends for a regular drinking-bout. But on the morning
of the day fixed for it he got a note from Julia begging
him to be with her the whole day, and come as early as
possible. She was ill and unhappy, she wrote, her nerves
were in an awful state, and so on. Though irritated, he
went to warn her that he could not stay with her, that he
had a great deal to do.

"Oh, of course! Dinner with Dumet, the theatre, sleigh-
riding, all very important business," she said mournfully.

"What's the meaning of this?" he asked angrily. "I believe you're having me watched. I'm not going to stand that!"

He rose as if to go.

"Wait, hear me out!" she said. "We must have a talk."

"I have no time."

"Just one minute! Sit down."

He sat down grudgingly on the edge of a chair.

Folding her hands she looked at him nervously, as if

trying to read in his face the reply to what she was going to say.

He fidgeted impatiently in his seat.

"Hurry up! I have no time," he said coldly.

She sighed.

"Don't you love me any more?" she asked, shaking her head slightly.

"The old song!" he said, smoothing his hat with the cuff of his coat sleeve.

"You've tired of me!" she retorted.

He got up and began rapidly walking up and down the room. A minute later the sound of sobbing was heard.

"That's the last straw!" he said furiously, stopping in front of her. "Haven't you tortured me enough?"

"*I* torture you?" she exclaimed, and sobbed still harder.

"This is intolerable!" said Alexander, preparing to go.

"I won't do it any more!" she said hastily, drying her tears. "Look, I'm not crying, only don't go, sit down!"

She tried to smile, while the tears rolled down her cheeks. Alexander was touched. He sat down, swinging his foot. He addressed a series of questions to himself, and came to the conclusion that he had cooled, he no longer loved Julia. And why? God alone knew! She loved him more and more every day—was that why? Great heavens—what a paradox! All the conditions for happiness were present. Nothing stood in their way, there was not even another feeling to distract him, and he had cooled. Such is life! But how was he to console Julia? Sacrifice himself? Drag out these tedious days with her forever? Pretend? But he was incapable of that, and not to pretend would mean incessant tears, reproaches, torture for her and himself. Expound to her all of a sudden his uncle's theory of unfaithfulness and the cooling off of love? No, thank you! She was crying as it was, what would it be then? What was to be done?

Julia, seeing him silent, took his hand and looked into his eyes. He turned away slowly, gently freeing his hand. Not only did he feel nothing for her—at the touch of her hand a cold unpleasant tremor passed over him. She redoubled her caresses. He did not respond to them and only became ever colder and grimmer. She suddenly flushed and tore her hand away from him. Feminine pride, wounded vanity, shame, had awakened in her. She held up her head, straightened her back and reddened with anger.

"Leave me!" she said curtly.

He rushed away without the slightest protest. But when the sound of his footsteps began to die away she rushed after him.

"Alexander Fyodorich! Alexander Fyodorich!" she cried.

He turned round.

"Where are you going?"

"You told me to go."

"And you were only too glad to escape! Stay!"

"I have no time."

She took his hand, and once more there was a stream of tender, passionate words, entreaties, tears. Neither by glance, word, nor movement did he display any sympathy, and just stood there stiffly, shifting from foot to foot. His imperturbability drove her frantic. Threats and reproaches were showered on him. Impossible to recognize in her the mild woman with the weak nerves! Her curls came tumbling down, her eyes shone with a feverish brilliance, her cheeks blazed, her features were strangely distorted. "How ugly she is!" thought Alexander with a grimace of distaste.

"I will have my revenge!" she cried. "Do you think you can toy so lightly with a woman's fate? You stole into my heart with flattery and hypocrisy, took possession of me completely, and then abandoned me, when I no longer have the strength to forget you. Oh, no, I will not leave you! I will follow you everywhere. You will never be able to escape from me. If you go to the country—I will follow you, if you go abroad, I shall be there too, always and everywhere. I shall not give up my happiness so lightly. Nothing matters to me any more. Whatever my life may be ... I have nothing more to lose now. But I will poison yours, too. I will take my revenge. I must have a rival, of course. You would not leave me just like that! I will find her, and you will see what I will do. You'll be sorry you were ever born! If you were to perish now, how delighted I would be! I could kill you with my own hands!" she screamed wildly, frantically.

"How idiotic, how ridiculous!" thought Alexander, shrugging his shoulders.

Seeing that threats left Alexander indifferent, she swiftly passed to a gentle mournful tone, and then stood looking at him in silence.

"Have pity on me," she said. "Do not leave me. What shall I do without you now? I shall not survive separation. I shall die. Think—the love of women is different from that of men, it is tenderer, stronger. For women—especially for a woman like me—love is all. Other women may flirt, enjoy society, noise, bustle—I am not used to all this, my nature is different. I love quiet, solitude, books, music, but above all else in the world—you."

Alexander showed signs of impatience.

"Good, then do not love me," she went on in animated tones. "But keep your promise, marry me, only be with me ... you will be free! Do whatever you like, even love anyone you like, only let me sometimes, every now and then, see you... Oh, for God's sake, have pity on me!"

She started crying and could not go on. Exhausted by her emotions she fell on the sofa, her eyes were closed, her teeth clenched, and her lips were convulsively drawn to one side. She was in a fit of hysterics. An hour later she came to, and opened her eyes. Her maid was hovering about her. Julia looked round the room.

"Where?.." she asked.

"Alexander Fyodorich has gone!"

"Gone!" she echoed forlornly and sat for a long time motionless and silent.

The next day note after note was sent to Alexander, but he neither put in an appearance nor sent any answer. The next two days were the same. Julia wrote to Pyotr Ivanich, asking him to come and see her on a very important matter. His wife she did not like because she was young, pretty, and Alexander's aunt.

Pyotr Ivanich found her ill in real earnest, almost dying. He sat with her for an hour or two, and then set off to see Alexander.

"Oh, what a hypocrite!" he said.

"What do you mean?" asked Alexander.

"And he behaves as if it had nothing to do with him! Says he doesn't know how to win a woman's love, and makes her fall madly in love with him!"

"I don't understand you, Uncle."

"Oh, don't you? You understand me very well! I've just come from Tafayeva—she told me everything."

"What?" muttered Alexander in great confusion. "Everything?"

"Everything. How she loves you! Happy man! Well now, you kept moaning that you could not find passion anywhere. And here's passion for you, so cheer up! She's going mad, wild with jealousy, weeping, frantic... But why do you mix me up in your affairs? You've begun foisting women on to me, and that's really too much. I wasted a whole morning on her. I thought it was about business, I supposed she wanted to mortgage her estate with the board of Trustees or something. She did mention it once ... and look what she really wanted me for! Is that business!"

"But why did you go?"

"She sent for me to complain of you. And really you ought to be ashamed of neglecting her like that. Stayed away four whole days—that's no joke! She is dying, poor thing. Go—go and see her at once."

"What did you say to her?"

"Nothing special—that you, too, love her madly, that you have long sought a tender heart, that you positively adore *sincere effusions*, and cannot live without love. I told her not to worry—you'd come back to her; I advised her not to be too possessive, to let you have your fling every now and then ... otherwise, I said, you'll get tired of each other ... just the usual thing people say in such cases. She quite cheered up and began chattering about your wedding, and told me my wife had taken an interest in it. And not a word to me from either of you! Well, never mind—good luck to you! This one at least has a fortune— enough for the two of you. I told her you would cer- tainly keep your promise... I did my best for you, Alexan- der, in gratitude for the service you did for me. I assured her that you loved her *so ardently, so dearly*..."

"What have you done, Uncle!" exclaimed Alexander, his face expressing horror. "I—I don't love her any more ... I don't want to marry ... I'm as cold as ice to her. I'd rather take a dive into the river than..."

"Heigh-ho!" said Pyotr Ivanich with affected aston- ishment. "Can this be you? Didn't you say—remem- ber?—that you despised human nature, especially female human nature? That there was not a heart in the world worthy of yours? What else was it you said? Let me see..."

"No more, Uncle, for God's sake! Reproaches are quite enough. Why moralize as well? D'you think I don't understand? Oh, people, people!"

Alexander suddenly began to laugh, and his uncle laughed with him.

"Come, that's better," said Pyotr Ivanich. "I told you you would be laughing at yourself one day—and here you are!"

And again they both laughed heartily.

"Come now, tell me," continued Pyotr Ivanich. "What do you think of that ... what's her name ... Pashenka, isn't it—with the wart?"

"Uncle, that's ungenerous!"

"I only wanted to know if you still despised her."

"For God's sake don't talk about that! Just help me to get out of the appalling situation I am in. You're so clever, so rational."

"Ah, compliments, flattery, now! No, you must get married this time."

"Not for the world, Uncle! Help me, I implore you!"

"Aha, Alexander! A good thing I've known for a long time what you were up to!"

"A long time!"

"Oh, yes! I've known of this from the very beginning."

"I suppose *ma tante* told you."

"Not a bit of it! I told her! Nothing special in that! I could read it all in your face. Never mind, never mind! I have done what I could to help you."

"What? When?"

"This very morning! Don't worry! Tafayeva will never bother you any more."

"What did you do? What did you say to her?"

"It would take a long time to tell you, Alexander, it would be a bore."

"But who knows what you told her? She will hate, despise me!"

"Why should you care? I consoled her—and let that suffice. I told her you were incapable of loving, that you weren't worth troubling about."

"And what did she say?"

"Now she's glad you have left her."

"Glad!" said Alexander thoughtfully.

"Yes, glad."

"You saw no signs of regret or sorrow in her? She doesn't care? How can it be?"

He began pacing the floor nervously.

"She's glad! She's calm!" he repeated. "Imagine! I'll go and see her this very minute."

"I like that!" remarked Pyotr Ivanich. "Follow the bidding of your heart they say, and everything will be fine. And now... Wasn't it you who told me you were afraid she would send for you? Wasn't it you who asked me for help? And now you're upset because she doesn't die of grief at the separation from you."

"She's glad, she's pleased!" muttered Alexander, pacing up and down and not heeding his uncle's words. "So she never really loved me! No grief, not a tear! I must see her."

Pyotr Ivanich shrugged his shoulders.

"Say what you will, I can't leave it at that, Uncle!" added Alexander, picking up his hat.

"All right—go to her! But you'll never shake her off again, and don't come to me begging for help! I shan't interfere any more! I only did so this time because it was I who got you into this situation. What! Still looking glum?"

"Life is a shameful thing!" said Alexander, sighing.

"Unless one finds real work to do," interposed his uncle. "Enough! Come and see us today! We'll laugh about your affair over dinner, and then we'll drive to the factory."

"How insignificant, how worthless I am!" said Alexander ruefully. "I have no heart! I am pitiable, a bankrupt soul!"

"And all because of love," interrupted Pyotr Ivanich. "A foolish occupation—leave it to people like Surkov! You are a clever chap, you could occupy yourself with more important things. You've done enough running after women."

"But you love your wife, don't you?"

"Of course I do! I'm deeply attached to her, but that does not prevent me from going about my business. Well, good-bye. Come and see us soon!"

Alexander sat on, confused and morose. Yevsei stole

into the room, his arm thrust into a boot.

"Look, sir!" he said happily. "What splendid boot polish! You can get a surface with it like glass and it only costs twenty-five kopeks."

Alexander roused himself, and looked blankly from the boot to Yevsei.

"Get out!" he said. "You're a fool!"

"Then why don't you send me back to the village?" said Yevsei.

"Get out, I tell you!" shouted Alexander, almost in tears. "You're worrying me to death, you'll drive me to the grave with your boots ... you ... barbarian!"

Yevsei retreated hastily to the hall.

IV

"Why doesn't Alexander ever come? I haven't seen him for three months," Pyotr Ivanich asked his wife one day, on his return from work.

"I have quite lost hope of ever seeing him again," she replied.

"I wonder what's the matter with him? In love again, perhaps!"

"I have no idea."

"Is he well?"

"I suppose so!"

"Write to him, I want to speak to him. There have been changes at the office again, and I suppose he knows nothing about it. I can't understand such carelessness."

"I've written to him again and again, and invited him here. He says he has no time, but he's always playing draughts or going fishing with a queer set of people. Better go and see him yourself! You could find out what the matter is."

"I don't feel like it. Send a servant."

"Alexander won't come."

"We'll try."

They sent a servant, who soon came back.

"Well—was he in?" asked Pyotr Ivanich.

"Yes, sir. He sent his respects."

"What's he doing?"

"Lying on the sofa."

"What, at this time of day?"

"His man says he lies on the sofa all day long."

"What does he do—sleep?"

"No, sir! At first I thought he was asleep but his eyes were open, and he was staring at the ceiling."

Pyotr Ivanich shrugged his shoulders.

"Is he coming?" he asked.

"No, sir. 'My respects to my uncle,' he says, 'and tell him to excuse me. I'm not feeling quite well,' and he sent his respects to you, Ma'am."

"Now what's the matter with him? It's really astonishing. Strange chap! Tell them not to unharness the horses. There's nothing for it but to go to him. But this really is the last time."

Pyotr Ivanich, too, found Alexander on the sofa. He sat up when his uncle came in.

"Aren't you well?" asked Pyotr Ivanich.

"Not quite," said Alexander with a yawn.

"What are you doing?"

"Nothing."

"And can you live without doing anything?"

"I can."

"Listen, Alexander—I heard today that Ivanov in your office is retiring."

"Yes, he is."

"And who will get his place?"

"Ichenko, they say."

"And what about you?"

"Me? Nothing."

"What d'you mean, nothing? Why shouldn't you get the place?"

"I have not been honoured. Can't be helped! I suppose I'm not considered worthy."

"But, Alexander, you must do something! Why not go to the director?"

"I won't," said Alexander, shaking his head.

"You don't seem to care one way or another."

"Not a bit!"

"But this will be the third time you have been passed over."

"I don't care! Let them!"

"We'll see what you say when your former subordinate starts giving you orders, or when you have to get up and bow when he comes in."

"Very well, then! I'll get up and bow."

"And what about your pride?"

"I haven't any."

"But I suppose you have some interests in life?"

"None whatever! I used to, but not any more."

"That's impossible—one interest takes the place of another. And how is it that you have lost yours, while others keep theirs? It's early days for that—you're not thirty yet."

Alexander shrugged his shoulders.

Pyotr Ivanich saw no point in continuing the conversation. He put everything down to mere whim, but he knew that when he got home he would be unable to evade his wife's questions, and therefore he reluctantly pursued the subject.

"Why don't you seek distraction, go out into society?" he said. "Or you could read."

"No desire, Uncle!"

"People are beginning to talk about you, they say you've ... er ... gone off your head from love, that you're up to all sorts of things, hobnobbing with a queer set... That alone would make me go and show myself to people."

"They can say what they like!"

"Listen, Alexander, joking apart—all that's a mere trifle! You can bow, or not bow, go out into society or not—that's not the point. But remember that, like everyone else, you have a career to make. Do you ever think about that?

"I do! I've made it already."

"What d'you mean?"

"I have outlined a course of action and do not wish to go beyond its limits. Here, I am master—that's my career."

"That's just laziness."

"Perhaps."

"You have no right to lounge about, when there are things you could do, while you have the strength. Is your work all done?"

"But I do work. No one can reproach me with idleness. I go to the office in the mornings, and to do any more than that would be a luxury—superfluous zeal. Why should I take the trouble?"

"Everyone takes trouble about something or other. Some because they consider it their duty to work while they have the strength, some for money, some for rank. Why should you be an exception?"

"Rank? Money? Especially money! What's the good of it? I have enough to eat, I am clothed—there's enough for that."

"And very badly dressed you are," remarked his uncle. "Besides that's not all you need!"

"That's all."

"And the luxury of mental and spiritual enjoyments, and art," said Pyotr Ivanich, imitating Alexander's way of speaking. "You are capable of developing. Your vocation is higher. Your duty summons you to noble toil... And strivings towards the sublime—have you forgotten?"

"The deuce take them, the deuce take them!" said Alexander restlessly. "You, too, Uncle, have begun speaking wildly. You used not to do that. You're putting it on for my sake, I suppose. Don't bother. I used to strive for the sublime—you remember? And what came of it?"

"I remember you wanted to become a minister straight away, and then a writer. But when you saw that the road to a high office is long and hard, and that a writer needs talent, you beat a retreat. Many fellows like you come here with lofty ideas, but are unable to see what lies under their very noses. As soon as it becomes a matter of office drudgery they take one look and are off. I'm not talking about you, you have shown that you know how to work, and could, in time, become a somebody. But this is tedious, it takes a long time. We want everything all at once. When it doesn't come off, we fall into dejection."

"But I have no ambition for a high post. I want to stay where I am. Haven't I the right to choose my own occupation? What does it matter whether it's beneath my abilities or not? So long as I do my work conscientiously, I am doing my duty. Let them reproach me for my inability to do more than that, I shouldn't care a bit even if it were true. You said yourself there was poetry in a modest lot, and now you reproach me for having chosen the most modest possible. What is to prevent me from descending a few steps lower still, and staying at the level that pleases me? I do not wish for a higher post—I do not wish for it, d'you hear me?''

"I hear you. I'm not deaf, but these are all pitiable sophisms."

"What do I care? I've found myself a place and will stay in it to the end. I have found simple, unsophisticated people, they may not be very clever, and a good thing, too! I play draughts with them and go fishing. What if, according to your ideas, I am punished for that, giving up rewards, money, rank, distinction, all that is so dear to you? I renounce them once and for all."

"You pretend to be calm and indifferent to everything, but your words are a cover for a raging resentment. Your speech is not words, but tears. There is much gall in you. You do not know whom to vent it on, for you alone are to blame."

"Amen," said Alexander.

"What d'you want? A man must want something."

"I want to be left alone in my obscure corner, to strive for nothing, and to be at peace."

"But that's not life!"

"And I don't consider the life you lead is life, either. So you see I, too, must be right."

"You want to shape your life according to your own ideas. I can just imagine how nice it would be! I suppose in your sort of world lovers and friends would stray in couples among rose bushes."

Alexander said nothing.

Pyotr Ivanich looked at him in silence. Alexander had grown thin again. His eyes were sunken. Premature wrinkles had appeared on his cheeks and forehead.

His uncle was alarmed. Not one to put much faith in spiritual sufferings, he feared that some physical indisposition was at the bottom of this depression. "The fellow may go off his rocker," he thought, "and then I'll have his mother to deal with. I imagine the correspondence! Before you knew it she'd be turning up here!"

"You're disillusioned, Alexander," he said. "I can see that."

"How can he be led back to his favourite ideas?" he thought. "Wait, I'll have a try."

"Listen, Alexander," he said. "You've let yourself go

terribly. Shake off this apathy! It's not right! And what's
the reason of it? Perhaps you took it too much to heart
when I sometimes spoke slightingly of love and friendship.
I was only joking, you know, chiefly to moderate your
raptures which somehow don't belong to our practical age,
especially here in Petersburg, where everything is weighed,
studied, appraised ... where limits are set to everything.
Why be the only one to outwardly deviate from these
general rules? Surely you do not really consider that I am
callous, that I do not acknowledge the power of love!
Love is an exquisite emotion. There is nothing more sacred
than the union of two hearts; or take friendship, now...
At heart I am convinced that feeling should be constant,
eternal."

Alexander laughed.

"What's the matter with you?" asked Pyotr Ivanich.

"You're talking nonsense, Uncle! Won't you have a cigar?
You can go on talking and I'll listen."

"What's the matter with you?"

"Nothing. You thought you would bait me. And you
once told me you thought me no fool. You want to play
with me as if I were a ball, and that hurts. One can't be
a youth for ever. The school I have been through has at
least taught me that much. And you start haranguing
me. D'you think I have no eyes? You thought you would
do a little conjuring, but I saw through you."

"This is not for me," thought Pyotr Ivanich. "I'd
better send him to my wife."

"Come and see us," he said. "My wife is longing to see
you."

"Sorry, Uncle, I can't."

"D'you think it's nice of you to forget her?"

"It may be very bad, but do please excuse me, and don't
expect me to come yet. Wait a little—I'll come."

"Well, just as you like," said Pyotr Ivanich, and went
home.

He told his wife that he had given Alexander up—let
him do what he likes; he, Pyotr Ivanich, had done all he
could, and now he washed his hands of him.

Alexander, after running away from Julia, had plunged
into the whirlwind of noisy pleasures. In the words of our
well-known poet, he exclaimed:

> *Away, to where joy reigns supreme,*
> *Where vain delights fill all of life,*
> *Where song and mirth flow in a stream,*
> *Where festive gaiety runs rife.*
> *In this false happiness engrossed,*
> *I'll grow as commonplace as most,*
> *And reconciled to fate by wine,*
> *I will not let my heart repine,*
> *I'll bid my thoughts to cease their flights,*
> *I will not let my yearning eyes*
> *Look at the shining heavenly heights.*

A host of friends appeared, and with them the inevitable goblet. The friends gazed at their own countenances reflected in the goblets filled with foamy liquid, and in their polished boots. "Away with grief!" they cried gleefully. "Away with cares! Let us squander, destroy, burn up, drink away our life and our youth! Hurrah!" Glasses and bottles crashed against the floor.

For a short time liberty, noisy company, carefree life made him forget Julia and disillusionment. But not for him was the monotonous round of restaurant dinners, the same bleary-eyed countenances, the same foolish drunken ravings of boon companions, and, to crown it all, the same perpetual indigestion. Alexander's delicate physique and nervous system, tuned to a melancholy, elegiac mood, could not stand these amusements.

He forsook the merry games at the cheerful board, and took to his room, alone with himself, with his forgotten books. But the book slipped from his hands, the pen found no inspiration. Schiller, Goethe, Byron had shown him the dark side of humanity—the bright side he had not noticed, he had been too busy for that.

How happy he had once been in this room! He had not been alone—a bright vision had hovered about him, sheltering him during the day's earnest toil, keeping watch over his pillow at night. Dreams had been his companions then, his future had been shrouded in mist, not the dense mist which is the precursor of bad weather, but that of early morn, veiling the bright sunrise. There had been a secret something concealed behind this mist—happiness, no doubt... And now? Not only his room, but the whole world had become empty, and within him were only coldness and melancholy.

He inspected his life, questioned his heart, his mind, and was appalled to discover that not a single dream, not a single rosy hope was left anywhere—all that was behind him. The mists had dispersed, and he was confronted, as by a desert, by naked reality. Heavens, what a boundless vista! What a dull, joyless prospect! The past had perished, the future was destroyed, there was no such thing as happiness. All was chimera—and yet one must go on living.

He did not know himself what he wanted—but there was so much that he did not want!

His head seemed to be in a mist. He did not sleep, but dwelt in a kind of trance. Gloomy thoughts dragged across his mind. He asked himself what was left for him to take an interest in; captivating hopes, carefree moods, no longer existed. He knew all that the future held for him. A career, ranks, ambitious strivings? What use were they to him? Was it worth struggling just for the sake of another twenty or thirty years of this life? And would all this warm his heart? Would his soul rejoice when a few persons bowed low to him, at the same time probably thinking: "The devil take you!"

Love? Nothing new in that! He knew it by heart, and anyhow he had lost the ability to love. His memory, as if to mock him, assiduously reminded him of Nadenka, not the innocent, naïve Nadenka—her he never remembered—but always the treacherous Nadenka, with her whole background, the trees, the garden path, the flowers, and, in the midst of it all, the snake with the familiar smile, the flush of tenderness and shame ... and all for another, not for him... He clutched at his heart with a groan.

"Friendship," thought he, "yet another folly! Everything is known, there is nothing new, the past will never return, and yet you've got to go on living!"

He believed in no one and nothing, could not lose himself in pleasure, which he tasted as a man with no appetite tastes some delicious dish, coldly, fully aware that afterwards would come boredom, that there was nothing to fill the emptiness in his soul with. If one believed in feeling, it deceived one, roused one needlessly, and added a few more wounds to those already inflicted. When he saw people united by love, in ecstasies of joy, he would smile sarcastically and say to himself: "Wait a bit! You'll come to your senses! After the first joys begin jealousy, scenes of reconciliation, tears! If you live together, you will bore each other to death, and if you part, your tears will be redoubled. You will come together again, and that will be still worse. Poor crazy things! Perpetually quarrelling, sulking, making jealous scenes, reconciled for a moment, only to quarrel still more violently! That's their love, their devotion! They foam at the mouth, sometimes with frantic tears, stubbornly calling this happiness! And the thing they call friendship... Throw them a bone, and they'll fight over it like dogs..."

He was afraid to wish for anything, knowing how often, at the very moment of fulfilment, fate wrenches happiness out of our hands and offers something quite different, something you never desired—some spurious trifle. And even if fate does bestow on us what we wished for, it is only after torturing us, wearing us out, humiliating us in our own eyes, and then flinging us a bone as if we were dogs, who are made to crawl up to the titbit, to look at it, to balance it on their noses, to roll in the dust, to stand on their hind legs, till they hear the command, "Take it!"

The periodical alternations of happiness and grief in life also alarmed him. He foresaw no joy, nothing but sorrow ahead, inevitable sorrow. All are subject to the same law, all, it seemed to him, receive an equal share of joy and sorrow. His portion of happiness was over, and what had it been? A will-o'-the-wisp, a delusion. Grief alone was real, and it lay ahead. The future held sickness and old age and all sorts of losses, perhaps even poverty. All these *blows of fate*, as his aunt in the country called them, were lying in wait for him—and what joys would there be? His lofty poetical vocation had failed him, a heavy burden had been imposed on him, and given the name of duty. Nothing but the most despicable benefits remained—money, comforts, rank... The devil take them! Oh, how sad to have seen through life, to have realized what it is, but not to know what it is for!

And he indulged in his spleen, seeing no escape from the slough of these doubts. Experience had only exhausted him; it had failed to increase his vitality, to cleanse the atmosphere, to give him light. He was at the end of his teth-er. He tossed and turned on the sofa, going over the names of his friends in his mind and falling still deeper into dejection. This one was doing very well at his office, and enjoyed respect and fame as an efficient official, another had a growing family and preferred a quiet life to all vain worldly blessings, envying no man, desiring nothing. Yet another ... but why go on? They had all succeeded and were proceeding along the trodden path they had chosen. "I alone ... ah, what am I?"

Here he began to delve into himself—was he capable of leading, of commanding a squadron? Could he be con-tent with family life? And he realized that none of these things could have satisfied him. Some imp stirred restless-ly within him the whole time, ever whispering to him that all this was beneath him, that he ought to aim higher ... but where and how he could not make up his mind. He had been mistaken about his literary talents. "What am I to do? How am I to begin?" he asked himself, and knew not how to answer. And he was perpetually pes-tered by a voice which told him he might still be a leader or the commander of a squadron ... but no, it was too late, it would mean beginning all over again.

Despair wrung tears from his eyes—tears of vexation, envy, ill-will to all, tears of anguish. He bitterly repented not having listened to his mother and stayed at home in obscurity.

"Mamma foresaw my sufferings instinctively," he thought. "At home, all these restless impulses would have remained sound asleep. There would not have been this complex, seething life. And although all the human feelings and passions—vanity, pride, ambition—would have visited me there too, it would have been to an infinitely lesser degree, within the narrow confines of our district, and all these feelings would have been satisfied. To be first in the district! Yes, everything is relative. The divine spark from the heavenly fire, which to a certain extent burns within us all, would have shone mildly in me and soon have been extinguished in that idle life, or would have flamed in devotion to wife and children. My existence would not have been poisoned. I would have pursued my vocation proud-ly. My path in life would have been peaceful, would have seemed simple and comprehensible, life would not have been beyond my powers, I would have endured the daily struggle... And love? It would have become a luxuriant blossom and filled my whole life. Sophia would have loved me in that quiet. I would not have lost my faith in anything, I would have plucked nothing but roses, never have felt the thorns, I would not have known jealousy, for lack of competition. What drew me so strongly and blindly to that remote misty unknown, to the unequal and unfamiliar struggle with fate? And how wonderfully I then understood life and human beings! I would still be understanding them as I then did, that is to say, not understanding them. I expected so much from life and if I had not seen it so close, I would to this day be expecting something. What treasures I discovered in my own soul—where are they all? I have exchanged them for the world's coin, given my heart's sincerity, my first passion— and what did I get in return? Bitter disillusionment, the knowledge that all is deception, all is unstable, that one can place trust neither in oneself nor in others—and I have come to fear both others and myself. I have not been able, along with this analysis, to accept the trivia of life and be content with them, as my uncle and many others are. And now..."

Now he desired only one thing—oblivion of the past, peace, slumber of the soul. He grew colder and colder towards life, and surveyed everything with drowsy eyes. The crowd of humanity, the noise of festivities held only tedium for him, he fled them, but tedium pursued him.

He wondered how people could make merry, be eternally occupied, be carried away by new interests every day. He was surprised that everyone did not go about drowsy-eyed and weeping, like himself, and, instead of prattling about the weather, did not speak of grief and sufferings, or that, if they did speak of sufferings, it was only about pains in their legs or elsewhere, about their rheumatism or their piles. The body alone was the subject of their care, they never gave a thought to their souls. "Shallow, worthless creatures, animals!" he thought. And sometimes he would be plunged in profound meditation. "There are so many of them, of those worthless creatures," he would say to himself with a certain anxiety. "And I am alone... Can it be that all these ... shallow creatures ... are wrong ... and I!.."

Here he would begin to feel that he alone was wrong, and this made him more unhappy than ever.

He stopped seeing his old acquaintances, and the approach of a new one made him shudder. After his conversation with his uncle he sank still deeper into apathy, and his soul wallowed in drowsiness. He gave himself up to a kind of stupefied indifference, living in idleness, stubbornly fleeing anything which might remind him of the educated world.

"What does it matter how one lives, so long as one does live?" he asked himself. "Everyone has the right to interpret life in his own way. And when one comes to die..."

He sought converse with those whose minds were jaundiced and embittered, whose hearts had hardened, and rejoiced only when he heard jeering remarks about fate. Or else he spent his time with persons not his equals either in mind or education, chiefly with old Kostyakov, whom Zayezhalov had wished to introduce to Pyotr Ivanich.

Kostyakov lived in Peski, went about in a cap with a varnished peak and a dressing-gown belted with a handkerchief. He played cards with his cook of an evening. If a fire broke out anywhere, he was the first to turn up and the last to leave. If he passed a church in which a funeral service was being held, he would squeeze through the crowd to have a look at the dead man's face, and later would follow the coffin to the cemetery. He was a passionate lover of rituals of all sorts, both gay and mournful. He liked, too, to be present at various emergencies, such as fights, fatal accidents, the caving-in of ceilings, and so on, and would read newspaper reports of such events with gusto. In addition to this he read books on medicine, in order, he said, "to know what there is inside us". In the winter Alexander played draughts with him, and in the summer went fishing with him. The old man would chat of one thing and another—the harvest, the sowing if they happened to be crossing a field, fish and shipping when they came to the river. In the streets he would make remarks on houses, building materials and profits—never anything abstract. He regarded life as a fine thing when one had money, quite the opposite when one hadn't. A

man like that was no danger to Alexander, and could not
arouse any spiritual agitation in him.

Alexander tried to mortify his spirit as assiduously as
hermits try to mortify the flesh. At the office he was taciturn, speaking no more than a word or two when he
met an acquaintance, and soon beating a retreat, saying
he was in a hurry. But his friend Kostyakov he met every
day. The old man either sat in Alexander's room all day, or
invited Aduyev to share his dinner of cabbage soup. He
taught Alexander how to brew cordials, and make delicious fish and meat stews. They would sometimes go together to the country, to some village in the
vicinity. Kostyakov had a host of acquaintances everywhere. He talked to the peasants about their daily life, and
joked with the women, showing himself to be really the
chatterbox Zayezhalov had called him. Alexander let him
run on as much as he liked, but spoke very little himself.

Thoughts of the world he had abandoned came to him
with lesser frequency and intensity and, finding no reflection in his surroundings, did not reach his tongue, but
died away, still-born. Within him all was wildness and de-
vastation, as in a neglected garden. A little longer and he
would have been in a state of complete petrification. A
few more months, and all would have been over. But then
something happened.

One day Alexander and Kostyakov were fishing as
usual. Kostyakov, in a robe and a leather cap, deposited on
the bank several fishing-rods of various sizes and lines for
deep fishing, some with floats, some with little bells, attached to them. He smoked his short pipe, and keeping a
watchful eye on this battery of rods, among which was
Alexander's, too, for Alexander was leaning against a tree
and looking away. They remained thus in silence for a
long time.

"You have a bite, Alexander Fyodorich!" whispered
Kostyakov suddenly.

Alexander glanced at the water and turned away again.
"It's only a ripple," he said.

"Look, look!" cried Kostyakov. "A bite—it *is* a bite!
Oh, oh—get it, hold it!"

And indeed the float plunged into the water, the line
was jerked after it, and with the line, the rod, which had

been stuck in a bush. Alexander seized the rod and then the line.

"Steady, not too hard, not like that—what are you doing?" cried Kostyakov, pulling at the line eagerly. "My, my! What a weight—don't tug! Careful, it might snap! That's the way—right, left—this way, on to the bank! Step back! Further! Now pull, pull, but don't jerk! That's the way! That's the way!"

A huge pike appeared on the surface of the water. It whirled round and round, its silvery scales gleaming, its tail lashing from right to left, splashing them both. Kostyakov turned pale.

"What a pike!" he cried in something almost like awe and, leaning over the water with outspread arms, he fell down, stumbling over his rods, catching at the writhing pike with both hands. "Come on, on to the bank, there—further back! We'll get it, it won't get away! Look how it wriggles—what a devil! What a creature! Oh!"

"Oh!" repeated a voice from behind them.

Alexander turned. Two paces away from them stood an old man leaning on the arm of a tall, pretty girl, hatless and holding a parasol in her hands. Frowning ever so slightly, she bend forward, following Kostyakov's every movement with evident sympathy. She did not even notice Alexander.

The unexpected apparition embarrassed him. He dropped the rod, the pike fell heavily into the water, waved its tail gracefully and plunged into the depths, taking the line with it. It all happened in the twinkling of an eye.

"Alexander Fyodorich, what have you done?" shouted Kostyakov frantically, seizing the line. He tugged at it but it came out of the water minus both hook and pike. Pale as death, he turned to Alexander, showing him the end of the line, and glaring at him furiously for the space of a minute. Then he spat.

"I'll be damned if I ever go fishing with you again!" he declared, and moved towards his own rods.

Just then the girl, noticing that Alexander was looking at her, blushed and retreated a step. The old man, evidently her father, bowed to Alexander. Alexander returned the bow morosely, threw down his rod, and went to sit on a bench beneath a tree, some ten paces away.

"Even here there is no peace," he said to himself. "An

Oedipus and an Antigone! Again a woman! No getting away from them! Heavens—what a lot of them there are everywhere!"

"A fine fisherman you are!" Kostyakov said, fussing with his rods, and darting resentful glances at Alexander. "You can't catch fish! You ought to catch mice, sitting on your sofa! And you go fishing! How can you catch it if you let it go? It almost jumped into your mouth, it only wanted frying! I'm surprised they don't get away when they're on your plate."

"Are they biting?" the old man asked.

"Look!" replied Kostyakov. "Not a miserable minnow so much as nibbles at one of my six rods! And look what Alexander Fyodorich got from the floats—a ten-pound pike and he let it go! They say that game runs to meet a good hunter. But is it true? If it had got away from me, I'd have taken it out of the water myself. And here was a pike fairly jumping into your mouth, and you go to sleep—and call yourself a fisherman! A fisherman! Why, a proper fisherman wouldn't run a hair if a gun were to go off beside him! A fisherman indeed!"

By this time the girl had discovered that Alexander was quite a different sort of person from Kostyakov. His clothes, his figure, his age, his manners, everything about him was different. She swiftly recognized in him the signs of breeding and read thought in his face. Even the shade of melancholy did not escape her.

"What made him run away?" she wondered. "Funny, I don't think I'm the sort people run away from."

Drawing herself up proudly, she lowered her eyelids, then raised them, darting an angry glance at Alexander.

She was quite vexed. Pulling her father away, she passed Alexander with a majestic mien. The old man bowed to him again, but his daughter did not even deign to look at him.

"Let him see that nobody is interested in him!" she said to herself, stealing a furtive glance to see if he was looking at her.

Alexander, though he did not look at her, could not help assuming a more picturesque pose.

"Fancy—he doesn't even look!" thought the girl. "What insolence!"

The next day Kostyakov came to fetch Alexander to go fishing again, in spite of his curses of the day before.

For two days no one disturbed their solitude. At first Alexander looked around him as if in fear, but, seeing no one, calmed down. The next day he caught a huge perch. Kostyakov was half reconciled to him.

"Still, it's not a pike," he sighed. "Your luck was in your grasp and you could not profit by it. Such things don't happen twice! And again I have nothing! Six rods—and nothing!"

"Ring your bells," said a peasant, pausing on his way to see how the fishing was going. "Perhaps the fish will hear the ringing, and ... bite, you know."

Kostyakov looked at him angrily.

"Shut up, ignorant dolt!" he said.

The peasant moved on.

"Blockhead!" shouted Kostyakov after him. "Stupid ass! Joke with your own kind, damn you! You're an ass, I tell you! A yokel!"

Woe to him who irritates a sportsman in the moment of failure!

On the following day as they were silently watching their rods, gazing fixedly at the water, a rustle was heard from behind. Alexander turned and started as if he had been bitten by a gnat. There were the old man and the girl again.

Alexander looked at them askance, hardly replying to the old man's bow, but he seemed to have expected this visit. As a rule he went fishing very carelessly attired, but today he had put on a new coat and tied a sky-blue kerchief round his neck; his hair was carefully dressed, perhaps ever so slightly waved, and he looked like a fisherman in an idyll. He stood where he was a short time, for the sake of decency, and then went to sit under the tree.

"*Cela passe toute permission!*" thought Antigone, reddening angrily.

"Excuse me," said Oedipus to Alexander, "perhaps we're in your way?"

"No," said Alexander. "I'm only tired."

"Any bites?" the old man asked Kostyakov.

"Bites, with talking going on so near!" replied the latter crossly. "Just now a yokel passed by and had to stop and blab, and ever since—not a bite! I suppose you live somewhere near?" he asked Oedipus.

"That's our house, the one with the balcony," replied the latter.

"Do you pay much for it?"

"Five hundred rubles for the summer."

"Looks like a nice house, in good repair, and plenty of outhouses. Probably cost the owner about thirty thousand."

"About that."

"I thought so. And is that your daughter?"

"Yes."

"I thought so. Nice young lady! Taking a walk?"

"Yes, taking a walk. If you live in the country you must go for walks."

"True, true, why not go for walks? The weather's good, not like it was last week. What weather—oh my, dear God! The winter crops must have suffered."

"With the Lord's help they will recover."

"Amen."

"So you have no catch today."

"I haven't, but he has—look there!"

He pointed to the perch.

"I tell you it's a marvel what luck he has! A pity he doesn't give his mind to it, with his luck we'd never go home empty-handed. To let a pike like that go!"

He sighed.

Antigone began listening more attentively, but Kostyakov said no more.

The old man and his daughter came more and more frequently. Even Alexander deigned to bestow his attention on them. He sometimes actually exchanged a few words with the old man, but never with his daughter. At first she was annoyed, then she was offended, and at last she was grieved. If Alexander had spoken to her, or simply taken some notice of her, she would have thought no more of him. As it was, everything was different. The human heart, it would appear, lives on contradiction alone—if it were not for that, one might suppose there was no such thing in the breast.

At first Antigone conceived a terrible plan of revenge, but gradually gave up the idea.

One day, when the old man and his daughter came up to our friends, Alexander, after waiting a little while, rested his rod against a bush and repaired as usual to his place under the tree, glancing involuntarily from father to daughter.

They were standing half-turned away from him. In the father he could see nothing special. A white shirt, nankeen trousers and a low hat with a broad brim, lined with green plush. But the daughter! How gracefully she leaned on the old man's arm! Every now and then the breeze stirred a curl against her cheek, as if to give Alexander a view of her exquisite profile and white neck, blew open her silk cape exposing her slender figure, or lifted the hem of her dress, so that her slim ankles could be seen. She stood gazing pensively at the water.

For a long time Alexander could not take his eyes off her, and felt a feverish tremor pass through his frame. He turned away from temptation and began cutting off the heads of flowers with a stick.

"I know all about it," he told himself, "only let myself go, and everything will start all over again! And the next thing will be love—what madness! My uncle is right. But I am not to be led away by mere animal lust—I shall not sink so low as that."

"May I fish?" the girl was shyly asking Kostyakov.

"Why, yes, Miss—certainly!" he replied, giving her Alexander's rod.

"Well, now you have a companion," her father said to Kostyakov, and went off to wander along the bank without his daughter.

"Mind you catch some fish for supper, Liza!" he called.

For some moments silence reigned.

"Why is your friend so sulky?" Liza asked Kostyakov in a low voice.

"He's been passed over three times, Miss."

"What?" she asked, her brows twitching.

"Why, you see, three times they haven't given him promotion."

She shook her head.

"It couldn't be that," she thought to herself. "Not that."

"You don't believe me, Miss? May God strike me dead!

And that's why he lost the pike that time—remember?"

"It couldn't be that," she said to herself with conviction. "I know why he lost the pike."

"Oh, oh," she screamed suddenly. "Look, it's moving, it's moving."

She pulled the rod, but there was nothing at the end of the line.

"Got away," said Kostyakov, looking at the rod. "See— it took the worm! Must have been a big perch. You don't know how to fish, Miss, you should have waited for it to bite properly."

"And does one have to know how to fish?"

"Like everything else," said Alexander involuntarily. She blushed, turning sharply, and letting the rod fall into the water. But Alexander was looking away again.

"And how can one learn?" she said, with a slight tremor in her voice.

"By practice," replied Alexander.

"Aha!" she thought, secretly thrilled. "That is to say, come here more often—I understand! Good, I will, but I will torment you, Mr. Boor, for all your insolence."

It was thus that her coquetry interpreted Alexander's reply, but that day he said not another word.

"She will be imagining heaven knows what," he said to himself. "Soon she'll be putting on airs and flirting—idiotic!"

After this the visits of the old man and the girl were repeated daily. Sometimes Liza came without the old man, accompanied by her nanny. She would bring her needlework, or a book, and sit down under a tree, displaying the utmost indifference to the presence of Alexander.

She thought in this way to tease her pride and, as she had said, torment him. She talked aloud to the nanny about the house and household affairs, to show that she did not even see Alexander. Sometimes he really did not notice her, or if he did, greeted her coldly, with hardly a word.

Seeing that this banal manoeuvre got her nowhere, she changed her plan of attack and once or twice addressed him herself. Sometimes she took his fishing-rod from him. Gradually Alexander began to be more communicative, but he was extremely cautious and did not let slip a single cordial word. Whether this was strategy on his part or whether, as he said, his former wounds were still unhealed, he was sufficiently cold in his converse with her.

One day the old man ordered a samovar to be brought to the river-bank. Liza poured out tea. Alexander glumly refused to have any, saying he never took tea in the evening.

"All this tea-drinking ends in ... making friends... I won't have it!" he told himself.

"What? You drank four glasses last night," said Kostyakov.

"I never drink tea out of doors," added Alexander hastily.

"Your mistake!" said Kostyakov. "This is delicious tea, scented tea, probably cost fifteen rubles or so. Another glass, please, Miss, and it would be nice with a drop of rum."

Rum, too, was brought.

The old man invited Alexander to his house, but met with a firm refusal. When Liza heard this refusal, she pouted, and tried to find out from him the reason of his unsociability. But cunningly as she led the conversation to this subject, Alexander evaded it still more cunningly.

The mystery merely stimulated her curiosity and perhaps some other feeling in Liza. On her countenance, hitherto as clear as a summer sky, there appeared a cloud of anxiety and care. She often fixed a mournful gaze on Alexander, and then looked away with a sigh, lowering her eyes, as if thinking: "You are unhappy, perhaps you have been deceived... Oh, how happy I would make you! How I would look after you, love you ... I would protect you from fate itself, I would..." and so on and so on.

Thus argue the majority of women and thus do they allure those who listen to their siren song. Alexander appeared to notice nothing. He spoke to her as he would have spoken to a man-friend, or to his uncle. There was not a shade of that tenderness which steals unconsciously into the friendship of a man and a woman and makes their relations something different from friendship. That is why it is said that there can never be friendship between a man and a woman, that so-called friendship between them is nothing but either the beginning or the remains of love, or, perhaps, love itself. To see Aduyev and Liza, however, one might have believed in the existence of such friendship.

Only once did he partially reveal to her, or begin to reveal to her the course of his thoughts. He picked up from the bench the book she had brought, and opened it. It was *Childe Harold* in a French translation. Alexander shook his head, sighed, and silently put the book down.

"Don't you like Byron? Are you against Byron?" she asked. "You don't like a great poet like Byron?"

"I didn't say a word, and you attack me!" he said.

"Why did you shake your head?"

"Oh, I was only sorry that you should have got hold of this book."

"Sorry for the book or me?"

Alexander made no reply.

"Why shouldn't I read Byron?" she asked.

"For two reasons," said Alexander after a pause.

He placed his hand on hers, either for greater emphasis, or because her little hand was soft and white, and began speaking in low measured accents, his eyes travelling from Liza's curls to her neck and to her waist: with each resting place his voice gradually grew firmer.

"In the first place," said he, "because you read Byron in French, and consequently the beauty and power of the poet's language are lost on you. See how vapid and feeble the language is in this translation! It is the ashes of the great poet. His thoughts seem to have been diluted with water. The second reason why I would not advise you to read Byron is that he might awaken in your soul chords which might otherwise have remained forever asleep."

Here he pressed her hand firmly and expressively, as if by way of adding weight to his words.

"Why should you read Byron?" he continued. "Perhaps your life will flow as quietly as this stream. See how narrow it is, how shallow! It reflects neither the expanse of the sky, nor the clouds. There are no cliffs on its banks, no abysses. It flows playfully. Only the tiniest ripple ruffles its surface. It reflects nothing but the trees on its banks, a patch of sky, a little cloud ... and thus, no doubt, your life would flow on, if you did not seek unnecessary emotions and storms. Do not strive to see life and human beings through dark-tinted glasses. Do not read this book! Look at everything with a smile, do not look into the distance, live for the present day, do not investigate the dark side of life and human beings, or..."

"Or what?"

"Nothing," said Alexander, as if checking himself.

"No, you must tell me. You have probably gone through something yourself."

"Where's my rod? Excuse me, it's time for me to go."

He seemed perturbed at having expressed himself so incautiously.

"One more word," pleaded Liza. "Should not a poet arouse sympathy for himself? Byron is a great poet, why don't you want me to feel sympathy for him? Am I so stupid, so insignificant that I shall not understand..."

She looked hurt.

"It's not that at all. Sympathize with something that is more natural to your feminine heart. Seek a heart in harmony with yours, otherwise terrible dissonances may be awakened ... both in your head and in your heart."

Here he shook his own head, as if hinting that he had himself been the victim of such dissonances.

"One will show you a flower," he said, "and make you enjoy its fragrance and beauty, while another will show you nothing but the poisonous juices in its calyx ... and then both beauty and fragrance will be lost on you. He will make you wonder ruefully why these juices exist, and you will forget about the fragrance. There is a difference between these individuals and the sympathy they inspire. Do not seek poison, do not dig into the origins of all that goes on within and around you. Do not seek unnecessary experience. It is not this which leads to happiness."

He stopped speaking. She had been listening to him with grave trustfulness.

"Go on, go on," she said, now all childish submissiveness. "I could listen to you for days, obey you in everything!"

"Me?" said Alexander coldly. "What earthly right have I to rule your will? Forgive me for having ventured to make a remark! Read whatever you like. *Childe Harold* is a very good poem. Byron is a great poet."

"No, no, don't pretend! Don't talk like that! Tell me what to read!"

Assuming a learned air, he named a few historical works,

and books of travel, but she said she had had enough of that sort of thing at boarding school. Then he proposed Walter Scott, Fenimore Cooper, some French and English authors and authoresses, and two or three Russian authors, displaying, as if involuntarily, his own literary taste and tact. After this they never had a conversation like this again.

Alexander made heroic efforts to escape.

"What do I care about women!" he said. "I can no longer love, I have outlived those days."

"All right, all right!" growled Kostyakov. You'll marry, and then you'll see! When I was young I thought nothing of playing about with women and wenches, but when my time came I was like one possessed, it was as if someone pushed me into marriage."

And Alexander did not run away. All his former dreams raised their heads again. His heart began to beat more rapidly. Liza's waist, her foot, one of her curls flashed past his eyes, and life looked bright once more. For three days running Kostyakov did not have to persuade him, it was he who suggested going fishing.

"The same old story," Alexander said to himself. "But I am firm." And yet he made all haste for the river-bank.

Liza always awaited the arrival of the two friends with impatience. Every evening a cup of fragrant tea and rum was prepared for Kostyakov, and perhaps it was partly due to this ruse of Liza's that they never missed a single evening. If they were late, Liza and her father would go to meet them. When bad weather kept the friends within doors the next day endless reproaches would be showered both on them and on the weather.

After much thought Alexander decided, though why, he did not rightly know, to put a stop to these outings, and neither he nor Kostyakov went fishing for a whole week. At last, however, they started going again. They met Liza and her nanny almost half a mile from the place where they used to fish. She cried out when she caught sight of them, and then, suddenly embarrassed, blushed. Alexander bowed coldly. Kostyakov began chattering.

"Here we are!" he said. "You weren't expecting us? Hee, hee! I see you weren't—no samovar! We haven't met for a long time, Miss, a long time. Are the fish biting? I kept wanting to go but Alexander Fyodorich here wouldn't be persuaded. Sitting in his room all day ... and not even sitting, lying down."

She cast a reproachful glance at Alexander.

"What's the meaning of this?" she asked.

"The meaning of what?"

"You haven't been for a whole week, have you?"

"About a week, I think."

"And why not?"

"I didn't feel like it."

"You didn't feel like it!" she repeated in amazement.

"No. And what about it?"

She said nothing, but seemed to be thinking: "Can it be that you really didn't want to come?"

"I wanted to send Papa to town to look for you," she said, "but I don't know where you live."

"To town, to look for me? What for?"

"Funny question!" she said in injured tones. " 'What for?' I wanted to find out if anything was wrong, if you were quite well."

"Why, what is it to you?"

"To me? Oh heavens!"

"Oh heavens what?"

"Well, you see I ... I have your books." She showed her embarrassment. "To stay away a whole week!" she said again.

"Am I bound to be here every day, then?"

"Yes, you are."

"What for?"

" 'What for', 'what for'! " She looked at him mournfully, repeating, " 'What for', 'what for'! "

He glanced at her. What was this? Tears, confusion, joy, reproaches? She was pale and had grown a little thinner, her eyelids were red.

"So that's it! Already!" thought Alexander. "I didn't expect it so soon." He gave a loud laugh.

" 'What for?' you say! Listen," she began.

Determination gleamed in her eyes. She was obviously preparing the way for some important utterance, but just then her father approached them.

"Till tomorrow!" she said. "I must have a talk with you

tomorrow. I can't today. My heart is too full ... will you come tomorrow? You won't forget us? You won't forsake us?"

And she ran off without waiting for a reply.

Her father looked steadily from her to Aduyev, and shook his head. Alexander gazed after her in silence. He seemed to pity her and to be vexed with himself for having imperceptibly led her along this path. The blood rushed, not to his heart, but to his head.

"She is in love with me," Alexander said to himself, on his way home. "Oh, God, what a bore! How idiotic! I shan't be able to go there any more now, and the fish are biting splendidly! Very annoying."

And yet he seemed to be inwardly not altogether displeased, and for some reason was very cheerful, chattering incessantly to Kostyakov.

His obliging imagination did not fail to draw him a full-length portrait of Liza—her voluptuous shoulders, her slender waist—nor was the tiny foot forgotten. A strange sensation stirred within him, once more tremors ran over his whole frame, but died away before reaching his heart. He analyzed this sensation from its source to its termination.

"Animal!" he muttered under his breath. "So these are the thoughts which haunt your mind. Bare shoulders, breasts, a tiny foot ... to exploit trustfulness, inexperience, to deceive ... very well, deceive, and then what? The same old boredom, and perhaps remorse as well, and what for? No! No! I will not allow myself, I will not lead her to... Oh, I will be firm! I feel that I have the purity of soul, the generosity of heart. I will not perish, nor drag her down with me!"

Liza awaited him the whole day in pleasant excitement, but at last her heart sank—she grew timid, why, she knew not, she fell sad, she almost hoped Alexander would not come. When the appointed hour came and there was no Alexander, her impatience changed into weary sadness. With the last ray of sunshine all her hopes vanished, and she wept.

The next day she awaited him again, again started the morning in gay spirits, but by evening her heart ached still more painfully, and she knew fear and hope. Again he did not come.

On the third and fourth days the same thing! But hope still lured her to the river-bank. If a boat appeared in the distance, or two shadows flitted along the bank, she would tremble and all but swoon from the burden of joyful expectation. But when she saw that it was not they who were in the boat, that the shadows were not theirs, she let her head droop sadly, and despair take a firmer hold on her soul. A minute later cunning hope whispered to her some consoling excuse for the delay, and once more her heart beat in expectation. And Alexander stayed away, as if purposely.

At last, when one day she was sitting in her place beneath the tree, with despair in her soul, she suddenly heard a rustling. Turning, she started in joyful trepidation—before her, his arms folded, stood Alexander!

She stretched out her hands to him with tears of joy and for a long time was unable to recover her equanimity. He took her hand, gazing thirstily, as much moved as she was, into her face.

"You have grown thin," he said softly. "Are you unwell?"

She trembled.

"You stayed away so long," she brought out.

"And did you expect me?"

"Did I?" she replied eagerly. "Oh, if you knew!.."

She completed the sentence with a firm pressure of his hand.

"I have come to bid you good-bye," he said, and stopped to see how she was taking it.

She glanced at him in terror and incredulity.

"It can't be true!" said she.

"But it is," said he.

"Oh," she said suddenly, with a timid look all round her. "Don't go away, for God's sake, don't go away! I'll tell you a secret! Papa can see us from the window. Come to our garden, to the summer-house ... it faces the fields, I'll show you the way."

They turned and walked away together. Alexander never took his eyes off her shoulders, her slender waist, and was conscious of a feverish trembling.

"What does it matter," he thought, as he followed her,

"whether I go or not? I'll just have a look—see what it's like in their summer-house. After all, her father invited me! I could go there perfectly openly. But I am far from temptation, far, God knows, and I will prove it. I went straight to her and told her I was going away ... though I'm not going anywhere. No, Demon, you shall not tempt me!" But here Krylov's little imp, emerging from behind the hermit's stove, seemed to whisper in his ear: "Then why did you come and tell her? There was no need for that. You should not have come—you would have been forgotten in a fortnight."

But Alexander imagined that he was acting nobly in not shrinking from a deed of self-sacrifice, in struggling with temptation face to face. The first trophy won by his victory over himself was the kiss he stole from Liza, and then he put his arm round her waist and told her he wasn't going away at all, that he had made it up to test her, to discover whether she had any feeling for him. Finally, to clinch the victory, he promised to be at the summer-house at the same hour on the following day. On his way home he thought over what he had done, going hot and cold in turns. He was overcome with horror and could hardly believe it. At last he decided not to go the next day—and turned up before the appointed hour.

August had already come, and dusk was beginning to fall. Alexander had promised to be there at nine, but arrived at eight, alone, and without his fishing-rod. He crept up to the summer-house like a thief, looking round furtively, and every now and then breaking into a run. But somebody was there ahead of him. Whoever it was ran panting into the summer-house and sat down on a bench in a dark corner.

Somebody seemed to be watching for Alexander. He opened the door softly, in a violent state of agitation, tiptoed over to the bench and gently took the hand of—Liza's father. Alexander started back, as if to run away, but the old man held him by the skirt of his coat and forced him to sit down beside him.

"What did you come here for, sir?" he asked.

"I ... for fish..." muttered Alexander, scarcely moving his lips. His teeth chattered. The old man was by no means awe-inspiring, but Alexander, like any thief caught in the act, trembled in his boots.

"Fish!" repeated the old man mockingly. "D'you know the expression 'fishing in troubled waters'? I have been watching you for a long time, and I think I understand you now. And as for my Liza I have known her all her life. She's kind-hearted and trustful, and you—you are a dangerous rascal."

Alexander tried to get up but the old man detained him with a hand on his arm.

"Don't be angry with me, my friend! By pretending to be unhappy and avoiding Liza, you won her affection, assured yourself of this, and intended to profit by it. Do you call that honest? What am I to take you for?"

"I swear on my honour I did not foresee the consequences," said Alexander in a voice which carried profound conviction. "I had no intention..."

The old man was silent for a few moments.

"Perhaps that is so," he said. "Perhaps you tried to turn the poor girl's head not from love, but simply from idleness, without knowing what the result would be. If you succeeded—well and good, if not—never mind! There are plenty of young fellows like that in Petersburg. Do you know how such dandies are dealt with?"

Alexander sat there with lowered eyes. He had not the spirit to stand up for himself.

"At first I had a better opinion of you, but I was mistaken, grossly mistaken. Look what a meek fellow you made yourself out to be! Thank God I found you out in time! Now listen to me—there is no time to be lost. The silly girl will appear at the rendezvous any moment now. I kept a watch on you yesterday. She must not see us together. You will go away and of course never come back. She will think you have deceived her and it will be a lesson for her. But mind—you must never come here again. Find another place for fishing, or else ... I will turn you out, and none too gently. Be thankful that Liza can still look me straight in the eyes. I've been watching her all day... Otherwise you would leave this place by another road! Good-bye!"

Alexander tried to speak but the old man opened the door and almost pushed him out.

The reader may judge for himself of Alexander's situation, if he is not ashamed to put himself in his place for a moment. My hero actually shed tears, tears of shame, fury with himself, despair...

"Why do I go on living?" he said aloud. "Hateful, atrocious life! And I ... I... But no ... I had not the strength of character to resist temptation ... but I still have strength enough to put an end to this useless, shameful existence."

He strode rapidly towards the river. The water was black. Long, fantastic, distorted shadows raced over it. At the place where Alexander stood the river was shallow.

"One can't even die here!" he said scornfully and went towards the bridge, about a hundred paces further on.

Alexander stood in the middle of the bridge, leaning against the rail, and gazing at the water. Mentally taking leave of live, he sighed for his mother, blessed his aunt, and even forgave Nadenka. Tears of emotion ran down his cheeks. He covered his face with his hands. Who knows what he might have done, if suddenly the boards had not begun to shake beneath his feet. He turned. Heavens! He was standing on the edge of an abyss. The grave yawned before him. The bridge parted and moved aside to allow some barges to pass; another moment and all would have gone over. He mustered all his strength and took a desperate leap, landing on the other side. Once there he stood panting and pressing his hand against his heart.

"What's the matter, sir—had a fright?" the watchman asked him.

"Oh, brother, I almost fell into the very middle," replied Alexander tremulously.

"God forbid—think of that!" exclaimed the watchman, yawning. "Last summer a bargeman did fall in."

Alexander made off, his hand still clutching at his heart. Every now and then he glanced at the river and the open bridge, and immediately turned away, trembling and hastening his steps.

Every evening Liza dressed herself up and went out, without either her father or her nanny, and sat under the tree till late in the night.

The evenings began to be dark. She waited and waited, but there was not the slightest sign of life from the two friends.

Autumn set in. The yellow leaves fell from the trees and carpeted the banks of the river. The grass withered;

the river turned leaden-coloured, the sky was grey, a cold wind blew, bringing with it a fine rain. The banks and the river were deserted. There was no sound of gay songs, laughter, or resonant voices. Light craft no longer scurried about. Not a single insect buzzed in the grass, not a bird twittered in the trees. There was nothing but rooks and crows with their dismal cawing. And the fish no longer rose to bite.

And still Liza waited. She felt she simply must speak to Alexander—she had a secret to tell him. She sat on the bench beneath the tree, a sleeveless jacket over her dress, and a kerchief tied under her chin. She had grown thin, she was hollow-eyed. Her father found her in this state one day.

"Come, you've sat here long enough!" he said, wincing and shivering with cold. "Look, your hands are quite blue! You're cold! Come, Liza! Do you hear me?"

"Where?"

"Home. We'll go back to town today."

"Why?" she asked in surprise.

"Why? It's autumn—we are the only ones left here."

"Oh, dear!" she said. "It'll be nice here in the winter, too! Let's stay!"

"Now what have you got into your head? Come, that'll do!"

"Wait a little!" she said in imploring tones. "The fine days will come back yet!"

"Listen to me," said her father, patting her on the cheek and pointing to the place where the friends had fished. "They will not come back."

"Not come back?" she repeated in mournful, questioning tones, and then she gave her father her hand and slowly, her head drooping, went back to the house with him, every now and then looking over her shoulder.

Aduyev and Kostyakov had for a long time been fishing somewhere in the opposite direction.

V

Alexander gradually forgot Liza and the unpleasant scene with her father. Once again he was tranquil, even cheerful, and often laughed at Kostyakov's flat witticisms. This man's attitude to life was a perpetual source of amusement to him. They even planned to go somewhere far away and build a hut on the bank of some river where the fish were plentiful, and there live out the remainder of their days. Once more Alexander's soul was steeped in the ooze of petty ideas and the material side of life. But fate was wide awake, and he did not sink utterly in this ooze.

That autumn he got a note from his aunt earnestly requesting him to take her to a concert, for his uncle was indisposed. A celebrated European musician had arrived.

"A concert!" exclaimed Alexander, deeply perturbed. "A concert! To plunge again into the crowd, into the very glitter of all that tinsel, falseness, hypocrisy! No, I won't go!"

"And it'll cost at least five rubles too," remarked Kostyakov who was in the room.

"The ticket'll be fifteen rubles," said Alexander. "But I would gladly give fifty to get out of going."

"Fifteen!" exclaimed Kostyakov. "The rascals! They come here to swindle us, to steal our money! Damned loafers! Don't you go, Alexander Fyodorich—have nothing to do with it! If it was something real—something you could take home, put on the table, or eat ... but to pay fifteen rubles just for listening... You could buy a foal for fifteen rubles!"

"People sometimes spend even more for the sake of an evening's pleasure," said Alexander.

"An evening's pleasure! I'll tell you what—let's go to the baths, we'll have a nice evening! Whenever I feel bored that's what I do and it's fine! You go there about six and come back at midnight, warm your bones, scrape yourself clean, and sometimes make a nice new friend. Some clergyman, or merchant or officer comes in, and the conversation turns on trade, or, say, the end of the world, and it's so nice you don't want to go away! And all for sixty kopeks a head! And people say they don't know what to do with their evenings!"

But Alexander did go to the concert. Sighing, he took out his last year's frock-coat, so long unworn, and drew on white gloves.

"Gloves, five rubles—that's twenty," reckoned Kostya-kov, who was present at Alexander's toilet. "Twenty rubles—and all thrown away in one evening! It's hard to believe!"

Alexander had got out of the habit of being decently dressed. In the mornings he went to the office in his comfortable uniform, and in the evenings donned some old coat or other. He felt awkward in a frock-coat. It was tight in one place, felt uncomfortable in another. The satin cravat made his neck hot.

His aunt received him cordially, grateful to him for having brought himself to leave his seclusion for her sake, but she said not a word about his way of life or occupations.

When he had found a seat for Lizaveta Alexandrovna, Alexander leaned against a pillar in the shade of some broad-shouldered music-lover, and gave himself up to tedium. He yawned softly into his hand, but before he could close his mouth a thunder of applause broke out to greet the performer. Alexander did not so much as glance at him.

The orchestra struck up an overture, which went on for only a few minutes. As its last notes died away other sounds joined in very softly, at first gay and playful, reminiscent of children's games. Childish voices, noisy and jolly seemed to be heard. The sounds grew more flowing and more virile—expressing, perhaps, the recklessness of youth, audacity, an excess of life and strength. Then they became slower, softer, as if pouring out the tender effusions of love, of spiritual converse, and, gradually dying away, were merged in passionate whispers, till, imperceptibly, they ceased...

No one dared to move. The audience was silent and entranced. At last an unanimous gasp was breathed out, and ran in a whisper through the hall. The audience began to stir but suddenly the music poured out in a crescendo, in a torrent, the sounds scattered in a thousand cascades, leaping, jostling, trampling on one another. They thundered as if with jealous reproaches, seethed with the fury of passion. Hardly had the ear caught them, when they broke off, as if the instrument no longer had any strength, any voice left. Now from the violin there escaped a hollow, broken moan, now tearful imploring sounds came from it, and all ended in a prolonged, painful sigh. The listeners' hearts were wrung. The sounds seemed to be singing of love foresworn, of hopeless grief. All the sorrow and sufferings of the human soul could be heard in them.

Alexander was profoundly moved. Raising his head he glanced through his tears over his neighbour's shoulder. The lean German bending over his violin confronted the crowd, and imposed his will on it. He stopped playing, and passed his handkerchief over his hands and forehead. Voices roaring "bravo" and thunderous applause shook the walls. And suddenly this great artist bent low before the crowd, and began assiduously bowing in gratitude to it.

"And he bows to this mob!" thought Alexander, glancing timidly at the hydra-headed monster. "He, who is head and shoulders above it!"

The violinist raised his bow and all fell quiet on the instant. The swaying crowd had once more become a motionless body. Other sounds flowed, majestic, solemn—sounds which made the listeners sit up straight and lift their heads higher. These sounds aroused pride in the heart, inspired dreams of glory. The orchestra came in with muffled sounds, like the hum of a distant crowd, like the voice of the people.

Alexander turned pale and let his head drop on to his chest. With utter clarity these sounds seemed to be relating to him, his own past, his whole life, so bitter and disillusioned.

"Look at that man," said someone, pointing to Alexander. "I can't understand how people can show their feelings so! I heard Paganini, and I never turned a hair!"

Alexander cursed his aunt's invitation, the violinist, and above all fate, for not allowing him to rest in oblivion.

"And what for—to what end?" he asked himself. "What does fate want of me? Why remind me of my futility, the uselessness of the past, which will never come back?"

After seeing his aunt home he made an attempt to go away, but she held him by the arm.

"Won't you come in?" she asked reproachfully.

"No."

"Why not?"

"It's late. I'll come some other time."

"And you refuse *my* request!"

"Yours more than anybody else's."

"But why?"

"It would take too long to explain. Good-night."

"Just for half an hour, Alexander—please! Not more! If you refuse it means you never felt the slightest friendship for me."

She asked him with such feeling, such urgency, that Alexander had not the heart to refuse, and followed her with a drooping head. Pyotr Ivanich was in his study.

"Have I really deserved nothing but contempt from you, Alexander?" asked Lizaveta Alexandrovna, seating him beside the fire.

"You are mistaken—it is not contempt," he replied.

"What is it then? What shall I call it? How often have I written to you, invited you here, and you never came, and at last even stopped answering my letters."

"It wasn't contempt."

"Then what was it?"

"Oh, nothing," said Alexander, and gave a sigh. "Goodnight, *ma tante*!"

"Wait! What have I done to you? What's the matter with you, Alexander? Why are you like this? Why are you indifferent to everything, why do you go nowhere, and keep unsuitable company?"

"I just do, and that's all, *ma tante*. This way of life pleases me. It's peaceful, I like it. It suits me."

"Suits you? You find nourishment for your mind and heart in such a life, with such people?"

Alexander nodded.

"You are pretending, Alexander! Something has grieved you deeply and you won't talk! In the past you found someone to confide your sorrows in. You knew you would always find consolation or at least sympathy. And now—have you no one?"

"No one."

"You don't trust anyone?"

"No one."

"And do you never think of your mother ... of her love ... her tenderness? Has it never occurred to you that here, too, perhaps, there is someone who loves you, if not as she does, at any rate like a sister, or, still more, like a friend?"

"Good-bye, *ma tante*," he said.

"Good-bye, Alexander! I will not keep you any longer," said his aunt. Tears came into her eyes.

Alexander picked up his hat to go, but suddenly put it down and looked at Lizaveta Alexandrovna.

"I cannot run away from you—I have not the strength," he said. "What have you done to me?"

"Be the old Alexander again, if only for one minute! Tell me, confide in me..."

"I cannot be silent with you. I will pour out my soul to you," he said. "You ask why I hide from people, why I am indifferent to everything, why I don't even come to see you? Why? Know, then, that I have long been sick of life and have chosen for myself a way in which life makes less demands on me. I desire nothing, seek nothing but peace, the slumber of the soul. I have tasted all the hollowness and wretchedness of life and I despise it heartily. *Whoever has lived and thought cannot but despise humanity.* Activity, cares, worries, distractions—I am sick of them all. I wish for nothing, I seek nothing. I have no aim, for one gains that which one is eager for—and sees that it is all illusions. Joys have passed for me, I have cooled to them. In the educated world, amidst human beings, I feel the disadvantages of life more strongly, but alone, far from the crowd, I turn to stone. In this trance anything can happen, I see neither others nor myself. I do nothing and do not notice the actions either of others or myself—and I am at peace, I am indifferent. There can be no happiness for me, and I will not succumb to unhappiness."

"That's terrible, Alexander!" said his aunt. "At your age to be so indifferent to everything!"

"Why are you surprised, *ma tante*? Turn your eyes for a moment from the narrow horizon by which you are confined, look at life, at the world—what is it? Yesterday's greatness is today's nothingness; what was desirable yesterday is not desired today. The friend of yesterday is the foe of today. Is it really worth worrying about anything, loving, forming attachments, quarrelling, making up—in a word, living? Is it not better to sleep, mind and heart? I sleep, and therefore I go nowhere, especially not to see you. I almost went to sleep for ever, and you aroused my mind and my heart, and pushed me once more into the whirlpool. If you want to see me gay, healthy, perhaps alive, perhaps even, according to my uncle's ideas, happy—then leave me as I now am. Let these agitations calm down, let aspirations die away, let the mind grow torpid, the heart turn to stone, the eyes forget what tears are, the lips forget to smile and then—in a year or two I will come to you ready for any test—then you will not be able to arouse me, try as you may ... but now..."

He made a gesture of despair.

"See, Alexander," his aunt interrupted him eagerly. "You have changed in a single moment! There are tears in your eyes, you are the same as you used to be! Do not pretend, do not repress your feelings, give them an outlet."

"What for? Shall I be any the better for it? I will only suffer the more. This evening has destroyed me in my own eyes. I see clearly that I have no right to blame anyone for my sufferings. It is I who have ruined my life. I dreamed of glory—why? God alone knows!—and despised my work. I rejected my modest vocation and can no longer set the past to rights—it is too late. I fled the crowd, despised it, but that German with his strong, deep soul, his poetic nature, does not reject the world, does not flee the crowd. He is proud of their applause. He knows he is a mere insignificant link in the endless chain of humanity. He knows what I know, too. He is acquainted with suffering. Did you hear him tell the story of his life in sound—its joys and its griefs, its happiness and spiritual sufferings? He understands life. How trifling, how insignificant I appeared in my own eyes today, with my grief, my sufferings. He aroused in me the bitter consciousness that I am proud—and helpless... Oh, why did you invite me? Good-bye, let me go!"

"Was it my fault, Alexander? Surely I could not arouse bitter feelings in you—not *I*?"

"That's just the trouble! Your angelic, sweet face, *ma tante*, your kind words, the friendly pressure of your hand—all this confuses and moves me. I want to cry, to live once more, to suffer—and what for?"

"What for? Stay among us for good! And if you consider me the least little bit worthy of your friendship, it means you will find consolation in someone else too. I am not the only one—you will find someone to appreciate you."

"And you think this will always console me! You think I shall be able to believe in this fleeting emotion? You are a woman in the noblest sense of the word. You were made for joy, to make some man happy, but can one count on such happiness? Can one be sure that it is solid, that today, tomorrow, fate will not overturn this happy life—that is the question! Can one believe in anything or in anyone, even in oneself? Would it not be better to live without hopes and emotions, expecting nothing, seeking no joys, and, consequently, weeping for no losses?"

"There's no getting away from your fate, Alexander. It'll follow you even where you are now."

"I know that. But there fate has nothing to play with, I myself can play with fate—now it is a fish which gets away from the hook, just as I am stretching out my hand to take it, or it rains when I was going to go to the country, or the weather is fine, but I have no inclination to go out ... and all this is merely funny."

Lizaveta Alexandrovna could find no more objections to raise.

"You will marry ... you will love," she said uncertainly.

"I marry! What an idea! Do you really think I would trust my happiness to a woman even if I loved her, which is an impossibility? Or do you think I would undertake to make a woman happy? No, I know very well we should deceive each other, and both be deceived. My uncle Pyotr Ivanich and my experience have taught me."

"Pyotr Ivanich—yes, he has much to answer for," said Lizaveta Alexandrovna with a sigh. "But you were not bound to listen to him ... and you might have been happy, married."

"Yes, of course—in the country. But now! No, *ma tante*, marriage is not for me! I am no longer able to pretend after I have ceased to love, and I have stopped being happy, and I would not be able to help seeing if my wife pretended. We would both dissemble as ... for example ... you and my uncle do."

"*We* do?" exclaimed Lizaveta Alexandrovna in astonishment and alarm.

"Yes, you! Tell me, are you as happy as you once dreamed of being?"

"Not as I dreamed ... but happy in another way, perhaps a more sensible, better way, perhaps—what does it matter?" replied Lizaveta Alexandrovna in confusion. "And you would be too!"

"More sensible! Oh, *ma tante*, it is not you speaking—it is the voice of my uncle! I know what happiness means according to his system—it may be more sensible, but is it better? Why, for him there is nothing but happiness—unhappiness does not exist. But never mind him! No, no! My life is finished. I am tired, weary of life."

They both fell silent. Alexander glanced at his hat. His aunt tried to think of a means to keep him.

"And your talent?" she asked with sudden animation.

"Oh, *ma tante*, how can you laugh at me! You have forgotten the Russian saying—don't hit a man when he's down! I have no talent, none whatever! I have feeling, I used to have an ardent imagination. I took dreams for creative power, and tried to create. Quite recently I came upon one of my early sins, and read it—I wanted to laugh myself. My uncle was right when he made me burn everything I had. Oh, if I could bring back the past! I would dispose of my life quite differently."

"Do not give way to utter disappointment," she said. "Each of us has a heavy cross to bear."

"Who has a cross to bear?" asked Pyotr Ivanich, coming into the room. "Hullo, Alexander! Is it you?"

Pyotr Ivanich's shoulders were bowed and he moved his feet with difficulty.

"Not the sort of cross you mean," said Lizaveta Alexandrovna. "I was speaking of the heavy cross which Alexander has to bear."

"Now what has he to bear?" asked Pyotr Ivanich, letting himself down with the utmost caution into a chair. "Oh, the pain! What a visitation!"

Lizaveta Alexandrovna helped him to sit down, tucked a cushion behind his back and placed a stool for his feet.

"What's the matter with you, Uncle?" asked Alexander.

"As you see, I bear a heavy cross. Oh, my poor back.

There's a real cross for you! A reward for my efforts! Oh, my God."

"You're chair-bound, that's why. You know this climate," said Lizaveta Alexandrovna. "The doctor told you to take more exercise, but no—you sit writing from morning to evening and then playing cards all night!"

"Am I to go gaping about the streets and wasting time?"

"Well—there's your punishment."

"There's no escape from it if you go in for business. Who is there whose back does not ache? It's almost a mark of distinction for every businessman. Oh, I can't straighten my spine! Well, Alexander, what have you been doing?"

"The same as before."

"Ah! Your back will never ache then! It's really a wonder!"

"What is there to wonder at? Aren't you yourself partly to blame for his becoming like this?" said Lizaveta Alexandrovna.

"Me? I like that! Was it I who taught him to do nothing?"

"Indeed, Uncle, there is no cause for wonder," said Alexander. "You did much to help circumstances to make of me what I am now. But I do not blame you. I blame myself for not knowing how, or rather, for being unable, to profit by your lessons as I should have, because I was unprepared for them. Perhaps you are partly to blame for trying to change me though you summed me up at first sight. As an experienced man you should have seen that it could not be done. You aroused in me a struggle between two opposing outlooks and could not reconcile them. And what is the result? All within me is doubt, chaos."

"Oh, my back!" groaned Pyotr Ivanich. "Chaos! What I wanted was to make something of this chaos!"

"Yes—and what did you do? You presented life to me at its seamiest, and at my age, when I should have seen nothing but the bright side!"

"That is to say, I tried to show you life as it is, so that you should not stuff your head with silly notions. I remember what a hot-headed fellow you were when you came from the country. I had to warn you that one can't go on like that here. I may have saved you from many mistakes and follies. But for me you might have perpetrated many more."

"Perhaps. But you overlooked one thing, Uncle—happiness! You forgot that happiness is made up of illusions, dreams and hopes. Reality does not make people happy."

"What nonsense you talk! You brought these views with you straight from the borders of Asia. In Europe they have long gone out of fashion. Dreams, toys, illusions—all that will do for women and children, but men must know things as they are. Do you believe it would be better to go on being deceived?"

"You can say what you like, Uncle, but happiness is woven from illusions, hopes, belief in others, confidence in oneself—also from love, friendship... And you assured me that love is nonsense, a hollow feeling, that it is easy, and even better, to live without it. That to love passionately is no great virtue, we'll never outdo the animals at it..."

"Just look back and remember how you wanted to love—writing such bad verses, and speaking in such stilted language, that you bored your ... Grunya, wasn't it?—to death! Is that the way to win a woman?"

"What is then?" asked Lizaveta Alexandrovna coldly.

"Oh, what painful twinges in my back!" groaned Pyotr Ivanich.

"And then you assured me," continued Alexander, "that profound mutual affection does not exist, and that everything is habit."

Lizaveta Alexandrovna gazed with silent intentness at her husband.

"That is to say I spoke to you for your own ... oh, oh, my back!"

"And all that," continued Alexander, "to a youth of twenty, for whom love was everything, whose activities, aim, everything revolved round this feeling! Whom this alone could have saved or utterly ruined!"

"Anyone would think you were born two hundred years ago!" muttered Pyotr Ivanich. "You ought to be living in the days of fairy-tales."

"You expounded to me," said Alexander, "your theory of love, deception, treachery, cooling off... So that I knew all this before I began to love, and when I did fall in love I analyzed my love as a student dissects a corpse under the guidance of his professor, seeing not the beauty of its forms, but only muscles, nerves..."

"And yet I seem to remember this did not prevent you from being madly in love with that, what's her name? Dasha, wasn't it?"

"True. But you would not allow me to deceive myself. I would have seen in Nadenka's treachery nothing but chance misfortune, and have gone on hoping until I no longer had need of her love, but you were on the spot with your theory, and showed me that this was in the order of things, and I, at twenty-five, lost faith in happiness and in life, and grew old in my soul. Friendship you denied, calling it, too, mere habit. You called yourself, no doubt in jest, my best friend, simply because you had already proved to me that there was no such thing as friendship."

Pyotr Ivanich listened, rubbing his back with one hand. He defended himself carelessly, like a man who knew he could crush all the accusations brought against him with a single word.

"And a fine idea you had of friendship!" he said. "You wanted your friend to play just such a comedy as those two fools of ancient times—what's their name?—are said to have done, one of them remaining as a pledge, while the other—what was it he did? Supposing everyone were to go on like that—why, the whole world would be a madhouse!"

"I loved people," continued Alexander. "I believed in their virtues, regarded them as brothers, was ready to open my arms to them in a warm embrace..."

"And a lot of good that was! I remember your embraces," interrupted Pyotr Ivanich. "You bored me to death with them!"

"And you showed me what they were worth. Instead of training my heart through affection you taught me not to feel but to analyze, to examine people and beware of them. I did so, and stopped loving."

"How was I to know you would be like that? That you'd go jumping to conclusions! I thought this would make you more indulgent to others. I know people, and you see I don't hate them."

"What, you love people?" asked Lizaveta Alexandrovna.

"I'm used to them."

"Used to them!" she repeated dully.

"And he would have got used to them too," said Pyotr Ivanich. "But he was already thoroughly spoiled in the country by that aunt of his with her yellow flowers, and so his development was retarded."

"I used to believe in myself," resumed Alexander. "You showed me that I was still worse than others, and I hated myself, too."

"If you had looked at things more coolly, you would have seen that you are neither better nor worse than others, which was what I wanted you to see. Then you would have hated neither others nor yourself, and would have borne human follies indifferently, and have been more conscious of your own. I know my own worth, I see that I am not so very nice, but I admit that I am very fond of myself."

"Ah, you're fond of yourself—you're not just used to yourself!" remarked Lizaveta Alexandrovna coldly.

"Oh, my back!" groaned Pyotr Ivanich.

"Finally, with a single blow, without the slightest warning, without pity, you destroyed my best dream. I thought I had a spark of poetical talent—you ruthlessly showed me that I was not born to be a high priest of the beautiful. You tore this splinter out of my heart in the most painful manner, and proposed work which was highly distasteful to me. But for you I would have gone on writing..."

"And would have become known to the public as a mediocre writer," interrupted Pyotr Ivanich.

"What do I care about the public? I would have done my best for myself, and attributed my failures to hostility, envy, ill-will, and gradually grown accustomed to the idea that I must not write, and would have gone in for something else. Why are you surprised that, on learning the whole truth, I was plunged into melancholy?"

"Well, what have you to say to that?" asked Lizaveta Alexandrovna.

"I don't feel inclined to say anything. How am I to reply to such nonsense? Am I to blame that you, on arriving here, fancied that all was yellow flowers, love and friendship, that people do nothing but write poetry or listen to it—occasionally, just for a change, going in for prose? I proved to you that a man must work—everywhere, but here especially—and work hard, work till his back aches ... there are no yellow flowers, there are ranks, money. And these are a great deal better! That's what I wanted to make you see! I did not despair of your understanding at last what life is, especially life as it is now understood. And you did, but when you realized that there were very few flowers and poems in it you decided that life was a big mistake, that you had seen this and were therefore entitled to mope, whereas others, apparently not having noticed this, remain in the best of spirits. Well, and why are you discontented? What do you lack? Another in your place would bless his fate. Neither need, nor sickness, nor serious grief has ever touched you. What is it you lack? Love? You still haven't had enough? You've been in love twice, and been loved. You have been deceived, and you have had your revenge. We have agreed that you have friends such as few have. Not false friends, even if they are not ready to go through fire and water for you, and not fond of embracing. All that's simply idiotic, understand it once and for all! But friends always ready with advice, assistance, even money. What better friends could there be? In time you will marry. You have a career before you, you have only to work. And a fortune will come with it. Do as others do, and fate will not ignore you. You will come into your own. It's ridiculous to fancy yourself a special, great man, when you were not born to be one. Well, what have you to grieve over?"

"I don't blame you, Uncle. On the contrary, I appreciate your intentions and am heartily grateful for them. It can't be helped if they failed, can it? But don't you blame me either. We have not understood each other, that's the trouble. That which pleases and suits you and many others, does not please me."

" 'Pleases me and many others!' You're talking nonsense, my dear fellow! Am I the only one to think and act as I have tried to teach you to think and act? Look round you! Look at what you call *the crowd*, not at those who live in the country, all this will take a long time to reach *them*, but at the modern, educated, thinking and acting crowd. What do they want, to what do they aspire? How do they think? And you will see that they act and think as I have tried to teach you. It was not I who invented all that I expect of you."

"Who then?" asked Lizaveta Alexandrovna.

"The age."

"And is everybody bound to obey whatever this age of yours invents?" she asked. "Is all this so sacred, is it all so true?"

"It is all sacred," said Pyotr Ivanich.

"What! It is true that we should think more and feel less? That we should not follow the bidding of the heart, but restrain its impulses? Not indulge in sincere emotion, not believe in it?"

"Quite true," said Pyotr Ivanich.

"Always act according to a system, trust others as little as possible, consider everyone unreliable, and live by oneself alone?"

"Yes."

"And is that a sacred truth, that love is not the principal thing in life, that we should love our business more than the person dearest to us, not put our trust in anyone's devotion, believe that love must come to an end in coolness, deception, or habit? That friendship is only a habit? Is all this true?"

"It has always been true," replied Pyotr Ivanich. "Formerly people would not believe it, and now it has become a truth universally acknowledged."

"And it is sacred that everything must be examined, reckoned, thought out, that we must never try to lose ourselves in oblivion, never dream, never cherish an illusion simply because it makes us happy?"

"Sacred because rational," said Pyotr Ivanich.

"It is true, also, that one should treat according to the dictates of reason even the woman who is dearest to one's heart—one's wife for example?"

"Never have I had such a pain in my back ... oh!" said Pyotr Ivanich, writhing in his seat.

"Your back! A fine age, I must say!"

"A very fine age, a splendid age! Nothing is done from mere caprice—everywhere are reason, cause, experience, gradual progress and, consequently, success. Everything working for perfection and good."

"There may be some truth in what you say, Uncle,"

said Alexander, "but it does not console me. I know everything according to your theory, I look at things through your eyes. I am a product of your school, and yet I find life tedious, hard, unbearable. Why is that?"

"You are not used to the new order. You're not the only one. There are still backward individuals—they are all *martyrs*. They are pitiable, indeed, but what's to be done about it? The majority cannot stay behind for a handful of people. For all of which you have just accused me," said Pyotr Ivanich, after a pause, "I have one general justification—do you remember when you came here how I, after five minutes' talk with you, advised you to go back? You did not obey me. Why do you now attack me? I warned you you would never get used to the prevailing order of things, but you wanted my guidance, asked for advice, spoke in highflown terms of the achievements of the brain, of mankind's aspirations ... of the practical trend of the age! And there you are! I could not mollycoddle you from morning till night. Why should I? I could not cover your mouth with a handkerchief at night to keep the flies off, and make the sign of the cross over you. I spoke sense to you, because you asked me to. And what came of it is not my business. You are not a child, and you are no fool. You can judge for yourself. And instead of setting to work, you either groaned over the deception of a silly girl, or wept at separation from a friend, suffered from spiritual emptiness one moment, or from a superfluity of sensations another. What sort of a life is that? Why, it's torture! Look at the young men of today—what fine fellows they are! What mental activity, what energy, how deftly and easily they cope with all that nonsense which in your old-fashioned language is called *agitation, sufferings,* and God knows what else!"

"How easily you reason," said Lizaveta Alexandrovna. "Aren't you at all sorry for Alexander?"

"Not a bit! Now if his back ached, that would be something to pity him for! That's no invention, no dream no poetry, that's real trouble! Oh!"

"At least tell me what to do now, Uncle. How would you solve my problem with your common sense?"

"Do? Why ... go back to the country."

"To the country!" repeated Lizaveta Alexandrovna.

"Are you in your right mind, Pyotr Ivanich? What would he do there?"

"To the country!" echoed Alexander, and they both gazed at Pyotr Ivanich.

"Yes, to the country. You would see your mother, comfort her. You say you want a quiet life. Everything here upsets you. And where could it be quieter than there, beside the lake, with your aunt. Go, for goodness' sake. Who knows, perhaps you would ... oh!"

He clutched at his back.

A fortnight later Alexander resigned his post and went to say good-bye to his uncle and aunt. Alexander and his aunt were mournful and silent. Tears hung on Lizaveta Alexandrovna's eyelashes. Pyotr Ivanich alone spoke.

"Neither career nor fortune," he said, shaking his head. "Was it worth coming? You have disgraced the name of the Aduyevs."

"That'll do, Pyotr Ivanich," said Lizaveta Alexandrovna. "I'm sick of you and your career!"

"Eight years, my dear, and nothing achieved!"

"Good-bye, Uncle," said Alexander. "Thank you for everything, everything!"

"No need for thanks! Good-bye, Alexander. You don't need any money for your journey?"

"No, thanks. I have enough."

"How is it you never take any money? It makes me quite angry. Well, God bless you, God bless you!"

"Aren't you sorry to part with him?" put in Lizaveta Alexandrovna.

"H'm," muttered Pyotr Ivanich. "I ... have got used to him. Remember, Alexander, that you have an uncle and a friend, d'you hear me? And if you should ever need a post, work and filthy lucre, don't hesitate to turn to me. You will always find any of these three things."

"And if you should ever need sympathy," said Lizaveta Alexandrovna, "consolation in grief, warm, tried friendship..."

"And sincere effusions," added Pyotr Ivanich.

"...then remember," continued Lizaveta Alexandrovna, "that you have an aunt and a friend."

"He'll have plenty of that in the country, my dear. It'll all be there—flowers, love, effusions, even an aunt."

Alexander was touched. He could not say a word. On taking leave of his uncle he would have put his arms round him, though not quite so eagerly as eight years ago. Pyotr Ivanich did not hug him, but only took both his hands in his own and pressed them more warmly than eight years ago. Lizaveta Alexandrovna dissolved in tears.

"Ugh! A weight off my back, thank God!" said Pyotr Ivanich when Alexander had gone. "It doesn't even ache quite so much!"

"What harm did he do you?" asked his wife through her tears.

"Why, he fairly tormented me! He was worse than my factory hands! If they misbehave at least they can be flogged, but what was I to do with him?"

Alexander's aunt cried all day and when Pyotr Ivanich asked for dinner he was told that the table was not laid, and that the mistress had locked herself into her room and refused to see the chef.

"And all because of Alexander!" said Pyotr Ivanich. "Nothing but worry with him!"

He growled and scolded, and went to dine at the English Club.

Early next morning the diligence rumbled slowly out of town, carrying with it Alexander Fyodorich and Yevsei.

Alexander, thrusting his head out of the carriage window, did his best to put himself in a melancholy mood and at last vented his feelings in an unspoken monologue.

They drove past hairdressers' shops, dentists' rooms, dress-making establishments, and posh mansions.

"Farewell," he said, shaking his head and clutching at his thinning hair. "Farewell, city of false hair, artificial teeth, stuffed imitations of nature, bowler hats, city of courteous arrogance, artificial feelings, meaningless bustle! Farewell, majestic tomb of profound, powerful, warm and tender impulses of the soul! For eight years I stood face to face here with modern life, but with my back to nature, and she turned away from me. I have wasted my vital forces and grown old at twenty-nine. But there was a time when... Farewell, farewell, the city

Where I have suffered, where I loved,
And where my heart lies buried!

To you I open my arms, broad, blessed fields and mead-
ows of my native countryside! Enfold me once again,
and I shall be revived, my soul will wake to life and hope
once more."

After this he spouted a poem of Pushkin's, "The clumsy
dauber with his languid brush", wiped his moist eyes,
and nestled into the depths of the carriage.

VI

It was a glorious morning. The lake the reader knows
so well, on the banks of which the village of Grachi is
situated, rippled faintly beneath a light breeze. The dazz-
ling brilliance of the sun's rays, reflected in iridescent
sparks on the surface of the water, made the passer-by
involuntarily screw up his eyes. The weeping willows
dipped their branches in the lake; here and there, along the
bank, it was overgrown with sedge in the midst of which
hid great yellow flowers, resting on broad, floating leaves.
Every now and then a light cloud passed across the sun,
which seemed to turn away from Grachi for a few moments, and then the lake, the copse and the village were
instantly plunged in shadow. Only the distance was radiant
with light. But the cloud passed on, and again the lake
gleamed, and the cornfields seemed to be flooded with gold.

Anna Pavlovna had been sitting on the balcony ever
since five in the morning. What had brought her there—the
sunrise, the fresh air, the singing of the larks? No—she
never took her eyes from the road running through the
copse. Agrafena came to ask for the keys. Anna Pavlovna
did not so much as glance at her, but, her eyes still on the
road, handed her the keys without even asking what she
wanted them for. The chef appeared—she gave him a number of orders, without looking at him. The last two days
dinner had been ordered for ten.

Anna Pavlovna was alone again. Suddenly her eyes
shone—her whole being, body and soul, was concentrated in
her eyes, for a black spot had appeared on the road. Something was approaching, but very slowly. Oh, it was only a wagon coming down the hill! Anna Pavlovna frowned.

"What's that wagon doing here!" she grumbled.
"There's a roundabout road, but no, everyone has to

come poking round our way."

Displeased, she sank into her chair again, once more fixing her anxious gaze on the copse, seeing nothing around her. Yet there was plenty for her to see—the scenery kept changing continually. The air of midday, laden with the sun's sultry rays, was becoming close and heavy. Now the sun hid itself. It grew dark. The woods, the distant villages, the grass, everything was shrouded in a uniform yet sinister grey.

Anna Pavlovna came to herself with a start. Oh, heavens! From the west, like some live monster, spread a hideous black stain, coppery red at the edges and advancing rapidly upon village and copse, as if on vast outstretched wings. All living things were unnerved. The cows drooped their heads, the horses shook their tails, dilated their nostrils, neighed, and tossed their manes. The very dust they kicked up did not rise, but scattered heavily, like sand, beneath the wheels of the carriages. The cloud approached menacingly. Soon a distant roll of thunder was heard.

All was still, as if in expectation of something extraordinary. Where were those birds that had just been flitting about and singing in the sunshine? Where were the insects which had hummed in such a variety of voices in the grass? Everything was hushed and hidden, even inanimate nature seemed to share the ominous forebodings. The trees ceased their tossing and jostling of one another's twigs, and seemed to draw themselves up. Only now and then they inclined their crowns as if whispering to one another a warning of the imminent danger. The cloud had by now covered the horizon and formed a leaden, impenetrable dome. The villagers were making for their homes with all possible speed. There was a moment of solemn, universal silence. And then, from the woods, came a fresh breeze, like a herald, cooling the face of the traveller, rustling the leaves, banging a gate on its way, whirling the dust on the street and then sinking to rest in the bushes. Immediately after it sped a violent whirlwind, slowly driving a column of dust along the road. Now it came bursting upon the village, knocking down a few rotten boards in fences, lifting a thatched roof, whipping the skirts of a peasant woman carrying water, and driving the cocks and hens before it down the street, their tail feathers aflutter.

It passed. Again silence. People and animals were making for shelter. Only a foolish ram in the middle of the street had no forebodings, but went on chewing the cud indifferently and staring at nothing, unaware of the general alarm. A feather and a straw whirled along the road, as if trying to catch up with the wind.

Two or three big drops of rain fell—and suddenly there was a flash of lightning. An old man got off the bench where he had been sitting, and hastily propelled his little grandchildren into the house. An old woman, crossing herself, shut her window quickly.

The thunder crashed, drowning with its imperious rolling all other noise. A terrified horse tore itself loose from its tether and galloped round the field with the rope trailing, pursued vainly by its master. And the rain came pouring, thrashing, faster and faster, drumming on roofs and windows, louder and louder. A delicate white hand timidly put some flowers—the objects of tender solicitude—out on a balcony.

At the first clap of thunder Anna Pavlovna crossed herself and went indoors.

"No good expecting him today," she said with a sigh. "He's probably sheltering from the storm ... but he might come towards evening."

Suddenly there was the sound of wheels, but not from the copse—from the opposite direction. Someone drove into the yard. Anna Pavlovna's heart stood still.

"Why from there?" she wondered. "Could it be he wanted to take me by surprise? No, no, there's no road there!"

She didn't know what to think, but soon all was explained. A minute later Anton Ivanich appeared. His hair was now frosted with silver, and he had put on weight, his cheeks were flabby from idleness and overeating. He wore the same overcoat and the same wide trousers as before.

"I've been waiting and waiting for you, Anton Ivanich," said Anna Pavlovna. "I thought you weren't coming— I was in despair."

"How could you think that? If it were anyone but you, now! You can't get me to go just anywhere—but to *you*! I was delayed through no fault of my own—you know I only use one horse now."

"How is that?" asked Anna Pavlovna absently, moving up to the window.

"Why, you see the piebald has been lame ever since the christening at Pavel Savich's. That coachman of theirs—perdition take him!—had the bright idea of laying the old door of the barn across the ditch ... they're poor folk, you see, they hadn't any new boards. And there was a nail or a hook or something left in the door, the devil knows what! The moment the horse stepped on the boards it shied, and almost broke my neck. The careless idiots! And it's been lame ever since. Some people are such skinflints! You wouldn't believe what their house is like! Why, any alms-house is better kept! And every year they spend ten thousand rubles in Moscow, on Kuznetsky Most!"

Anna Pavlovna listened to him absent-mindedly, and shook her head slightly when he had finished.

"I've had a letter from Sashenka, Anton Ivanich!" she burst out. "He says he'll be here about the twentieth—and I'm so happy I don't know what to do with myself."

"So I heard, my dear! Proshka told me, at first I couldn't make out what he was trying to say. I thought he was here already. I fairly broke out into a sweat from excitement."

"God keep you, Anton Ivanich, for loving us!"

"Of course I love you! Why, I dandled Alexander Fyodorich on my knee! He's just like my own!"

"Thank you, Anton Ivanich! God will reward you! I haven't slept these two nights and I don't let the servants sleep. Supposing he was to arrive and we all asleep—that would be a fine thing, wouldn't it? Yesterday and the day before I went to the copse on foot and I would have gone today, but that accursed old age has got the better of me. I'm worn out with sleeplessness. Sit down, Anton Ivanich. Why, you're wet through! Won't you have something to drink, some breakfast? Dinner may be late, for we must wait for the beloved guest."

"Well, just a bite! As for breakfast, you know, I must admit that I've breakfasted."

"Where did you manage to do that?"

"I stopped at Marya Karpovna's on the way. I had to pass her house, anyhow, you know. I stopped more for the horse than for myself. I had to give it a rest. No joke rattling for twelve versts in this heat. And once I was there, I had a bite. A good thing I didn't listen to them and stay, try as they did to keep me, otherwise the storm would have held me up the whole day."

"And how is Marya Karpovna?"

"Quite well, and she sends you her greetings."

"Much obliged. And how's her daughter, Sophia Mikhailovna and her husband, how are they?"

"They're all well, my dear. The sixth child is on the way. It's expected in about a fortnight. They asked me to come round about that time. And such poverty in the house—I can hardly bear to go there! You'd think they had enough children—but no!"

"Really?"

"I assure you. All the doors are warped, the floor boards move wherever you step, the roof leaks. And no money for repairs, and all you get for dinner is soup, curd-pies, and mutton—nothing more. And yet you should see how they press you to come!"

"She used to be after my Sashenka, the old crow."

"As if she was a match for an eagle like him! I can't wait to see him! A handsome fellow he is, I wager! Let me see, Anna Pavlovna—hasn't he got himself engaged to some princess or countess, oh, and isn't he now coming to ask for your blessing and invite you to the wedding?"

"Anton Ivanich!" exclaimed Anna Pavlovna, overcome with joy.

"I'm sure of it!"

"Oh, you darling—God give you health! Oh, I almost forgot. I meant to tell you—I knew there was something, but I kept forgetting—what a good thing you said that, I should never have remembered. Will you have breakfast first, or shall I tell you now?"

"Just as you like, my dear—while I'm having breakfast would do. I won't miss a bite ... I mean a word."

"Well, then," began Anna Pavlovna, when breakfast had been brought in and Anton Ivanich was seated at the table. "I dreamed..."

"Aren't you going to have anything yourself?" interrupted Anton Ivanich.

"As if I could think of eating! The food would stick in my throat. I couldn't even finish my cup of tea this morning. Well, then, I dreamed I was sitting like this, and opposite me stood Agrafena with a tray in her hands. And I said to her, 'Agrafena,' I said, 'why is your tray empty?' And she didn't say anything but kept looking at the door. 'Dear me,' I said to myself, in my dream, 'why is she staring over there?' And then I followed her glance—and suddenly Sasha came in looking ever so sad, and he came up to me and he said, as plain as if it wasn't a dream, 'Goodbye, Mamma,' he said. 'I am going far away, over there,' and pointed to the lake. 'And I shall never come back again,' he said. 'Where are you going to, my love?' I asked him and my heart ached something terrible. He didn't say anything but just looked at me, very strangely and pitifully. 'And where have you come from, my darling?' I asked him then. And he sighed, the dear, and pointed to the lake again. 'From the slime,' he said, very low. 'From the water-sprite.' Then I began to shake all over, and woke up. My pillow was wet with tears. And for a long time I couldn't get over it! I sat up in bed, crying my heart out. When I got up I at once lit the icon-lamp in front of our Lady of Kazan. May she, our merciful protectress, keep him from all misfortune and calamity! I'm so worried, I can't make out what it means. Could something have happened to him? Such a terrible storm!"

"Why, it's lucky to cry in a dream! It's a good omen," said Anton Ivanich, breaking an egg against his plate. "He's sure to be here tomorrow."

"And I was wondering if we shouldn't go to the copse after breakfast to meet him. We'd get there somehow. But look at all that mud!"

"No, he won't be here today. I've had a sign that he won't."

Just at that moment the wind brought the distant jingling of a bell, and again all was silence. Anna Pavlovna caught her breath.

"Oh," she cried, giving vent to a sigh. "I wondered if it wasn't..."

Again the jingling.

"Oh Lord, oh Lord—can it be a bell?" she said, rushing out to the balcony.

"No," said Anton Ivanich, "it's the foal pasturing somewhere near, it has a bell on its neck. I noticed it on my way. I shooed it off, or it would have wandered into the rye. Why don't you have it hobbled?"

Suddenly the bell seemed to be jingling right under the balcony and the sound grew louder and louder.

"Oh, dear, it is, it is! It's coming here! It's he, it's he!" cried Anna Pavlovna. "Run, Anton Ivanich! Where's everybody? Where's Agrafena? There's nobody about! He might as well be coming to a strange house, dear God!"

She was almost frantic. The bell seemed to be jingling in the room now.

Anton Ivanich jumped up from the table.

"It's he, it's he!" he cried. "That's Yevsei on the box! Where's your icon, and the bread and salt? Get them, quick! What shall I take out to him in the porch? He must be met with bread and salt—it's an omen. Why aren't things done properly here? Nobody remembered? And you, Anna Pavlovna, why do you stand there, why don't you go to meet him? Run, run!"

"I can't," she brought out with difficulty. "My legs won't move!"

With these words she sank on to a chair. Anton Ivanich snatched a piece of bread from the table, placed it on a plate, added the salt-cellar, and dashed to the door.

"Nothing prepared!" he scolded.

But at the very door he was met by three menservants and two maids, rushing in.

"He's coming! He's coming! He's here!" they shouted, as pale and terrified as if it were highwaymen who had come.

Immediately after them appeared Alexander himself.

"Sashenka, my dear one!" exclaimed Anna Pavlovna, but checked herself and looked at Alexander in astonishment. "Where's Sashenka?" she asked.

"Here I am, Mamma!" he said, kissing her hand.

"Is it you?"

She gazed at him intently.

"Is it really, really you, my beloved?" she repeated, embracing him.

Then she took another look at him.

"But what's the matter with you? Are you ill?" she asked anxiously, still holding him in her embrace.

"I'm quite well, Mamma."

"Well, just look at yourself, my darling! Is that how I sent you away?"

She pressed him to her heart and wept bitterly. She kissed his head, his cheeks, his eyes.

"Where is your hair? It was like silk," she moaned through her tears. "Your eyes shone like twin stars, your cheeks were like milk and roses. You were like a ripe apple. Wicked men must have wished a sickness on you, they envied your looks and my happiness! What was your uncle thinking about? I gave you into his care, believing him a man of sense. He didn't take proper care of my treasure! My darling!"

The old woman wept and showered caresses on Alexander.

"So it's not always lucky to dream of tears!" thought Anton Ivanich.

"Why are you keening over him as if he were dead?" he whispered. "Don't do that! It's unlucky."

"Welcome home, Alexander Fyodorich," he said. "God has willed that we should meet again on this earth."

Alexander gave him his hand in silence. Anton Ivanich went to see if everything had been taken out of the carriage and then went to summon the household servants to greet their master. But they were already crowding the hall and the entrance. Anton Ivanich made them line up and told them what to do—who was to kiss the master's hand, who his shoulder, who the hem of his coat, and what they were to say at the same time. One lad he sent packing right away, saying, "First go and wash your face and wipe your nose."

Yevsei, wearing a leather belt, exchanged greetings with the other servants, who came crowding round him. He handed out his Petersburg gifts—a silver ring for this one, a birch snuff-box for that. When he saw Agrafena he stood as if transfixed and looked at her in silent, sheepish rapture. She glanced at him sideways, frowning, but the next moment her expression changed in spite of herself, and she first laughed for joy, then almost cried, and again turned away huffily.

"Why don't you say something?" she said. "What a blockhead! You don't even say a word of greeting to me!"

But he could not speak. He went up to her with the same

sheepish smile on his face. She hardly allowed him to give her a hug.

"Turned up like a bad penny, he has!" she said crossly, darting furtive glances at him, but her eyes and her smile showed how great her joy was. "I suppose they've turned your heads, yours and your master's, there in Petersburg. Look at the moustache you've grown!"

He produced a small cardboard box from his pocket and handed it to her. In it was a pair of brass ear-rings. Then he took a parcel containing a big shawl out of his bag.

She seized it and thrust both gifts into the wardrobe without looking at them.

"Show us your presents, Agrafena Ivanovna!" said some of the servants.

"What is there to show? Haven't you ever seen a present before? Off with you! What are you crowding round here for?" she shouted.

"And here's some more!" said Yevsei, handing her another parcel.

"Show us, show us!" they insisted.

Agrafena tore off the paper and several packs of cards fell out, used but still almost new.

"Couldn't you find anything better?" said Agrafena. "You think I have nothing to do but play cards! The idea! As if I would play with you."

But she put away the cards too. An hour later Yevsei was once more seated in his old place, between the table and the stove.

"Lord, what peace!" he said, stretching and bending his knees. "There's no place like home! We had a dog's life over there in Petersburg! Would you give me something to eat, Agrafena Ivanovna? We haven't had a bite since the last stopping-place."

"So you haven't given up your old habits? Here you are! Look how he falls on it! I can see you haven't been fed at all!"

Alexander made the round of all the rooms, and then went through the garden, stopping at every bush, at every bench. His mother accompanied him. Looking into his pale face she sighed, but was afraid to weep: Anton Ivanich had told her it was bad luck. She questioned her son about his life, but could not get at the cause of his having become so thin and pale, and having lost so much of his hair. She offered him food and drink, but he would not touch anything, saying that he was tired after his journey and wanted to sleep.

Anna Pavlovna went to see if his bed had been made properly, scolded the maid because it was hard, made her do it all over again while she looked on, and did not go away till Alexander had lain down. She went out of the room on tiptoe, adjuring the servants, with many threats, not to dare to speak, not even to breathe too loud, and to take off their boots. Then she sent for Yevsei, who came accompanied by Agrafena. Yevsei bowed low to his mistress and kissed her hand.

"What's happened to Sashenka?" she demanded fiercely. "Why does he look so ill, eh?"

Yevsei said nothing.

"Why don't you answer?" said Agrafena. "Don't you hear what the mistress says?"

"Why is he so thin?" asked Anna Pavlovna. "Where has his hair gone?"

"I cannot say, Madam," said Yevsei. "It's the master's business."

"You can't say! And where were you all this time?"

"Look who you trusted in, Madam," put in Agrafena, gazing affectionately at Yevsei. "As if he were any good! What did you do there? Come on, tell the mistress! Or you'll get it!"

"And didn't I do my best, Madam?" said Yevsei timidly, glancing from his mistress to Agrafena. "I served him truly—ask Arkhipich."

"And who's Arkhipich?"

"The yardman there."

"Hark to him!" cried Agrafena. "Take no notice of him, Madam! Lock him up in the shed, he'll soon find something to say."

"I'm ready not only to serve my masters but even to die for them," continued Yevsei. "I will swear on the icon."

"You're all good at talking," said Anna Pavlovna, "but when it comes to doing, where are you? I can see how well you looked after your master! You let my darling lose his health. Looked after him! You just wait..."

She shook her finger at him.

"I didn't look well after him, Madam? In eight years only one of his shirts has been lost, even the worn-out ones are all there."

"And where was it lost?" asked Anna Pavlovna fiercely.

"At the washerwoman's. I told Alexander Fyodorich at the time to deduct it from the bill, but he didn't say anything."

"The hussy!" said Anna Pavlovna. "I suppose she was tempted by such good linen."

"I didn't look well after him!" repeated Yevsei. "If only every one did his duty as well as I! Why, every morning while he was still asleep I ran to the baker's."

"What sort of rolls did he eat?"

"White ones, very good."

"I know they were white—but were they rich buns?"

"The dunce!" said Agrafena. "Hasn't a word to say for himself, and he from Petersburg!"

"No, no!" said Yevsei. "Plain rolls."

"Plain! You rascal, you! You robber!" cried Anna Pavlovna, crimson with rage. "You couldn't even buy him rich rolls! And you say you looked after him well."

"But he never told me to, Madam!"

"Never told you! He doesn't care what you put in front of him, the darling will eat anything! And it never came into your head. D'you mean to say you forgot that he always ate rich rolls here? Buying plain rolls! No doubt you spent the money elsewhere. Oh, what a rogue! Well, what else, tell me."

"After he had his tea," continued Yevsei, much subdued, "he went to his office and I fell to polishing his boots. I polished them the whole morning, all of them, three times over sometimes. And when he took them off in the evening I polished them again. You say I didn't look after him, Madam! Why, I never saw such boots on any other gentleman! Pyotr Ivanich's boots weren't so well polished, and they have three menservants!"

"But why does he look so ill?" asked Anna Pavlovna, somewhat mollified.

"It must be from the writing, Madam."

"Did he write a lot?"

"A lot—every day."

"What did he write—papers?"

"It must have been papers."

"And you didn't try to stop him?"

"I tried, Madam. 'Don't sit there, Alexander Fyodorich,' I told him. 'Why don't you go out? It's lovely weather, ever so many ladies and gentlemen are out walking. What's the good of all this writing? You'll ruin your chest. Your Mamma will be angry.'"

"And what did he say?"

"He said, 'Get out! You're a fool!' he said."

"And so you are a fool!" commented Agrafena.

At this Yevsei glanced at her, and then turned his gaze upon his mistress again.

"And didn't his uncle try to stop him?" asked Anna Pavlovna.

"He, Madam! If he found the master not doing anything when he came he would be at him at once. 'What, doing nothing? This isn't the country,' he says. 'You must work, and not lie about! Always dreaming!' And he'd go on and on scolding him."

"Scolding him!"

"'Provincial,' he says, and he'd go on and on, scolding him so that sometimes it made me sick to hear him."

"A curse on him!" said Anna Pavlovna, and she spat vehemently. "He should have raised a brood of his own to scold. Instead of taking care of him, he ... goodness gracious me! Who is one to trust nowadays when one's own kin are worse than the wild beasts? A dog looks after its puppies, but an uncle made his own nephew sicken! And you, you poor fool, couldn't you tell him not to dare to scold your master, to leave my boy alone! Why didn't he shout at his wife, the hussy! He found the right person to nag at, 'Work, work!' Let him wear himself out with working! The cur, the cur if there ever was one, God forgive me! Trying to make a slave of my boy!"

After this silence ensued.

"Has Sashenka been so thin for a long time?" she resumed.

"About three years," replied Yevsei. "Alexander Fyodorich became very down-hearted, ate badly, and grew thinner and thinner, wasting away like a candle."

"What made him down-hearted?"

"God alone knows, Madam! Pyotr Ivanich spoke to him about it. I tried to listen to what he said, but it was no good. I couldn't understand a thing."

"Well, and what was it he said?"

Yevsei thought a moment, his lips moving, apparently trying to remember.

"He called him something ... but I've forgotten what."

Anna Pavlovna and Agrafena looked at him, waiting impatiently for his reply.

"Well," said Anna Pavlovna.

Yevsei said nothing.

"Say something, you dolt," added Agrafena. "The mistress is waiting."

"Dis ... dis ... illusioned," brought out Yevsei at last.

Anna Pavlovna looked in astonishment at Agrafena, Agrafena looked at Yevsei, Yevsei looked from one to the other, and none of them spoke.

"What?" asked Anna Pavlovna.

"Dis ... dis ... illusioned, that was it, I remember now," said Yevsei firmly.

"And what sort of affliction is that? Heavens! Is it an illness?" asked Anna Pavlovna dismally.

"It doesn't mean bewitched, does it, Madam?" asked Agrafena hurriedly.

Anna Pavlovna turned pale and spat.

"Blast your tongue!" she said. "Did he go to church?"

Yevsei showed signs of embarrassment.

"I can't say he went so very often, Madam," he faltered. "I might almost say he never went. The gentry don't go to church much, there."

"So that's it," said Anna Pavlovna, sighing and crossing herself. "It seems my poor prayers were not enough for the Lord. Dreams never deceive—he really has been in the slime, the darling!"

At this moment Anton Ivanich came in.

"Dinner's getting cold, Anna Pavlovna," he said. "Isn't it time to wake Alexander Fyodorich?"

"No, no, for mercy's sake!" she replied. "He asked us not to wake him. 'Eat by yourselves,' he said. 'I have no appetite, I'd rather sleep,' he said. 'Sleep will strengthen me—perhaps I may feel like eating in the evening.' And you, Anton Ivanich, don't be angry with an old woman like me! I'll go and light the icon-lamp and say a prayer while Sashenka sleeps. I don't feel like eating. Have your dinner by yourself."

"Very well, my dear, I will. You can rely on me."

"And will you be so kind," she continued, "you are our friend, you love us—send for Yevsei and try and find out from him why Sashenka has grown so grave and so thin, and why his hair has gone. You're a man, it'll be easier for you. I wonder if anyone was unkind to him there? You know what a lot of bad people there are in the world—find out everything."

"Very well, my dear, very well! I'll get it out of him, I'll ferret out the truth. Send Yevsei to me while I'm having dinner, I'll do everything you ask me."

"Hullo, Yevsei," he said, seating himself at the table and tucking his napkin into his collar. "How are you?"

"Good-afternoon, sir. What sort of a life was ours? A poor one! Look how fine and stout you got, living here."

Anton Ivanich spat over his left shoulder superstitiously.

"Don't tempt Providence, brother—anything may happen," he said and started on the cabbage soup.

"Well, how did you get on there?" he asked.

"Nothing special—not very well."

"The food was good, I suppose. What did you eat?"

"What did I eat? I used to go to the shop and buy brawn and cold pie—and that was my dinner."

"To the shop? Didn't you have your own stove?"

"We didn't do any cooking at home. Bachelor gentlemen never do there."

"Fancy that!" exclaimed Anton Ivanich, laying down his spoon.

"It's true—the master had his dinners sent in from the restaurant."

"A gipsy life. No wonder he's thin. Here, drink up!"

"Thank you humbly, sir! Your health!"

Silence ensued. Anton Ivanich went on eating.

"How much are cucumbers there?" he asked reaching for one.

"Forty kopeks for ten."

"No, really?"

"Cross my heart! Why, it's a disgrace to say it, sir,

but sometimes pickled cucumbers were sent from Moscow."

"Oh heavens! How could anyone help getting thin?"

"You'd never see one like that there," went on Yevsei, pointing to a cucumber. "Not in your sleep, you wouldn't. Sickly little things. You wouldn't so much as look at them, and the gentry eat them there. There are very few houses, sir, where they bake their own bread. And as for storing cabbage or salting pork, or pickling mushrooms—why, there's no such thing!"

Anton Ivanich shook his head but said nothing, for his mouth was as full as he could cram it.

"How can that be?" he said, when he had got it all down.

"You buy everything at the shop, and what you can't find there you get at the sausage-shop, or else at the pastry-cook's. And if there's none at the pastry-cook's you go to the English shop. The French have everything, too."

Silence.

"Well, and what do sucking-pigs cost?" asked Anton Ivanich, helping himself to almost half a sucking-pig.

"I couldn't say, sir. We never bought one. They're very dear, about two rubles, I believe."

"Goodness, how could any one help getting thin? How expensive!"

"The gentry don't eat much—only the officials do."

Again silence.

"Well—and so it was bad there," suggested Anton Ivanich.

"God knows how bad! Why, the beer there is thinner than the kvass here. And as for the kvass it sort of rumbles in your stomach all day. The only thing that is good there is the boot-polish. You never saw such boot-polish! And how it smells—good enough to eat."

"No, really?"

"Upon my word!"

Silence.

"Well, and how was it?" asked Anton Ivanich after a pause for mastication.

"Nothing special."

"The food was bad?"

"Very bad. Alexander Fyodorich hardly ate at all—he quite lost the habit of eating. Didn't eat even a pound of bread at dinner."

"Just try not to get thin!" said Anton Ivanich. "And all because it was expensive!"

"It was expensive, and people don't eat their fill there every day. The gentry eat on the sly-like, once a day, if they have the time, at five o'clock, or sometimes even six. But generally they just have a bite and that's all. Eating is the last thing they think of—first they do all their business, and only then eat."

"What a life!" said Anton Ivanich. "Just try not to get thin! It's a wonder you didn't both die! And is it like that all the time?"

"Oh no! You should see the gentry, when they get together on holidays! They dine in some German restaurant, and they say they eat up a hundred rubles' worth. And the stuff they drink, my God! Even worse than we poor fellows do! At Pyotr Ivanich's the guests would sit down to table about six o'clock, and only get up at four in the morning."

Anton Ivanich stared.

"Really!" he said. "Eating all the time?"

"Eating all the time."

"I'd like to see that—it's not our way! And what do they eat?"

"Why, nothing much to look at, sir. You don't know what you're eating. The Germans put God knows what into the food, you wouldn't want to touch it! Even their pepper is different. They pour stuff from all sorts of foreign bottles into the sauce. Pyotr Ivanich's cook once gave me a taste of what he serves to the gentry, and I was sick for three days. I saw there was an olive in it, and I thought it was just an olive, like we eat them here. I tasted it, and what do you think—there was a tiny fish inside it. I was disgusted and spat it out. I took another, just the same thing! And the same everywhere, damn them!"

"And do they put it in on purpose?"

"God alone knows! I asked, and the fellows laughed, and said, 'They grow like that.' And what food! First they serve soup, all very nice, with pies, but pies not much bigger than a thimble. You stuff half a dozen into your mouth at one go, and before you start chewing them there's nothing left, as if they had melted. After the soup all of a sudden comes the sweet course, and then beef and after that ice-cream, and then some sort of green stuff, and then again roast meat... Such a mess!"

"So you didn't cook at home! No wonder he's thin!" remarked Anton Ivanich, getting up.

"I thank thee, o Lord," he said aloud, sighing deeply, "for feeding me with divine blessings ... oh my, what am I saying ... earthly blessings, and for not depriving me of thy heavenly kingdom." Then he addressed Yevsei.

"Clear the table. The master and mistress will not dine. Order another sucking-pig for the evening—or perhaps there's a turkey. Alexander Fyodorich used to like turkey. I should think he'll wake up hungry. And now bring an armful of fresh hay to the attic. I'll rest for an hour or two. You can wake me for tea. If Alexander Fyodorich so much as stirs ... give me a push."

After his nap he sought out Anna Pavlovna.

"Well, Anton Ivanich?" she asked.

"Thanks, my dear, my humble thanks for your bread and salt ... and I've had a good sleep. The hay was so fresh, so fragrant..."

"You're welcome, Anton Ivanich! Well, and what does Yevsei say? Did you question him?"

"Of course I did. I got it all out of him. It's nothing. It'll all pass. It all comes from the food there being so bad."

"The food?"

"Yes. Judge for yourself! Cucumbers forty kopeks for ten. Sucking-pig two rubles, and all the meals from the pastry-cook's—and never eating one's fill. No wonder he got thin! Don't worry, my dear, we'll put him on his legs here, we'll cure him. Have plenty of birch-cordial made. I'll give you the recipe. I got it from Prokofy Astafich. You can give him one or two wine-glasses morning and evening, and there'll be no harm in giving one before dinner, too. You can serve it with holy water. Have you any?"

"Yes, yes! You brought us some yourself."

"So I did! Give him the richest food possible. I ordered sucking-pig or turkey for supper."

"Thank you, Anton Ivanich."

"Don't mention it, my dear. Shouldn't you order pullets with white sauce as well?"

"I will."

"Why should you trouble? What am I for? I'll see to it—do let me."

"Do that, dear friend, help me!"

He went out of the room and she remained deep in thought.

Her woman's instinct and mother's heart told her that food was not the chief cause of Alexander's dejection. She tried to draw him out in a roundabout way with artful hints, but Alexander refused to understand them, and said nothing. Two or three weeks passed thus. Vast quantities of sucking-pigs, pullets and turkeys were consumed by Anton Ivanich but Alexander remained as thin and grave as ever, and his hair did not grow.

Then Anna Pavlovna decided to be frank with him.

"Sashenka, my dear," she said one day. "You've been here a month now and I have never once seen you smile. You go about like a dark cloud, your eyes cast down all the time. Does nothing please you here at all? I suppose you liked it better away from home. Is that what you're pining for? It breaks my heart to look at you. What's the matter with you? Tell me—what do you lack? I will spare nothing to get it for you. Has anyone done you wrong? I'll see to that, too."

"Don't worry, Mamma," said Alexander. "It's nothing, really. I've grown older, become more thoughtful, that's what makes me so grave."

"But what has made you so thin? And why has your hair gone?"

"I can't answer that ... it's impossible to recount all that happened in eight years. Perhaps my health has suffered a little too."

"Where do you feel pain?"

"I feel pain here, and here." He pointed first to his head and then to his heart.

Anna Pavlovna put her hand on his forehead.

"No fever," she said. "What could it be? Do you have shooting pains in your head?"

"Oh, no, I just..."

"Sashenka, let's send for Ivan Andreich."

"And who's Ivan Andreich?"

"The new doctor. He came here two years ago. He's a marvel! He hardly ever prescribes any medicine. He just makes up some tiny pills himself, and they help. Foma here had the stomach-ache—he bellowed for three days and nights, and three of Ivan Andreich's pills cured him instantly. Go to the doctor, my darling."

"No, Mamma, he won't be able to help me. It'll pass of itself."

"But what makes you so sad? What has come over you?"

"Oh, nothing."

"What is it you want?"

"I don't know myself. I just feel bored."

"What can it be, dear Lord?" said Anna Pavlovna. "You say you like the food, you have every comfort, you hold a good rank... Anybody'd think that was enough... Yet you are bored. Sashenka," she said softly, after a pause, "isn't it time for you to get married?"

"What? Oh, no, I shall never marry."

"And I have my eye on such a nice girl for you—as pretty as a doll, rosy and sweet. Such a tiny waist, and so slender! She's been to boarding school in the town. She has a dowry of seventy-five serfs and twenty-five thousand rubles in money, besides a splendid trousseau, all made in Moscow. And nice relations too. What d'you say, Sashenka? I've already spoken to her mother over a cup of coffee, just dropped a hint, in fun as it were. She was so delighted, you should have seen her prick up her ears."

"I shall never marry," repeated Alexander.

"What, never?"

"Never."

"Great heavens! What will come of it? Everybody behaves like everybody else, all except you. What's the matter with you? How happy I should be if the Lord answered my prayers for grandchildren! Come, do marry her! You'll fall in love with her."

"I shall not fall in love, Mamma. I've got over all that."

"Got over falling in love and not married? Who did you fall in love with there?"

"A girl."

"Why didn't you marry her?"

"She betrayed me."

"Betrayed you? But you weren't married to her!"

Alexander made no reply.

"Fine girls they have over there—loving before they

marry! Betrayed you, the nasty thing! Happiness was there for the taking, but she couldn't appreciate it, the worthless chit! If I were to see her I'd spit in her face, I would! What was your uncle thinking about? Where could she find someone better, I should like to know! But she's not the only one, is she? You can fall in love another time."

"I did, Mamma."

"Who with?"

"A widow."

"Well, and why didn't you get married?"

"This time it was I who betrayed her."

Anna Pavlovna looked at Alexander and could think of nothing to say.

"Betrayed," she repeated. "I suppose she was some loose creature," she whispered. "Slime! Slime! God forgive me. Loving before the wedding, without the church service—betraying! The things that go on in this world! It must mean the end of the world is near! Come now, tell me, isn't there anything you want? Perhaps the food isn't to your liking. I'll hire a chef in the town."

"No, thank you. Everything's all right."

"Perhaps it's lonely for you all by yourself. I'll invite the neighbours."

"No, no. Don't worry, Mamma! I like it here, it's peaceful, it'll pass... I haven't had time to look around me yet."

And that was all Anna Pavlovna could get out of him.

"Ah," thought she, "we cannot take a step without God, it seems." And she invited Alexander to go to church with her in the nearest village, but twice he overslept, and she could not bring herself to wake him. Then she asked him to go with her to evening service. "Very well," said Alexander and off they went. The mother entered the church and stood right up in front, while Alexander remained at the door.

The sun was setting, its slanting rays playing over the gilded icon covers, lighting up the austere dark countenances of the saints, putting to shame the feeble and uncertain flickering of the candles. The church was almost empty. The peasants were at work in the fields, and there were only a few old women in white kerchiefs, huddled in a corner near the entrance. Some of them, with sad faces, their cheeks propped on their hands, sat on the stone step of a side-chapel, heaving loud, mournful sighs every now and then, either for their sins, or their domestic affairs. Others prayed lying prostrate on the ground.

A fresh breeze blew through the iron bars in the windows, lifting the cloth on the altar, playing with the priest's grey hair, shuffling the pages of his book and extinguishing a candle. The steps of the priest and the deacon on the stone floor resounded through the empty church. Their voices rose dismally to the domed roof. Overhead in the cupola, the rooks cawed loudly and the sparrows chirped as they flew from one window to another, and the noise of their wings and the tolling of the bells sometimes drowned the words of the service.

"So long as a man's vital strength is at its peak," thought Alexander, "so long as his desires and passions have free play, he lives the life of the senses, fleeing the soothing, profound and solemn contemplation to which religion leads us. He turns to it for consolation with exhausted, wasted strength, shattered hopes and the burden of years."

Gradually the sight of so many familiar objects aroused reminiscences in Alexander. He passed in review his childhood and youth up to his departure for Petersburg, remembered how, as a child, he had repeated the prayers after his mother, how she had told him of the guardian angel who watches over the human soul, ever warring against the Evil One, how, pointing to the stars, she had told him that they were the eyes of god's angels who looked down at the earth and counted the good and bad deeds of human beings, and that the saints weep when the account shows more evil than good deeds and rejoice when the good exceeds the evil. Pointing to the blue distance of the horizon she used to tell him it was Zion... Alexander emerged from these reminiscences with a sigh.

"If only I could still believe all that!" he thought. "The infantile faith has been lost and what new, true things have I learned? None. I have found doubts, interpretations, theories ... and am still further than ever from the truth. What's the good of this dissension, this philosophizing! My God! When the warmth of faith no longer warms the heart, how can one be happy? Am I happier than I used to be?"

After the service Alexander was still sadder than he had been when he left home. Anna Pavlovna did not know what to do. One morning, waking up rather earlier than usual, he heard a rustling beside his pillow. Looking up he saw an old woman standing over him, her lips moving in a whisper. She disappeared instantly as soon as she saw that she had been noticed. Under his pillow Alexander found some herbs, there was an amulet round his neck.

"What's the meaning of this?" Alexander asked his mother. "Who was that old woman in my room?"

Anna Pavlovna showed some confusion.

"That was ... Nikitishna," she said.

"Who's Nikitishna?"

"She ... now don't be angry with me!"

"What is she? Tell me!"

"They say she's helped lots of people... She only whispers over some water and breathes on a person when he's asleep, and everything passes."

"Two years ago," put in Agrafena, "a fiery snake came down the chimney of the widow Sidorikha's house."

Anna Pavlovna spat to avert the Evil One.

"Nikitishna," continued Agrafena, "laid a spell on it and it stopped coming."

"And what about Sidorikha?" asked Alexander.

"She gave birth to a child. The baby was so thin and dark. It died in three days."

Alexander laughed for perhaps the first time since his return to the country.

"Where did you get her from?" he asked.

"Anton Ivanich brought her," replied Anna Pavlovna.

"How can you listen to that old fool?"

"Fool? Oh, Sashenka, how can you? Aren't you ashamed? Anton Ivanich a fool? I wonder you can bring yourself to say such things! Anton Ivanich is our benefactor, our friend."

"Here, Mamma, take the amulet and give it to our friend and benefactor. Let him put it round his own neck."

From this moment he took to locking himself into his room at night.

Two or three months passed. Gradually solitude, quiet, home life and all the material blessings accompanying it helped Alexander to put on weight. And idleness, freedom from responsibility and the absence of all moral shocks whatever, instilled in his soul the peace he had so vainly sought in Petersburg. There, fleeing from the world of ideas and art, confined within four walls, he had hoped to sleep the sleep of the mole, but had been continually aroused by envy and impotent desires. Every phenomenon in the world of science and art, every new celebrity had aroused in him the question, "Why is this not I?" There, at every step, he had encountered people with whom he could not help comparing himself unfavourably ... there, he had slipped so often, had seen, as in a mirror, all his failings ... there, was his inexorable uncle, criticizing his way of thinking, his slothfulness, his utterly groundless conceit. There was the elegant world, a lot of gifted men amidst whom he played no role whatsoever. Finally, there, people tried to subject life to certain conditions, to elucidate its dark and obscure places, they did not give rein to the senses, passions and dreams, thus depriving life of its poetic allurements, and imposing upon it tedious forms, which were barren, monotonous...

And here—what freedom! Here he was better, cleverer than anyone else. Here, he was the idol of all for miles around. And here, wherever he went, his soul, in the face of nature, was unsealed to absorb peaceful, consoling impressions. The voice of the stream, the rustling of the leaves, the coolness, sometimes even the very silence of nature—all gave birth to thought, aroused sensation. In the garden, the fields, at home, he was haunted by reminiscences of childhood and youth. Anna Pavlovna, who sometimes sat beside him, seemed to guess at his thoughts. She helped him to bring back to life the trifles so dear to his heart, or related something he did not remember at all.

"Those lime-trees there," she said, pointing to the garden, "were planted by your father. I was expecting then. I would sit here on the balcony and watch him. He worked a bit and then looked at me, and the sweat came pouring down his face. 'Ah, you're here,' he would say, 'no wonder I'm enjoying my work so!' and then he would start again. And there's the meadow where you used to play with the village children. You were so touchy! If the slightest thing upset you, you would bawl your head off. Once Agashka—she's married to Kuzma now, theirs is the third house from the end of the village street—gave you a push, and your nose bled. Her father thrashed her and thrashed her, I could hardly stop him!"

Alexander mentally supplemented these memories with his own. Over there on that bench, he told himself, I used to sit with Sophia and was happy then. And over there, between the two lilac bushes, I kissed her for the first time... It all seemed to be going on before his eyes. He smiled at these memories and sat on the balcony by the hour, greeting the sun when it rose, bidding it farewell when it set, listening to the birds singing, the lake splashing against the shore, and the invisible insects humming and buzzing.

"God, how good it is here!" he would cry, stirred by these mellow impressions. "Far from vanities, from that petty life, that ant-hill, where people

> *...In swarms, hemmed in,*
> *Breathe not the cool of morn,*
> *Nor verdure of the fields.*

"How weary one gets of life there, and how one's soul rests here, in this simple, unsophisticated life. The heart renews itself, one breathes more freely, the mind is not tormented by anguished thoughts and wearisome conflicts with the heart—they're in harmony. Here there is nothing to ponder on. One is carefree, with no sad thoughts, heart and mind are drowsy; one's glance moves lightly from copse to ploughed fields, from ploughed fields to hillside, and then loses itself in the infinite blue."

Sometimes he would go up to the window and look out on the yard and the village street. There the picture was different, a Teniers canvas, full of busy domestic life. The dog lay in front of his kennel, overcome by the heat, his nose on his front paws. Dozens of hens greeted the morning, clucking in turns. Cocks fought. The herd was driven down the street to pasture. Sometimes a cow, falling behind, lowed dismally, standing in the middle of the street and looking all round. Men and women with rakes and scythes on their shoulders went to work. Every now and then the breeze carried a word or two up to the window. A farm wagon rumbled thunderously over the little bridge, and after it a load of hay crawled lazily past. Boys, with coarse, flaxen hair, waded in the puddles, lifting the hem of their shirts. As he looked upon this scene Alexander began to grasp the poetry of *the grey sky, the broken fence, the wicket gates, the muddy pond, the folkdance*. He changed his elegant tight-fitting frock-coat for a loose, home-made dressing-gown. And in every manifestation of this peaceful life,. in every impression, in the morning, in the evening, at meals and during rest time, the vigilant eye of maternal love was present.

His mother could scarcely contain her joy to see Alexander beginning to put on weight, the colour returning to his cheeks, the peaceful light coming back to his eyes. "But the hair will never grow any more," she said, "and it used to be like silk!"

Alexander often took walks in the neighbourhood. Once meeting a crowd of women and girls, going to the woods to pick mushrooms, he joined them, and spent the whole day with them. When he got home he praised a girl called Masha for her simplicity and agility, and Masha was taken into the house *to attend to the master's needs*! Sometimes he went to watch the work in the fields, and learned from experience the things he had so often written about and translated for the magazine. "What a lot of nonsense we used to write," he thought, shaking his head, and he began to look more steadily and deeply into things.

One day, when the weather was bad, he sat down to write, and was extremely pleased with the beginning he had made. He needed a book for reference—he sent to Petersburg for it, and the book came. He began working in earnest. More books were sent for. Anna Pavlovna tried in vain to persuade him not to write, or he would *ruin his chest*. He took no notice whatever. She sent Anton Ivanich to him, but Alexander would not heed even him, and went on writing. When three or four months had passed and, far from wasting away from all this writing he had grown actually fatter, Anna Pavlovna's fears were allayed.

Thus passed a year and a half. Everything seemed to be going well, but at the end of this time Alexander became splenetic again. He had no desires at all, or if he had any they were such as were easily satisfied. They never went beyond the domestic circle. There was nothing to worry him—neither cares, nor doubts—and yet he was bored. Gradually he grew tired of the narrow domestic circle. His mother's solicitude became tiresome, and he was quite sick of Anton Ivanich. He was sick of work, too, and nature no longer charmed him.

He would sit silently at the window, glancing indifferently at his father's lime-trees, and listening with irritation to the lapping sound of the lake. He pondered on the cause of this new melancholy, and discovered that he was pining for ... Petersburg. Now that he was so far from the past he began to regret it. The blood still raced in his veins, his heart beat, his body and soul demanded activity. More problems! He almost wept at this discovery. He had hoped his melancholy would pass, that he would get used to country life, but nothing of the sort—the longer he lived there the worse his heart ached, and once again he craved for the whirlpool he already knew so well.

He had reconciled himself to the past—it had become sweet in memory. Hostility, morose looks, grimness, unsociability were all softened by solitude, by meditation. The past appeared before him cleansed and purified, the traitress Nadya herself all but wore a halo. "And what am I doing here?" he asked himself peevishly. "Why should I wither away? Why should my gifts fade into insignificance? Why should I not shine there with my work? I have become more reasonable. In what way is my uncle better than I am? Am I incapable of finding a path for myself? I didn't manage to, because I undertook what was not for me—so what of it? I have now come to my senses. The time has come. But how my departure will sadden my mother! And yet I simply must go! I cannot stay here and perish. All kinds of people have made their way there. And my career, my fortune? I alone lag behind—and what for? Why?" He was restless with melancholy, and did not know how to break to his mother the news that he was going away.

But his mother soon relieved him of this worry—she died. And this is what he wrote to his uncle and aunt in Petersburg.

To his aunt:

"Before my departure from Petersburg, *ma tante*, you pronounced, with tears in your eyes, words which have been engraved on my memory. You said, 'If ever I needed warm friendship, sincere sympathy, there would always be a corner in your heart for me.' The moment has come for me to understand the full value of these words. The place you have so generously given me in your heart is for me a pledge of peace, quiet, consolation, tranquillity, perhaps happiness, for the whole of my life. Three months ago my mother died—I will not add a single word. You know from her letters what she meant to me and will understand what I have lost in losing her. I shall now flee this place for ever. And whither should I, lonely pilgrim, direct my steps, but to that place where you are? Tell me one word—shall I find you the same as I left you a year and a half ago? Or have you driven me out of your memory? Will you undertake the tedious task of healing a fresh, deep wound with your friendship, which has more than once saved me from grief? I place all my hope in you and in another powerful ally—activity.

"You are surprised, are you not? It seems strange to you to hear this from me. To read lines written in a calm tone so unlike myself. Do not be surprised, and do not fear my return. It is not a madman, a dreamer, a disillusioned person, or a provincial who is coming back to you, but simply a man such as Petersburg is full of, such a one as I ought to have become long ago. Mind you assure my uncle, in particular, of this! When I look back on my life I am overcome by confusion and shame. But it could not have been otherwise. And see how late I have come to my senses—at the age of thirty! The hard school through which I passed in Petersburg, and my meditations in the country, have made my destiny quite clear to me. Keeping my uncle's lessons and my own experience at a respectful distance I have pondered over them here, in solitude, and now see more clearly where they should long ago have led me, and how wretchedly and irrationally I digressed from my true aim. Now I am at peace. I do not torture myself, but I do not boast of this. Perhaps this peace still only comes from egoism. But I feel sure my outlook will clear up to such an extent that I shall discover new and purer sources of peace. I cannot help feeling sorry now that I have, alas, already come to that dividing line where youth ends and the time of meditation, testing and analysis of all emotions, the time of consciousness begins.

"Although my opinion of others and of life may perhaps not have changed very much, many hopes have vanished, many desires left me, in a word, I have lost my illusions. Consequently, there are not many people or things left for me to be mistaken about or deceived in, and that is extremely consoling in its way. And so I have a clearer vision of the future. The worst is behind me. Emotions are no longer alarming, for very few remain to me. The chief ones have been outlived and I bless them. I am ashamed to remember how, imagining myself a martyr, I cursed my lot in life. Cursed! What miserable puerility and ingratitude! How late I have understood that suffering purges the soul, that it alone makes a man tolerable both to himself and others, that it elevates him! I admit now that not to know suffering is not to know the fullness of life. It contains many important elements, the significance of which we perhaps shall not see in this world. I see in these emotions the hand of Providence, which, it seems, sets humanity the infinite task of progressing, achieving an aim imposed from above, while incessantly struggling with deceptive hopes and maddening obstacles. Yes, I see how necessary this struggle, these emotions are, how without them life would not be life, but stagnation, slumber... When the struggle ends, life, too, ends: a man was busy, he loved, enjoyed, suffered, worried, went about his business, and consequently he lived.

"See how I argue! I have emerged from the shadows and see that my whole life up to now has been a kind of painful preparation for the true path, a wise lesson for the remainder of life. Something tells me that the rest of the way will be easier, calmer, clearer. The dark places have been lit up, the intricate knots have become unravelled. Life begins to appear a blessing and not an evil. Soon I shall again be saying: how good life is! But I shall say it, not as a youth drunk with fleeting pleasures, but in the full consciousness of its true joys and sorrows. And then death itself will hold no terrors—it will no longer be a bogey, but a splendid experience. A calm hitherto unknown to me is already being wafted into my soul. The puerile

vexations, the outbursts of wounded vanity, the childish irritability and comic rage against the world and its
inhabitants, like the rage of the puppy against the ele-
phant, have all vanished.

"I have reconciled myself to those with whom I have
long been at enmity—human beings—who, by the way,
are much the same here as in Petersburg, only cruder,
coarser, absurder. But I do not criticize them here, either,
and have long ceased to criticize those I met in Petersburg. Here is an example of my meekness: a certain crank
called Anton Ivanich visits me, stays with me, presumes to
share my grief. Tomorrow he will go to a wedding at some
neighbours and share their joy, and then to some other
place, where he will perform the duties of a midwife. No
matter what the occasion is, one of grief or joy, he will
anyway eat his four meals a day at whoever's house he is.
I see that it is all one to him—whether a man dies, is born,
or weds, and I regard him without disgust, without irritation. I bear with him and do not drive him away. A good
sign this, is it not, ma tante? What will you say on reading
this self-praise of mine?"

To his uncle:

"My dear, kindest of uncles, and at the same time Your
Excellency!

"With what joy I learned that your career, too, has been
crowned with success. You have long ago wrung success
from fortune. You are a Councillor of State, you are the
head of a government office. Dare I remind Your Excellency of the promise you gave me when I left? 'If you ever
require a post and an occupation, or money, come to me,'
you said. And now I need both post and occupation, not
to mention money! The poor provincial ventures to ask for
a post! What will be the fate of my request? Will it be that
which once met Zayezhalov's letter, in which he asked you
to see to his affairs? As for literature, which you were so
cruel as to refer to in one of your letters—are you not
ashamed of reminding me of long-forgotten follies, when I
myself blush for them? Oh, Uncle, oh, Your Excellency!
Who has not been young and more or less foolish? Who has
not *cherished* strange secret dreams destined never to come

true? Take my neighbour here, to the right of me—he fancied himself a hero, a Nimrod, a mighty hunter in the face of the Lord ... he thought to astonish the world with his achievements ... and it all ended in his retiring with the rank of ensign, never having been to war, and peacefully cultivating potatoes and sowing turnips. My other neighbour, to the left, dreamed of remaking the whole world, including Russia, according to his own ideas, but, after spending some time copying out documents in a government office, has returned home, and to this day has been unable to repair his old fence. I myself believed I was endowed with the creative gift, and longed to confide new secrets to the world at large, never suspecting that they were secrets no longer, and that I was no prophet! We are all ridiculous, but who would attempt without blushing for himself to brand these youthful, noble, passionate, if not very reasonable dreams as disgraceful? Who has not, in his day, cherished futile desires, imagined himself a hero performing valiant deeds, in whose honour a triumphant song is composed and a plangent lay is written? Whose fancy has not carried him back to fabulous, heroic times? Who has not wept in sympathy with the lofty and the beautiful? If such a man exists, let him throw the first stone at me—I do not envy him! I blush for my youthful dreams, but I also revere them! They are the pledge of purity of heart, the sign of a noble soul, disposed to good.

"I know these arguments will never convince you. You require something definite, practical. Well, here it is— tell me how talent would be recognized and developed if the young were to suppress in themselves these early tendencies, if they did not freely voice their dreams, but slavishly followed the path laid down, without testing their powers! And, finally, is it not a law of nature that youth should be restless, excitable, sometimes eccentric, always foolish, and that in time such dreams die down, as they have in my case? Were these errors, then, unknown to your own youth? Look back, search your memory! I can see you shake your head, your glance, as always, calm and imperturbable, as you say, 'Nothing of the kind!' But allow me to trip you up here—what about love? Will you deny it? You cannot. The clues are in my hands.

Remember I have been able to investigate the matter on the spot. The theatre of your amorous adventures is before my eyes—this lake! The yellow flowers still grow there. One of them, dried and pressed, I have the honour to send Your Excellency herewith, as a tender memento. I have in my possession an even more terrible weapon against your denunciation of love in general, and of my love in particular, and that is a document. You frown? And what a document! You turn pale. I stole these withered relics from my aunt's no less withered breast, and shall bring them with me as an eternal clue incriminating you, and as a defence of myself. Tremble, Uncle! And this is not all—I know in detail the whole history of your love. Every day, at breakfast and at supper, before going to bed, my aunt tells me some interesting detail. I intend to gather up all this precious material in a special memorandum. I shall not fail to hand it to you personally, together with a work on agriculture on which I have been occupied for the last year. For my own part I consider it my duty to assure my aunt of what she is pleased to describe as the unchangeableness of your *feelings*. When I am so fortunate as to receive from Your Excellency a favourable reply to my request, I will have the honour of appearing before you with a gift of dried raspberries and honey, and with a few letters which my neighbours promise to give me, stating their needs—all but Zayezhalov, who died before his case was completed."

EPILOGUE

And here, four years after Alexander's second arrival in Petersburg, is what happened to the principal characters in this novel.

One morning, Pyotr Ivanich was pacing up and down the floor of his study. This was not the former brisk, well-built Pyotr Ivanich, with his imperturbable glance, his proudly held head, and erect carriage. Whether from age or circumstances, he seemed to have deteriorated. His movements were no longer so lively, his glance not so firm and confident, as before. Numerous grey hairs shone in his whiskers and on his temples. It was obvious that he had already celebrated the fiftieth birthday. He stooped a little in his walk. But strangest of all was to see on the face of this calm, stern man, as we had until now known him, an expression which was more than careworn, which was almost dejected, although it had in it something that was peculiarly characteristic of Pyotr Ivanich.

He seemed to be in a state of perplexity. Taking two steps he suddenly stood still in the middle of the room, or again started rapidly pacing the room, as if visited by some unaccustomed thought.

Seated in an armchair not far from the writing-table was a stout man in a tightly buttoned frock-coat with a cross on his chest suspended from a ribbon, his knees crossed. All that he lacked was a stick with a big gold handle, that familiar stick by which the reader immediately recognized the doctor in old novels and stories. This

stick, with which he strolled about for want of anything
better to do, or sat by the hour at bedsides, comforting
the patients and not seldom uniting in himself two or three
roles—the doctor, the practical philosopher, the friend of
the house, and so on—might be highly appropriate to a
doctor. But this was all very well where people lived at
their leisure, with plenty of space round them, where
people were seldom ill, and where the physician was more
of a luxury than a necessity. But Pyotr Ivanich's physician was a Petersburg doctor. He did not know what it
was to stroll, though he prescribed exercise for his patients.
He was a member of some council, the secretary of some
society, a professor, medical adviser to several government departments, and to the poor, and was invariably
summoned to take part in consultations. Besides this he
had a huge practice. He seldom removed the glove from
his left hand and would not have taken it off the right one
either but for the need of taking pulses. He never un-
buttoned his coat and seldom sat down. He had already
crossed and uncrossed his knees several times impatiently. It was high time for him to go, but Pyotr Ivanich
said nothing. At last:

"What's to be done, Doctor?" asked Pyotr Ivanich,
suddenly stopping in front of him.

"Go to Bad Kissingen," replied the doctor. "It's the best
thing you can do. Your attacks have become too frequent."

"Oh, you are still thinking about me!" Pyotr Ivanich
interrupted. "I'm talking about my wife. I'm over fifty
but she's in her prime, she wants to enjoy life. And if her
health has begun to fail at this early age..."

"To fail?" said the doctor. "I only spoke of my fears
for the future, at present there's nothing. I only meant
to say that her health—or rather not her health—she ...
seems to be in a state that is not quite normal."

"It's the same thing! You merely let slip a remark,
and forgot all about it, but since then I have been watching
her closely and every day I discover fresh, disturbing
changes in her—and I have known no peace for three
months. How it is that I never noticed anything before, I
can't understand. My work and business have robbed me
of my time and health ... and now, perhaps my wife..."

He again took to pacing the floor.

"Did you examine her today?" he asked after a pause.

"Yes, but she has not noticed anything herself. At first I supposed there was some physiological cause—she has never had any children. But there doesn't seem to be any. The cause is probably purely psychological."

"Worse still," remarked Pyotr Ivanich.

"On the other hand it may be nothing. There are absolutely no suspicious symptoms. You know what it is—you have lived here too long in this marshy climate. Go to the south. Have a rest, accumulate fresh impressions, and see what comes of it. Spend the summer in Bad Kissingen, taking the waters, the autumn in Italy, the winter in Paris. I assure you, the accumulation of mucus, the irritability, will all disappear."

Pyotr Ivanich scarcely heard him.

"Psychological cause," he said under his breath, and shook his head.

"I'll tell you why I say psychological," said the doctor. "A person who didn't know you might suspect some sort of troubles—at least not troubles, but suppressed desires. Sometimes there is need, deprivation, I only wanted to draw your attention..."

"Need, desires!" interrupted Pyotr Ivanich. "Her every desire is forestalled! I know her tastes, her habits! Need—h'm... You see our house, you know how we live."

"A fine house, a splendid house!" said the doctor. "A wonderful chef, and what cigars! Has that friend of yours who lives in London stopped sending you sherry? I don't remember seeing it on your table this year."

"How treacherous fate can be, Doctor! Was ever anyone so solicitous for his wife as I?" said Pyotr Ivanich with unwonted ardour. "I may say I have always weighed every step ... and now everything is shattered and at such a moment! When everything has been such a success, and at the peak of my career!"

He made a gesture of despair and resumed his pacing.

"What makes you so nervous?" asked the doctor. "There is absolutely no danger. I repeat what I said the first time—her constitution is sound, there are no destructive symptoms. Anaemia, a certain weakness—that's all."

"A mere trifle!" said Pyotr Ivanich.

"Her symptoms are negative, not positive," continued

the doctor. "And is she the only one? Look at all the people who live here but are not Petersburg-born! They're
all in a bad state! Take her away, take her away! And if
you can't do that, distract her, don't let her stay at home
too much, amuse her, make her go out! More exercise for
body and soul! Both are in an unnaturally comatose state
in her. Of course in time it might settle in the lungs or..."

"Good-bye, Doctor. I am going to her," said Pyotr
Ivanich and hastened towards his wife's room.

At the door he stopped, parting the curtains softly
and fixing an anxious glance on his wife.

What was it that the doctor had noticed about her?
Anyone seeing her for the first time would have thought
her a woman like so many other women in Petersburg.
Pale, it is true, her glance a little dim, the gown falling loosely
and evenly over her narrow shoulders and flat bosom,
her movements slow, almost languid. But rosy cheeks,
shining eyes and impetuous movements have never been
the distinguishing marks of our beauties. And lovely
curves? Neither Phidias nor Praxiteles would have found a
model for Venus among them.

No, it is not shapeliness which must be sought in our
northern beauties! They are not statues. Not theirs are the
classical poses which immortalize the beauty of Grecian
women, nor the irreproachable curves which make these
poses possible. Voluptuousness does not stream from their
eyes in ardent rays, there is not the naïvely sensual smile
on their parted lips which burns on those of southern wom-
en. Our women have been endowed with another, a higher beauty. The sculptor's chisel has never fixed the gleam
of thought impressed upon their features, the struggle
'twixt will and passion, the play of inexpressible impulses
of the soul and innumerable subtle mischievous nuances,
assumed simplicity, anger and good nature, hidden joys
and sufferings ... all those fleeting flashes of lightning that
burst from the over-intensity of the soul.

However this may be, no one seeing Lizaveta Alexandrovna for the first time would have noticed anything
wrong with her. Only one who had known her before,
who remembered the freshness of her colour, the sparkle
of her glance, making it difficult to determine the colour
of her eyes, drowned as they were in quivering waves of

light, who remembered her gorgeous shoulders and high bosom, would now have looked at her in painful surprise, his heart wrung with pity, unless he were a mere stranger, as now perhaps Pyotr Ivanich's heart was wrung, though he was afraid to admit it to himself.

He went softly into the room and sat down beside her.

"What are you doing?" he asked.

"I am looking through my accounts," she said. "Fancy, Pyotr Ivanich, we spent about a thousand five hundred rubles on food alone last month! Really it's a disgrace!"

Without answering a word he took the account-book from her and laid it on the table.

"Listen!" he said. "The doctor thinks my illness will get worse here, he advises going abroad for the waters. What do you say to that?"

"What can I say? In this case I suppose the doctor's word carries more weight than mine. You must go since he advises it."

"And what about you? Would you like to make this voyage?"

"I wouldn't mind."

"Perhaps you'd rather stay here?"

"Very well, I'll stay."

"Which would you rather?" asked Pyotr Ivanich not without impatience.

"Do as you like—for yourself and for me," she answered in dreary indifference. "I'll go if you say so, if not, I'll stay here."

"You can't stay here," said Pyotr Ivanich. "The doctor says your health too has suffered slightly ... from the climate."

"What makes him think so?" asked Lizaveta Alexandrovna. "I'm quite well, there's nothing wrong with me."

"A long voyage might exhaust you, though," said Pyotr Ivanich. "How would you like to stay with your aunt in Moscow while I'm abroad?"

"I don't mind. I think I'll go to Moscow."

"Or should we both go to the Crimea for the summer?"

"That would be nice, too."

Pyotr Ivanich could stand no more. He got up from the sofa and began pacing the floor as he had done in his study, and then stopped in front of her.

"Is it all the same to you where you are?" he asked.

"Quite."

"But why?"

She did not answer, and picked up the account-book again.

"You can say what you like, Pyotr Ivanich," she said, "but we shall have to cut down expenses—a thousand five hundred rubles on food alone..."

He took the book from her and threw it under the table.

"Why does it worry you so?" he asked. "Do you grudge the money?"

"How can I help worrying? Am I not your wife? You taught me yourself ... and now you reproach me for worrying... *I'm doing my work.*"

"Listen to me, Liza," said Pyotr Ivanich after a short pause. "You are trying to change your nature, to force yourself—that's not right. I have never compelled you. You will not convince me that this sort of thing," he pointed to the account-book, "can interest you. Why force yourself? I allow you complete freedom."

"My God! What's the use of freedom to me?" said Lizaveta Alexandrovna. "What should I do with it? Up till now you have always disposed both of yourself and me so well, so wisely, that I have forgotten I have a will. Go on doing that. I don't need freedom."

They were both silent.

"It's a long time," resumed Pyotr Ivanich, "since I heard any request from you, the expression of any desire or whim."

"I need nothing," said she.

"Have you no particular ... secret desires?" he asked kindly, looking steadily at her.

She seemed to hesitate.

Pyotr Ivanich noticed this.

"Tell me! For God's sake, tell me!" he said. "Your desires shall be my desires, they shall be law!"

"Very well," she said, "if you would do this for me, put an end to our Fridays—these dinners fatigue me."

Pyotr Ivanich paused for thought.

"As it is, you live the life of a hermit," he said. "And when our friends stop coming to us on Fridays you will be utterly alone. But since you wish it—it shall be so.

What will you do with yourself?"

"Give me all your bills and account-books and things—I'll see to them," she said, trying to reach under the table to pick up the account-book.

To Pyotr Ivanich this seemed mere clumsy dissembling.

"Liza!" he said reproachfully.

The account-book remained under the table.

"I was thinking you might revive some of our old acquaintances which we have quite dropped. And I thought of giving a ball, so that you should have some amusement, start going out yourself..."

"Oh, no, no!" said Lizaveta Alexandrovna in alarm. "For heaven's sake, don't do that! A ball—what an idea!"

"Why does it upset you so? At your age a ball should be still enjoyable. You're still young enough to dance."

"Pyotr Ivanich, don't do that, I beg you!" she cried hotly. "To bother about a new frock, to dress, to receive a crowd, to go visiting—God forbid!"

"Do you want to live in a dressing-gown the rest of your life?"

"Yes—if you didn't mind, I'd wear nothing else. Why dress up? Expenses and unnecessary trouble for no good reason!"

"I'll tell you what," said Pyotr Ivanich. "They say Rubini is coming here this winter. We shall have a permanent Italian opera. I've asked them to reserve us a box—what d'you say to that?"

She said nothing.

"Liza!"

"You shouldn't have," she said uncertainly. "I think I should find that exhausting too. I tire so..."

Pyotr Ivanich, his head on one side, went up to the mantelpiece, and leaned his elbow on it, looking at her ... how shall we say? Not exactly in anguish, but with alarm, with anxiety.

"Liza, why this..." he began and broke off, not liking to pronounce the word "apathy".

He looked long at her in silence. In her blank, lifeless eyes, in her face, where there was no play of living thought or feeling, in her listless pose and slow movements, he read the cause of this apathy about which he feared to ask. He had guessed the reply as soon as the doctor hinted at his fears. Then he had searched his memory and realized that, in systematically shielding his wife from all deviations which might be detrimental to their marital interests, he had failed to offer her any compensation for those joys, perhaps unlawful, which she might have known outside the domestic circle, that her home had become a kind of prison, owing to the regime he had devised, surrounded by barriers and guards which rendered impossible the most legitimate outpourings of feeling.

The methodical and dry manner in which he treated her had developed, without his knowledge or will, into cold, refined tyranny—and over what? The heart of a woman. For this subjection he had paid her with wealth, luxury, with all the external conditions of happiness, as he visualized it—a terrible error, the more so that it arose not from ignorance, not, he was sure, from a coarse interpretation of love, but from neglect and egoism. He had forgotten that *she* neither went to work nor played cards, that *she* had no factory to keep her occupied, that excellent food and the best wines have very little value in the eyes of women, and that the life he had forced upon her was thoroughly uncongenial.

Pyotr Ivanich was a kindly soul. He would have given anything, if not from love for his wife, then from a sense of justice, to set the right this wrong. But how was this to be done? He had spent more than one sleepless night since the doctor had expressed fear for his wife's health, in trying to find some way of reconciling her heart to her present situation and restoring her failing strength. And now, as he stood leaning against the mantelpiece, he was still thinking about this. It occurred to him that perhaps the germ of a dangerous disease was already lurking inside her, that this hollow, insipid life had been slowly killing her...

A cold sweat broke out on his forehead. He sought desperately for remedies, at the same time feeling it was the heart that had to invent them, not the head. But was the heart he had able to do it? Something told him that if he could fall at her feet, take her in a loving embrace and tell her passionately that he lived for her alone, that all his labours, his career, his thriftiness, had been for her alone, that his system of behaviour had been inspired solely

by the ardent, insistent, jealous desire to secure love...
He realized that such words would have sufficed to revive
a corpse, that she would instantly blossom out into health
and happiness, and there would have been no need to go
abroad for the waters.

But to say and to prove are two very different things.
To prove all this, the passion must really exist. And Pyotr
Ivanich, searching his soul, could not find in it the sligt-
est trace of passion. All that he felt was that his wife was
necessary to him, and this was true enough, but on a level
with the other necessities of life, she had become necessary from habit. He was willing to pretend, to play the role
of a lover, ridiculous as it would be at fifty to suddenly use
the language of passion, but how could one deceive a woman
with passion when there was none? Would he have enough
heroism and skill to drag out this role of passionate lover
until the need for it passed? And would not her wounded
pride kill her when she saw that that which, a few years
before, would have been a magic potion for her was now
being offered her as a remedial draught? No, after weighing the pros and cons of this too-late step he found himself unable to venture upon it. He thought of trying to
do the same thing in a different way, since it was necessary now and possible. For three months he had been pon-
dering an idea which would have seemed absurd to him before, but now matters were different. He had saved it up
for an emergency; the emergency had arisen, and he decided to carry out his plan.

"If this doesn't help," he thought, "then there is no way
out. I will try it, come what may!"

Pyotr Ivanich approached his wife with resolute steps
and took her by the hand.

"You know the part I play at the office, Liza," he said.
"I am considered the most efficient person in the department. My name will be proposed for Privy Councillor this
year and of course I will receive the promotion. Do not
think that this will be the end of my career—I can still advance ... and I would, if..."

She looked at him in astonishment, wondering what he
was leading up to.

"I never doubted your ability," she said. "I am perfectly sure that you will not stop half-way but will go for-

ward to the end."

"No, I will not. In a few days I shall hand in my resignation."

"Your resignation?" she repeated in astonishment, sitting up.

"Yes."

"Why?"

"Let me tell you. As you know I have bought out my partners and the factory belongs to me alone. It brings me in about forty thousand, clear profit, without the slightest trouble. It works as smoothly as a machine."

"I know—what about it?" asked Lizaveta Alexandrovna.

"I shall sell it."

"Sell it, Pyotr Ivanich! What's come over you?" asked Lizaveta Alexandrovna with ever increasing astonishment, regarding him with terror-stricken eyes. "Why should you? I'm overwhelmed, I can't understand!"

"Cannot you really?"

"No," said Lizaveta Alexandrovna.

"You can't understand that I, seeing how unhappy you are, how your health suffers ... from the climate, would give up my career and my factory and take you away from here?.. That I should wish to devote the rest of my life to you? Surely you don't think me incapable of sacrifice, Liza?" he added reproachfully.

"So it's for me!" said Lizaveta Alexandrovna, recovering her equanimity with difficulty. "No, Pyotr Ivanich," she said, deeply agitated. "For heaven's sake, don't make any sacrifices for me! I won't accept them—d'you hear me? I just won't! For you to stop working, distinguishing yourself, getting rich—and because of me! God forbid! I am not worthy of the sacrifice! Forgive me—I have been too shallow, too insignificant, too weak, to understand and appreciate your lofty aims, your noble labours... You needed a different sort of wife."

"Magnanimity again!" said Pyotr Ivanich, shrugging his shoulders. "My mind is made up, Liza!"

"Oh God, oh God, what have I done? I have been a stumbling-block to you! I am in your way! What a strange fate mine has been!" she added, almost in despair. "If a person does not want to live, he ought not to live ...

surely God will have pity and take me! To be in your way..."

"You are quite wrong if you think this sacrifice is hard for me. I have had enough of this rigid life. I need rest, peace. And where should I find peace if not alone with you? We will go to Italy."

"Pyotr Ivanich," she said almost in tears, "you are good, noble... I know you are capable of generous hypocrisy ... but perhaps this sacrifice will be futile, perhaps it is ... too late, and you will have given up everything..."

"Spare me, Liza, and don't follow up that thought!" said Pyotr Ivanich. "Otherwise you will see that I am not made of stone... I repeat, I want to live not by reason alone. Not everything in me is quite frozen, yet."

She gazed at him steadily, incredulously.

"And is this ... sincere?" she asked, after a pause. "You really do want peace, you are not going away solely for my sake?"

"No—for my own, too."

"Because if it's for me, I wouldn't for the world..."

"No, no! I'm ill, tired ... I need a rest."

She gave him her hand. He kissed it warmly.

"So we'll go to Italy," he said.

"Very well, let's," she replied dully.

Pyotr Ivanich felt as if a weight had fallen from his shoulders. "Now we'll see!" he thought.

They sat on for a long time not knowing what to say to one another. There is no telling who would first have broken this silence if they had remained alone longer. Suddenly hurried steps were heard in the next room, and Alexander came in.

How he had changed—how fat, rosy and baldish he had become! With what dignity he bore his rounded belly and the star on his chest! His eyes sparkled with joy. He kissed his aunt's hand with particular feeling and pressed his uncle's hand.

"Where have you sprung from?" asked Pyotr Ivanich.

"Guess!" said Alexander meaningfully.

"You seem to be in wonderful spirits today," said Pyotr Ivanich, looking at him inquiringly.

"I bet you anything you'll never guess," said Alexander.

"I remember you coming to see me like this eleven or twelve years ago," remarked Pyotr Ivanich. "You even broke something on my table—then, I guessed at once that you were in love, but now ... surely not again? No, it can't be! You're too clever to..."

He glanced at his wife and fell suddenly silent.

"You can't guess?" asked Alexander.

His uncle looked at him and tried to think.

"You're not going to ... get married, are you?" he said uncertainly.

"Quite right!" exclaimed Alexander triumphantly. "Congratulate me!"

"And who is the lady?" asked his uncle and aunt together.

"Alexander Stepanich's daughter."

"Indeed! Well, she'll be a wealthy bride," said Pyotr Ivanich, "and her father—what does he say?"

"I've just come from them. What could her father have against me? He listened to my proposal with tears in his eyes. He embraced me and said he could now die in peace, because he knew to whom he was entrusting his daughter's happiness. 'Follow in your uncle's footsteps,' he said."

"Is that what he said? You see! Uncle helped even here!"

"And what did his daughter say?" asked Lizaveta Alexandrovna.

"Oh, she ... like all girls, you know," replied Alexander. "She didn't say anything, only blushed. And when I took her hand her fingers seemed to be playing the piano in mine ... as if they were trembling."

"Didn't say anything?" said Lizaveta Alexandrovna. "D'you mean to say you never took the trouble to find out her feelings before proposing? Don't you care? What are you getting married for?"

"What d'you mean what for? Am I to remain bachelor all my life? I'm sick of living alone! The time has come, *ma tante*, to settle down, to set up a home, to fulfil my duty. The girl's pretty and rich. Uncle here will tell you why people marry. He explains it all so clearly."

Pyotr Ivanich tried to stop him with a furtive gesture, but Alexander took no notice.

"Supposing she doesn't like you!" said Lizaveta Alexandrovna. "Supposing she cannot love you—what have you to say to that?"

"What am I to say? You speak better than I do, Uncle,

so I'll quote your own words," Alexander went on, taking no notice of his uncle's uneasy fidgeting and significant coughs. " 'Marry for love but love will pass and you will live by habit. Marry not for love and you will arrive at the same result—you will get used to your wife. Love is one thing, and marriage is another. These two things do not always coincide and it is better that they never should.' It's true, isn't it, Uncle? Isn't that what you taught me?"

He looked at Pyotr Ivanich and was suddenly silenced by his uncle's furious glare. His mouth open in astonishment, Alexander glanced at his aunt and back at his uncle, and fell silent. Lizaveta Alexandrovna shook her head pensively.

"So you're going to get married!" said Pyotr Ivanich. "Just at the right time and may God bless you! And you wanted to marry at twenty-three!"

"Youth, Uncle, youth!"

"Of course it was youth!"

Alexander who seemed to have been lost in thought suddenly smiled.

"What are you smiling at?" asked Pyotr Ivanich.

"Nothing. A certain absurdity came into my head."

"What?"

"When I was in love," replied Alexander thoughtfully, "my marriage did not come off."

"And now you are going to get married, but the love won't come off," contributed his uncle and they both laughed.

"From this it follows, Uncle, that you are right in considering habit the chief..."

Again Pyotr Ivanich made a fierce face at him. Alexander stopped talking, not knowing what to think.

"To marry at thirty-five," said Pyotr Ivanich, "is perfectly in order. But remember how you raved and writhed in convulsions, screaming, how unequal marriages infuriated you, when a child-bride was dragged to the altar like sacrificial lamb, adorned with flowers and diamonds, and pushed into the embraces of an elderly man, for the greater part an ugly, bald fellow. Let's see your head!"

"Youth, youth, Uncle! I didn't understand the essence of marriage then," said Alexander, smoothing his hair with the palm of his hand.

"The essence, you say," continued Pyotr Ivanich. "Remember how much in love you were with that, what's her name?—Natasha, wasn't it? 'Mad jealousy, impulses, divine bliss.' Where's all that gone to?"

"Uncle, Uncle, that'll do!" said Alexander, blushing.

"Where are the vast passion, the tears?"

"Uncle!"

"What? No more surrendering to 'sincere effusions', enough of plucking yellow flowers? Now it's—'I'm tired of living alone'!"

"For that matter, Uncle, I can prove that I am not the only one who has loved, raged, been jealous, wept ... wait a minute, I have it here in writing."

He took out his pocket-book and after searching for some time among the papers in it, extracted an old, yellowing tattered sheet of paper.

"Look at this, *ma tante*," he said. "A proof that my uncle was not always such a rational, sarcastic and sober person. He, too, once indulged in *sincere effusions*, and even committed them to paper, not bond paper, and in a special kind of ink. I have carried this scrap of paper about for four years, waiting for a chance to show my uncle up. I would have forgotten all about it if you hadn't reminded me yourself."

"Nonsense! I don't know what you're talking about," said Pyotr Ivanich, casting a glance at the paper.

"Well, then, take a look!"

Alexander held up the paper to his uncle's eyes. Pyotr Ivanich's countenance suddenly darkened.

"Give it to me, Alexander!" he cried, trying to snatch at the tattered fragment. But Alexander jerked back his hand. Lizaveta Alexandrovna watched them both with curiosity.

"No, Uncle, I won't give it to you!" said Alexander. "Not till you admit here, in front of my aunt, that you, too, were once in love, like me, like everyone else. If you don't, I will leave this document in her hands as an eternal reproach to you."

"Barbarian!" shouted Pyotr Ivanich. "How can you treat me so?"

"You won't?"

"Very well! I was in love! Give it to me!"

"No, no! And you raged and were jealous?"

"Very well! I raged and was jealous," said Pyotr Ivanich, with a grimace.

"And wept?"

"No, I didn't weep."

"You did! My aunt told me! Admit it!"

"I can't say the words, Alexander. You'll make me cry in good earnest."

"*Ma tante!* Accept this document."

"Let me see it," she said, stretching out her hand.

"I wept, I wept, give it to me!" howled Pyotr Ivanich despairingly.

"Beside the lake?"

"Beside the lake."

"And plucked yellow flowers?"

"I did! The devil take you! Give it to me!"

"That's not all. Give me your word of honour that you will consign to utter oblivion my follies and never taunt me with them again."

"My word of honour."

Alexander yielded up the scrap of paper. Pyotr Ivanich seized it, lit a match and burned it on the spot.

"At least tell me what it was," asked Lizaveta Alexandrovna.

"No, my dear, that's a thing I will not even mention at the last judgement," replied Pyotr Ivanich. "Surely it wasn't I who wrote that! It's impossible!"

"You, you, Uncle!" struck in Alexander. "I can tell you what was in it, I think. I know it by heart. 'Angel, my adored.'"

"Alexander! I shall quarrel with you forever!" cried Pyotr Ivanich angrily.

"He's ashamed as if it were a crime, and what of?" said Lizaveta Alexandrovna. "Of his first tender love."

She shrugged her shoulders and turned away from them.

"There's so much that is ... silly in that sort of love," Pyotr Ivanich said to her gently, insinuatingly. "Now, there wasn't a hint of those sincere effusions, and flowers, and moonlight walks with you and me ... and yet you do love me, don't you..."

"Oh, I've got quite ... used to you," replied Lizaveta Alexandrovna absently.

Pyotr Ivanich stroked his whiskers thoughtfully.

"Well, Uncle," whispered Alexander, "isn't that just how it should be?"

Pyotr Ivanich winked at him as if to say, "Be quiet."

"It's one thing for Pyotr Ivanich to think and act like that," said Lizaveta Alexandrovna. "He's been that way a long time and I don't suppose anyone ever knew him any different. But from you, Alexander, I did not expect such a change."

She sighed.

"Why do you sigh, *ma tante*?" he asked.

"For the former Alexander," she replied.

"Surely, *ma tante*, you would not wish me always to be the person I was ten years ago," objected Alexander. "Uncle was right in calling me a foolish dreamer."

Pyotr Ivanich's countenance again grew fierce. Alexander said no more.

"No, not the person you were ten years ago," said Lizaveta Alexandrovna, "but the one you were four years ago. Do you remember the letter you wrote me from the country? How nice you were!"

"As far as I remember I was still dreaming then," said Alexander.

"No, you weren't! You understood life and gave your own interpretation of it. You were splendid, noble, wise... Why didn't you stay like that? Why was it all only words, only on paper and not in deeds? The best in you showed like the sun from behind a cloud, for one moment..."

"Do you mean, *ma tante*, that I am not wise ... and ... noble, any more?"

"God forbid! Not that! But now you are wise and noble in a different way ... not my way."

"What's to be done, *ma tante*?" said Alexander, heaving a loud sigh. "It's the age. I am abreast of the age—one can't lag behind. I refer you to my uncle, I quote his words."

"Alexander," said Pyotr Ivanich fiercely. "Come into my study for a moment. I have a word to say in your ear."

They went into the study.

"What possessed you to keep on quoting me today?" said Pyotr Ivanich. "Can't you see the state my wife is in?"

"What's the matter with her?" asked Alexander in alarm.

"Don't you notice anything? Why, I'm resigning, giving up all my affairs, everything and going away with her to Italy."

"Uncle!" exclaimed Alexander in astonishment. "Why, you'll be made a Privy Councillor this year!"

"Yes, but you see Madame Privy Councillor is in a bad way."

He paced the floor of his room three times in deep thought.

"Ah, well!" he said. "My career is over. The thing is done. Fate does not mean me to go any further. So be it!"

He made a gesture of despair.

"Let's talk about you instead," he said. "It appears you are following in my footsteps."

"It would be a good thing if I could," interposed Alexander.

"Yes," continued Pyotr Ivanich. "Collegiate Councillor at a little over thirty, a good income from the state, you earn a lot of money on the side, and are marrying well just at the right age. Yes, the Aduyevs know what they're about. You're just like me—all but the pains in the back."

"I get them, too, sometimes," said Alexander, touching his own back.

"All that is, of course, very fine, but for the pains in the back," continued Pyotr Ivanich. "I admit I never thought any good would come of you when you first arrived. You had your head crammed with a lot of other-world notions, you were soaring in the clouds ... but that's all over, and thank God for it. I would like to advise you—go on following in my footsteps, only..."

"Only what, Uncle?"

"Nothing ... I only wanted to give you a little advice ... about your future wife."

"Oh! That's interesting."

"On second thought I won't," said Pyotr Ivanich after a pause. "It might only make things worse. Do the best you can. Perhaps you'll find out for yourself. Let's talk about your marriage. They say your bride will have a dowry of two hundred thousand rubles—is it true?"

"Yes—two hundred thousand from her father, and her mother left her another hundred thousand."

"Why, that's three hundred thousand!" cried Pyotr Ivanich in awed tones.

"And he told me today that he would put all his five hundred serfs at my disposal. I am to pay him eight thousand annually. We shall live together."

Pyotr Ivanich jumped out of his chair with unusual liveliness.

"Wait a bit," he said, "you overwhelm me! Did I hear you right? Say it again—how much?"

"Five hundred serfs and three hundred thousand rubles," repeated Alexander.

"You're not joking?"

"Of course not, Uncle."

"And the estate ... isn't mortgaged?" asked Pyotr Ivanich softly, without stirring.

"No."

His uncle gazed respectfully, his arms folded, at his nephew for a few minutes.

"Career and fortune," he said almost as if speaking to himself, but still gazing at Alexander. "And what a fortune! And all of a sudden! Everything! Everything! Alexander," he added, proudly, solemnly, "you are of my blood, you are an Aduyev! It can't be helped—you must embrace me."

And they embraced.

"The first time, Uncle," said Alexander.

"And the last," replied Pyotr Ivanich. "This is an extraordinary occasion. And now do you mean to say you don't need any filthy lucre? Ask me for a loan, if only once!"

"Oh, I will, Uncle—I have so many expenses. If you could let me have ten or fifteen thousand."

"At last! For the first time!" cried Pyotr Ivanich.

"And the last, Uncle! This is an extraordinary occasion."

1845-1846

THE END

"Better Late Than Never"

(Excerpts from a Critical
Article by I.A.Goncharov)

...This critical analysis of my books is based upon the preface I intended for the edition of *The Abyss* which was to be brought out in 1870, but was not then published. In 1875 I returned to this preface, made certain additions, and again laid it aside.

Now, on rereading it, I consider it may serve as sufficient elucidation of, and reply to, the many remarks and questions addressed to me from various sources, both privately and in print, some of which were flattering, exaggerated praise, but most of which consisted in criticism, misunderstanding, reproaches, both as regards the general significance of my literary aims and the characters and certain details in my books.

I am far from setting up this analysis of my work as a categorical ciritical criterion, I impose it upon no one, and even foresee that many of my readers will, for various reasons, disagree with much in it. My only desire in presenting it is that they should know how I myself regard my novels, and should accept it as my reply to the questions put to me, and that there should remain nothing more for anyone to ask me.

If my readers find that the key I have made to my own works is not the right one, they are welcome to choose one of their own making. If, contrary to my expectations, I should ever find myself compelled to republish my collected works, this analysis may serve as the author's preface.

I may be told that I am rather late with such a preface; but even if it does not seem superfluous now, then—"better late than never".

...I will now approach the question of what I myself see in my three novels (*The Same Old Story, Oblomov* and *The Abyss.—Tr.*), the question of their general significance.

I see ... *not three novels, but one*. They are all connected by a single thread, a single, consistent idea—the transition from one period of Russian life, known to me from personal experience, to another—each of them contains the reflection of insignificant phenomena in my imagination, in portraits, scenes and smaller details.

In the first place, the following artistic principle must be borne in mind and expounded: if images are typical, they cannot fail to reflect, on a larger or smaller scale, the period in which they occur, for this is what makes them typical. In other words, the phenomena of social life, morals and manners are reflected in them, as in a mirror. And if the artist has sufficient depth himself, they will also display the psychological side of life. I hasten to remark that I make no pretensions to such depth, and modern critics have already remarked in print that I am shallow.

I myself, and the atmosphere in which I was born and bred and spent my life, are unconsciously reflected in my imagination, as a landscape is reflected through the window in a mirror, as a vast panorama is sometimes reflected in a small pond—the inverted bowl of the sky above the pond, with its design of clouds and trees, a hill-side, and the buildings on it, people, animals, movement and stillness—all in miniature likeness.

And this simple physical law is fulfilled in myself and my novels, in some way of which I am scarcely conscious.

While working on *The Same Old Story*, I naturally had in mind myself and many like myself, who received an education at home or at a university, lived in a backwater, beneath the wings of a kind mother, were abruptly torn away from this idyllic atmosphere, from hearth and home, and seen off with tears (as in the first chapters of *The Same Old Story*), next to appear on the main field of action— Petersburg.

Here, too—in the encounters between the dreamy nephew, cosseted in idleness and luxury, and the practical uncle—may be found the embryo of the theme then only just beginning to emerge against a background of the busiest place of all—Petersburg. This theme is the faint glimmerings of the consciousness that work—real work, not mere routine, but active work in contending against the stagnation prevailing all over Russia—was essential.

This was reflected in my tiny mirror in the life of average officialdom. There is not the slightest doubt that the same things, in the same spirit, tone and character, but on another scale, were going on in other spheres of Russian life, both higher and lower.

The exponent of this theme in society is the uncle. He has achieved a considerable position in his office, he is a financial director, a Privy Councillor, and in addition to all this, he becomes an industrialist. At that time, from the twenties to the forties of the nineteenth century, this was a bold innovation, there was nothing humiliating in it. (I am not speaking of those gentlemen industrialists, whose factories and mills were part of their hereditary estates, and helped to swell the income from them, while they themselves had nothing to do with them.) Very few privy councillors went in for this. Their rank would not allow them to, and the name of merchant was not considered distinguished.

The struggle between uncle and nephew reflects both the break—then only just beginning—with old conceptions and morals, with sentimentality, the absurd exaggeration of the feelings of love and friendship, the poetry of idleness, the family and domestic fictions of affected, in reality non-existent, emotions (e.g., the spinster-aunt's idea of love, etc.), the time wasted in visiting, unnecessary hospitality, and so on.

In a word, all the idle, dreamy, affected side of the old morals with the usual youthful impulses towards the lofty, the great, the aesthetic, the striving after effect, the thirst to express everything in sparkling prose, and, even more, in poetry.

All this had become a thing of the past, and faint gleams of the new dawn, of what was sober, practical, necessary, had begun to appear.

The former, that is the old, is represented by the nephew, who for that reason stands out more vividly.

The latter—the sober consciousness of the necessity for deeds, work, knowledge—is expressed through the uncle; but this consciousness has only just come into being, only the first symptoms have appeared, complete development is as yet far off, and, as is natural, these beginnings find but a faint, inadequate reflection, here and there, in single individuals and small groups, and so the uncle-image is paler than the nephew-image.

Nadenka, the girl who is the symbol of Aduyev's love, is also a reflection of the period. She is no longer the daughter utterly submissive to her parents. Her mother is wax in her hands and barely able to preserve the merest semblance of maternal authority, though always declaring *that she is very strict, even if she says nothing,* and that Nadenka *never takes a single step without her permission.* She feels herself that this is not true, that she is weak, and she is so blind that, while allowing her daughter complete liberty, both as regards Aduyev and the count, she has no idea of what is really going on.

The daughter is a few steps ahead of her mother. She falls in love with Aduyev *without waiting for permission,* and hardly troubles to conceal this from her mother, merely holding her tongue for the sake of propriety, considering herself entitled to dispose *of her inner life* as she likes, and domineering over Aduyev, whose measure she has taken. He is her obedient slave, gentle, weakly, good-natured, not without promise, just a vain, simple, ordinary youth, whose name is legion. She might have accepted him, become his wife, and all would have followed the usual course.

But the count appears on the scene—wise, deliberate, deft, brilliant. Nadenka sees that Aduyev cannot bear comparison with him, as regards mind, character, or manners. Nadenka's life has not afforded her opportunities to form any sort of ideals as to masculine dignity and strength.

Indeed, no such ideal existed at that time, for there was no independent life. Onegin and his like were the only ideal characters—dandies, celebrities, scorning the pettiness of work, and not knowing what to do with themselves.

Nadenka now saw that the young Aduyev was not a real force, that in him was reproduced everything that she had seen a thousand times in all the other youths with whom she had danced and mildly flirted. There was a brief interval in which she listened to his poems. The writing of verse was in those days a passport to the ranks of the intelligentsia. She expected to find power and talent there. But his verses turned out to be only just tolerable, no one had ever heard of them, and he actually harboured a secret grudge against the count for his simplicity and cleverness, and for knowing how to behave. Nadenka went over to the count's side and this was the first *conscious step taken by the Russian girl*—tacit emancipation, a protest against her mother's authority, which was no longer binding for her.

But here ended her emancipation. She became *conscious*, but *did not convert her consciousness into activity*, and so remained *unenlightened*, for the note of the period just then was one of unenlightenment. People did not yet know what to do with themselves, where to go, what to take up. Onegin and his fellow "idealist characters" merely languished in inaction, having no definite aims or work, and the Tatyanas were unenlightened.

"What will come of it?" Aduyev asks Nadenka, aghast. "The count will not marry you."

"I don't know," she replies wearily. The Russian girl really did not know how to act consciously and rationally in any given case. She could only vaguely feel she might sometimes protest against *being given in marriage by her parents*, and could only, unconsciously, of course, like Nadenka, express this protest, by rejecting one man and yielding to her feelings for another.

Here I have left Nadenka. I no longer require her as a type, and her personality has nothing to do with me.

Belinsky, too, remarked upon this. "So long as he needs her he takes trouble about her," he told someone, when speaking of me in my presence, "and then he flings her aside."

Many people have asked me what happened to Nadenka. How do I know? It was *not Nadenka, but the Russian girl of a certain circle, at a certain moment of the period in whom I was interested*. I never knew a single Nadenka personally, or I knew a great many.

I shall be told that she and other characters are insignificant, and do not represent types. This is very likely, and I am not in a position to argue the point. I can only state what they meant to me.

In the beginning of the forties, while I was meditating and writing this novel, I had not as yet seen clearly into the next period, which had not begun, though anticipations of it were already stirring within me, for, soon after the publication in the *Sovremennik* (1847) of *The Same*

Old Story, I had the plan of *Oblomov* ready, and in 1848 (or, perhaps, I am not sure, 1849) I published *Oblomov's Dream*—the overture on which the whole novel was based—in the *Sovremennik's Illustrated Review*, showing that I was mentally reacting to this period also, and intuitively conscious of what was to come. Now I can relate "what happened to Nadenka".

Look into *Oblomov*—Olga is the reincarnation of Nadenka in the next epoch...

Aduyev ended up as most people then did. He heeded the practical wisdom of his uncle, took a post in a government office, contributed to the magazines (but no longer verses), having *survived* the era of youthful agitation, gained all sorts of worldly benefits, like the majority of his contemporaries occupied a solid position in his office, and married well—in a word, managed his life efficiently. And this is the gist of *The Same Old Story*.

Among my books this is the first gallery, acting as an anteroom to the next two galleries or periods of Russian life closely connected as they are—*Oblomov* and *The Abyss,* or *The Dream* and *The Awakening.*

...In conclusion I still have to reply to the last questions put to me from all sides. These are: why did I take so long—up to ten years—to write my novels? And, next: why do I not write any more?

The answer to the first question, or reproach, is partially given in what I have already written here.

I would merely add that if anyone takes the trouble to discover the meaning of my novels, and find in them even a little of the significance I myself see in them, he will not require to be an author himself in order to appraise and define the invisible but enormous labour which the construction of such a literary edifice requires.

...Belinsky once said, "...Another would have found material for ten novels—he puts it all into one."

He said this of the shortest of all my novels—*The Same Old Story.*

What would he have said of *Oblomov* or of *The Abyss*, in which I have put as it were the whole of my own life and that of many others?

Whether this is good or bad is another question (it is not for me to answer it). But if prolonged periods—from the 'forties to the 'seventies—are covered by my novels, it may be asked whether the description of scenes, undergoing development and being written side by side with the current of life itself, could have been accomplished in a year or two of work? Of course it could not.

The last question: why have I not written and why am I not writing any more?

I cannot, I do not know how to. That is to say I cannot write, and do not know how to write òther than in images, scenes, and at great length, so that I must write slowly and with difficulty.

A certain freshness of powers and aspirations are required for the creation of images and scenes—and there is a time for everything. Towards the end of his life man grows weary in the struggle with everyone and everything which sets obstacles in his path, with all who do not understand him, are hostile to him.

I am no journalist, no professional critic, I have lived and written mainly under the influence of imagination—and beyond the sphere of this my pen has little force, refuses to move.

My collaboration in magazines in the capacity of reviewer and contributor should never have been asked—I tried, and nothing came of it but a few lifeless articles which could not bear comparison with the products of the lively pen of skilled journalists.

Nor were the subjects for a novel suggested to me of any more use. "Describe such and such an event, such and such a life, take up this or that problem, this or that hero or heroine."

I cannot, I do not know how to. *All that has not grown up and matured within me,* that I have not seen and observed, by which I have not lived, is foreign to my pen. I have (or had) my own field, my own background, just as I have my own native land, atmosphere, friends and foes, my own world of observations, impressions and memories— and I have written only *what I knew from experience, what I have thought, felt, loved, what I have seen and known intimately*—in a word I have written *my own life and that which adhered to it.*

1879

Notes

Lei 23

Mikhail Zagoskin (1783-1852), a Russian writer, author of several historical novels.

Marlinsky—the pen-name of Alexander Bestuzhev (1797-1837), author of romantic stories who took part in the Decembrists' uprising in 1825.

St. Isaac's Cathedral in St. Petersburg, built in 1818-1858. The architect was A. Montferrand.

The Bronze Horseman, the equestrian statue in Senate Square, St. Petersburg, created by Etienne Maurice Falconet and set up in 1782 as a monument to Peter the Great.

Peterhof (renamed Petrodvorets), a town founded on the shore of the Gulf of Finland early in the 18th century. The aristocracy and big officials of St. Petersburg built their summer villas there.

Les Martyrs (1809), a novel by François René Chateaubriand (1768-1848).

Dictionnaire philosophique by Voltaire (1694-1778).

Le Manuscrit vert by Gustave Drouineau.

Les sept pêches capiteux by Eugène Sue.

L'Ane mort et la femme guillotinée by Jules Janin.

Idylls by the Swiss poet and painter Salomon Gessner (1730-1788).

The Complaints or Night Thoughts on Life, Death and Immortality by Edward Young (1683-1765).

Christian Felix Weisse (1726-1804), a German children's writer.

Antioch Kantemir (1708-1744), a Russian poet, a dean of Russian classicism.

Alexander Sumarokov (1717-1777), a Russian poet and playwright.

Lei 53